PRAISE FO

MW00426535

"*Chick Magnet* has one of the best epilogues I've ever read, and it's a perfect demonstration of why writers keep going back to small-town settings. Because underneath all the cupcakes and cruel memories, there is one great promise at the heart of a small-town romance: there's always a first time for second chances."

—*New York Times*

"Barry is insightful when she hints at the painful social shifts initiated by the pandemic, infectiously cheerful while describing Nic's interactions with her clucking comrades, and especially evocative when she tackles Will's internal struggles . . . A comforting small-town romance, with chickens."

—*Kirkus Reviews*

"Barry handles both characters with care and delivers a powerful message about seeking help for mental illness even as she infuses the story with ample comic relief. Pet-loving romance fans should flock to this one."

—*Publishers Weekly*

"One of the chief pleasures of being a romance reader is getting to watch Emma Barry's complex, honorable characters forging themselves into stronger, happier versions of themselves. *Chick Magnet* is Emma Barry at the peak of her powers: hilarious and humane, it will restore your faith in the power of love."

—Jenny Holiday, *USA Today* bestselling author

"Intoxicating and deeply romantic, *Chick Magnet* delivers a riveting opposites-attract, slow-burn-with-the-hot-guy-next-door small-town romance. I fell in love with Will Lund from the first grumpy meeting."

—Zoe York, *USA Today* and *New York Times* bestselling author

PRAISE FOR *FUNNY GUY*

"This ingenious friends-to-lovers romance . . . [is] a fresh take on a favorite trope that perfectly marries humor and heartache."

—*Publishers Weekly* (starred review)

"It's a tug-of-war that would be hard for a less adept writer to pull off, but Barry's work has always thrived on this kind of interplay. She seems to be feeling her way to a new kind of structure here, one that's organic and messy but still generates a vital catharsis."

—*New York Times*

"With *Funny Guy*, Barry achieves that rare specialness found in the best romances: writing main characters who you come to love like they are people you know, for all their frustrating flaws and foibles. Sam and Bree have crackling chemistry together and a deep, abiding love for each other (another tough balance to strike, and Barry manages it beautifully), and I rooted for them to find themselves and to find their way together. A layered, lovely love story infused with sharp wit and soft humanity."

—Kate Clayborn, author of *Love Lettering*

"Sharply drawn characters and moments of sweet, aching vulnerability. *Funny Guy* is the friends-to-lovers romance of my dreams."

—Mia Hopkins, author of the Eastside Brewery series

BAD
REPUTATION

OTHER BOOKS BY EMMA BARRY

Stand-Alone Novels

Funny Guy

Chick Magnet

Political Persuasions Series

The One You Want

The One You Need

The One You Hate

The One You Crave

BAD
REPUTATION

Emma Barry

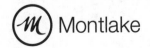
Montlake

Text copyright © 2024 by Emma Barry

Published by Montlake, Seattle

www.apub.com

Amazon, the Amazon logo, and Montlake are trademarks of Amazon.com, Inc., or its affiliates.

ISBN-13: 9781662520839 (paperback)
ISBN-13: 9781662520846 (digital)

Cover design by Caroline Teagle Johnson
Cover image: © Alessandra Taryn Bea / Getty; © Linear /
Getty; © Muhammad Syarif Hidayat / Getty; © VGstockstudio / Shutterstock

Printed in the United States of America

To my English, drama, and choir teachers
who looked at would-be censors and said no

Chapter 1

INT. CROWDED FAN-CONVENTION HALL

Cole James had a lot of regrets. Enough to field a Little League team. Enough to pack a Costco-size case. Enough to fill a keg . . . which made sense because several of those regrets featured kegs. But behind a signing table at Aughties Con, Cole would've put playing his doppelgänger, Cody Rhodes, on *Central Square* at the top of the list.

Sure, the part had made Cole famous in a star-of-a-soapy-teen-drama way. The kind of famous that landed you on the cover of *Us Weekly* and at the People's Choice Awards. The kind that had him in demand for fan conventions two decades later.

But Cody was the Halloween costume that Cole could never get off. Their names even sounded the same.

Take right now. The woman at the head of the autograph line stumbled forward. She was about Cole's age, in her early forties. From her Team Cody shirt to her reluctant giggles, she was clearly psyched to meet him and mortified to be so clearly psyched.

Sympathy mixed with the coffee in Cole's gut. That morning, he'd gotten on the elevator with Park Chan-wook, one of his dream directors to work with, and Cole had nearly forgotten his own name. Celebrity was a hell of a drug.

With the smile the fan expected, Cole extended his hand. "Hey, how are you doing? I'm Cole."

The woman blinked, hard.

"It's nice to meet you . . . ?" He trailed off, hoping she'd supply her name. It was so much better when they gave Cole their names. It made this feel more like a conversation and not an appointment, which, okay, it *was*.

The woman was still doing an ice-sculpture impression—and the people behind her in line were growing impatient.

"I'd love to sign that for you." Cole pointed to the poster she was clutching.

Without speaking, the woman pushed a poster from *Central Square*'s second season at him. Ah, the year when MIT had kicked Cody out because they thought he was running his sometime girlfriend Madison's cheating ring. Falling on that grenade won him her eternal love . . . until he lost it by sleeping with her best friend. Again. Things had ended with a cliff-hanger when Cody fell asleep while his joint lit his duvet on fire. In those twenty-two episodes, Cody had made some *bad* choices.

Life imitated art, he supposed.

Cole held up a sparkly gold gel pen. "Should I sign as Cole or as Cody?"

At that, she regained the power of speech. "Oh, please sign as Cody."

Of course. It was always Cody.

Because no matter how many times the character had kissed the wrong girl at a party, fought with his grandfather about his inheritance, or gotten sucked into a Lithuanian crime syndicate, fans forgave him. They got Team Cody tattoos and had his vow to Madison—*through thick and thin, baby*—engraved in their wedding bands. Through all ninety-two episodes of banana-pants drama, they loved Cody Rhodes. And for almost twenty years now, they had shared that same devotion with Cole.

"Of course." With a smile, Cole wrote *Cody Rhodes* across the tight black T-shirt he wore on the poster. The color had varied, but it had always been tight. The shirt was almost as much of a draw as the biceps under it. "Thanks for coming out today."

"I wouldn't miss it for anything."

Cole's career would've withered if that hadn't been true. He hadn't been much of an actor in his *Central Square* days—he wasn't much of an actor now—but things had come easily to him then. And the combination of stardom and being twenty had been corrosive.

Showing up to work drunk after all-night parties in hotel rooms? Yeah, he'd done that a few times—and he'd had to live with his terrible performances, tabloid coverage, and pissed-off coworkers. His first agent talking him into investing in an RPG adaptation that had gone *way* over budget and bombed? That was a rite of passage for jackasses. Being so clueless and self-obsessed that he'd missed the showrunner being garbage to the female writers? He'd discovered that after *Central Square* had gone off the air, when Cole had been broke, unemployed, and without an agent at twenty-four. Exactly where he deserved to be.

Two things had gotten him through: the enduring popularity of Cody Rhodes, and Drew Bowen, the agent who'd agreed to sign Cole when he'd been lying in the gutter. Everything that had come afterward, Cole owed to them . . . and Cody wasn't even real.

The fan gave Cole a sheepish grin. "These things must be awful for you."

"Nah. I really enjoy them."

Cole had stayed in the business because making television and movies was fun. Filming was about relationships, about people. Cons were for the last and most important link in the chain: the fans.

"Who else are you here to see?"

No one else from *Central Square* was at Aughties Con, as far as Cole knew. Lexi Harper, Cole's longtime on-screen love interest, was doing some play on Broadway. His on-screen bestie, Glenn Stokes, was filming a fantasy movie in Poland. He texted Cole sometimes to complain about the Dodgers. And Ben Hayes, who'd played Cody's rival for Madison's affections, wasn't acting anymore. The last Cole had heard, Ben was flipping houses—and not even on television.

"Just . . . you," the woman admitted. "It's been almost two decades, and I know the show was cheesy. But all through college and my first marriage, and my babies who wouldn't sleep, and awful coworkers, and quarantine, *Central Square* was there for me."

This was something Cole heard over and over again, and for the kazillionth time, he was walloped by guilt that he'd been such a prick on the show. He'd been so casual, so thoughtless about work that meant a lot to so many people. *Trashy television*—trashy according to who?

"It meant a lot to me too." He left out *I've never messed up so bad, and it made me grow up*. People didn't want that from him, he'd learned. They wanted him to smile, to be the good-time guy. They wanted him to confirm their experience of *Central Square*, not his own.

Trying to be that guy, the one the fan wanted to meet, Cole asked, "What's your favorite episode?"

"Oh, the one where you propose to Madison."

"The first or the second time?"

"The first time. *So* romantic."

A popular choice. Cole wasn't going to ruin the illusion by explaining that back then, Lexi Harper couldn't stand him. He'd made things better by apologizing, taking full and complete responsibility for being basically a frat boy with a TV contract. It helped that Lexi had moved on to bigger and better things, like acting in sad Norwegian plays. It was easy to be generous when you were winning Tonys.

Meanwhile, Cole made the streaming equivalent of direct-to-video movies involving explosions and drug kingpins and sand. So much freaking sand. Cole had gotten *really* good at looking concerned and running while holding a bazooka. At acting in front of green screens and with people in motion capture suits. There'd been commercials, too, and even supporting roles in kids' movies. Cole had never gotten close to fatherhood in real life, but he'd played it on television.

They'd been lean, humiliating years, but Cole had stuck to Drew's rules and developed his own too. Hand over hand, role after role, he'd made himself into a professional.

Cole wasn't talented. But in this business, showing up, doing the work, and being gosh-darn disciplined made up for a lot. Drew had managed to convince everyone Cole was a well-meaning himbo who'd let youth and fame go to his head but that he was better now. That wasn't far from the truth, but Cole was ready to leave the himbo designation behind and just be . . . Cole.

This year, he was finally going to emerge from the hole he'd dug, and *Waverley* was the ladder he was going to use to climb to the top.

"Well, if you like romance, you're going to dig *Waverley*."

Waverley had burst onto Videon two seasons ago. It sounded like *Masterpiece Theatre*, being adapted from the novels by Sir Something or Other. Pure class, at least before you got to all the sex. Sure, the show had an old-timey Scottish setting, and there were fancy speeches and poetry. But the characters fucked, and they fought with swords, and they plotted revolution. Add in a soundtrack that blended bagpipes with contemporary pop hits, and it wasn't like anything else. Quite frankly, Cole had to stop himself from fawning over the showrunner during his auditions.

And this season, Cole was going to play Geordie Robertson, a nobleman turned smuggler and revolutionary, and his BFF, Tasha Russell, was going to play his lover, Effie Deans.

While Cole might've limped along on the B- and C-lists for years, Tasha was a verified movie star, and they'd basically stopped making those. Getting her to do the show was a big deal for Videon and a bigger deal for Cole.

The woman's bright smile flash froze. "I saw that." A strained pause. "I love the show. And you and Tasha Russell together again? That'll be . . . great. Tasha will be amazing."

Oh.

Oh.

The blood went chunky in his veins. This woman, along with the jerks at *Variety* and the *Hollywood Reporter*, wasn't sure if *Cole* was right for the show.

She looked almost as sick as Cole felt about it. "It's just that it was a book first, right? And you haven't done a lot of book shows."

Cole had done more video-game-to-film adaptations than book-to-film ones, sure. But *Waverley* was going to be his new start. It had to be.

"You're right," Cole said gently. He wasn't mad, not at the woman. He was annoyed with himself—that he had messed up so badly that, two decades later, people were still acting as if Cole might get grubby fingerprints all over anything classy if he touched it.

All Cole could do was stick to the rules, his and Drew's, and do the part well. That was the only way to change anyone's minds.

"Me wearing breeches? Country dancing?" Honestly, Cole was looking forward to those things, but he knew that wasn't his reputation.

The woman barked out a laugh—a real one—which seemed to shatter both her fear that he was going to be mad and her cocoon of awe. "You'll look good."

Right on cue, there was the other thing people brought up at cons.

Cole wasn't going to pretend that his face and his transverse abs hadn't been the major driver of his career so far. Heck, if everything fell apart, his backup plan was to become a celebrity trainer. He'd certainly spent enough time working with one to qualify.

"Well, see, there's that," he said.

"And I bet you'll have fun."

But she didn't bet that he'd be *good*.

Everyone trusted Cole to get the party started, but they thought he was about as deep as a mirror—all flash, all reflection, and nothing else.

Trying to hide his wince, Cole gave the fan a sad smile. "It was nice, meeting you today."

"Oh." She must've just realized their time together was over, and it brought her up short. Trying not to look disappointed, she fished her phone out of her back pocket. "Can we get a selfie?"

"Of course."

The eighteen inches of folding plastic table between them eliminated the possibility of physical contact, for which Cole was grateful. He knew many fans saw him as a commodity, one they'd paid thirty dollars to meet. But that fee didn't include pinching his butt or squeezing his biceps. Cole had always struggled to find a nice way of saying *Please don't.*

After the woman snapped a pic, Cole sent her on her way with a wave, and he finished up with the rest of the people in his line. When the last one was done, Drew materialized with Brett Vaughn, Cole's PR guy, in tow. Cole's agent had an almost magical ability to show up at precisely the right moment. *Make a big appearance and melt away*—it was one of his rules.

Fifteen years ago, what Cole had needed most was a plan, and Drew had one, along with enough confidence to fuel a rocket ship to the moon. Cole had followed every syllable of Drew's advice. The few times they'd disagreed, Cole had quickly deferred to Drew, and now he was on the edge of what they both hoped was going to be a great comeback.

Brett strung the red velvet rope across the end of the aisle while Drew strolled up to Cole's table. "How bad was it?"

"Not very." Having to spend a day marinating in Cody Rhodes was not Cole's favorite thing, but seeing as how Cody had given Cole everything—even the golden parachute out of the mess he'd made of his own life—it was hard to dislike the guy.

Drew's nose wrinkled as he regarded the coffee that Cole was gratefully finishing. "I thought we talked about caffeine. Your pores."

Cole's pores looked fine to him, but he knew Drew meant well. "Needed an afternoon pick-me-up." Whatever else these days were, they were exhausting.

"And now you won't sleep tonight."

"I'll put in a few extra miles on the treadmill."

Drew pursed his lips. "Hmm. How's the training going?"

Learning to sword fight had been a multimonth commitment, and it was kicking Cole's ass. "I thought my thighs were in decent shape"—excellent shape, actually—"but this is an entirely different thing. Listen." Cole leaned his forearms onto the table. "I'm not saying I'm feeling insecure, but can I do this? Can I really play Geordie?"

"What are you talking about?" Brett said, laughing. It was as if the question didn't make sense to him, because it probably didn't. "Of course you can."

Brett was nicer than Drew, too nice for Hollywood. It was why Cole liked him—well, that and the fact that every entertainment reporter in the world was his bestie. Cole knew Brett believed in Cole. But his belief was a penny: easily given and not worth much.

Drew looked up from his phone, lines of disbelief crinkling across his forehead. Someone had missed his latest Botox appointment. "This is what we've worked toward for years," he said. "I wouldn't have put in all that effort if I didn't think you could."

That wasn't an answer about *Cole* at all, but it was comforting. Because at the end of the day, Drew wasn't lying. He didn't represent clients who didn't make money for him.

Years ago, at a party in Los Feliz, Cole had met a caterer who Drew had dumped as a client. "He'll only keep you around as long as you're useful to him," he'd warned.

It had spooked Cole until he'd realized . . . of course that was how this worked.

"I always did wonder why you took me on." It was clear what Cole had gotten out of the relationship, but it had taken a long time for Cole to be worthwhile for Drew. Even now, even with *Waverley*, the big payoff wasn't quite there yet. It would come with the next projects—if it came at all.

"I wanted to see how good I was," Drew said, shooting the cuffs of his shirt. "You were like this undeveloped mountain, and I was fairly convinced there was gold in them thar hills."

"Jeez, Drew, that's mercenary," Brett said. "I don't think you're supposed to say that part out loud." Brett certainly wouldn't. He was far more careful about his words and much gentler with people's feelings.

Drew's look of disdain expressed how little he thought of that. "Cole's a pro. He knows the score. And besides, it's worked out. It's only rude to say it if it fails—you can write that down."

There it was: another Drew Bowen maxim. He ought to put together a book of them, a Hollywood version of *The Art of War*.

Cole wasn't much for battle himself. These days, he preferred to step lightly and carefully. But he understood where his agent was coming from, and he had benefited from Drew's ruthlessness.

"Just don't go telling the press that Cole's your gold mine," Brett said. "That's not the line we're going for."

"Cole and I understand each other." Drew locked eyes with his client. "Don't we?"

"Yup, boss."

It was too late to abandon the strategy that had gotten them this far. At the end of the day, if Drew thought Cole was going to be worth the investment, one that he'd paid into for almost twenty years, then Cole's career was going to take off.

It had to.

Chapter 2

INT. TALK SHOW GREENROOM

After more than a year of television appearances, radio interviews, and podcasts, Maggie Niven still hated getting miked up. No matter where they clipped the box or how they draped the cord, she felt ridiculous.

She'd gotten through being fired and endured a wrongful termination lawsuit. But she didn't enjoy being the most well-known opponent of the high school theatre censorship movement.

"All set," the PA said. "How does that feel?"

"Fine," Maggie lied.

The guy led her out of the greenroom and into the studio. The set of *Hear Her* had to be the shiniest place on earth. Everything about it screamed *This is the number one morning talk show for thirty-five- to forty-four-year-old women.* The gleaming hexagonal table. The four hosts with their shimmering hair and perfect lip gloss.

Maggie was extremely dull and matte in comparison.

"Maggie!" Grace Choi waved carefully so as not to disturb the makeup person who was touching her up. "You're by me."

Grace was the only real journalist on the panel. She'd come to *Hear Her* from the White House beat, and they leaned heavily on her during segments about real news. That was probably why she had on a serious navy suit, albeit one that was better tailored than any item of clothing Maggie had ever touched.

Gingerly, Maggie took her seat and focused on the morning's important business: not puking when confronted by three massive arachnid cameras and the bank of stage lights.

"We're glad to have you," Grace said. "It's an important story."

"Yeah, it's . . . good to be here." Maggie almost choked on the word.

Grace's smile was knowing. "Just remember, some of us are on your side."

"Some?"

Across the table, Rylee Lagrange was straightening the lapels of her metallic silver suit. A former pop star, Rylee had moved into info-tainment, but she always seemed to be reminding everyone she used to pack arenas.

"And some of us," Rylee said, "are thinking about parents and *their* rights." Her smile was sweetly aggressive, like a Vera Bradley pattern.

A few weeks after her firing, Maggie had endured an especially painful interview on *Built Right*, the most popular current-events podcast among angry dads. That had been when Maggie still believed her firing was some kind of misunderstanding—that if she could just explain that the play in question wasn't smutty or inappropriate, it would all blow over and she'd get her job as a high school drama teacher back.

That interview had been the first time Maggie had come face to face—voice to voice, actually—with Parent Led. In nineteen exquisitely uncomfortable minutes, she'd learned this wasn't about the situation at her school. It wasn't even about whether *Covering the Spread* was a bad choice for high school students to perform. Something much bigger was at stake.

It felt grandiose for Maggie to cast herself as the canary in the coal mine, chirruping about students' freedom and the expertise of teachers in determining curriculum, about whether there was a right to expression and whether a small knot of angry people could decide what was okay for everyone else to read and watch and perform and listen to.

But these days, she was feeling sort of like Tweety Bird.

Rylee was still going. "I just think it's important for our viewers to hear a *balanced* story, and I—"

"Let's wait for the cameras to turn on," Denise Strong interrupted. An Oscar winner for her work on an Ida B. Wells biopic, Denise was thoughtful, empathetic, and smart. For all that she was pushing seventy, she was still stunningly beautiful. Her long braids might be frosted silver, but her face was still unlined.

Maggie really had to be more consistent with her nighttime skin-care routine.

Under her breath, Maggie asked Grace, "Who else is going to be on?" Maybe they could be a buffer against Rylee.

"Zoya Delgado."

Maggie had watched Zoya's show, of course. Everyone had. *Waverley* was Videon's biggest hit in years. During the trial, when Maggie had trouble sleeping, she'd put it on almost every night. The combination of political intrigue and romance, mixed with Scottish scenery and fabulous costumes, was hard to resist.

That wasn't going to help Maggie today, though. *Waverley* had nothing to do with her.

"Thirty-second warning, everyone," a producer cried.

Zoya Delgado arrived. She was young to be the showrunner of a cultural juggernaut, probably younger than Maggie. With her glossy curtain of black hair, stunning features, and stylish pink A-line dress, she could've starred in a Videon series in addition to writing and directing one.

"And we're live in five, four . . ." A producer signaled the last three counts, and Maggie reminded herself to breathe. She'd faced Parent Led's talking points before. She could do it again.

Maybe she'd buy herself a new plant to celebrate, like that slipper orchid she'd been lusting over but hadn't bought yet because more crucial things—such as paying her mortgage—had come first.

Damn responsibility. French fries were going to have to be a good enough bribe to survive this.

A light near the camera flipped from red to green, and they were on the air.

"Welcome back," Denise Strong said. "Conversations about content in the media are nothing new. From the Hays Code to movie ratings, we've struggled with what's appropriate in movies, on television, and at the theatre. Our answers have changed over time, but lately, things have taken a sinister tone. In the last few years, we've seen book bans, attacks on teachers, and media boycotts, all related to questions about subject matter and community standards. Joining us today are two people who've experienced this backlash firsthand: Oregon teacher Maggie Niven and Hollywood showrunner Zoya Delgado. Ladies, thank you."

Maggie muttered something incoherent, while Zoya offered a smooth "I'm so pleased to be here."

Denise pivoted in her chair. "I'd like to start with you, Maggie. Can you tell us about what happened to you?"

"Well, I was a high school drama teacher for sixteen years." The number was somehow too short and too long. But forty-eight main-stage productions, countless one-act plays and improvisational pieces, and thousands of students were the tally of Maggie's career.

The cliché was right: teaching wasn't a job; it was a calling. It had been *her* calling. For all that she'd disappointed her parents with her small ambitions, Maggie had always known her job was important.

"In that time, I won several district and state awards for teaching, and I mentored countless students."

The first face that sprang to Maggie's mind was Amira Kirby. Her parents hadn't wanted her to take drama. During back-to-school night, they'd been clear that acting was irrelevant for their future-physician daughter. But in class, it was equally clear acting lit Amira up in ways chemistry and biology never could.

Amira had been one of dozens of students who'd protested Maggie's firing. She'd told the school board that being in theatre was the only reason she felt confident enough to object. Studying drama empowered kids. *That's* why it was dangerous.

"Last year, I was fired when a parent complained about a production I directed, *Covering the Spread*."

The funny part was when Maggie had picked the plays to do that season, she'd worried far more about *Radium Girls*, with its messages about how science was perverted by commerce and the exploitation of workers, than she had about *Covering the Spread*. She'd been so naive.

"I've seen it," Denise said. "But for people who might not know the play, can you describe it?"

"It's a musical about a high school debate team. It's become a standard for community theatres and high schools because it has a small cast and really great songs. There's also an audience participation component and some improvisation, so it's a good teaching piece." That had been how Maggie had seen it, anyhow. "It does have some mature themes about poverty and parental pressure, and the characters—much like actual high school students—are coming to terms with their sexuality, but the tone is light."

"Maggie." Rylee was really good at conveying through a single word that someone had messed up big time. "You're being pretty casual about content that many people, many *parents*, have concerns about. Some might call *Covering the Spread* pornographic."

It would be extremely boring porn. As tempting as it was to be sarcastic, however, Maggie knew it wouldn't help.

"If anyone said that, they would be misrepresenting the truth." Maggie's voice was confident and calm, but sadly, she felt neither of those things. Her stomach was churning like the sea during a hurricane. "There's no nudity, sex, or violence in *Covering the Spread*. I've directed productions of Molière that were edgier. While there are a few profane words, if it was a movie, it'd probably be rated PG-13."

"They take the Lord's name in vain." Rylee clearly couldn't think of a worse offense. "And this 'play'"—she put sarcastic air quotes around the word—"normalizes teens having sex. It also represents alternative *lifestyles* as if they're no big deal."

Didn't *Hear Her* normalize lifestyles, at least Starbucks-swilling and yoga-doing ones?

Maggie wiped her sweaty palms on the cushion of her chair. *Don't be snarky. Don't be snarky.* "The play, with its language and the way it addresses a variety of families—and yes, even with the romantic sub-plots—represents life as it's experienced by many, if not most, of my students. It's real in a way that's also age appropriate."

"According to *you*."

Maggie had a master's degree in theatre education, so she was an expert in the subject. "Yes."

Luckily, Grace Choi stepped in. "If Rylee's correct, you should have encountered widespread outrage. Were there a lot of complaints?" Somehow, Grace made this sound evenhanded and not sarcastic, which Maggie suspected it was.

"Only one. To be clear, participating in the play and attending it were optional. I did offer extra credit to students who came. But one student's parents thought the content was too extreme, and after they went to the school board, I was fired."

"Which is when you tried to cash in," Rylee said.

Maggie had to blink back the emotions threatening to pour out of her eyes. She knew she'd done nothing wrong, that she'd been right ped-agogically, and that a few yahoos on the school board had been looking for an opportunity to make a statement. Even Maggie's parents, who would rather have had their daughter writing education policy than teaching, had seen the value in the lawsuit. It was one of the first times in Maggie's life when she'd felt as if she hadn't been disappointing them.

The money she'd gotten in the settlement had barely covered her legal fees. In a few months, the small nest egg Maggie had managed to squirrel away was going to disappear, and, not to put too fine a point on it, she'd be totally broke.

"I wasn't looking for a sweet payday. I sued for wrongful termination—and won—because it was a fight that had to be won." She was here today for other teachers who might find themselves in the same situation. As much as Maggie hated this, she had to be public about her win. It might give someone else the confidence to fight.

"Oh really," Rylee sneered. "Then why didn't you return to teaching?"

"I thought I was going to. But my case shows how things have changed in American public schools. Teaching is hard under the best of circumstances. I taught three classes of drama and two of stage-craft every year. Most school years, I directed two plays and a musical. I've sewed costumes and painted sets and hung lights. My days were regularly twelve hours long, once I tacked rehearsals and construction meetings onto the end of a regular school day." Maggie hadn't realized how hard she'd been working, the constant furious paddling she'd been doing, until it had stopped.

"My word," Denise said.

"That's not unusual, by the way. Almost every elementary, middle, and high school teacher has a schedule like that. Many of us coach or lead clubs or spend extra time mentoring or tutoring, in addition to our teaching. But when I won my case, the idea of going back to that schedule in such a hostile environment—I just couldn't." She'd been wringing herself dry, all while vipers had waited in the grass to pounce.

"Because you were too busy promoting yourself and your agenda?" Rylee demanded.

"I don't have an agenda." Maggie sounded almost desperate. "But the things the school board didn't like in *Covering the Spread* are real. Queer families exist. Parents sometimes pressure their kids in unhealthy ways. People use strong language. Teenagers kiss and break up and learn who they are outside the roles society and their families want to put them in. But that's the point: drama is about our very humanity. Art can't be art, it can't teach us anything or entertain us, if it denies those things. If we scrub all the so-called difficult content out, it's just a puppet show—and not a very good puppet show."

Rylee was steaming mad now. She was trying to hide it, but a vein in her temple had started to bulge. "So anything goes?"

"That isn't my position at all. I was always acutely aware of the responsibility I had to my students to pick works they could understand thematically and artistically, and *Covering the Spread* did that."

"And the court agreed with you," Denise put in.

"Yes." That was why Maggie had to sue. She had to make sure that some other teacher had the precedent of Maggie's case for protection.

"You have an answer for everything, don't you? But I've done my research, and I know that you'd been planning this for years," Rylee spit out. "You did a study, right? About teaching high school students to kiss?"

She'd been braced for this. Rylee's "research" had clearly consisted of downloading Parent Led's talking points.

"No, I didn't." Maggie certainly wasn't going to let Rylee lie about her. "I wrote my master's thesis about the challenges and best practices for directing *Romeo and Juliet* with a teenage cast. It was based on my experiences and those of two other drama teachers. How do you make sure everyone is comfortable with the blocking? What does negotiating consent look like?"

"You mean intimacy coordination?" Denise asked.

"Yes. Most high schools won't have someone doing that exclusively, the way they do on Broadway or in Hollywood, but you still need to think about *how* to direct those scenes and the feelings of everyone involved. Not because there's something dirty or wrong about kissing, but because you want to do it well, for the actors and the audience."

"If I could get in here," Zoya Delgado said, piping up for the first time. "I totally agree with Maggie. Sex is part of human experience, so it would be weird if film, television, and theatre didn't represent it at least some of the time. But you have to be responsible about it."

"Do you use an intimacy coordinator on *Waverley*?" Denise asked.

"We haven't," Zoya said slowly, as she watched Maggie with a gleam in her eye. "But we should."

Across the table, Rylee was incensed. "I can't believe you are all pretending that this is normal. It's disgusting. Teenagers kissing in front of an audience while you applaud? What filth. I, for one, am glad you aren't teaching anymore."

And there was the toxicity that made returning to teaching impossible.

Maggie's classroom had felt like a space where anything was possible. She had helped her students grow, and they had produced truly beautiful art together. But she had no idea how she was supposed to go back there knowing it was a minefield. Whatever bonds of trust she'd needed to be a good teacher had been shredded.

Even now, faced with the vitriol in Rylee's eyes, it was hard to imagine how any of those bonds could be remade. The woman, and the people who agreed with her, despised Maggie and everything she stood for. Maggie knew her own position was right, but seeing that hatred felt awful.

"I . . . disagree. And so did the court. But I have to say, it doesn't feel like a victory. It feels like we all lost something."

Denise let the sadness in Maggie's answer sit in the air for a minute before saying, "Well, after a break for some local headlines, we'll talk to Zoya Delgado, the showrunner for Videon's hit *Waverley*, which has also come under fire for some risqué content."

Lana Larkin, the boozy grandma of the panel who'd become famous doing fashion commentary during red carpets, piped up for the first time. "It's all the butts! People tuned in for the butts."

That was . . . succinct and probably true. The cast of the show had some very nice butts.

Denise ignored Lana. "We'll talk about how they film those steamy scenes, and the drama around the cast for the upcoming season, including the casting of Tasha Russell and Cole James."

"Woo-hoo, that man," Lana said with a wolf whistle. "I cannot wait to see his—"

"And we're out," the producer called as the light by the camera flipped to red, and thus the world would never know which Cole James body part Lana was dying to see.

Maggie pressed her hands to her cheeks and tried not to look at Rylee, who was stage-whispering to her makeup person about how everyone on the panel was *so mean*. She might have thrown the word *floozy* in there too.

Maggie wouldn't mind being a floozy, actually. It sounded fun. But instead, she was going to have to settle for a double order of fries.

If only Maggie were better at this. More charismatic. More persuasive. More like her parents wanted her to be. But there would never be any convincing the Rylees of the world—Maggie knew that for sure. You couldn't give facts to someone whose argument was built on a foundation of bad faith. They didn't want them.

Besides, there weren't going to be many more moments like this one. Interest in the lawsuit and in Maggie was fading, and she'd soon have to decide what to do with the rest of her life and how to pay her bills.

And that was probably the scariest thought of all.

"You can get some air if you want," Grace said. "Local affiliates have a few minutes for headlines."

With a grateful sigh, Maggie stood and slipped behind the cameras. The temperature dropped at least twenty degrees once she was on the other side of the set. She truly had no idea how the hosts of *Hear Her* could stand it. She was slick with sweat. She listed against the wall, where she was out of everyone's way, and took a few deep breaths.

But someone else clearly had the same idea. "Maggie," Zoya Delgado called. "I'm glad I caught you. It's great to finally meet you."

It was as if the mall Santa told you he was excited to meet you when you went up for a picture. "Um, I'm pretty sure that's my line. I'm a big fan of the show."

If Maggie weren't still feeling green from her confrontation with Rylee, she would've had a zillion questions about the upcoming season. At some point, she was going to regret not asking them—after all, how many times was she going to meet Zoya freaking Delgado?—but she was too wiped at the moment.

"And *I'm* a big fan of the stuff you've been saying about how art should represent human experiences—all human experiences. If you're not going back to teaching, I have to ask: Have you ever thought about working in Hollywood?"

Maggie was grateful for the wall under her shoulder; otherwise, she might have fallen flat onto her tailbone. The months she'd spent suppressing her gag reflex let her keep her voice even when she replied, "What did you have in mind?"

Chapter 3

INT. POSH TOWN CAR

Three Months Later

London made Cole feel like a hick. The mix of massive stone buildings and modern skyscrapers and intersections called circuses was dizzying. When the English called a building old, it was, like, actually old. And then there were the British accents.

It was just so *classy*, it made Cole feel like a dirty lumberjack. He kept wanting to apologize for the Boston Tea Party or for not going to college.

"Stop fucking fidgeting." Tasha was sitting next to him in the back of the town car on the way to a rehearsal space. With her blonde hair in some kind of perfect twist and in white from head to toe, she looked as if she belonged in London. Tasha absolutely didn't have a class problem . . . except for the part where she swore like a pirate. A perfectly arranged, foulmouthed pirate.

Cole ought to be swabbing the decks. It hadn't occurred to him before he'd gotten into the car with Tasha that jeans and a leather jacket weren't fancy enough for this meeting. He probably shouldn't have brought them to England at all. It should've been all frock coats, all the time. "This was a mistake."

"Not taking separate cars? Yes. I'd forgotten how jittery you get before filming."

"No, me taking this part. I can't play the son of a baron. Who am I fooling?"

"No one. You'll be fine. They hired you for these." She poked him in the stomach affectionately.

"Ouch." Cole was pretty sore. It had been an abs day.

It was always an abs day.

"See? You've been working your ass off to prepare for this part in the ways that matter. You have to walk in there as if you own the place. Like you're going to win an Emmy."

"But I'm not." He might hand Emmys out, but he didn't win them. *Hot frat boy* and *action hero* weren't the kind of roles that raked in golden statues, but those were what Cole had spent the bulk of his career playing. The truth was, it didn't even make him sad. He knew he wasn't that kind of actor.

Tasha rolled her eyes. "Then you have to project the attitude that you not winning was a goddamn oversight. You're doing them a favor. You have to believe that."

For Tasha—beautiful, bankable, and with multiple Oscar nominations—*Waverley* was a detour. While she'd denied it up and down, Cole knew she'd taken the part to help him. It was maybe the nicest thing anyone had ever done for him.

But for Cole, this was the mountain peak he'd been climbing toward, and he wasn't sure he could summit. Just look at this place, at the rows of creamy stone houses and the literal palaces and the warehouses converted into hip museums. He didn't belong here.

His doubt had him breathing hard, as if the oxygen in the car was slowly depleting—which sounded like a scene in some crap movie he'd make.

When they stopped in front of the rehearsal space, a couple of bored paparazzi were congregated near the door, smoking. They put out their cigarettes with obvious annoyance, as if Cole and Tasha had arrived too early.

Cole hopped onto the sidewalk and held the car door open for Tasha. In keeping with their usual shtick, she kept close and Cole let his hand linger on her lower back while the paps dutifully snapped a few pictures. In ten minutes, those images would be doing the rounds on social media, making a dozen hashtags trend around the world.

It was a little game they played together. It had started by accident, but Tasha had insisted they keep it up because it kept Cole's name in the press—in a good way. Every few years, they'd go through another intense cycle of *Cole and Tasha are getting serious this time* before the story became *Tasha's broken Cole's heart—again!*

Honestly, it wasn't fair. One of these times, Cole ought to be the one to break *her* heart, but the fans preferred to think of Tasha as a cold ice queen, with him as the golden retriever panting behind her.

Cole didn't enjoy lying, but he and Tasha never said anything about it at all. They just arranged a scene every once in a while, and fans supplied the rest, seeing things that weren't there in Cole's and Tasha's body language and facial expressions. It was kind of amazing, actually, the level of detail some people would pull out of the pics and the theories they'd come up with.

And it wasn't like there was anyone in Cole's life for this to bother. It sounded like a dodge, but Cole had been so focused on his career, he hadn't had time to date the last few years. Besides, when he'd been a little less focused and he had met women, they hadn't seen the real man who was under Cody Rhodes or whatever G.I. Joe he'd been playing that day. His friendship with Tasha was about as good as it got, and he was okay with that. He had to focus on his career. That was what mattered.

Zoya Delgado met them at the door of the rehearsal space. "Cole, Tasha, it's good to see you again."

The auditions had gone on for several months, and Cole had gotten to know Zoya fairly well. The show was her baby. She'd adapted it, and she even wrote and directed some of the episodes. Zoya was deeply invested in *Waverley* being good, being right. After making so many projects that no one seemed to truly care about, Cole appreciated that this one was different.

"I'm glad you two could get here before the table read. It's going to be such a long shoot, I know." They'd rehearse in London before moving to Edinburgh and the Scottish Highlands for the exterior shots and finally to a Glasgow studio for the interiors. Altogether, it was going to take almost four months to shoot the season's nine episodes. "But I wanted to touch base, and I thought it would be good for you two to meet Maggie Niven."

"Maggie?" Tasha said. "Who's that?"

Zoya signaled, and a woman approached them with a tentative smile. Honey-brown hair fell almost to her elbows, curling a bit at the ends, and framed her pale heart-shaped face. She had light eyes, though she wasn't close enough for Cole to make out if they were green, blue, or gray.

Her gaze slid over Cole, and she focused on Tasha. "Hey, it's great to meet you. I'm your intimacy coordinator."

Cole's heart tripped into his ribs.

Dammit. This was not the moment for his libido to jerk awake after a long hibernation. It was the time for him to kick ass at his job.

"What?" Tasha demanded.

Zoya wasn't bothered by his friend's tone. "Didn't Greta"—Tasha's agent—"tell you? We decided to add an intimacy coordinator this season. Maggie will help you, Cole, and the rest of the cast block and rehearse the scenes with nudity and simulated sex, but she's also going to be a liaison between the actors and the production."

Maggie nodded. "It's my job to make sure there's no friction."

"You could've just bought a can of WD-40." Tasha directed that right at Zoya, as if Maggie didn't exist.

That was a little rude. What was Tasha's problem?

Although maybe Cole should also be pretending Maggie didn't exist, because he kept noticing the way her sweater fell over her curves or the freckle crowning her lip, and he didn't like it. Dating someone on set was something he'd done back when he was young and stupid. It was a bad idea, much like embezzlement or participating in celebrity group videos singing "Imagine."

Cole dragged himself back to what was safe: being easy to work with and kind to all crew members. "I think this is great." He said it partially to defend Maggie—who he'd met ten entire seconds before—but also because he honestly thought having an intimacy coordinator for the show was an excellent idea.

Cole's body *was* his career. It had always been that way, and he'd never been confused about why he got hired for jobs, what was expected of him, or how he was going to be filmed. But having someone on set whose entire job was to advocate for him? Cole was down with that.

"Maybe for amateurs," Tasha shot back. "You an amateur, James?"

"No, but—"

"Because I've been making movies since I was seventeen. I don't get why we need this."

Cole was confused. This didn't feel like a diva thing, which would be par for the course for Tasha. It smelled more . . . anxious than that.

"Rhiannon Simmons is a relative newbie," Zoya said of the twenty-two-year-old who was going to play Madge Wildfire. Geordie was going to seduce her too. That guy got around. "She and Cole have love scenes. And Owen Roy has some concerns that we discussed during his audition."

"Isn't he part of the chaste, boring B-couple?"

Zoya swallowed a laugh. "Yes, but I still don't want to be the subject of his tell-all memoir in a few years. I don't want him to *write* a tell-all memoir in a few years. *Waverley* is a strictly no-trauma zone."

Tasha muttered something under her breath. Cole couldn't make out every word, but her tone was skeptical and profane.

"This is becoming the industry standard," Zoya said.

"So it's *required*?"

Interesting. Cole had never seen Tasha be this difficult about anything other than her willingness to do her own stunts. The woman was fearless.

So Zoya thought they needed some extra help during the love scenes. What was the problem?

Maggie was watching Tasha and Zoya's exchange without any emotion. They might as well have been discussing something that didn't affect her at all. Her eyes—they were light green—shifted to Cole, and she caught him watching her. She tipped her head to the side, and while she didn't smile, the lines around her mouth grew deeper.

Cole's answering grin was reflexive, and it made him feel like a doofus, but he couldn't have smothered it if he'd tried. Maggie was really pretty, and she'd absolutely caught him checking her out.

Beyond the hint of amusement, though, Cole couldn't tell what she was thinking. She was better than he was at keeping her expression neutral.

Cole's cheeks were heating now, apparently unaware that he was too old—way too old—to get a crush on a coworker.

She wet her lips, and he—

"Don't you think, Maggie?"

Maggie startled and turned back to Zoya. "Yes." She said it firmly. It wasn't a question; it was an answer. A confident answer. Maybe she was better at multitasking than he was and she actually knew what she was committing to, because he didn't have a clue.

Her conviction was pretty hot.

"So let's just sit down and talk through the process," Zoya said to Tasha. "Then you, Cole, and Maggie can figure out how to move forward from there."

Tasha harrumphed, but, like, in a chic way, and they all took seats around the conference table.

Maggie folded her hands on top of a stack of scripts. Little colored paper flags stuck out of them, and he'd guess she had an entire system. Blue probably meant one thing and red another and green something else. He wanted to ask about it, just as a matter of professional curiosity, but next to him, Tasha was a gray cloud, threatening a thunderstorm.

Right, he had to smooth things over with his best friend, who seemed spooked for some reason, and then he could have a completely Drew-approved conversation with the intimacy coordinator.

"Whatever happened to 'You're doing them a favor'?" he muttered to Tasha.

"You're looking at it."

"You okay?"

"Fucking peachy."

If the peach had grown prickles and a bad attitude, sure.

But across the table, Maggie was proceeding as if everyone in the room was totally on board. "Before we get into the details of how you'd like to work, I wanted to hear about what drew you to this project."

She looked at Tasha expectantly. Tasha just glared.

"I'll go first." For a beat, Cole imagined saying *It seemed really cool, and it's super popular but also bookish, and I think that would be good for me.* He liked to be honest, but that was obviously too honest. "Zoya's approach sold me," he said instead. "The show's fresh and different, and I wanted to be involved in *Waverley* in one way or another as soon as I saw it."

"What do you find compelling about Geordie?" Maggie asked.

"At the start of the season, he's selfish. He lets his friend take the fall for their smuggling operation. He breaks Madge's heart, and he gets Effie pregnant and doesn't marry her at a time when that's, like, really bad. But he's going to grow—to accept responsibility for his actions, to become a husband and father, and to take his place running the family estate. It's his growth that made me want to play him."

"That's great, Cole," Maggie said. "I agree that Geordie and Effie are fascinating, and we can use the love scenes to show their arcs. How they go from being two volatile people who share intense chemistry to being two people who've matured and are making a commitment to each other. At the end of the season, I believe they're in love and are going to parent their baby and build a life together. I mean, I know it's sexy and thrilling, but it's also really moving."

That was everything Cole wanted for his character . . . and probably also for himself. Maybe not the love part, but definitely the growth and redemption.

Next to him, Tasha's posture had softened. Her hands were folded in her lap, and she was at least following the conversation now.

Maggie must have picked up on the shift, too, because she said, "I was thinking we could begin by talking through the nudity and the love scenes. Zoya can walk us through the rough blocking and costume stuff, and you can red-flag anything that you have concerns about. Obviously we'll go through these in greater detail later, and you can always come to me if any worries pop up, but we wanted to take a five-thousand-foot view to start. I have them marked."

Of course she did.

She held up the script for the first episode. "So let's start with the moment when Geordie leads the mob into the jail and tries to free Effie." Effie was going to refuse, but the script had Geordie and Effie going at it up against a wall first.

One thing Cole could say for Zoya: she knew what the audience wanted, and she had no hesitations about giving it to them. And what they wanted was him naked. Early and often.

"Right." Tasha held up her hand. "I'm certain you're nice and you're good at what you do, Maggie." Her tone hinted she was not actually certain about that. "But—"

"This is only my third job," Maggie said. "And really, it's my first one not as a shadow or an assistant."

"Excuse me?"

"I'm changing careers. I was a high school drama teacher, and—"

She'd been a high school drama teacher? Adorable.

The job, not Maggie.

Well, also Maggie.

"*Excuse me?*" Tasha repeated, and they were back to her "petulant, anxious diva" routine.

And she'd accused *him* of being jumpy.

Maggie smiled sweetly, as if they were having a normal exchange, and said, "Yup."

"She's working with Bernard Caldwell, one of the best in the business," Zoya put in. "He's the senior intimacy coordinator, and she's the junior IC. Sadly, Bernard broke his leg in a recumbent bike accident, so he didn't want to travel to the UK, but he did all the preproduction and is consulting with Maggie every step of the way. We're lucky to have her."

Zoya was trying to make it clear she'd made her decision and she didn't intend to hear any debate on the matter.

But, of course, Tasha ignored Zoya's will in the way some people ignored those warning labels on pillows that said *Don't remove this*. "I was never on board with the idea of an intimacy coordinator, but you have got to be kidding me with this. I'm a professional, Cole's a professional. Let's just *go*."

With a sweep, she rose from the table and blew out of the room.

Silence settled while Cole tried to decide what was the best way to apologize for Tasha's behavior without having it sound like he was criticizing her, because he was certain she had a good reason for being a brat to Maggie. He just needed to pry it out of her, and then they could fix it together.

Before he could figure out what to say, Zoya got to her feet with a sigh. "Let me chat with her. Maggie, don't worry, this isn't about you. You keep talking with Cole, and I'll be back in a few minutes with our leading lady."

They watched Zoya leave, and then Cole said, "Tasha isn't normally—no, okay, she's normally like this. She's kind of . . . dramatic." Although the fireworks were typically more like a mask. This felt real.

"She's an actor." Maggie didn't seem to be offended, which was good because Cole didn't want to trash his best friend. "I've been watching your old work. You've done a decent amount of intimacy—a lot of nudity and some simulated sex."

"Yeah, it's kind of . . . expected, I guess, with the type of parts I do."

"And how do you feel about that?"

"It's the job."

Her eyes narrowed. That hadn't been what she'd asked, but she didn't push him on it. Instead, she said, "Tasha, though, hasn't. The movies you made together, *Chaos Principle* and *Fuse*, there was some kissing, but no nudity, no simulated sex."

There had been a love scene in the first version of the script for *Fuse*, but Tasha had convinced the director to cut it. Cole hadn't asked why. He'd been too grateful to be making the movie. The truth was he hadn't thought he'd had enough power to make any kind of demands. If they wanted him to get naked, he did. If they wanted him in bed with this costar or that one, he got in the damn bed.

Whatever Maggie was implying, it almost didn't make sense.

"Tasha was worried about getting typecast in rom-coms." He was fairly certain she'd said something like that to him once.

"Hmm." Maggie clearly didn't believe the explanation, and Cole didn't really either.

Huh, how *had* Tasha avoided getting naked on screen for so long?

"Do you think she has concerns about the scripts for *Waverley* as written?"

"I don't know," he admitted.

"Super fair." A pause. "Do you have concerns about the scripts as written?"

"Not really."

"No—or not really?"

Cole scratched his cheek before doing something that made him feel as if he were stripping down to his boxers: telling Maggie the truth. "I don't think so, but no one has ever asked me that. At least not anyone who cares about the answer."

Once again, he forced himself to meet her eyes, and he and Maggie shared a long look.

Finally, with almost painful gentleness, Maggie said, "I'm so sorry that happened to you."

Cole cleared his throat. He readjusted his jacket. He crossed and uncrossed his arms. Every part of him was suddenly screwed on too tight. "It's fine."

"It really isn't." She let that sit between them for a minute. "But I'm here for you and for Tasha, and also for Owen, Rhiannon, and Leanne. This *is* a new role for me—Tasha's right to be skeptical—but I care a lot about getting this right. I want the production to be safe for you."

Safe.

The word could've been from a language Cole didn't speak. His career hadn't been anything like safe, both because of the choices he'd made and also the choices no one had thought to give him.

For Maggie to offer that to him now? Some soft space opened in his chest that he hadn't known had been there.

"I—thank you." His voice was quiet, as if it came from far away.

"My pleasure."

When the door opened and Zoya stuck her head in, Cole jumped. He'd forgotten other people were supposed to be in this meeting.

"Tasha's done for the day. She took your town car, Cole. Since we have time, we should pack it in and try again tomorrow. I can run you back to the Rosewood, if you want."

"Um, yeah. That'd be great."

"I appreciate your openness." Maggie stood up and started to gather her stuff. "I'm just this random person, and you don't know me, but I hope I'll be able to make a difference."

Cole was tempted to say something ridiculous, such as *You already have.* But he kept that inside. It would be too much, and the goal—his goal—was to be professional.

What he needed to do here, what Drew would tell him to do, was to get Tasha on board so that Maggie could do her job and he and Tasha could do theirs.

"Look, Tasha and I have a reservation tonight at Troncos. It's a Brazilian place where we know the chef. It's a few blocks from the Rosewood. Are you staying there too?" He had no idea if they put the crew up at the same hotel as the cast—though he was going to feel like an ass if the production team had dumped her in a Motel 6 in the burbs.

"Yes."

"Great. Why don't you come with us? Maybe we can . . . get on friendly terms and thaw Tasha out. Let's meet in the lobby at eight."

Maggie had slid her scripts into a canvas bag. She was staring fixedly into it, as if she didn't want to look at him.

That bothered Cole more than it should have.

"She's not going to mind if I crash your dinner?"

"No." Actually, yes. But it didn't matter. Maggie was great. Once Tasha talked to her more, she'd realize it, and whatever was going on today would resolve. "And once she gets to know you, it'll work out. Trust me."

Cole hadn't realized how invested he was in Maggie's answer, or that he'd been holding his breath waiting for it, until she said, "Okay."

The entire ride back to the hotel, he told himself he only cared because it was what a professional would feel.

Chapter 4

INT. FANCY RESTAURANT

"So have I made a terrible mistake?" Maggie asked.

"Ma'am," the waiter said carefully, the vowel drawn out so long he might as well have been addressing the Queen. "I can show you the way to the chef's table now." Because it turned out that the waitstaff at Michelin-starred restaurants couldn't offer you vital career reassurance, even if you demanded it after you'd gotten lost on your way back from the bathroom, where you'd been hiding from the actress who wanted to disembowel you.

"Yes. Of course. I'm sorry to . . . dump on you."

"Very good."

It could be considered good only because Tasha hadn't stabbed Maggie yet.

Ten minutes ago in the hotel lobby, Tasha had taken one look at Maggie, and the temperature had dropped into the range that could only be measured in kelvins. Maggie would've declared a tactical retreat right then if it hadn't been for Cole. He'd clapped Tasha on the shoulder, told her that she looked amazing, and hustled both women into the waiting town car.

I think I've annoyed an Amazon warrior, Maggie had texted her best friend, Savannah, during the ride to the restaurant.

If your murderer has great hair, you're ten times more likely to be featured on a true crime podcast, Savannah had replied.

Which was probably an underestimate. True crimers couldn't resist beautiful murderers.

The waiter Maggie had cornered pushed the door open to the chef's table and ushered her inside. The private dining room was sleek and understated, with a single long table. The chairs were all on one side so everyone could look out the glass wall that separated it from the kitchen.

There, at least a dozen people were flying around the counters and cooking surfaces, chopping, sautéing, and plating dishes. The kitchen was a whirl of copper pans and a rainbow of produce, of fire and steam and noise. The mad choreography of it was mesmerizing.

And unlike in the main dining room, no one here was watching Maggie's famous dinner companions. This, despite the fact that in person, Tasha Russell was actually breathtaking. Her blonde hair and her pale skin seemed to emit light, like a saint in a Renaissance painting. Cole James wasn't hard on the eyes either. As long as Maggie didn't look directly at him, her heart rate stayed only slightly elevated, and that was just how it was going to have to be for the next four months.

Elevated . . . and curious. Maggie would've had to be living under a rock to miss the pictures of Cole and Tasha together. Her concern about their relationship was merely professional, of course. It would complicate her job if they were exes.

But now, Maggie didn't know what the hell she was dealing with. After the disastrous meeting, she'd had a long call with Bernard Caldwell. He had decades of experience as an intimacy coordinator, and Zoya had arranged for Maggie to be his apprentice. The last three months, he'd mentored Maggie on negotiating consent and managing conflict, and she'd been his shadow and then his assistant on two smaller indie projects in order to get her SAG card.

Technically, Maggie and Bernard were both intimacy coordinators for this season of *Waverley*. When he'd decided not to come to the UK, she'd had the giddy sense of graduating, at least until Tasha had refused to work with her.

Whatever their history might be, Maggie suspected that Cole and Tasha weren't together now. But they also weren't what Bernard had prepped her to expect: Cole James wasn't some Hollywood himbo, and while Tasha Russell was playing the diva, the drama felt like an attempt to hide something.

Maggie had seen that move from students all the time. Except she had a premonition that when she managed to pry up this stepping stone, she'd find maggots underneath.

"Tash and I know the chef from way back," Cole said as Maggie took her seat next to his. "The food's supposed to be good here."

Maggie almost barked out a laugh. Two Michelin stars, and that only rated a "good"? Movie stars: they're just like us.

"Forget the food. Let's hope the wine cellar's loaded," Tasha muttered.

"I'd bet Jose has both reds *and* whites."

"Good. I'll take a bottle of each, and maybe a rosé, too, just for kicks."

"If you have a hangover at our riding lesson tomorrow, Ryan will be pissed at me." Then to Maggie, he muttered, "He's the stunt coordinator. We've worked with him before."

Cole might be trying to pretend Tasha wasn't annoyed with him, but Maggie suspected he cared very much about Tasha's feelings—and, strangely, about Maggie's too.

Maggie had been prepared for Cole to be good looking; he was basically professionally hot. But what didn't translate to the glossy spreads in magazines or his high-testosterone movies was his sweetness. If Tasha intrigued Maggie because of her evident badassery, Cole held her attention because he was too easy to like.

People were mostly awesome, or at least that had been Maggie's hypothesis until she'd been fired. In that instant, the world had turned into Whac-A-Mole but with assholes.

Cole's innate sweetness was a fall of rain on the hard plain of Maggie's soul. Even now, green shoots were popping up inside her. *This. This is what you used to feel like—and maybe could again.*

Maggie reached for her water and took a long drag as a tall, slim, gorgeous man entered from the kitchen.

"Tasha, love, I've been working over a hot stove all day for you."

"You have no idea how excited I am." Tasha jumped up and kissed Chef Jose Alpin on both cheeks.

"Jose catered the set for *Chaos Principle*. We shot it here, at Shepperton," Cole explained in a whisper to Maggie. "We've wanted to check out this place ever since he started it."

Cole's breath made Maggie's cheek tingle, and it was hard not to trace the path of the sensation with her fingers.

"And who did you bring along without giving me a heads-up?" Jose asked, his tone mild.

"Hiya, man." Cole stood up to shake Jose's hand. "This is Maggie. She's our intimacy coordinator."

"Your what?"

"See." Tasha snapped her fingers decisively. "This is my point. How can you need something if you don't understand what it is?"

The chef rolled his eyes at the starlet before leaning across the table to shake Maggie's hand. "I'm sure Maggie's indispensable if Cole brought her along."

At that, Maggie hit her limit for the number of smoldering men she could handle today.

But Jose was still smiling that panty-melting grin, and Maggie had to say *something*. Trying not to sound breathless, she offered, "If me being here messes up your menu, I'm happy to just have a salad." She'd perused the menu online, almost died when she'd seen the prices, and then told herself that you only live once. But it would be far healthier for her bank account if she ate like a rabbit.

"Nonsense." Jose shot Cole a look. "I get why you needed intimacy coordination at dinner. I may get one too."

Tasha threw herself back into her chair. "Less chitchat, more eating."

"Your wish is my command, princess."

Jose held the door open, and three servers entered. In unison, they set a plate and a cocktail down in front of Tasha, Cole, and Maggie.

"To start, we have carabineros," Jose explained. "It's an Atlantic prawn, and I've prepared it with a sauce made from Sardinian Camone tomatoes and a tomato vodka that we make here on site. The drink pairing for this course is a caipirinha. Enjoy."

When Cole had said they were going to a Brazilian restaurant, Maggie had imagined steaks, salsa verde, and potatoes. Had she ever heard a chef mention what kind of tomatoes a sauce was made with before?

No, but then again, she'd never seen a sauce that was so vividly, almost painfully red. It smelled like sunshine, with the barest hint of pepper and the beach.

Jose and his merry band of servers exited, and Tasha immediately scooped up her prawn. She took a bite and moaned. "This is why we put up with Jose."

Cole reached for his cocktail. "You just don't like that he isn't impressed with you."

"I know, right? It's fucking uncanny. But so is this carabinero."

Seafood wasn't Maggie's favorite, but it wasn't as if she'd ever have the chance to eat the supersecret, superspecial chef's tasting menu at a two-Michelin-star restaurant ever again. And it was so beautiful, her mouth was watering despite herself.

She took a tentative bite, and it turned out Maggie didn't mind seafood if Jose prepared it. Intense tomato flavors exploded in her mouth, perfectly balanced between sweetness and brightness, with the prawn— lightly salty and buttery and not at all fishy—harmonizing with it all.

"What do you think?" Cole had watched her trepidation, and he hadn't touched his own food while he'd waited for Maggie's response.

"I don't normally go for seafood, but this tastes like summer in the best way."

"Catering can be hit or miss," Cole said, "but *Chaos Principle* is the best I've ever eaten on a set."

When they finished their first plates, those were instantly whisked away, and another set was delivered.

"How many dishes is Jose planning?" Tasha asked one of the servers.

"Fifteen."

Maggie emptied her glass.

When they had finished the fanciest Caesar salad Maggie had ever had, the dressing for which had been basically the Platonic ideal of creamy, Cole leaned back in his chair. "So the meeting this afternoon didn't go as planned. I thought we could have a nice meal, and then—"

"Nope," Tasha interrupted. "I don't want to talk about that. It'll just make me angry. What I want to do is enjoy this food and recover from my jet lag."

"Tasha doesn't do well with international travel," Cole said to Maggie.

He kept doing that, offering context or explanation, as if he knew that Tasha needed to be translated. He obviously understood Tasha, but he was also being very considerate of Maggie.

There her stomach went again—missing the bottom stair and wiping out.

Luckily, the servers materialized again, now with plates of roast chicken. The skin was golden and crispy, and the aroma had unlocked some feeling in Maggie's chest that could only be characterized as *home*. She felt like that mean critic in *Ratatouille*, except without the whole being-a-food-writer thing.

The entire meal had her feeling grubby and ignorant. And it wasn't just that she was sitting next to two people whom she'd seen a thousand pictures of. It wasn't just the white-glove treatment the staff lavished on them. It wasn't just that each dish was more elaborate than the last, containing flavors and aromas and ingredients Maggie had never heard of. It wasn't even the cocktails going to her head . . . though, okay, it was that too.

It was that this meal felt like a personality quiz in the back of an old *Cosmo*. Tasha was chic and discerning, Cole was affable and open, and Maggie was a peasant.

It didn't help that Tasha kept resisting all Cole's attempts to talk about Maggie's role or filming the show.

When she'd been dealing with a student with opposition defiance, Maggie would try to establish common ground with the kid and to offer them choices, all while trying to figure out what was causing the resistance. This afternoon, Tasha's temper tantrum had almost wrecked Maggie's fragile confidence. But because she'd been here before, she knew that the real key was you couldn't, under any circumstances, get dragged into a power struggle. It was sincerely one of those situations where you won by not playing. Solving someone's resistance took time.

But Cole barreled right in during the dessert course. "So I gotta ask, why are you so opposed to this? You'll do what the production wants when it's training, but—"

"Please," Tasha scoffed. "I'd rather wax my cunt."

Maggie was grateful she hadn't had any food in her mouth.

"Something that's supposed to be about protecting actors: that's where you draw the line?"

Tasha sipped her wine and ignored Cole.

A beat passed. Then another. Then ten.

Finally, Tasha said, "I don't have a problem with intimacy coordination *in theory*."

Cole looked at Maggie and beamed, as if to say *Now we're getting someplace*.

Maggie's heart leaped into her throat.

Resting, Cole's face had a sculpted beauty, with his high cheekbones, straight nose, and architectural brows. But when he smiled, his features went goofy. Happiness, like the kind he was trying to share with her now, muddled his cheekbones and wrinkled his nose.

He suddenly looked boyish, but somehow so much better looking. Cole was *touchable* when he smiled.

Except Maggie had no business thinking that.

Which was why it was a relief, totally a relief, when he took that smile with him as he turned back to Tasha. "So you have a problem with Maggie?"

"No."

Now that oxygen was getting to Maggie's brain again, she could tell Tasha meant that.

"But I was blindsided this afternoon, and I don't think it's necessary for us to work with Maggie. If other people on the set want her, like Owen and Rhiannon, that's fine. I'm sure that she's . . . fine. But can we just eat our baba in peace?"

The golden custard looked amazing—everything had been amazing—but Maggie would much rather go down this rabbit hole, even if she was simply observing this conversation and not participating in it.

"No," Cole said to Tasha. "This is a weird thing to dig in about. Also, I realized today that you haven't done much nudity since *Cosa Nostra*."

That was, in the mildest sense, a lie. Maggie had pointed it out to him. But she suspected Cole was saying this not to take credit for Maggie's observation but in order to shield Maggie from any more of Tasha's wrath.

Tasha ground her teeth, slowly, making a show of it so that Cole and Maggie would realize she didn't want to talk about this. It wasn't a power thing, not quite. Maggie had the sense that she was doing it for herself as well as for them.

"How did you get this job?" she finally asked Maggie.

That was fair. Maybe if Tasha trusted Maggie, this would go better. "I met Zoya on *Hear Her*, and she thought I would be a good fit for this."

Her parents still weren't over their shock. If her being a high school teacher had been mildly disappointing, going to work in Hollywood, especially like this, was spitting in their eyes.

"Because you were fired for directing a sexy play?" Tasha asked. "Yeah, I looked you up."

That was almost a relief. "You know, it isn't even a sexy play. I was fired for doing a play. Whatever other excuses the school board might have come up with, the empathy and imagination you need for theatre were the real problems."

Tasha considered this. "Have you ever been on a television set?"

"I've always liked movies and theatre. An older cousin of mine was a PA at Sony for a while, and then he worked as an assistant director on a couple of indie films. I did an 'internship' for him one summer when I was in college. Mostly I got coffee and flirted with grips."

Maggie considered detailing her time with Bernard, but Tasha didn't want Maggie's résumé. Tasha was after something more elemental here.

"The truth is, as a performer, I had debilitating stage fright and not very much talent. My Cali summer was fun, but it didn't feel real. And then it dawned on me, there were other ways to have a life in theatre."

"So you became a drama teacher?"

"Yup. Then a lightning rod. And now I'm here." Maggie licked her lips, trying to pick her words carefully. As if there were some combination of syllables out there that would defuse the tension and make Tasha see that Maggie was on her side. "This can be whatever you want it to be. I can be as involved as you want in the scenes, or we can touch base about your hard limits and you never have to see me again. You define how this goes. I'm just here to support you."

Maggie had the sense that Tasha might not even know what her hard limits *were*. But she was now stone-cold certain that Tasha's resistance wasn't about Maggie's lack of experience as much as about on-screen nudity itself. But she wasn't going to tip her suspicions now.

Hey, so I've noticed you might be traumatized would go over about as well as an IED.

Tasha pushed her spoon through her custard, considering Maggie's offer. "Where were you during *Cosa Nostra*?" she finally mumbled.

Now they were getting somewhere.

"What happened during *Cosa Nostra*?"

Maggie had seen the movie, of course. Tasha had played the daughter of a mafia don who'd been forced into an unhappy marriage with a rival family's son and rebelled by seducing several soldiers and capos. It had struck Maggie as a fearless performance, especially given that Tasha had been a teenager when she'd given it and that she'd spent a distressing amount of the film naked or in bed with this guy or that one. It was the part that had made her career.

Several pieces suddenly clicked into place for Maggie, enough to make the picture of the puzzle come into focus. It was still missing chunks, but Maggie suddenly could see the outline of what they were working on.

"Nothing." Tasha got to her feet. "Absolutely nothing, except I got an Oscar nomination. Now I'm going to complain to Jose, because this is clearly not reserve caviar."

"What was all of that about?" Cole asked when the door swung shut behind her.

"I'm not sure." Maggie could speculate, but none of her guesses were good.

"She gets like this before filming sometimes. It's not you. Once the camera's rolling, she'll settle down. Tash is a total professional."

"Uh-huh." Maggie wanted to know what being a "total professional" entailed—and what it might have cost Tasha.

When Cole and Maggie had finished their meal, Jose came in along with the servers. "I just saw Tasha, and she asked me to pass along her regrets."

"For?" Cole asked.

"Taking your car and heading back to the hotel." Jose scratched his cheek. "She did pick up the bill, if that eases the blow."

At the very least, that helped Maggie's credit card.

Cole laughed. "She always does this."

"Did you enjoy the meal?" Jose asked Maggie.

"I honestly have never eaten so well. You had flavors in there I hadn't even *imagined*." Going back to eating normal-person food was going to be disappointing now that she knew what she was missing.

42

"Beyond imagining, huh? We should take out ads with that line." Jose rolled his shoulders, pleased by the praise but also accepting it as his due. He was good looking, and damn, could he cook, but he was arrogant. "You two should come back while you're in town," he instructed Cole. "I can try to blow her mind again."

Maggie shot a sideways look to Cole, who, she was certain, would never bask in a compliment like that.

The actor met her eyes and shrugged, as if to say *You brought this on yourself.*

It took a second for Maggie to put herself back together. She still wasn't used to what happened in her gut when he acknowledged her. He was worse than the nitrous oxide at the dentist.

Maggie had no doubt Jose could succeed in exploding what she thought food was a second time. But not wanting to try to parry his mild flirting, she said to Cole, "I can call an Uber. Or it's what, like eight blocks? I don't mind walking."

"Let's do that."

On the street outside Troncos, Maggie stopped to button her coat. England clearly hadn't gotten the memo that by May, things should've warmed up, and Cole was regretting not bringing his own jacket.

"Are you going to get mobbed?" Maggie asked.

Cole almost laughed before choking it down. That might sound rude. Maggie was new to Hollywood, and she probably didn't get that he wasn't famous, not in the way Tasha was. "That's more of an issue for, like, Harry Styles. *Central Square* was never big over here, and the rest of my stuff . . . it's been lower profile."

"You don't seem low profile to me."

"Compared to Tasha, I am."

Cole shot a sidelong glance at Maggie. The town houses lining the street were built of sandy-colored stone, and her silhouette glowed against it. The cheeky tilt of her nose, the rosy pout of her lips, the proud jut of her chin: her profile was a question mark.

The woozy feeling in Cole's gut was the answer.

This is a work dinner, you dweeb, he reminded himself for what seemed like the millionth time tonight. If it felt like something else, something more, that was only because the neighborhood could've been a studio back lot. The charmingly narrow rows of houses, the converted Victorian brick factory across the way, and the inky sky above them, studded not with stars but with twinkle lights. It was the place doing this to Cole, not the woman. He needed to remember that. Anyone could get swoony when they were walking through this wonderland. That was why unwashed Americans, such as himself, ought to avoid it.

Maggie sighed—and not in a swoony way.

"You're not letting Tasha get to you, are you?" Cole asked.

"No." Maggie sounded as if she meant it. "I don't think her hesitation about working with me is personal. I just want to figure out how to help her."

"She'll get on board." Cole gently maneuvered Maggie around an uneven bit of pavement. "Tonight was a *terrible* mistake." If he'd thought dinner would soften Tasha up, he couldn't have been more wrong—as per usual.

"You were trying to help."

"But not actually helping."

"You did, though. I have a much better idea of what's going on with Tasha now."

"Good, because I don't." Something serious was up with his friend, something that had her spooked and anxious.

But he and Maggie weren't going to solve that mystery tonight. Maggie would crack Tasha eventually. He was certain of it. She clearly had good intentions and a knack for this.

He was curious about Maggie's previous gig. "I didn't know there was some mess at your old job. I should've googled you."

Maggie's eyes went wide. "It's really . . . unpleasant, how it ended. Please don't look it up."

"I won't." If anyone knew how false stories, or true stories shot in an unflattering light, could haunt you, it was Cole. If Maggie didn't want him to probe her past, he wouldn't. "I understand how it can be when you get a bad reputation and people think they know you," he said, very softly. "Especially when you don't think you're that person at all."

For a second, he wasn't certain if she was going to respond to that, which was fair enough. She didn't owe him anything.

But at last, she said, "Feel free not to answer this, but how do you handle it?" She'd matched his tone: quiet, without posturing or restraint. Like a whisper in the dark. Like a confession by a lover.

The jet lag, the food, and the wine were mixing with this pictur-esque setting. They were making Cole feel as if he knew this woman already. As if he could trust her.

It made no sense—it made absolutely no sense—but this night was stripping away the mask he usually wore around people. And for all that he didn't know Maggie, he suspected that she was taking off her mask too. That they were both speaking more freely, more honestly, than they usually did.

It was a little terrifying . . . and something else. Something equally visceral, equally raw, that he didn't want to name.

"Hmm." They'd gone another half block before Cole worked up the courage to keep telling her the unvarnished truth. "I made up rules, like a code, for the person I wanted to be. The person I thought I . . . was. And I follow them. If I can be that man every day, then eventually they have to realize that's who I am, right?"

"Right." She said it as if she understood completely.

His words started coming faster then. "When I laid it out for myself like that, it helped me know what was true. I think I lost reality there for a while, because I kept hearing all these stories about who I was. And maybe I even believed them for a bit. But I won't let myself get confused again."

Even if that meant denying himself. This goal, he had to feed it everything. Ambition was a hungry mofo.

They came to a corner. Across from them, a busker was playing "Some Enchanted Evening" on the trumpet. Cole would normally find all of this sappy, but tonight, it fit. It did feel like an enchanted evening.

"Hey, he's pretty good." Cole patted his pocket and pulled out a couple of bills. He loped across the street to drop them in the guy's case.

When he returned to Maggie, the expression in her eyes—he didn't have the words for it. It was heat and longing, all the things he'd spent the better part of twenty years not letting himself have. Not trusting himself to have. Not feeling worthy of *having*.

"Shall we dance?" Cole had meant it as a joke about the way he was feeling. The spell that this night had cast on him. But his words came out stilted and formal—and needy, so stupidly needy—and it turned into a real question.

He wanted to dance with her.

Heat swept down his body, from his hairline to his toes. Brisk spring night? Nah, Cole might as well have been hiking the Grand Canyon in August.

For a second, he thought Maggie was going to play along. That she wanted to play along. She took a step toward him, and his palm was itching to touch her.

Then she shook her head, and when she looked at him again, he knew she was being reasonable. Her eyes were cool, her expression no longer dazed. "That's a different song. Both are by Rodgers and Hammerstein, though." She was saving them both by pretending to misunderstand him.

Smart. Maggie was really smart.

"Oh, oh—right."

Maggie started walking faster. "I've directed most of their musicals at one point or another. Occupational hazard!" Her voice was high and cheerful and kind. So kind.

But it didn't matter. Cole was going to relive this humiliation for the rest of his life. For one minute, he'd let himself want something— want someone.

This was embarrassing. Like naked-in-front-of-the-class-nightmare level of embarrassing.

At least the sting of the cold night air on his cheeks was sobering. Harsh, but sobering.

"I understand what you were saying about wanting to stay . . . focused." Maggie was clearly trying to get them back to a more professional footing. "To live your values."

"I can't imagine you getting confused." Obviously she was more grounded than he was. Much wiser.

"You don't know me very well."

"I'd like to."

Oops.

It was *true*, but it wasn't helpful. In fact, it was the exact opposite of what he needed to be doing here. He should fill the hole in, not dig it deeper. "As friends, I mean," he added clumsily. "For us to work together, we'll have to become closer." God, how was he making this worse? It was already so bad.

"I knew what you meant." But Maggie's tone was too brittle to be convincing. She was probably regretting every second of this night, and he couldn't blame her. He was out of practice being around normal people.

Thankfully, they rounded a corner, and the hotel, with its stone carvings and cupola, popped into view. "Here we are, no thanks to Tasha." Cole offered Maggie an apologetic smile, trying to decide how to best fix everything he'd just awkwardly broken.

But Maggie was there, better and smoother than he was. "Thanks for dinner. It was out of this world." She gave him a small wave. "I'm going to take the stairs."

Because she couldn't wait to get away from him. Awesome. Reasonable.

It was going to be a *long* four months if Cole kept shoving his foot in his mouth around Maggie.

Chapter 5

INT. REHEARSAL ROOM

"Wait, we can shoot it without showing my boobs?" Rhiannon Simmons looked at Cole as if she wanted him to confirm that Maggie wasn't talking nonsense when she said the actress didn't have to display her nipples to everyone with a Videon subscription.

Cole's costar was almost impossibly young—the kind of young he could barely remember being. But Rhiannon was about a zillion times more together than Cole had been in his early twenties, and someone was taking time and care with her that they never had with him.

He was so, so glad the industry had changed . . . and maybe also the tiniest bit jealous.

"I mean, I'm not saying I don't want to," Rhiannon added quickly. "But I didn't know that was an option."

Across the table, Maggie was watching Rhiannon with a mixture of warmth and motherly concern. Cole understood, since Rhiannon made him feel like the Cryptkeeper. It was one thing to know your coworkers had been in kindergarten when you'd gotten your start. But then they introduced themselves and said your early work was "classic," and your heart shriveled up to a raisin in your chest.

Cole didn't want to be classic. Classics joined the AARP and had opinions about the best brands of over-the-counter meds for aches and pains—which was ridiculous, because it was clearly Bayer Back & Body.

"Of course," Maggie told her. "Zoya has a vision for the scene, for what it shows us about your characters, but this is collaborative. If there are elements you don't want to do for whatever reason, it's my job to help you negotiate those and to find a way to film this that's comfortable for you."

Rhiannon again turned to Cole. *Are you hearing this?* her expression screamed. "I'm feeling a little green."

"I can't tell," he said.

Maggie snorted. "Look, if anyone's the newbie here, it's me. As written, you'd be nude from the waist up, and the blocking—it would be pretty intense. Zoya sees Madge as being debased by her relationship with Geordie. She's exposed, literally and emotionally, and we can tell he already has one foot out the door. When Geordie leaves Madge for Effie, that's going to destroy her."

"Not very heroic of me," Cole said, trying to make a joke.

"No." Maggie gave him a courtesy smile, but Cole knew they were both focused on Rhiannon.

His costar considered the script under Maggie's hand. Cole knew this was Rhiannon's first big film or television role. During their chemistry read, she'd been amazing, but she was also walking into a world she didn't know at all.

For a second, Cole thought about what Tasha had said last night about *Cosa Nostra*. Tasha was so fierce—and she'd grown up in Hollywood—so it was hard to see her and Rhiannon as having much in common. But suddenly, those distinctions hardly seemed to matter. They had both been young women in an industry of vampires.

"I've done nudity on stage," Rhiannon said, "in *The Bald Soprano* when I was at uni. My gran came one night, and that was . . . awkward. But this feels different."

"Because the play didn't have an international audience?" Maggie asked.

"Yeah."

Maggie nodded. "Again, the goal is to show something with the intimacy that we can't reveal another way. But your nipples aren't necessary to achieve Zoya's vision, and I'll be discussing what we decide during a production meeting tonight."

Rhiannon processed this. Nodded. "And Zoya won't be mad? I signed the nudity waiver already. My agent . . . I mean, we didn't even have a discussion about it. *Waverley* is big for me, and this is just what you do."

Drew had certainly never told Cole that he could decline a scene or negotiate nudity. Cole's abs were practically a résumé item for him. The idea that he might not smack them up on screen was almost comic.

Almost.

But there was a gap between the cartoon version of Cole, all muscles and good vibes, and the real person, who might feel embarrassed or self-conscious about it. And given how much of his life Cole spent caught in between them, he didn't find it that funny.

"No," Maggie said. "Zoya won't be mad."

"And who cares if she is? If it isn't something you want to do, you shouldn't do it." Oops, Cole shouldn't have said that.

One of Drew's key rules was *Be easy to work with*. This wasn't because Drew believed kindness to be inherently important or anything so slushy, but because in a world without many backup options, you didn't want to give them a single reason to axe you.

If he were here, he would lose his mind that Cole had suggested Rhiannon put her own wants ahead of the showrunner's.

But . . . she should.

"Sorry," Cole said, trying to decide how much of that to walk back. "I don't mean to give you bad advice. Of course you want Zoya to be happy. But your feelings are important too." Cole sounded like a goddamn after-school special. If this went on any longer, he was going to tell Rhiannon to stay away from drugs and not to text and drive.

But when he glanced across the table, Maggie was watching him with a slightly dazed smile on her face, as if he were a butterfly she'd seen in October after she'd assumed they'd all flown south for the winter.

Well, he couldn't have messed up too badly, not if his words had Maggie looking like that.

"Cole's right," Maggie said.

It was all he could do not to puff his chest out.

Maggie turned her attention back to Rhiannon, and for a second, he was almost tempted to say something else reckless to get it back. But he'd done enough. He had to go back to following the rules.

"We can *always* modify the waiver. It's my job to have those conversations for you and to get everyone on the same page."

Next to Cole, Rhiannon considered this, twisting a lock of her red hair between her fingers. "I need to think about it."

"That's totally fine. That's why we're starting this now, before we even get into the full rehearsals. Whatever you decide, I want you to feel good about it. Is there anything else you want to discuss?"

"Nope."

"Okay, then." Maggie turned to Cole. "On to Geordie."

Her tone was more removed than last night, and Cole wanted to press Maggie until she went soft, like she had been when they'd walked back to the hotel, under the twinkle lights with the romantic trumpet serenade and all the wine going to his head. Before he'd made an ass of himself, of course.

He was making up for it now and proving that he wasn't a total fool. To keep doing that, he had to focus. And in, like, twenty seconds, he was going to do exactly that and stop indulging in the schmaltzy crap that had gotten him into trouble in the first place.

"We're going to be good friends by the end of this shoot, Cole. You have a lot of nudity and intimacy on the books. But let's start with this scene with Madge from episode two. Just top line, how do you feel about the costuming?"

The script said he'd bare his ass, but that ship had sailed. Cole had shown his ass to anyone who'd wanted to see it from *Central Square* on. And it didn't bother him . . . though it did seem odd that no one had ever asked how he felt about it before.

"I'm comfortable with it," he said. "I've signed the waiver. I don't need a body double."

"Okay. But it's the same thing I just talked about with Rhiannon: you aren't locked in."

"I appreciate that." And he did. "But I'm not worried about the nudity on my end." At least the script didn't call for full frontal—because *that* he'd need to think about.

"You'll keep your pants on for this scene with Madge, but with Effie, you'll be more exposed. What's most comfortable for you in terms of coverage when we're filming?"

"The genital barrier is fine. Can we get Penelope Bullock for that? We've worked together before." Having a strapless thong pasted over your junk was the kind of job where trust was important.

Maggie made a note. "I need to check, but I'll put in that request."

"Thanks."

She riffled through the script. "So we just have a rough description of the choreography. We'll get into the details in the next few weeks. I know that Zoya is going to direct episodes one and four herself. Kevin Combs will handle episodes two and three. Access to the set will be quite limited on the days with intimacy, but do either of you have any hard limits?"

Rhiannon lowered her eyes, and Cole got the sense that she was deferring to him, waiting to see what he would say. Cole was a senior talent here, and if he showed a willingness to negotiate, to think about how stuff was written, that could help Rhiannon.

"I don't . . . I don't love the moment when Madge is performing oral sex on Geordie and he's basically ignoring her. This isn't a hard limit. I know *how* we'll film it, and I know why we need it."

Cole had prepared for this role for months, and part of what he loved about it was how much Geordie was going to grow. But the way this scene was meant to draw a clear line between the sex that Geordie had with Madge and the kind he had with Effie, it struck him as kind of gross.

"What don't you love about it?" Maggie wasn't disagreeing with him. Her question was open and curious.

"I'm playing an asshole," he said flatly.

She tipped her head to the side. "Are you worried about how people will respond?"

Strangely, he wasn't. Cody Rhodes had frequently been an asshole, and that hadn't put people off the character. Far from it.

But you still had to identify with a character to play them. Cole didn't want to rattle around inside himself to find the bits of selfishness that matched Geordie's. He knew they were there, but he'd rather not rip them out and hold them up to the light.

He probably should've decided that before he'd taken this part.

"No, but I guess I worry about finding too much of Geordie in me. Like, I read the script, and part of me goes, 'Why did I want to play this jerk?'"

A beat, then Rhiannon burst into laughter. "I have to tell you, I reread episode two on the way here, and he's such an asshole! I'm like, 'Girl, run.'"

Cole covered his face with his hands and groaned. "He's Mister Red Flag."

"But oh so sexy," she teased.

That didn't seem like much of a trade-off.

"Why *is* that?" Cole asked, looking over his fingers from Rhiannon to Maggie. "Why are we okay with his behavior if he's sexy?"

"I don't think we are," Rhiannon said. "It's entertainment. Just because you enjoy watching it on Videon with a glass of wine to unwind doesn't mean you want it in real life."

Cole caught Maggie's eye. This probably wasn't what she wanted them doing in this rehearsal. "I'm sorry. I'm slowing us down, asking these questions that aren't really about anything, and I—"

"They're very much about something." There was steel under Maggie's words. "This is exactly what we wrestle with in acting."

"Absolutely," Rhiannon agreed. "I mean, Madge isn't exactly a saint. She's going to steal your baby and frame your lover for murder. That's some pretty dark shite."

Rhiannon wasn't wrong. *The Heart of Midlothian* was a weird swirl of darkness and cotton candy. The book's main character was Jeanie, who walked barefoot to England to beg the queen for a pardon for her sister. But Zoya had pushed Jeanie and her bland love interest, Rueben, to the edge of the series because, well, they weren't very interesting. They were, however, much nicer people than Geordie, Effie, and Madge.

"So why did you want to play Madge?" he asked Rhiannon.

"Setting aside the, you know, evilness of some of her choices, I identify with her. I mean, haven't we all had a relationship that wasn't emotionally equal? Haven't we all thought 'I'm going to do everything they want, and then they'll love me'? I mean, I have. I want to find a way to give her dignity, even if Geordie isn't giving her that."

Cole was pretty sure he'd been both people in that scenario, the one having fun and the one in over their head, but love had stopped being fun for him a long time ago. He could understand that Rhiannon, who hadn't blown out twenty-three birthday candles, probably wasn't there yet.

Geordie was certainly someone who still enjoyed the thrill of the chase, and Cole was going to get to play him while he grew the fuck up.

There was that.

"When he apologizes to Madge," Cole asked, "do you think it's sincere?"

Cole was still trying to decide how to play that moment. He'd talked to Zoya about it, and she wanted him to try it where it was absolutely sincere. She thought it would show he'd learned a lot.

Some tiny piece of Cole—the piece that probably identified the most with his character—was less sure Geordie had. He'd probably ask for some takes that were more skeptical, where Geordie was saying the right words but maybe didn't fully understand them yet.

"I want to believe he is," Rhiannon said, which was generous.

"It doesn't help that by that point, she's basically . . ." Cole tried to decide what was the polite way to describe Madge's mental state in the back half of the season.

"Having a mental health crisis?" Rhiannon supplied.

"Yup. I mean, it sort of undermines his apology if he's broken her." Cole reached for his script so he'd have something to do with his hands. He was feeling suddenly self-conscious. "Sorry. I know you're all pros, and you know I'm not him. But we're talking about this, breaking down all the beats, and it's hitting me how awful he's going to come across."

"More even than the moment when he watches Andrew, his partner in smuggling, hang?" Maggie asked.

"Maybe. Yes. I mean, sex . . . it isn't always making love, I get that. But you should have respect for the people you take to bed. That's like the floor of good-personing, and Geordie can't do it. At least Andrew is an adult, and he chose to be a smuggler. Madge didn't sign up to get crushed. So yeah, Geordie was way worse to Madge and Effie than to Andrew. No question."

Maggie set one of her hands over her mouth, and he knew she was doing it to buffer her emotions from him. He didn't know her, not really, but he was certain of it.

Did she think he was being silly? Unprofessional? Unserious? He wanted to ask.

He shouldn't.

"What are you thinking?" Well, that had just popped out. It was too personal a question, but he wanted to know.

After a beat, Maggie dropped her fingers to her neck and looked at the ceiling, considering how to answer.

He tried not to think about how soft the skin under her neck looked.

"Actors are empathetic," she said. "You absorb emotions. That's what makes you good at your jobs. But sometimes, I think performance is about shedding civilization—dropping the rules, the stuff that in most cases we might say makes us good people. We have to turn the volume down on that when we're performing and try to reveal the truth instead, the messy shit underneath. So it's good to ask these questions, Cole. It speaks highly of you as a person. But at some point, you have to let those worries go, because they'll get in the way of your performance."

Cole had next to no formal training in acting, which hadn't mattered when he'd been playing a guy who looks good in a tight polo. He'd tried to think about "technique" sometimes, but this conversation was on another level.

He might not be a novice, but Cole hadn't walked through every beat of this before. He hadn't had someone to help him communicate with the director or someone whose job it was to balance his feelings with what was good for the production. Maggie was taking him seriously, as a person and as an artist, and it made him feel hot and cold at once.

He desperately wanted to be worthy of this conversation, and he worried that he wasn't.

"I'll try." His voice was a bit gruff. He cleared it, taking a sip from his water bottle, while Maggie shuffled through the pile of scripts in front of her.

"Let's jump for a minute to the scene from episode six—though we'll come back to episode two. There's no nudity in this one, but there's some kissing and more of that humiliation dynamic you don't dig."

She gave him a sympathetic smile, and Cole's heart crinkled.

Gosh, but Maggie was thoughtful. Last night, he'd watched her watching him, watching Tasha. Not even really enjoying her dinner but trying instead to figure them out.

Cole was so familiar with how people watched him—full of expectations they were confident he'd meet—that he'd forgotten what it felt like for someone to be unsure with him, to check if they were getting the right answers, and to gauge his feelings and wants.

He was used to how the world watched him, but he preferred how Maggie did it.

"Let's do it. More of *The 'Geordie Robertson Is the Worst' Hour*."

"Yay," Rhiannon cheered.

When they'd finished with the scripts, Maggie pulled out another notebook, which she flopped open in front of them. "I've been working with this mentor to learn how to, you know, do this job, and he suggested I try these."

She'd broken the page into panels, as if it were an erotic cartoon strip peopled by stick figures. At least Cole suspected they were supposed to be stick figures.

And supposed to be erotic.

Rhiannon leaned over the table to inspect them more closely. "Is that an arm, or does he have three legs?"

Maggie squinted. "It's an arm."

"And is that a shirt, or is it one of those puffy coats? Wait, did they have puffy coats in 1700s Scotland?"

"Arg." Maggie tried to close the notebook, but Rhiannon had slapped her hands on the pages and was holding it open.

She was cackling now. "Maggie, I'm sorry, but these are the worst drawings I have ever seen, and I have a three-year-old nephew."

"I don't think they're that bad," Cole put in. They were, actually, but he was trying to be nice. "Is that a bush behind us?"

"It's a campfire. I was thinking about the light." Maggie sounded so glum as she sagged in her chair and began tapping around on the floor for something. "No, you're right, they're hideous. Bernard uses pictures as a way to agree on rough blocking before you do it for real, but we're going to have to try something else."

Maggie straightened and, without warning, heaved an exercise ball at Cole. He snagged it out of the air, and Maggie managed a crooked smile, one that he felt in his gut.

Having her here helped so much, but that smile was pure trouble.

Maggie rifled through the box of props and costumes she'd brought with her. "I have a period-appropriate shirt if you want it, Cole." The linen scratched her palm. Hopefully the real one would be softer than the mock-up.

"Sure." He stood and began to take off his sweater, doing that thing where he stretched his hands over his back and pulled it off over his head. And what that did to his abs—it was indescribable. Just a ripple of muscles and golden skin.

Maggie made herself look away, but they were in a dance studio. There were mirrors *everywhere*. The art of Cole's torso was inescapable.

Don't lust after the actors. But she wasn't having trouble not lusting over the actors generally, just Cole specifically.

She was starstruck. That was it. She couldn't believe that she was here. She couldn't believe she was doing *this*. She'd had a terrible year, and somehow, this magic dream had become real. No wonder she was dizzy.

The previous night, Maggie had almost let herself get carried away. It had been the fault of that once-in-a-lifetime meal and all the booze, but when Cole had made a chivalrous joke about how they should dance, Maggie had almost said yes.

Which would've been embarrassing because he hadn't meant it. Thank *God* she'd figured that out at the last second.

No, she had to concentrate on her job. No more emotionally reveal-ing conversations. No more entirely-too-romantic late-night walks.

Work, work, work: that was the ticket. Once Maggie got her sea legs, this silly crush would go away, as surely as the nausea faded the second day of a cruise. It had to.

Luckily, Rhiannon had hopped up onto the exercise mats and was still teasing Maggie for her bad drawings. The words *unintentionally Cubist* were getting thrown around a lot, and that was a blast of cold water over Maggie's libido.

Bernard had been adamant that storyboarding was a necessary pre-rehearsal step, but Maggie knew when something was a lost cause. At least she felt confident about handling the blocking.

For the next bit, they walked through the dialogue and the kissing that preceded the love scene. It was like choreographing a dance, which Maggie had done for her productions because her high school didn't have a dedicated dance teacher, but it was more complicated than on stage because of the different kinds of shots and camera positions. *Are you comfortable with this movement?* and *How does it look from this angle?* Maggie was taking notes madly.

The truth was that sex scenes on TV and in the movies were broken down into so many tiny bits, rehearsing them didn't feel sexy. The rough blocking had an establishing shot with kissing, a tracking shot of Cole's hand tugging up Rhiannon's skirt, a close-up of Rhiannon's face in ecstasy, a medium over-the-shoulder shot from one point of view and then the other, a series of close-ups of various body parts touching and thrusting, and then a close-up of Cole gasping, before a high-angle shot looking down on the postcoital couple.

And each one would be scarcely longer than a GIF.

But when they were stitched together and processed and scored, they would be swoony. Or at least Maggie had to believe that this was going to, somehow, turn out swoony. Because right now, she couldn't see it.

Cole and Rhiannon ran through the blocking again.

"I don't think you can kiss her like that, Cole." Maggie tapped her pen against her cheek, considering. "It's too . . . tender."

Maggie couldn't think about whether this was how Cole James would kiss a woman in real life. What she had to think about was this shot, and Geordie wouldn't kiss Madge like that, as if she were precious. With that much sweetness and intensity. Even if Maggie was certain that every woman in the audience—herself included—would vaporize if he did, the feel of it wasn't right, not for these characters.

Cole raised his brows in amusement at Maggie's comment. "How should I do it, then?"

"Well, don't cradle her neck. Maybe if you put one hand on the back of her head? You have to be more controlling."

Cole rearranged, his fingers splayed across Rhiannon's hair—and whoa, those were some thick, sculpted fingers.

Not the point.

"Like this?" he asked.

She cleared her throat. "Yup, that's better. Rhiannon, you good?"

The actress gave a thumbs-up, and they ran through the sequence again. This time, Cole was more distanced, less affectionate. His movements were rougher, more demanding.

"That was good. Much more Geordie. I think we can call it a day."

"Hold on." Cole rolled back on his heels, and with the V of his old-fashioned shirt hanging open and his hair mussed and his lips flushed, he looked like a romance cover model come to life.

Maggie whimpered in her mind.

"Toss me a pen," he deadpanned. "I gotta write *When in doubt, be a selfish ass* in my script."

Which she could tell that he loathed because it was contrary to every reflex she'd seen him act on. Even when he was being a little too direct and told Rhiannon to put her own feelings ahead of the director's, his impulse had had good intentions.

"That's why they call it acting," she reminded him as she began packing up.

He looked as if he wanted to disagree, but then he swallowed whatever self-deprecating response he'd wanted to make. Cole wasn't as obviously or deeply wounded as Tasha, but somewhere along the way, someone had done a number on him too.

As long as Maggie managed to keep things aboveboard, she needed to try to help him as well. So when Cole returned the prop shirt, she told him, "I really appreciate everything you brought into the room today. I don't think most people would be as willing to share those worries as you were, but it helped with—" She covertly pointed to Rhiannon. The actress was quite possibly the most Scottish-looking person ever, with pale-white skin, long red hair, and bright-green eyes. This rehearsal had driven home for Maggie how young she was, how vulnerable. "So thank you."

Cole shrugged, as humble as ever. "It was no big deal. I honestly wasn't even trying to break the ice or whatever. Those are real things I'm stressed about."

"That's what made it work. It wasn't a put-on. You're sincerely a nice guy."

That much she felt comfortable saying, even though it was exactly why this crush was going to linger. She liked him, in addition to being attracted to him. It would've been easier if he'd been simply the hot, vacuous guy she'd assumed he was, but the real Cole James wasn't the Cole James brand. Not at all.

"Now we just have to get Tasha to do the same," he said.

When Maggie hadn't been able to fall asleep last night, she'd spent the wee hours contemplating the Rubik's Cube that was Tasha Russell.

This first episode of the season included a Geordie-Effie love scene in her jail cell. The audience needed to see the history between them but also their desperation, which was no small order. Since the table read for episode one was just a few days away, Maggie and the actors needed to start work on the blocking immediately.

"I'm going to take another swing at her, one on one."

"You sure?" Cole was impressed, and it took a lot of self-control for Maggie not to preen.

"Yup. I have some theories about what's going on, and I need to test them without witnesses."

"Okay, but maybe you should get that gear baseball catchers use. The pads and the mask."

"Do you have fencing gear to practice the sword fighting? Maybe I could borrow some from Ryan Baris." Maggie hadn't met the stunt coordinator yet, but from the way Cole talked about him, it was clear he and Tasha liked and trusted him. She was kind of jealous about that.

"Actually, no. We're not using sharp swords, but they have me training with the stuff that we'll use for filming. No masks or eye protection or anything. The gear for the sex is more hardcore."

"Whoa."

Cole shot another look at Rhiannon, but she wasn't paying attention to them at all. She was smiling at her phone, probably texting someone.

He set a hand on the table and leaned closer to Maggie. Close enough that she could smell his deodorant. "I'm really glad you're here, Maggie Niven. I don't think I've talked about the hows of acting or creating characters more than I have today."

Maggie's voice came out soft. Intimate. "That, Cole James, is a crime."

For a long moment, they stood there, watching each other. The sun had shifted during the morning, and the room was now all soft grays and blues. Cole's hair looked less blond and more brown and gold than this morning. Maggie wanted to push back the lock that had fallen over his forehead.

But Maggie needed this job. She needed to be *good* at this job.

So she just waved her hand awkwardly. "Have a good day."

She made that big, including both actors. And then she left before she accidentally said something else too revealing.

Chapter 6

INT. CONFERENCE ROOM

Esme McCullough—Zoya's assistant—read the description that brought the first episode of the third season of *Waverley* to an end: "CLOSING MONTAGE: AN ANGUISHED GEORDIE LEANING AGAINST THE WALL OF THE TOLBOOTH PRISON, AN ANGRY MOB POURS THROUGH THE STREETS OF EDINBURGH, A DETERMINED EFFIE ALONE IN HER CELL, MORE SHOTS OF THE MOB, A FRIGHTENED JEANIE HUDDLES IN HER COTTAGE, AND THE FEET OF THE HANGED MAN SWINGING. OUT."

The room was silent. Maggie had no problem imagining it, and if everyone here did their jobs, it was going to be awesome.

Someone whooped, and the cast and crew broke into applause.

"Great work," Zoya shouted over the clapping. "I don't know about you all, but I'm pumped."

Maggie might be pumped, but the nausea was doing a good job masking it.

Next to her, the stunt coordinator sat up. *Ryan Baris*, according to the paper tent in front of him—the guy who'd worked with Cole and Tasha several times. He folded his arms onto the table in a mirror of Maggie's posture and said, under his breath, "You feeling all right?"

Great. Her face must be broadcasting her trepidation for everyone's amusement. "I don't think I realized how *big* this is." Maggie had known that there would be fifty people at the table read, and even more on set once they started filming, but the sheer size of *Waverley* was only beginning to hit her.

"It's like being back in Afghanistan."

"I didn't realize you'd served." Since she'd never spoken with him before today, she couldn't've known, but she still felt vaguely guilty.

Ryan snorted. "Why would you?"

She shrugged in apology. "I guess it's obvious I'm a little overwhelmed."

"Yup."

Someone had mentioned that Ryan had gotten his start as Cole's stand-in, and Maggie was having trouble believing it. The men had a superficial resemblance, sure, insofar as they were both tall and fit with dirty-blond hair. But they had completely different energies. Cole was a teddy bear, all soft warmth and self-deprecating smiles. Ryan had an edge that felt genuinely intimidating.

But maybe it was a front, because the look Ryan shot her was kind. "Just keep faking it, and one of these days, you'll realize you know what you're doing."

"Did that work for you?"

"Yup. Just be aware, once you get a taste for this"—he gestured at the room—"it's addictive."

The jury was still out as far as she was concerned.

"Can you tell me something? Why are we shooting wildly out of order?" They wouldn't finish with all the stuff for the first episode until four months from now.

"When we're in Edinburgh in a few weeks, we have to get all of the location stuff. Then we move to the Highlands for all the pretty vista shit, and we wrap up with the interiors in the studio in Glasgow. I don't know how they do it." He pointed to the actors. "It would mess with my head."

There, way down the ring of conference tables, was Tasha Russell, whom Maggie hadn't seen since the disastrous dinner at Troncos. The actress rolled her neck before giving Cole, on her right, a small smile. Tasha had been absolutely focused during the read-through, alert and determined, like a bird of prey. But Cole was in a full-on serious mode that Maggie had never seen from him before. While most of the actors had been giving a half-strength version of their performances, feeling out the beats and logistics of the script as much as anything else, Cole had been giving it his all.

It had been exhilarating to watch. For all his worries about this part, and the moments of vulnerability that he'd shared with her, he was nailing this role.

The former-director part of Maggie was happy for him. The now-in-timacy-coordinator-who-might-be-credited-with-supporting-him was delighted. But under both of those roles, Maggie was also a person. A person who'd come to care about him a totally normal amount for a couple of days of acquaintance. He was a charming, sweet guy—of course she wanted him to be amazing in this role.

That was all the tenderness in her gut was. Nothing else.

"I gotta check in with the sword guys," Ryan said, "but holler if you need anything."

"Thanks. I appreciate it."

Maggie flipped through her script and added a note. *Check with David re: camera angles.*

During the table read, she'd followed along on a clean copy of the latest version of the script. This sat next to her annotated, working, and slightly-out-of-date copy, but that one was already thick with highlighting, sticky tabs, and notes. If she'd added anything else to it, it would've been unusable.

Zoya, who'd been accepting congratulations, stood, and the room fell silent. "Thanks, everyone. That was great work all around. Actors, you're free to go. Any meetings that you have with wardrobe will be delayed for a bit until I can finish conferring with Alexa. Same with Ryan on stunts and Maggie for intimacy."

Alexa Pratt was a legend who needed no introduction. An older white woman with a stylish gray bob and chunky red-framed glasses, Alexa was currently deliberating with several assistants, who were sitting in the outer ring of chairs around the table. Ryan and Maggie were not famous. Zoya pointed to them, and they gave obligatory waves, but no one paid attention. The conference room had melted back into a mix of overlapping conversations and laughter.

Cole caught Maggie's eye, and for a second, a smile passed over his face—just a flicker of the man underneath the movie star—and Maggie's breath lodged in her throat. She nearly choked when he began walking through the crowd, which parted around him as he made his way over to her.

"Did you get it?" he asked her.

"Get what?"

"The Wordle. I saw you working on it when you came in."

Cole James—the movie star—wanted to know if she'd solved today's Wordle.

Life, it comes at you fast.

"Yup, in four. *SAVVY.*" It had been a *tricky* one. "How many five-letter words have double *V*s?"

"Bevvy," he offered.

"And divvy. Damn, there are more than I thought."

"Well, regardless, good work." Then, because she was only barely holding it together as it was, he leaned closer. "You okay? You were a little green. Saw Ryan checking in on you."

At some point, when sensation returned to her body, Maggie was going to be mortified that everyone apparently could sense how out of her depth she felt. But with Cole smiling down on her, everything seemed okay with the world.

"Cole? You ready?" It was Tasha, trying to reclaim her best friend.

Which was fine. It was where his attention ought to be. Maggie wasn't miffed at all. Nope.

"I'm fine." Maggie considered adding some white lie, like *Must have been bad fish pie*, but she didn't want to lie to him. Not even about something trivial.

"Good." Then he returned to Tasha.

They left the room with the rest of the cast trailing behind, as if the actors were a royal court taking the lead of their king and queen.

The doors closed behind them while Zoya jotted notes on her tablet. When she finished, she paused, read over what she'd written, and gave a satisfied nod. Her eyes popped up and skimmed over the room, her expression bright and lively. "What'd you think?"

The crew began talking at once.

"That last action sequence is going to be a bear—"

"They're still not ready for the sword choreography—"

"I have concerns about the location shooting—"

"We really have to start thinking about music—"

"Okay." Zoya projected her voice over the din. "Let's start with David, and then we'll go to Kevin."

David Keith, a Black British man who was always impeccably put together, was the director of photography and would be shooting the show. "I only have a few notes. Shirley tells me that the production is still waffling on two locations for exterior shots. The National Trust is being difficult about Gladstone's Land, so Tom is scouting a backup plan. Alas, it's in Glasgow, so it'd completely cock up the schedule."

"Fuck, I don't like to hear that. Let me send you the most up-to-date version. I wanted to have things finalized by the end of next week."

"I don't think that's possible."

"Understood."

They were going to spread the nine table reads out over the weeks of rehearsal before they moved to Scotland. Zoya was planning to direct the first, fourth, and ninth episodes, but the directors for the rest were listening from the edges. This really was like shooting several movies at the same time.

Zoya chatted with the directors, with Alexa about wardrobe, then with Ryan for stunts.

"And Maggie, how are things coming on your end?"

"Well," Maggie said carefully, "we're not as far with the choreography as we'd like, but since that's a much larger conversation, I don't want to bog down this check-in."

"I have time now. We good, everyone else?" Zoya asked. The room muttered assent. "Great. I'll see you all back here Wednesday for the episode-two read-through."

As the crew left, Zoya patted the spot next to her at the table. Maggie moved over and arranged her drawings between her two copies of the script.

"What's going on?" Zoya asked.

"Tasha Russell is being . . ."

"Tasha?"

"Yeah. She's made it clear she thinks this is unnecessary, even as she's also . . . look, I'm reading between the lines here, but I think she's got some issues with nudity. Can I ask if anything came up during negotiations?"

Zoya shot a look at Esme to confirm before saying "No. We went into the nudity waiver discussion with her agent thinking there would be some pushback, but basically, she was really committed to the part. She signed the show's standard rider."

"It's just that she hasn't done nudity since *Cosa Nostra*. That's a long time for an actress not to take her clothes off on screen, especially someone who takes the kinds of parts she does."

Quite frankly, most action movies were pretty male-gaze-y. For Tasha to have maintained such a vise-tight grip on her image was impressive.

"Hmm." Zoya wasn't agreeing or disagreeing. Just digesting.

"You're well connected. Did something . . . happen on that set?"

Zoya smiled faintly at the flattery, seeing it as the ploy it was but accepting the offering anyhow. "What do you know about Vincent Minna?"

"That he's won a lot of Oscars."

"I shouldn't say anything, really. He's technically a producer for *Waverley*, though it's really Elmer Meyers at Silverlight who's shepherding the show. But as long as you understand that this isn't confirmed and it has to stay buried, there are certainly . . . rumors about his relationships with the actresses he discovers. And he discovered Tasha. He produced that movie. I mean, I can't say for sure that they had an affair or whatever, but there's a lot of smoke for there to be no fire."

Maggie considered this. Tasha's mom had been one of the biggest stars of her era, and her daughter seemed more like a finely honed knife than a woman. It was hard to imagine Vincent Minna steamrolling someone that well connected and fierce.

But then Maggie recalled Rhiannon, who was also strong and self-possessed with a good agent who was supposed to be advocating for her, and Rhiannon hadn't even realized that she could object if she didn't want to bare her entire breasts on screen.

No, this industry sucked for anyone without power. And at the beginning of her career, Tasha had had very little power, especially compared to Vincent Minna.

"That would make sense," Maggie said. "It'd be more disappointing than surprising. But even if we're right, it could also be that I'm just not a good fit for Tasha. It could be personal. Maybe she doesn't like me—"

"I really doubt it's personal."

"I wouldn't be offended or anything." Maggie was a grown-up. She didn't expect everyone to like her. "But it's a hard industry for young women."

"It's a hard industry for everyone. How's Cole doing?"

Maggie took a second to make sure her I'm-an-expert-not-a-woman-with-a-crush mask was on tight before answering. "He's sweet. Every rehearsal, he's very professional, very conscientious of Rhiannon and of me. He clearly wants to do a good job, and he's talented. In the meetings I've had with him and Tasha, I can see the relationship between them, the mutual concern. But I worry if she and I don't have a breakthrough soon, we're not going to get to a point where I can help. And . . . this is my job."

At its core, Maggie was here to put the humiliation of her firing behind her and to build a new career. If she couldn't get Tasha to come around, Maggie wasn't exactly making a strong case that she'd be a good intimacy coordinator.

It had taken way longer—way, way longer—for her to feel like a bad teacher. Even at the end of that job, she hadn't thought she was objectively not good at it. The problem was that the field was hostile and toxic. But she couldn't start over yet *again*. She was way too old for that.

"Also, Tasha truly seems to need support." While it would be professionally embarrassing for Maggie if she couldn't make this work, there was an angle of this that was much larger than her piddling professional anxiety. "The entire goal of me being here is to address this dynamic—to make the intimacy easier to film and not traumatic—and I'm feeling like . . . a spleen. That's a vestigial organ, right?"

Zoya had listened to Maggie's monologue with a focused expression that gave nothing away, but at this, she laughed. "You're not a spleen."

"Fine, but I am feeling stuck. I dunno, how do you get through to someone like this?"

Maggie's high school students had been all open enthusiasm. Sometimes a kid who didn't care ended up in one of her classes, but in her experience as a director, it was lack of talent or discipline that had been the major issues.

She had no capacity to understand the inner workings of movie stars, and Bernard hadn't covered this subject in his lessons.

"I'd just jump into the choreography," Zoya said. "Tasha is absolutely not a touchy-feely person. Cole, Rhiannon, Owen, Leanne: they're going to want to work through the emotions with you. Tasha has emotions—at least, I think she does—but she doesn't want to share them. She hates to come across as vulnerable in any way. Maybe even invite David to your next meeting. Frame it as a craft question. Where is the camera going to be? How are we going to light the scene? It helps that we aren't filming this until we're in the Highlands. The on-location scenes at Midlothian, plus Cole and Rhiannon's stuff, comes sooner, so you have a longer time to figure out what's going on with Tasha. But no one expects you to solve the riddle of Tasha Russell, I promise. Just do your best."

That made sense.

"Is there anything else?" Zoya asked.

"Yeah. I'm sorry. I feel like the squeaky wheel. But for the Madge-and-Geordie love scene, Rhiannon and Cole found the script as is to be . . . underdeveloped."

Zoya's eyes sparkled. She was listed as the lead writer on that episode. "Is that so?"

"Yeah. So here's what we've worked out." Maggie pushed her sketches across the table. "I apologize in advance for the quality of my art." Maggie had bought colored pencils and had painstakingly redrawn the pictures. They weren't better, but they were in color.

After a few beats, Zoya asked carefully, "Are they snow people?"

Esme, who was young and bright and had a mass of brown curly hair, was trying very hard not to laugh. "No, it's Stay Puft Marshmallow Man porn. It's only missing the jaunty hat."

Maggie whined. "Bernard insists storyboarding is necessary."

"I think he's, like, a classically trained artist."

Maggie had seen his portfolio. She believed it. "Okay, what about this?" She offered her shorthand notes instead. They were broken down shot by shot and move by move, the way she used to write down dance choreography. It listed which hand went where and what it did, from the beginning of the sequence to the end.

Cole's words to Rhiannon kept echoing in her head: *Your feelings are important too*. Maggie had planned to follow Bernard's instructions to the letter, but just as Rhiannon had, Maggie clearly had to find her own way.

"What does *RL* mean?" Zoya asked.

"Right leg."

"Oh, of course."

Zoya skimmed through the notes, then went back to the beginning and reread more slowly, consulting with the script. "This looks great. I'm really comfortable with the blocking here."

"You can see that we changed the wardrobe to give Rhiannon a bit more coverage."

"Yup. That's the kind of thing that we tend to work out in the moment when we're filming, or even in the editing room."

That had been exactly what Bernard had predicted Zoya would say. "Directors all trust themselves to handle these things while shooting," he'd speculated when he and Maggie had talked last night. "But that's not good for an actor who can't advocate for themselves, or might be lying there with no clothes on—with a disinterested crew standing around, watching—while they have a discussion about boundaries. I mean, maybe some established star can work in those conditions, but that's not going to be the best option for a twenty-year-old kid who needs this job to pay their rent or get their SAG card."

But when it came to how someone's lack of power might affect their ability to speak truth to someone with power, Maggie was the pot calling the kettle black.

This was it, the heart of the job. Was Maggie able to tell Zoya she was wrong? And would Zoya accept that criticism with grace, or would she bristle?

Maggie was about to find out.

"Look, I know that I'm new at this," Maggie said. "And I don't want to speak out of turn. But I think it would be better to have this level of detail"—she tapped her choreography notes—"in the script. Not in a way that's set in stone, because there needs to be some ability for the actors, the intimacy coordinator, and the director to improvise and reject and make changes. But . . . if we don't have a clear, beat-by-beat, shot-by-shot starting point, it leaves the process open for problems."

Zoya was quiet for a long time. A long, inscrutable time.

Then, in a completely neutral tone, she said, "Like whatever went down at *Cosa Nostra*?"

"Yes. Exactly. I don't mean to be unfun or whatever, but I don't know how an actor could know what they're signing on to, how they could weigh a nudity waiver, if the script basically says *They make passionate love*. That could look so many different ways. Like is it a fade-to-black Hallmark Christmas movie or *Fifty Shades of Grey*? You're not telling them."

Oops. That was probably too much.

After a beat, Zoya's lips twitched. "I love it when I'm right."

"Excuse me?" Maggie asked.

Zoya looked at Esme. "Did I call it or what?"

"You totally called it," Esme agreed.

"Did I bet someone about this?" Zoya asked her. "Do I have some money to collect?"

"No, no one will bet you anymore because you always, always win."

"I have no idea what's going on here," Maggie put in.

Zoya gave Maggie a smug smile. "I left the set of *Hear Her* that morning, and I texted Esme and told her we had to find room in the budget for you. Esme was skeptical, and the production company was skeptical—basically there was skepticism everywhere—but much like Cassandra when Agamemnon met his fate, I have been vindicated. I was right." She punched the air with a fist. "You're great at this. A natural. And the show is going to be stronger because you're here."

"Wasn't Cassandra's vindication . . . murder?"

"You're missing the key part: I was right."

Maggie's mind was still picking through every sentence of Zoya's speech as if it were a table at a flea market. "They didn't want to hire me?"

"That's not the point! The point is that I was right." Zoya looked at her assistant and sniffed. "Someone really ought to be giving me five bucks."

Maggie had no idea what Zoya was making as the showrunner, director, and writer of *Waverley*, but it was presumably a lot more than five bucks.

Zoya pushed the sketches and notes across the table to Maggie. "I can see your point. Next time, we'll bring you in sooner, when we're still writing, and you can write out the choreography for all the intimacy and nudity for us. It's good for the actors, but it's also good for production and design too. I'm impressed you were willing to stand your ground with me like that. Very plucky."

"Zoya admires pluck," Esme said. "It's why she keeps me around."

"I . . . really appreciate you saying so. After the stuff with Tasha, I needed that vote of confidence."

Maggie had to do this job well. She just had to. Zoya might want the vindication, but Maggie needed it. Maybe Zoya could call Maggie's parents and mention that she was good at this and also that it was a legitimate and important job.

"You got this. I know it. And as we've established, I'm never wrong."

Maggie let the compliment light up the rest of her afternoon.

Chapter 7

INT. GYMNASIUM

"Again," Cole demanded.

Ryan let loose another volley of flashing steel.

The stunt coordinator was about an inch shorter and substantially less bulky than Cole. He was all lean muscle, and Cole was more decorative brawn. But only one of them had done their homework—and for once, it wasn't Ryan.

Cole had known Ryan for more than a decade, from when he'd gotten his start doing stunts and stand-in work for Cole. From a distance, they looked alike. Up close? Not so much. And with swords in their hands? Well, Cole suspected for once, he might be the better man.

The stunt coordinator struck, and Cole parried. Ryan lunged, and Cole parried again. When Ryan advanced a third time, it was with all the finesse of a child clutching a fake lightsaber. Cole just stepped out of the way. A feint from Cole, and Ryan fell for it—and almost tumbled to the ground. From there, it was easy to launch a riposte that had Ryan stumbling backward.

Through it all, Cole kept his knees bent, his joints loose. Leonard Pierce and Amin Cordova were teaching and choreographing the sword fighting and historical combat on *Waverley*, and they had emphasized that the real key was Cole's stance and grip. There wasn't going to be that much swordplay on the show, and the choreography wasn't that complex. Cole didn't have to be Errol Flynn—thank God. But he had to get the basics right, because that was how professionals spotted actors who were merely hacking away at each other.

Cole's hack days were behind him.

"Ryan," Leonard warned as Cole pressed his attack. "Cole looks great, but your stance sucks. You're jerking around like Frankenstein."

"Like a zombie," Amin corrected. "A slow one. Keep the sword closer—it's gotta be an extension of your arm."

Ryan made an inarticulate *gahhh* that conveyed a full rainbow of profanity.

Cole continued to advance until Ryan stumbled backward in retreat and dropped the tip of his sword to the ground.

"Goddamn it, stop." Ryan bent over, his hands on his hips, breathing hard.

"You yield?"

Ryan flipped Cole off.

"I think that makes five for me," Cole said, mildly.

"I'm not even supposed to be doing this."

The actor playing the British exciseman, and Cole's soon-to-be on-screen sparring partner, had a cold, and Ryan was just filling in. So Ryan had a point, but Cole was still going to rub his superiority in.

"Nice work," Leonard said with evident pride.

Cole had certainly put in the effort, the time.

"Pay attention to your footwork, though," Amin warned. "You need better turnout."

"Like a ballerina?"

"Exactly."

Ryan had caught his breath. He straightened and glared at Leonard. "Why aren't you or Amin doing this with him since Reynold is out?"

Cole was the *him*.

Leonard was struggling not to laugh. "Because we're old men. And if you have to double for him in some of the shots—"

"I'm going to do all of my own shots," Cole insisted.

"—then you have to be up to speed."

"I hate all of you." Ryan fumbled for his water bottle. "I never should have agreed to do this. Guns and bombs and planes are where I live. I'm not taking another project that's not all guns and bombs and planes."

Since it was clear they were done for the moment, Cole picked up his own water. "You're just jealous because, for once, I'm better at something than you are."

"Give me another few days, James, and I'll kick your ass." But it was an empty threat. Ryan didn't have time for extra training. He had enough stuff to worry about with the coming shoot.

"I think we're done for the day, gentlemen," Cole said to Leonard and Amin. "See you tomorrow at ten?"

"We'll bring the ballet barre."

When they'd left, Cole slid down to sitting, leaning his back against the wall.

"You've worked your ass off," Ryan said. "I'm impressed."

From anyone else, this would have carried a rancid air of surprise. *Cole, I can't believe you worked so hard.* But he'd known Ryan long enough—and had quite literally just kicked his butt several times in a row—so Cole wasn't offended.

He took a long drag from his water bottle. "This one has gotta work. If it doesn't—I don't have many more in me."

For years, Cole and Drew had made plans. Cole would take this part or meet that casting director, and it would lead to another part. Slowly, each of these moves would take him another rung up the ladder. When he got to the top, he'd be back where he was supposed to be. And he would've finally wiped the slate clean.

Not every step had been right. Some of the gambles hadn't paid off. But in taking this part on *Waverley*, with how much time he was investing in it and how high profile it was, it was like going all in on a roulette spin.

Cole had gotten up off the dirt before. But if this one didn't work, he didn't have the energy for yet another backup plan.

It was this or nothing.

Ryan watched Cole steadily. They'd known each other long enough and liked each other well enough that Cole didn't have to explain all that to him.

"It's going to work," the stunt coordinator said. "This show . . . it's a phenomenon."

"That's what Tasha said."

And the reason that Tasha had agreed to take the part of Effie.

Cole carefully trained his attention on a piece of fluff on the floor halfway across the studio. "You working with Tasha on her riding?"

Effie, meaning Tasha, didn't have many stunts. The character's badassery came from not compromising. Since Tasha had spent most of her career literally kicking butt, this was going to be a change of pace for her.

But it also meant that she and Ryan weren't working together much—which was a shame.

"Yeah. But she already rides well."

The unspoken part was that Ryan thought Tasha did everything well.

Cole had never once doubted the guy's feelings for Tasha. It was in Ryan's face every time he looked at her. It was in his hands when he'd touch her in the course of his job. It was in how his voice changed when he spoke to or about her.

"You think it's finally time to say something?"

"About?"

"You being in love with her."

Ryan scowled. "What?"

"Come on, man. It's *me*."

A few seconds passed. Then a few dozen more.

"She doesn't want to hear that from me," he finally said.

Cole wasn't surprised Ryan wouldn't try to deny it—his feelings for Tasha were sort of undeniable. But Cole was surprised to have a fact so obvious, if silent, be open for discussion at last.

If Cole's own love life was shoved to the back burner, Tasha's was frozen. Her few relationships had the cadence of high school love affairs, but Cole supposed that made sense. For all that she might be in her thirties, Tasha had devoted about as much time to herself as a sixteen-year-old.

"Besides," Ryan said, "during her last riding lesson, she was pissed because I wouldn't let her canter. I told her she was going to have to use a stunt double for that part."

"Yeah, she hasn't heard no a lot. Actually, that's not true." Few people's lives had been as limited as Tasha's and yet as privileged. She'd grown up in a solid platinum cage, and everyone had wanted to point and laugh. "But she doesn't like feeling as if anyone is trying to control her, even if your motives are good."

"I just want her to be safe."

"I'm not her dad. I can't give you permission."

Ryan flicked a quick glance at Cole. "But she cares about your opinion more than she does her father's."

"Her dad's a schmuck." Tasha's father had been Beth Russell's second and briefest marriage. He was a record producer without much talent, except when it came to ignoring his kids—at that, he was basically a prodigy. Beth Russell might be an unpredictable addict, but at least she loved Tasha even if she lacked the emotional range to truly be there for her.

"The thing about Tasha is she's strong until she's not," Cole explained. "And when she needs you to step in, it's going to happen all at once. She'll be fine, and then she'll need a break, and there's no space in between."

Ryan had to suspect some of it. There'd been enough stories about Beth Russell's stints in rehab, and for all the complete crap written about the family, some of them were true. But Tasha was going to have to sort that out for Ryan—Cole wasn't going to do it.

"You sure do know her well." Ryan knotted his hands together and turned his scowl on Cole. "The reason why all her relationships fail—it's not you, is it?"

"It's never been like that." That was a game they only played for the press. They'd never tried to deceive people who really knew them. "Her relationships fail because she goes after assholes. She thinks a man wanting to use her is the same as him needing her."

"I don't want to use her, and I don't need her. I *want* her. Just her." Ryan spoke with such conviction, his words could almost be inside a Valentine's card.

"Well, she's not going to know what to do with that."

"And so we're back where we started. No, I won't be saying anything to her."

The man loved Tasha, and Cole would be willing to bet that she loved him back, but no one would say it.

Words—they were hard.

And fair enough! Cole would much rather spend a few hours fencing than talk about his feelings.

Cole got to his feet and rolled his shoulders. For all that he'd stretched and done cardio this morning, he was still sore. But even feeling every day of his forty-one years, he was still in better shape than Ryan.

When it came to his body, Cole was a master. Give him a grueling exercise plan to follow, or a set of detailed ancient fencing figures to memorize, and he was happy as a clam. Working hard, staying disciplined, putting in the hours: that was the path Cole knew, the place where he felt confident.

But if his mouth was involved, he felt . . . stumble-tongued. Incapable. He was grateful to Maggie for the care she was showing him and the rest of the cast, but their sessions left him feeling more naked than naked. Who knew that talking about your feelings was more exposing than taking off your pants?

Not wanting to argue, Cole hoisted his bag onto his shoulder. "I'll see you tomorrow morning."

He wove through the tangle of studios and rehearsal spaces. Stopping in the breezeway, he dug around in his bag for his phone.

At the door. Where are you? he texted his driver.

Outside, the sky was the color of wet concrete, and gusty winds had the trees undulating like waves. They appeared to be seconds away from a storm.

His phone dinged with a reply from his driver: **Two minutes away.**

Cole answered an email from Drew about a script he'd sent him, and he was still looking at his phone when the lightning hit. The screen reflected the bolt, and the thunder was still echoing in his ears when he raised his head. The flash and the crash had been almost simultaneous.

He was turning toward the door when someone barreled through it and into him. Cole wrapped his arms around the figure so he didn't go over backward, and it was only when she tipped her chin back that he realized it was Maggie.

Cole was holding Maggie.

Her eyes went wide. At the short distance, the irises were very green around the rim of her pupils, an herbal eclipse. Her mouth dropped open, and her lips were flushed a deep shade of rose. She was slim, pressed against him, and her body seemed to be holding most of the energy on earth. Or maybe that was just the rushing of his own pulse.

"Oof?" It came out like a question.

Was that an oof? Or was it something else?

Cole was dizzy, and it wasn't the proximity of the lightning and the smell of the rain that had just started to come down outside.

It was entirely the woman in his arms.

Her hands, which had been raised to push the door open, flattened against his chest, and Cole found himself staring down at them. The neat curve of each nail, the soft pink of the cuticles, the architecture of her fingers. It was as if he'd never seen hands before. As if no one had.

"Oof," he repeated, but the sound was gibberish.

Maybe it was the only way to describe the stew of things he was feeling. Attraction, yes, but also just bone-deep concern. And relief that she wasn't out in the storm. And . . . tenderness. Maggie made his insides into a honeycomb, gooey and buzzing.

He raised his gaze to meet hers. Maggie's breathing was shallow, each inhale a tiny sip, and her expression was so confused.

Probably because he was cradling her like a doofus.

Cole raised his hands from where they had been clenched on her back and took a few steps away from her. It didn't help. He still felt all golden and glittery.

"Sorry," he said. "I was trying not to—sorry. Are you okay?"

"Yeah." Maggie shook her head. "You don't have to apologize. I'm the one who ran into you. I wasn't even looking. I'm sorry."

"Don't worry about it. I hate lightning. It's like a top-five fear for me."

Her smile was grateful. "I'm not too fond of it either. It started to feel like it was about to storm when I was walking toward the Tube station. Then the temperature dropped, and I could smell the rain, and I decided to turn around. The last few feet, the hair was starting to stand up on the back of my neck. I knew I was in trouble."

Cole almost hauled her back into his arms. He shoved his hands into the pockets of his jacket instead. "I'm glad you're okay."

"Me too." She wiped at her eyes. "That was *not* what I was expecting this afternoon."

"Did you have a session with Tasha? I thought she was with wardrobe." If Tasha was going to meet with Maggie again, he really ought to be there, if only to protect Maggie.

"Leanne and Owen," she explained. "Wedding-night choreography."

"Our jobs are so weird."

Lightning split the sky again, and Maggie tugged her coat around herself. "I may just spend the night here. Seems safer."

"My driver's on the way. I'm happy to drop you at the hotel. And he'll wait for us until the lightning passes. We don't have to rush out in"—a bolt of electricity cracked the sky again—"that."

"Thank you, I'd appreciate it. I don't normally mind the Tube. I like it, actually, but . . . maybe not today."

"I'll give you my number. We can carpool every day."

Maggie's answering smile was soft, but it wasn't directed at him. Instead, she'd turned her attention to the toes of her shoes. "You're very sweet to offer, but I'm okay."

Is she declining the carpooling, my number—or both?

Cole knew it was safer, more professional, for her to pass. Because the things he'd felt when he'd held her, they'd been dangerous. Just as he wouldn't want to take a stroll outside right now, it would be risky for him to draw Maggie closer . . . even if he wanted to.

Maybe he'd developed some respect for Ryan's position. Sometimes, it was smarter to keep your mouth shut.

Chapter 8

INT. MAGGIE'S HOTEL ROOM

Maggie carefully arranged her checklist, script, pens, and sticky tabs on the hotel desk. She wasn't nervous; her mind was too busy to be nervous. She did want to get through filming this first scene; then maybe she'd be able to find a quarter of calm, just a sliver, where she could catch her breath.

She picked up her phone and dialed. "Hey, Rhiannon. I'm calling to check in."

Over the last three weeks, Maggie had worked every day. Every moment of intimacy or nudity was fully choreographed and rehearsed—except for Tasha Russell's scenes. On that front, there had been absolutely no movement. Even Tasha's assistant, an impossibly chic and stoic young woman ironically named Merrit, seemed to feel sorry for Maggie at this point.

But never mind that. Maggie had worked with Zoya and the other episode directors, with Alexa in wardrobe. She'd talked to the director of photography, to the show's composer, and even to the catering staff and security crews.

As Ryan had encouraged her to do, she'd faked it until she almost—almost—felt comfortable with the language of moviemaking. Until she was only dazzled by the famous people about 10 percent of the time.

Then she'd packed her London hotel room, and this morning, they'd arrived in Edinburgh. The first scene of the show was filming tonight—the much-debated love scene with Rhiannon and Cole.

"Hiya, Maggie." Rhiannon sounded cheerful, which was hugely relieving. "You caught me at the gym. Yup, we're all set."

"Do you have any last-minute questions or concerns?"

"No, actually. I feel . . . good about it. Which I sort of can't believe."

Warmth unfurled in Maggie's chest. "We've all done our jobs, then. And I'll be there the entire time if anything comes up."

"I'll see you in a few hours."

"Don't hesitate to call if you need me sooner."

The cast had a few more hours of downtime before they had to drive up into the hills around Edinburgh to the outdoor set for the Jacobite camp—and then Madge and Geordie were going to get steamy beside a campfire.

Maggie had no idea why they were kicking off principal photography for season three of *Waverley* with *this* particular scene, but she had a very clear place in the production's pecking order: at the bottom.

Maybe next season—if they asked her back—she'd have enough power to say something about this, to insist that they didn't need to start with something so emotionally charged. And also that maybe asking actors to take off most of their clothing and get frisky in the Scottish Highlands was cruel.

Zoya was right: Maggie did seem to have a knack for this job. If only she could crack the nut that was Tasha Russell, she'd feel as if she'd earned an A in Intimacy Coordination: The Rehearsal Period.

But the actual filming posed an entirely new set of challenges.

She crossed *Check in with Rhiannon* off her list. Then with trembling fingers, she dialed the next number.

"This is Cole." His tone was friendly but with a heaping of professional distance—because he didn't know who was on the other end.

"Hi, it's Maggie." For all that they'd worked together for weeks, they'd arranged all the logistics over email. Calling or texting him had seemed too . . . intimate.

Even now, if she closed her eyes, she could conjure the sensation of Cole's arms banded around her back. In her defense, they were some arms. She'd seen those biceps, directed them, actually, and she could testify that they were aesthetically perfect.

But what had her weak kneed wasn't his musculature, but how Cole hadn't hesitated to hold her. The warmth of him. The certain heft.

It was infatuation. Puppy love, really. Maggie had been through a major life upheaval, and now she was surrounded by literal movie stars. Of course she'd gotten all gooey about the nicest one.

That didn't mean she had to indulge it in any way.

Over the line, she could hear Cole breathing. His intake and exhale were rapid and even. Maybe she'd caught him at the gym too.

"I hope it's okay I'm calling. I wanted to do a quick check-in." Maggie was going to have to work on her chipper voice. She sounded like a Chipmunk.

"Yeah, of course. I'm feeling solid."

He was solid in absolutely every way.

"I caught up with Esme and David in the lobby. They're going to have warm-up stations. They estimated that it'll take about two hours to film."

She'd checked about this several times now. She hated being cold, and the idea of being cold, nearly naked, and having to act—it was basically a hell dimension, as far as she was concerned.

Maggie liked Zoya, but it was possible the woman was a bit of a masochist.

Silence over the phone. Then, "I've made a few TV shows." But there wasn't any annoyance in Cole's voice. More amusement that she'd brought this up several times.

"Sorry, I know. I'm feeling anxious." Which was why she was babbling.

"You shouldn't be."

Of course not: she wasn't the one taking her clothes off. But also, he shouldn't be reassuring her. That was her job.

"Ha, too late for that." Trying to get this conversation back on track, she asked, "Do you have any questions? Worries?"

"Not about the scene."

Maggie reminded herself that whatever the rest of Cole's issues were about, it wasn't any of her business. "If I can help, let me know. I'm here for whatever you need." She hoped her tone conveyed that she meant it in a friendly yet detached way.

This was just like when he'd offered to commute to rehearsal with her. There'd been the storm and the lightning, and Cole was a kind and thoughtful person who'd made an offhand suggestion. Certainly he hadn't spent any time since, dissecting that moment into each discrete, clinical detail, before shuffling them and reexamining from a different perspective. He probably didn't even remember that he'd said it or that she'd declined.

She was being ridiculous. Right there in the *Oxford English Dictionary* under *ninny*, there was probably a picture of Maggie. Sample sentence: *The high school drama teacher reinventing herself in Hollywood who develops a pointless crush on the polite but disinterested movie star is a ninny of the highest order.*

"I appreciate that."

Because he was perfect—and not for her. So completely not for her.

"I'll see you on set?"

"I'll be the big guy in the robe."

And that . . . she wasn't going to think about. Nope.

It took another half hour to complete the rest of her calls. Then Maggie kicked off her shoes—she always put them on for work calls for some reason—and sprawled out on the bed. It was softer than the bed in London had been, broken in, more like her mattress at home.

She'd been ignoring an email from her parents—which was par for the course—and a series of texts from her best friend, Savannah Harris. That was less normal.

Savannah was the choir director at Maggie's old school. Music and drama had occupied a building connected to the main building by a breezeway, and it had felt like mutual exile. As the tone had changed in the school and the history curriculum and the library's collection had come under scrutiny, Maggie and Savannah had worried. But it had been easy to pretend those problems were happening in some distant land not directly connected to theirs.

Until Maggie's world had been torn open.

All through the trial and everything that followed, Savannah had been there for Maggie—been there even as people in the community had made that difficult and painful.

Woman, I need details, Savannah's most recent text read. Every. Single. Detail.

It's currently 21 degrees Celsius, Maggie replied. The barometric pressure is 1011mb. Visibility 9 km. And there's 82% humidity.

After a minute, Maggie's phone dinged. I deserved that.

Maggie glanced at the clock. It was midmorning in Oregon. "You did, actually," she said when Savannah answered her phone.

"I can't help it. You're living the dream and making my favorite show—and you can't say *anything*? I'll have you know, I'm very discreet."

Which was true. Maggie couldn't have imagined a better friend or support system than Savannah.

Even still: "I don't think so. The NDA I had to sign to get the scripts was incredibly scary. It was gold and glowing, and I inked it with a fish bone. It's possible Ursula is their lawyer. They may take my voice if I break the rules."

Savannah laughed. "Fair enough. But the first scene shoots tonight?"

Maggie had felt safe sharing that. Someone would probably post pictures of the production vans on TikTok. "Yup. It's make-or-break time for me. This is when we find out if I can do this."

"You keep saying that, but things aren't that dire. If this gig falls through, they're always hiring at Starbucks."

Maggie had almost gone that way during the trial. "I don't even like coffee that much."

"Don't tell them that during the interview. Seriously, though, how are you holding up?"

"It's like the first year of teaching." Meaning that Maggie felt underprepared and as if every step was taking her three times as long as it needed to. "I want to be good at this. I want to be good at this so badly."

"You *are* good at this. You're good at everything."

If that was true, why had Maggie found herself unemployed and humiliated? Why was she remaking herself in her late thirties, when she really ought to have been on the cusp of getting bored with her life and having a midlife crisis instead?

"You have to say that. You're my best friend."

"I don't have to say crap. And besides, the fact we're friends proves your awesomeness."

Savannah wasn't suffering from a lack of self-confidence. Well, one of them should be well adjusted.

"Enough about me, how is Emily?" Emily was the concertmaster for the local symphony orchestra and Savannah's on-again, off-again girlfriend.

"Exploring things with her ex from college."

"Ouch." That had to have hurt.

"It's okay. I may be too bi for her anyhow."

Savannah was playing it off, but from previous iterations of this fight, Maggie knew that it stung. "You want to talk about it?"

"Nope."

What she needed was a girls' night—and Maggie was halfway around the world.

"Got it." With Emily off the table—and with her, music, the farmers' market, and brunch were off the table too—what was safe to discuss? "How are my verdant babies?" When Maggie had taken this job, she'd sublet her place and put most of her things in storage. Savannah had been kind enough to take possession of her collection of houseplants.

It had started during quarantine with one or two pots, but it had quickly spread to every windowsill and side table of her condo. Maggie had thought she'd missed the green thumb gene, but it turned out you could learn how not to kill plants. There were books and YouTube channels and everything.

"You literally left me a calendar with daily instructions."

"You wouldn't want to confuse the ferns and the snake plant." For starters, one had to be watered daily, and the other would only need to be watered twice during Maggie's entire absence.

"You labeled every pot with the inhabitant's name and a QR code I can scan for a complete dossier on the variety." Savannah's tone was dry, but really, she knew what Maggie was like.

"I just wanted to make it easy for you. Plus, you know, educational. How are things otherwise in Eugene?" Savannah would know that was code for *How are my former students?* As bruised as Maggie still was by her old job, she did miss everyone.

"Excellent. Amira got into Berkeley."

"Have her parents relaxed?"

"Of course not. They still have to ensure she gets all As for med school. They've probably started stressing about whether she'll land the right residency."

How exhausting for Amira . . . but also for her parents. When every step of your life was about what came next—when nothing was worth celebrating or brought security, because there was always another thing and then another—where was the achievement in that? The rest? The fun?

Maggie tried not to think about the agenda that was sitting on the hotel desk . . . and the similar agendas for every other day of the shoot that were in her accordion files.

This was different. Totally different.

"And the school board?"

"Our benevolent overlords would never act contrary to the good of the people."

"That bad?"

"I've never seen a group of people in charge of something who seem to hate it as much as those bozos hate public education. Honestly, you got out just in time. Do you think I could set up a private choir?" As it was, Savannah taught voice lessons in her "free" time, but that income didn't come close to covering her teaching income. Side hustles were a crock.

"You could be like Harold Hill! You could travel around setting up choirs and selling uniforms and pitch pipes and seducing librarians."

"If the librarians are cute, I'm in." A pause. "I miss you. I mean, I'm deeply jealous you're hanging out in Scotland with Tasha freaking Russell and Cole 'The Abs' James. But I also miss you."

Maggie had a flash from the before times—before COVID, before everyone decided teachers were the enemy—to a Friday happy hour at Chili's with Savannah and the other cool teachers from their school. She missed her best friend so much. She missed her old job more than she would let herself admit. But the ache in her chest was also for *that*, for the sense of being a part of something larger than herself. The camaraderie, the jokes, the confidence that they were in a job where they made a difference and improved lives.

She had none of those things here. Maybe she *could* have them, someday, but she still felt so insecure.

She was playing a role, and even several months in, she still felt badly miscast. Some part of Maggie's heart was still pinwheeling madly postfiring, desperate to know which way was up and which was down and which direction she ought to be going.

Ever since college, Maggie had *known*. The very nature of teaching was predictability. If it was spring, she'd be teaching the film unit in her intermediate drama class, and doing scenes with her beginning students, and directing a musical. Her calendar had been as certain as the daffodils popping up when the snow melted.

Maggie had had moments in the last few months where she felt as if she were getting that conviction back, but then along had come Tasha to make her feel dizzy all over again.

"I miss you too." After a poignant beat, Maggie tried to sound cheerful as she added, "I'll be back in three months!"

"Not soon enough. This pothos is looking sad."

"You should've picked pretty much any other plant: pothos is impossible to kill. Just check the soil, and—"

"Maggie, I was kidding."

"Right, right. I knew that. I was kidding too." She hadn't been. "But I do have to go. It's a night shoot . . . and that's the only detail you get."

"Ooooh, that's enough for me to build an entire dream scenario. I will take it. Talk soon, Niven!"

Maggie took a quick nap, and before leaving for the bus that was going to take the crew up to the location, she dashed off a quick email to Bernard.

> Going into the first day of shooting, I feel as prepared as it's possible to feel when I don't really know what I'm doing. As long as everything goes according to plan, I feel confident. But I have absolutely no ability to improvise, and that's what worries me the most. With teaching, it took years before I trusted my ability to respond to whatever might happen in the classroom. I wish Zoya were directing this episode as we have the best working relationship, but I'm glad that I'm starting with Rhiannon as Tasha still isn't speaking to me.

They were almost at the last moment for the star to change her mind about that. It felt like a distant mountain that Maggie wanted to climb, one that kept poking through the clouds and taunting her.

Every time Bernard asked about it and Maggie had to repeat that no, nothing had changed, Maggie hadn't made any progress, she wanted to cry. She'd almost begged Bernard to get on a plane to see if he could make any headway. Maggie didn't have any ego here—okay, she had a small and reasonable amount of ego—but at this point, her worries weren't just about herself but also about Tasha.

Maggie wanted to make sure that Tasha was going to be okay.

She blew out a long breath, watching the hair around her face stir. She couldn't control Tasha's reaction. She could only keep making herself available and do a good job with Rhiannon and Cole.

In the last year, so much had been outside Maggie's control. She'd spent so much time literally making herself sick over people's feelings—which she couldn't dictate—and other people's choices—which weren't hers to make. The helplessness had almost destroyed her, until she'd realized that if she could embrace it, then she had more energy for the stuff she could control. Seeing her limits, affirming them, it *increased* her power.

I'm still feeling stymied about that, she wrote, but that's a problem for another day.

And quite frankly, it was a problem Tasha had to solve on her own. All Maggie could do was keep her hand outstretched and hope Tasha would eventually grasp it.

She hit send on the email to Bernard, packed her bag, double-checked its contents, and headed out—because those were the things she could do.

Tonight, they had to be enough.

Chapter 9

EXT. *WAVERLEY* SET—NIGHT

Kevin Combs, who was directing this episode, leaned out from behind the monitor and asked, "You ready?"

Cole surveyed the set as he waited for Rhiannon to respond. It was supposed to look like a 1730s Jacobite camp, all hand-spun bedrolls, swords, and bonfires. On the other side of them was the twenty-first century—the state-of-the-art camera, the monitors, and the boom mic. When they filmed the daylight scenes, the set would be full of horses and people. Tonight, it was just Madge, Geordie, and a skeleton crew.

"Yup." Rhiannon gave Kevin a firm nod.

"I'm good," Cole said.

They'd already run through the blocking for the scene fully clothed; then they'd filmed the shots of talking and kissing that led into the love scene. They'd filmed the slow dance of undressing. They'd removed a layer, like Geordie's shirt, which spilled out in front of them, and shot for a bit. Then they'd paused to move the cameras and the lights for the next shot.

So now they'd arrived at the blow job, the part he'd gone over so many times with Maggie and Rhiannon during rehearsal and about which he was still not thrilled.

"David, you ready?" Kevin asked.

The DP gave a thumbs-up.

Maggie stood behind the director, her expression fixed into something friendly, distanced, and on top of things. It was how she'd sounded on the phone this afternoon, and Cole was grateful for it. But it was also vaguely unsatisfying in a way he didn't want to ponder.

Whatever. He had a job to do. He didn't need to be wasting time wishing for another thunderstorm so Maggie might seek shelter against his chest again.

Cole shrugged off his robe and handed it to a PA. He was nude from the waist up, and for all that there was a huge bonfire just to the left of the bedroll, it was nippy. Scotland at night was freaking cold.

Penelope Bullock, a tech on the hair and makeup team whose no-nonsense air of authority suggested a middle school vice principal, applied a quick skim of gel to Cole's chest. "I'm trying not to overdo it. We don't want you to look like you've recently retired from *Magic Mike*."

"Believe me, I'm familiar with UltraSweat." It was basically his professional calling card.

When she'd finished, he settled on his mark.

Rhiannon handed her robe to a PA and slid into place—straddling Cole's legs. "Remember, don't be gentle," she warned him.

"I won't." The words were brave. Cole wasn't.

After he'd voiced his initial concerns that first day they'd worked on the blocking, Maggie had made sure they'd rehearsed this to the point of routine, but it was different on the set, with the lights, the fire, and the crew.

Cole wasn't a Method actor. Being your character every moment for weeks or months at a time? Frankly, the idea made him want to poke his eyes out. But way back on *Central Square*, he'd realized while he could—and probably should—understand what his character might be thinking in a scene, when they were filming, the key thing was being present. Acting was that simple, and it was that hard.

Decades of doing this, and Cole had become hyperaware of his body. Of the line he made during a shot. Of whether he was clenching his abs. Of whether that was an attractive grimace or an ugly one. But that same awareness made his acting self-conscious and shitty.

Cole had to be a roguish, sexy jerk in this scene. He had to blot out everything in him that wasn't *that*. It was the only way to give a half-decent performance.

In the previous shot, Cole's and Rhiannon's fingers had tangled together, unlacing the fastening of his breeches. Now, the crew had reset for a wider shot. She was going to kiss down his chest until he put his hand on the back of her head, forcing it downward, and they simulated her performing oral sex on him.

In reality, her head would be over his thigh. The placement of the camera would make them look far closer together than they were. But this was the shot he was least excited about in the entire damn show.

His stomach was revolting, his muscles cagey. He didn't normally feel this tense filming intimacy, but he had to trust Kevin and the production team, trust Rhiannon, trust Maggie, and above all, trust himself.

He locked eyes with Maggie, and she nodded. *You got this.*

He hoped she was right.

"Picture's up."

It was time.

Cole tipped his head back, Rhiannon leaned against his chest, slate was called, and Kevin shouted "Camera set!"

They were filming. Cole blotted everything out and let muscle memory take over.

The shot was a blur, and it felt far longer than the minute Cole knew it took.

Kevin yelling "Cut!" broke the bubble.

Cole immediately lifted his hand, and Rhiannon rolled back onto her heels. Production assistants were there with their robes instantly.

"You okay?" he asked Rhiannon once she was covered.

"Perfect." She patted his forearm. "You're the sweetest."

But having concern for your scene partner wasn't sweet. It was the absolute bare minimum.

"Let's go again." Kevin's eyes were glued to the monitor, rewatching the footage they'd just shot. Tall and slim with a buzz cut and a penchant for wearing black turtlenecks, Kevin always looked as if he were cosplaying Steve Jobs. "This time keep your expression more neutral, Cole. Almost disassociating."

Since that had been what Cole thought he'd been doing, he could only nod and say "Sure."

What he'd learned from Tasha was to make every take a little different. Give more or less emotion. Phrase his lines differently—at least until they said *Exactly like that.*

"The director makes your performance in the editing," she'd said.

Cole had never really thought about it until she'd said that to him, but she'd been right. She was almost always right, except for the part where she was stonewalling Maggie. That was just bizarre.

Kevin signaled they were ready to go, and they filmed the shot again and then a third time.

Cole felt queasy. His insides were roiling. But he gritted his way through it.

"Got it," Kevin called. "Let's reset for the next bit."

The next part of the sequence had Geordie tugging Madge's dress and underthings off. This bit was tricky because Rhiannon had decided she wasn't comfortable having her nipples on screen. Kevin had fully supported the change, despite her signed nudity waiver, but it took four takes to get it right.

"Your arm has to be higher to hide her pasties," Maggie instructed.

Damn, this was a weird business.

Then Maggie was there with the exercise ball that would sit between Cole and Rhiannon for the next shot—the onset of the actual thrusting. They had to film that from the side and from the back, before getting close-ups of Rhiannon's face and then Cole's. There was the inherent awkwardness stemming from the fact that Cole was still clothed from the waist down, and Rhiannon was naked except for a few bits of Lycra and toupee tape.

The entire thing was worse than a game of Twister. Where should his hand be to shield this bit or that one from the camera? Where should Rhiannon put her left knee? How could they get the angle right but keep the ball invisible?

At least all the technical concerns were enough to make Cole's nausea fade. This was so clearly a group exercise, he didn't have to feel bad, as if he specifically were using someone.

After what felt like a dozen takes, Geordie put Madge on her knees. In the flow of the work, Cole was able to shove down another wave of discomfort. The shot came with another set of lights and camera moves, all while the design team had to keep the fire stoked at the same height for continuity. Penelope kept touching up Cole's fake sweat, and the makeup and hair people kept fussing over Rhiannon.

When the last shot of thrusting was done, the awkwardness faded, and people started to crack jokes. Cole felt himself smile for what might've been the first time all night. His body was almost loose, almost *his* again. He could almost take himself back from Geordie.

They were on the last part of the sequence—the cuddling. The camera reset to be overhead, looking down at the couple in their shared bedroll. Wordlessly, he and Rhiannon had to convey that Madge was triumphant, in love, satisfied. She was fully convinced that giving herself to this man meant they were together forever. But Geordie needed to feel like a sleeping lion, as if he was only content for the night.

"That seemed fast," Rhiannon said while they waited for Kevin to shout *Camera set*.

"About two hours, I think." Cole wasn't sure if he'd ever shot an involved love scene so quickly. Even the moments he'd been most hesitant about had been basically fine. Maggie had prepped them well.

"At least we get a blanket now."

"It scratches like hell, though." The crew had staked a ground cover underneath the bedroll and sprayed for midges—disgusting tick-like insects that were all over the Highlands. If Cole got midge bites on his nether regions, he was going to be extremely pissed off.

"I cannot wait to get into that warming station." Rhiannon chafed her arms. "Thank God for Maggie."

Next to them, a grip finished tending the fire.

"I owe you ten bucks on the Lakers, right?" Cole asked him.

"Yeah, but I'd guess you don't have your wallet on you."

"I left it in my other crotch sock."

Everyone was still laughing when Kevin said "Let's get this in the can."

It took five shots, largely because Cole was feeling tired and unfocused. He'd never felt good at these kind of moments when he just had to emote, and he could only hope he didn't look as if he had indigestion.

At last the director announced they were done.

A PA handed Cole his robe, some sandals, and a cup of tea. He didn't really drink the stuff, but he appreciated how it was thawing his hands, so he took it back to his trailer. He set the canister of warmth down long enough to change into sweats, and then he curled up at the small dinette table, clutching the paper cup.

After filming, it always took a while to quiet his mind. It was good that they'd gotten everything they needed in a single evening. A few night shoots in a row could mess up his sleep for weeks.

A knock sounded on his trailer door.

"Yeah?" he called.

"Cole? It's me."

Me being Maggie.

"It's open."

He really should have locked the door when he'd changed, but since the crew had seen most of his body tonight, that hadn't seemed important.

Maggie poked her head in and smiled at him. Her hand still on the knob, she asked, "How are you doing?"

"A little cold," he admitted.

"Apparently last night was even chillier. So I guess we're lucky."

"Do you want to come in?"

"Sure. May I?" She pointed to the bench across from him and only sat once he'd nodded. "Rhiannon is in the warming station. I'm sure she'd be happy to share."

"I'm okay. I have tea." He held up his cup. "How did the footage look?"

"You know, I wasn't paying attention to the monitor. But Kevin sounds really pleased."

"One down . . . a lot to go." Cole had never bothered to count how many scenes he was in, but he was number one on the call sheet. He was going to be a busy man during the next three months.

"You got off to a great start. Listen, I wanted to stop by because you had some concerns about the scene when we were rehearsing. Now that it's done, how are you feeling?"

Apparently a postfilming check-in was one of the duties of an intimacy coordinator.

Cole set his tea on the table so he could scratch his face. He wasn't certain how to answer Maggie's question. He didn't feel like celebrating, but mostly, his feelings were blank. "Playing someone who's so different from me is . . . look, on the one hand, if I can pull it off, maybe I'm a better actor than I thought I was. But on the other hand—"

"You're a damn fine actor, Cole." Which Maggie meant. Absolutely. Her fiery belief was—well, it felt nice.

Her belief in him wasn't enough to obliterate the discomfort in his gut, though. The queasiness lingered, like film on a glass when you drained it. "It doesn't feel natural. I'm not a man who'd shove a woman's face in my crotch."

"I'm certain you aren't."

Awareness pulsed in the air, like a bomb had detonated but without the destruction. Just the blast of energy and heat.

Cole was attracted to Maggie. Had been from the first moment he'd clapped eyes on her. He wasn't going to act on it, but it was there, the shimmering gold version of whatever gilt thing he'd faked tonight.

All the restlessness in his limbs, in his mind, began to pool in the pit of his abdomen. *Her. You want her,* it said.

But he wasn't going to get her.

He took a sip of his tea, which had gone lukewarm, and almost gagged. Nothing was quite as unpleasant as liquid that wasn't hot and wasn't cold. The taste equivalent of beige. "Well, to play Geordie, I have to find the part of me that would do that to a lover. And I don't dig it." It wasn't much different from what he'd said while they were rehearsing, but it was still true.

Maggie's fingers danced over the Formica tabletop for a second. Maybe she played piano?

Then, finally, she said, "I directed a production of *Oklahoma!* once, and the kid playing Jud said a similar thing to me."

"I haven't seen that one in a while." He wasn't really into musicals.

"Ah. Well, Jud assaults Laurey twice, and he strongly implies that he killed another woman and her family when she turned him down. This kid was one of the nicest kids I've ever directed. He was playing way against type. We had endless conversations about those moments. How far did we need to go so the audience would get it? What would be comfortable for the actress playing Laurey? How to stage it? How to block it? How to use the music? The girl playing Laurey, she got right with it very quickly. From her perspective, it was so important because sexual violence could make this old play feel relevant to teens now. But for him, it was the relevance that made him want to crawl out of his skin."

Lots of actors liked playing villains. Relished it, really. But Cole never had, and he suspected he never would. Geordie's moral grayness was as far as he was comfortable going—and he obviously wasn't comfortable with that.

"So how did he deal with it?" Because Cole was feeling so insecure, he'd take acting advice from an actual teenager.

"It helps that Jud is the villain in *Oklahoma!* And since it was a school production, it was supposed to teach the students something. So we talked about what he was learning, the technical challenges of the role. But ultimately, I asked him *why* he thought we did plays. Like, what human impulse demands drama?" Maggie turned her gaze from the window to Cole. "What do you think?"

Cole almost took another sip of his tea, but nope, it would only be disappointing. He set it down again. "I assume you're not going to let me say I make movies because I enjoy it."

"Nope—though I get that. But I think there's something deeper, more existential here."

Cole closed his eyes and pictured the set. "I love the collective effort it takes to make television. I mean, tonight was fairly sparse, but wait until we get to those big crowd scenes. I know when people watch it, they'll just think about Rhiannon and me. But dozens of people were involved in filming that. So many folks, so much expertise." When he watched a movie, he always stayed through the entire credit sequence, trying to see every name. From the assistants to the caterer to the sparks and the grips, they all had made that movie. They were all important.

"So it's a group endeavor," Maggie said. "Like building a cathedral or something. What else?"

"Movies, television"—probably theatre, too, but he'd never done plays—"they say something about who we are. Like, as humans. Why we do the things we do."

"Humanity and psychology." Maggie ticked those off on her fingers.

"Sure. And to be selfish for a minute, I wasn't a very good actor at first."

Maggie started to disagree, but Cole cut her off. "No, really, I wasn't. But I've gotten better, and sometimes when I'm really in a scene, everything else goes away, and I can be in the moment."

Her eyes were gleaming, as if they'd caught every bit of the electric lights outside and compressed them.

Cole had caught the thread she'd been trying to get him to find, and he was speaking quickly now. His body was still humming with lust, but maybe also with some professional know-how. "Have you ever been in an accident, and you remember every single millisecond of it? As if time has slowed down or something? Performing can be like that. And other times, it's an out-of-body experience, and I don't come back to myself until it's over. Either way, I feel ten times more alive. It's standing on a mountaintop but without the climb." Even tonight, with its moments of discomfort, his body was still rushing. Cole wouldn't be able to sleep for hours.

"And now?"

"It's a smaller buzz." Cole laughed. "Sex scenes, fight scenes, stunts—they're too technical to be truly . . ."

"Transcendent?" she offered.

"Yeah." That was a good word for it.

"I hope you get some of those moments during this shoot, Cole," Maggie said softly. "They sound amazing."

There was a note of jealousy in her tone that had him curious. "Was it like that when you were teaching?"

"Yes. Maybe even amplified because I felt extra pride in my students. I didn't know my heart could be that full before that job."

"I bet you were incredible at it."

"Not to brag, but I was." Maggie's expression was smug, and for an instant, he was the jealous one.

Cole never found it easy to be kind to himself, probably because he'd made such big mistakes at the start. He wouldn't give himself higher than a B-minus at pretty much any task or role he'd ever had.

But while she kept a smile pasted on her face, Maggie's eyes dimmed. "Now I have to settle for being incredible at this."

"You are. Oh my God, I should be saying thank you. I'm sitting here whining about how I don't like playing a selfish lover, and I'm not acknowledging *you*. Maggie, I am so sorry."

"For what?"

"That scene went so much better than it would have without you. It's what Zoya wanted and the show needed. And that's because of you."

She shook her head and got to her feet. "It was you, Cole. You and Rhiannon. I just hope I helped."

"Wait, leaving so soon?" Cole said it jokingly, but under the question, he knew he was serious. He wanted Maggie to stay, to keep chatting with him, to tell him more about the kids she'd worked with and the plays she'd directed. To give him the perfect word when he couldn't think of it.

The moment stretched out. Her standing, one hand still on the table. Him sitting, staring up at her, with what was probably a pathetically needy look on his face.

But honestly, he was feeling pretty pathetically needy.

Maggie's gaze on him . . . he couldn't have begun to make sense of it. She was watching him so intently, she might as well have been sending sonar waves through him. He could only hope his echo sounded good.

Please.

But he didn't even know what he was asking for.

After a few beats, Maggie yawned, comically exaggerated. "You may be used to movie star hours, James, but I am not. And I have more work to do tomorrow."

He almost wrapped his fingers around her wrist. But before he could do something so stupid, Maggie was gone.

Which was . . . good. She'd been kind, professional. Her work had made the shoot go well, and then she'd helped him set down his stress about the character. And that, and only that, was all Maggie owed him.

Whatever he'd been imagining in her face had been exactly that—imagining. Cole might want her, but he wasn't going to have her. He had to bury those feelings deep and pretend they didn't exist.

Chapter 10

INT. HOTEL CONFERENCE ROOM

If Tasha had scheduled this meeting in the hotel parking garage, Maggie would've been certain it was the pretense for a hit job. Since it was in a conference room, the odds of that were only, like, 33 percent.

Maggie pushed the door open. "Tasha?"

The lights weren't on. A folding table leaned against the wall. A few chairs were strewed about the room almost randomly. But just before Maggie left, chalking it up to Tasha changing her mind or Maggie having the wrong place or time, she noticed the starlet standing at one of the windows.

In her movies, Tasha never seemed to stop moving. She was a creature of constant action, always punching someone, kicking a door open, or jumping out of a plane. *Tasha Russell does stuff* was practically a genre category on Videon.

But now, she might as well have been a statue. One of Tasha's hands was curled around the base of her throat. The other held the flimsy curtain open a crack so she could see the street below. She was so still, she was almost camouflaged.

"I thought I had the wrong room." Maggie closed the door behind her.

"Traffic is really soothing. To watch, I mean. Not to sit in."

For about the one hundredth time since taking this job, Maggie wished she were a psychologist. Tasha was like one of those glacial lakes: far deeper than she appeared from the outside yet strangely disconnected from the rest of the world. But the only way for Maggie to do her job was if she better understood Tasha's hang-ups, which were clearly numerous and painful. Maggie had to dive in.

"Why?" she asked.

Tasha took and released a deep breath. "In traffic, everyone works together. They follow the rules . . . ish. We make allowances for the rat bastard that's speeding or the lady who didn't use her damn turn signal. I'm honestly amazed there aren't more car accidents. It's kind of uncanny we all get into murder tanks every day and more people don't die."

"In fairness, driving is probably the most dangerous thing we all do daily."

"But we don't think of it as being scary. When you consider how much humans hurt each other in other ways, you'd think it'd be like *John Wick* on the 405. I guess I'm perverse, but that soothes me."

That we should hurt each other more—and we don't?

But Maggie was going to keep tiptoeing after Tasha's lead here, hoping they ended up plumbing the contours of this lake of secrets.

Tasha finally turned toward Maggie, and it was honestly unfair for anyone to be that beautiful. She didn't have on a lick of makeup, her hair had clearly dried after her shower without any styling, and she was more arresting than any person Maggie had ever seen in her life. People who looked like Tasha had called movies into being. It was the only explanation. Humans had had to create some medium to record their beauty. Tasha was *that* lovely.

"I'd never thought about traffic like that," Maggie said. "But I'm guessing that's not why you wanted to chat."

"No."

As a teacher, Maggie had made friends with silence. In her first few years on the job, she'd ask a question, and if someone didn't answer it immediately, she'd want to fill the void—to rephrase her question or to offer a little hint or to just answer the damn thing herself. But sixteen years later, she felt none of those impulses.

Ten seconds slipped by. Maybe a minute.

Finally, Tasha offered, "I ran into Rhiannon at the gym this morning."

Maggie was the only person here who didn't hit the treadmill first thing. The gym was obviously the *Waverley* equivalent of the water-cooler. "Filming went well last night."

The call sheet that had arrived in Maggie's inbox earlier today said the second unit was shooting B-roll, and then there was a bunch of Jacobite stuff shooting at the set they'd used yesterday.

No kissing and no nudity meant no Maggie.

"That's what Rhiannon said." Tasha appeared to be murderous about it. "I had a text from Cole too."

Cole was definitely trying to help out Tasha and, by extension, Maggie. Her heart did a hop, skip, and a jump about that, but Tasha's trauma had to come before Maggie's drama.

"I realize I'm being a bitch, and it isn't personal."

"I never thought it was," Maggie said quickly.

There was another epic silence. Then Tasha said, "Have you seen *Cosa Nostra?*"

"I have."

"Do you remember those Oscars?"

"I remember your dress." It had been an engineering marvel: strapless peach silk that was minimalist in the front but somehow backless with a sweeping train. Tasha had worn what appeared to be a royal vault's worth of diamonds: in her hair, around her neck, dripping down her arms. She'd been fresh and radiant, beyond beautiful—and she hadn't left public consciousness since that moment.

After those awards, her style had never again been that overtly feminine. A decided edge of I-could-fuck-you-up-if-I-wanted-to had crept into her persona, and on screen she'd become a professional ass kicker. But that movie, that night, had started it all.

Or maybe it had ended something.

"I remember you came with Vincent Minna." That was risky, injecting him into this conversation, but Maggie suspected she'd been right when she'd said to Zoya that that movie was the key to unlocking Tasha's pain.

"Uh-huh." Tasha betrayed no emotion. She didn't so much as bat an eyelash or flinch. She was obviously used to taking a high-definition close-up.

It had been almost twenty years ago, and Tasha was younger than Maggie. "How old were you?"

"Eighteen at the Oscars. Seventeen during filming."

Maggie managed not to gasp but only barely. "That's pretty young."

Something broke in Tasha's face. Her eyes shot to the ceiling, to the floor. She found her composure again, but her voice was reedy when she spoke. "You know when you're a kid and people say 'You have an old soul' or 'You're so mature' or 'You grew up in this business, you're already a pro,' and it feels like a compliment? None of those are fucking compliments."

The time for patient silence was done. Tasha was asking Maggie to ask, so she did. "What happened when you filmed that movie?"

"I never talk about *Cosa Nostra*, you know. When people ask me, I change the subject. I talk about something else instead, fitness or my hair—as if I care about my freaking hair. You'd think people would've noticed, would've pressed me or asked other people about it, but no one ever does. I guess I shouldn't be surprised. No one ever fucking sees *me*. I'm like a Rorschach test."

No, Tasha was more like Mount Saint Helens, rumbling and smoking and about to level the place when she blew. The force of her rage was palpable. A seismometer could've measured it.

"*I* see you," Maggie insisted. "I see that you haven't done a nude scene since *Cosa Nostra*. I see that you're scared. I see that I could help you." That last bit was hubris: Maggie hoped it was true, but she wasn't certain.

Tasha scoffed, not dismissively, but sadly. "I know *Waverley* won't be like *Cosa Nostra*. I trust Zoya, and I trust Cole. He'd never hurt me or make me uncomfortable. Ever. And even though I don't really know you"—she took a breath—"I'm not afraid this will be like that."

What was *that*, though? Tasha hadn't answered the question.

Maybe Maggie didn't need her to. "I don't want you to talk to me about what happened if you don't want to. Honestly. I think we can work together even without that disclosure. But I think that if you're not talking to someone about it—like a therapist—then you're probably not healing. And it's clear you have an open wound."

Bernard had impressed upon Maggie that her main concern had to be what was good for the production, but it was impossible not to see someone in as much pain as Tasha and not worry about her on a human level.

It's what Cole would have done.

"I've been injured on sets a lot," she said, wryly. "Black eyes, broken toes, cracked ribs, a concussion once. It was easier to treat all of those. To feel as if I *needed* to treat them."

A pause.

Then Tasha rushed into it. "When they brought the script for *Cosa Nostra* to me, they were upfront that it was going to be 'edgy.' I mean, I can't say I didn't know what the part was going to be. And I fucking *wanted* to play her. Here was this woman who had so little power in a world that doesn't respect women, and she was using her body and sex to challenge that shitty system. Something about that seemed . . . radical. But I didn't understand that, sure, she acts out of desperation and survives—but to portray that, I'd have to be pushed to my limits. Experience humiliation. It isn't a revolution when the caged animal bites, you know?" She drew a sharp breath, her first as she'd delivered the monologue.

"No, it isn't." Maggie understood what it was like to be powerless and face down a bully.

When she'd been fired, she'd realized that all too often, it was the worst people in the world who were making the decisions. It wasn't that she'd been ignorant about those people existing. It was that she'd thought we all knew better than to listen to them. It had been shocking to realize they were actually in charge. That when we'd all been distracted, they'd seized the levers of control.

"I don't know why they bothered to have wardrobe for me on that fucking movie." Tasha rolled her eyes. "Most of my costumes were lingerie. I was on screen with, like, half a dozen different men, most who were fine." She paused, and Maggie had trouble not spitting out that an adult man who was appearing in intimate scenes with a literal child was not actually "fine" until Tasha added "But."

"But?" Maggie echoed.

If the first part had come out almost in a rush, now her story was a series of choppy spurts. "The real issue was Vincent, that fucking bastard. He and my mother had a relationship—a complex, messy relationship. It was professional, at the start. Then came the sex. They fucked and used each other for decades. Now, it's whatever these things turn into when you despise each other but you still work together sometimes and sleep together when you're drunk or desperate. Vincent has the most obnoxious I've-seen-you-naked shit-eating grin. It's astonishing no one has knocked his teeth out."

There was a largeness to this world Maggie was only just now coming to understand. The amounts of capital, the number of people, the sheer size of the entertainment industry was more expansive than Maggie had realized—and she'd spent her life working in the theatre. What Tasha was saying, and the fact that it was an open secret in Hollywood that Zoya could speculate about even while still working with him . . . it made her dizzy.

This was dangerous. For Tasha to have experienced. For Maggie to know.

Maggie added *fear* to the list of swirling emotions she was feeling.

"Did he hurt you?" Maggie's question was painfully bald but still euphemistic. *Hurt* covered all kinds of crimes.

"Not like you're thinking. He was on set constantly. All the fucking time. He loves to give back rubs to his stressed-out stars, and it turns out I must have been very stressed."

"How . . . thoughtful." How disgusting.

"Remember, I went into this movie calling him 'Uncle Vince.' Of all the goddamn names, it was *uncle*."

"And now he's watching you act naked and giving you back rubs."

"Yup. And bringing along the other producers, too, the douche. It was . . . I wanted that part, I really did. But I didn't know how it would feel."

Maggie had a lot of suggestions, but she didn't want to name Tasha's emotions for her. What the actress needed right now was unconditional support.

"You were a child, Tasha. This isn't your fault. There was an entire industry that should've responded to this and stopped it." Stopped him.

"My mom, my own fucking mom, was on set when some of it went down, Maggie. And she and I and my agent signed whatever they put in front of me without blinking. The press . . . they've picked up the tension between my lovely mother and me, but they've never connected it to *Cosa Nostra*."

Of course Tasha was livid about it.

"She should've protected you."

"Maybe. She could have fucking warned me at the very least. I feel like everyone assumed I knew the score because she's my mom, but I honestly had less information than anyone else about what he was, what this industry is. My mom told me jack shit."

Maggie wanted to scream on Tasha's behalf. She wanted to burn down the fucking room and kick Vincent Minna's ass. But Tasha was watching her, waiting for that exact response. It would've been expected, and in some ways, not enough.

What Tasha, and probably so many other women, had experienced was soul destroying. What did justice even mean? What would Maggie's rage *do*, beyond making Maggie feel better?

What Maggie could actually provide to Tasha was validation. During those moments when Maggie had been at her lowest, the way Savannah had simply told her over and over again that she hadn't done anything wrong and put the blame where it belonged, that had been the only thing that had helped.

"Tasha, if this was a Reddit AITA post, the answer would be that everyone in this story except you sucks. They all suck so much." Comic understatement wasn't enough, but in this moment, it was what Maggie could give.

There was an extended pause. Then Tasha laughed, hard and long. A laugh that was a sob.

"You did not deserve that," Maggie went on. "Even if you read that script and wanted to play that character, you did not deserve to be treated like shit on the set. Vincent Minna should not have harassed and pressured you in any way. He had absolutely no business touching you. None. Your mother, your agent, and every professional on that set failed you. I'm joking to defuse the situation, but if you want to put together a team of mercenaries to exact justice . . . I mean, I don't think I'm very scrappy, but I'm aces at travel research. I can probably get us a group rate."

Tasha covered her face. After several deep breaths, she put her hands on her hips. She'd composed herself again into ruthless beauty. "I have never talked about this with anyone. Not my old agent, not my new agent, not Merrit, not Cole, not anyone. It's been the cone of fucking silence."

"Again, I am so sorry that this happened to you. And I will never repeat any part of this conversation." Maggie wasn't able to project emotions into a space the way Tasha could, but she meant it. Tasha had shown tremendous trust in telling Maggie all this. The least Maggie could do in return was to keep her mouth shut.

"Thank you."

That felt like the end of one chapter in their relationship and the beginning of another one. As a director, Maggie knew that necessitated a scene change.

She crossed to one of the chairs and dragged it toward another one. She sat down and pulled a notebook out of her purse. "With that context, if you're ready to talk about it, I'd really like to think about what you need for *Waverley*—what the production can do to support you and protect you while you're acting."

Tasha sat down across from Maggie. The morning sunlight streaked over her cheekbones and down the column of her throat lovingly, as if she were in a Dutch master's painting. "Well, I don't want Vincent Minna to be on set."

"I don't think that will be a problem. But he is . . . I mean, he owns Silverlight, and they're producing *Waverley*."

"I know." Tasha muttered a string of curses under her breath. "But he's mostly retired."

"Feel free not to answer this, but why did you take this part? With them as the production company and all the sex and nudity in the script, those both seem like they'd be dealbreakers."

"I took it for Cole," she said simply. "But also, Effie Deans is a badass—and not in the way 'strong' female characters usually are. She doesn't set off explosives or roundhouse kick anyone. But she knows what's true, and she says it, even when it costs her. She refuses to escape from prison because that would admit guilt, and she knows she's not guilty. She's selfish and immature, like Geordie, at the start, but she becomes a better person. I know Zoya reworked the book, made Effie the focus rather than Jeanie and gave Effie a happy ending, and I just felt as if she deserved that. I realized I'd be pissed if anyone else got to play her."

"That makes sense."

Tasha probably identified with her character in much the same way Cole did with his.

Tasha smiled a deadly sort of smile. "For a long time, I did action movies because, while I had to wear tight clothes, I didn't have to get naked. They're all PG-13, so there'd be some kissing, maybe, but nothing else. And they let me be . . . powerful, albeit in a pretty limited way. But I've killed, like, hundreds of shitty men on screen."

"Did you picture them all as Vincent Minna?"

"Half. The rest are Supreme Court justices—you can guess which ones."

"Super fair."

Now that Tasha had let her guard down, it was easy for Maggie to see why Tasha and Cole were such close friends. The real Tasha was charmingly profane.

"I don't want to be afraid anymore. Effie Deans, *Waverley*: they're going to be the way I finally get past this. And again, I really do trust Cole. And Zoya. And I think you too. I needed some time to warm up to the idea of an intimacy coordinator. And maybe to figure out that strength isn't just holding things in."

"Noted. And I want to earn that trust. So no Vincent. What else do you need?"

"Rhiannon said you wrote out all the blocking, touch by touch."

"Yup. I know it'll be tricky, but if you and Cole and I could find some time in the next few days, we could choreograph your stuff. There are, um, several scenes." Zoya had literally described episode four as including a bonk-fest montage.

"Effie and Geordie are really hot for each other."

"They are," Maggie said diplomatically.

Tasha nodded. "It would help me to have predictability, a closed set, and veto power over the wardrobe. I guess what I'm saying is I need to know if I speak up, someone will hear me."

That was all anyone needed, and it was amazing how rare it was to get.

Maggie leaned back in her chair. "I wouldn't have taken this job if Zoya hadn't convinced me that the people at the top of the production care. I was worried they were bringing me on to paper over something messy or unsalvageable. I haven't been here very long, but I don't think that's the case."

It hadn't been during the preproduction or rehearsal, at any rate.

"And look, I should also say, while I will do everything in my power to make filming go well for you, I can't . . . I'm not a therapist."

Tasha snorted. "I can barely talk about my piece-of-shit mother and her psychopath ex with you—I'm definitely not going to do it with a total stranger."

"They'd only be a stranger for a few minutes."

"Everyone's a stranger to me, except maybe Cole. He's a marshmallow, that guy, and I love him like a brother. That's why I took this part for him, to help with his career, even if I loathe so many things about it."

Maggie could see the love and concern between them. Now, knowing more about Tasha's history, she was even more stunned by it. "It's one of the most sincere acts of friendship ever."

"I expect my fucking Nobel Peace Prize to arrive any moment."

But because no one knew about what had happened with Vincent, no one except Maggie would ever appreciate how much sacrifice had been involved.

Maggie shoved the thought away. It wasn't her job to mediate Tasha and Cole's friendship, or make sure Tasha got credit for how brave this performance was going to be. It was her job to protect Tasha on set—and today had been an object lesson in why that mattered.

She'd worried that if she didn't go back to high school teaching, she'd never find a job that felt that important again. But Maggie had been very wrong.

This job was every bit as crucial.

"Okay, let's set up meetings with wardrobe and makeup and find a rehearsal space and a window for you, Cole, and I to get to work."

Chapter 11

INT. COFFEE SHOP

Dinna fash was driving Cole up the wall. He'd figured out that it meant *Don't worry* and was interchangeable with *Nae bother*. But did that mean his request was a bother but a small one he shouldn't worry about, or that it was actually no bother?

Scotland was incomprehensible.

The man behind the counter of the coffee shop handed Cole a drink caddy with a few more words of Gaelic—which raised another possibility: Cole was on the receiving end of some well-earned teasing.

"Who's the second coffee for?" a soft, familiar voice came from over Cole's shoulder. He turned to find Maggie Niven smiling at him.

"Hey, I didn't see you come in." Cole tried to arrange the two to-go cups and the white paper bag of scones on the caddy. "My driver."

"Doesn't he normally get coffee for you?"

"Nah, that's not his job. And he's doing me a favor."

"That's kind." She gestured around. "I see Merrit shared the good news about this place with everyone."

She had indeed. "That woman ought to run the United Nations."

"Not enough of a challenge."

"Tropical Storm Tasha is more her speed," he agreed. "But always trust Merrit's recs. I don't know how she does it, but she finds the best places in any city. If you need to buy a case of plastic pink flamingos or eat the best tapas, she'll know where to get 'em."

"Pink flamingos?"

"Don't ask. But speaking of Merrit's boss, I'm glad you and Tash are getting along." They'd all had a conversation the day before that had been so smooth and friction-free, he'd almost asked his best friend for identification. "Did Merrit manage that too?"

The guy behind the counter delivered Maggie's coffee and wished her a good day in totally comprehensible English. So the barista had been messing with Cole. Well, he was an American strolling in to play a Scottish literary hero. They could mock him if they wanted to.

It was good Zoya wasn't making the American actors do accents on the show. Cole would never have heard the end of it.

He and Maggie headed toward the door together.

"I wish I could take credit for the change," she said, "but it worked out because Tasha decided it should. I'm as shocked as you are."

If her words were a little careful, Cole decided to leave the matter alone. They had a blocking rehearsal on the books for Monday, and that would be the sink-or-swim moment for Tasha and Maggie.

"That sounds about par for the course, then." They stepped out into the street. "What are you up to?" The production had the day off. Depending on the weather, this likely wouldn't happen often. The schedule had them filming two pages of the script per day, and they didn't have many free days if they were going to nail that.

"I was planning to play tourist and go see the castle."

Because Cole wanted to keep talking to her, he did something stupid: he looked at Maggie's shoes. They weren't boots, but they laced and had thick soles. His gaze traveled up her body. Maggie was wearing jeans, a sweater, and a raincoat—a solid outfit for what he had in mind.

"Do you have a hat and gloves?" he asked.

"Yup?" Her tone was quizzical.

"Forget the castle. You wanna go climb a hill with me?"

Maggie's face scrambled. "A . . . hill?"

"Yeah, like go hiking. I'm meeting my driver in a second; that's why I grabbed him a coffee. He's putting together a pack for me with water and snacks. He's going to drop me at the trailhead and then pick me up a few hours later. It's supposed to have the best views of the city and the sea."

Maggie blew into her coffee, and for a second, Cole wondered if he'd overstepped. Or maybe she really wanted to see the castle.

But when she looked back at him, those worries disappeared.

Gosh, he liked her eyes.

"That sounds fun, but I'm not really an experienced hiker. Are carabiners involved? Or, um, crampons?"

It was hard not to laugh. "No, it's a beginner hike."

"Good, because I honestly have no idea what crampons are."

"Spikes that go over the soles of your shoes."

Her eyes went wide. "My God, I don't think I will ever be badass enough to do any activity that requires shoe spikes."

"It's good this isn't one of those things, then." He nudged the toe of her sneaker with his. "Come on, Maggie, go hiking with me."

She looked away, a smile playing over her mouth. It was a breezy morning, and the wind was blowing color into her cheeks. Finally, she turned her eyes back to him. "Okay."

Cole felt the word everywhere, but his car showed up then, which kept him from touching her again. He opened the back door for Maggie and leaned into the front to give Phil his coffee and scone.

"You didn't have to do that." Phil was a burly guy who looked as if he warmed up for the day by tossing a few cabers. Cole probably should've gotten him more than one scone.

"Sure I did. This is beyond your normal duties."

"I have to show off the city to best advantage."

"Do I have enough water for two? I talked Maggie into coming along."

"Oh, aye. You'll be grand. Try not to get lost."

"Will do."

"Do you normally do things like this?" Maggie asked Cole.

"Yeah. You have to pass the time somehow."

Cole didn't know if he was more of an introvert or an extrovert, but his career had forced him into a fairly solitary nomadic lifestyle. Every project was like a little family, where you built a place for yourself for the weeks or months it took to film. When one project ended, the family dissolved. Then it was on to the next role, the next little family, and the next and the next and the next.

He'd been running so hard for so long, he'd gotten tunnel vision. Did this life suit him? Did that even matter? But as he buckled his seat belt, he glanced at Maggie, and doubt ran a cold fingertip up his spine.

During the drive, Cole chatted with Phil about the route, about the Edinburgh Festival Fringe—which they were going to miss—and about the weather. In California, the weather was too boring to be much use for conversation. But here, a single day could contain every season. Maggie joked with them both, and she produced an elastic from her pocket and braided her hair. Cole tried not to watch the progress of that too closely.

Finally, Phil pulled in to the parking lot of what was, in winter, a ski lodge.

"Where are we, anyhow?" Maggie asked.

"The Allermuir Hill trail," Cole explained. "It's a loop, or nearly so. Phil's going to pick us up in this village—"

"Swanston," Phil supplied.

"Yup, that's the place. We should be there . . . in three or four hours." Cole had originally planned to do the trail faster, but he added some time to account for Maggie.

"If you're not, I'll send out a search party."

"Last chance to ditch me," Cole said, getting out of the car and putting on the backpack of supplies he'd borrowed from his driver. "Phil can take you back to the hotel."

Please don't go back to the hotel.

But after a beat, Maggie unbuckled her seat belt and climbed out. "I don't know if you've properly prepped me for this scene, James."

"Do you have any hard limits?"

"Shoe spikes. We already went over that one."

They stopped at the trailhead, and he snapped a picture of the map with his phone. Maggie did the same and texted it to someone.

"Savannah, my best friend," she explained. "I'm telling her if I don't text again in four hours to call the police. It's our date protocol."

"Date protocol, huh?" He rubbed the burn that had started in his belly.

"Can't be too careful." There was something faux chipper in Maggie's tone, as if she didn't like this subject any more than he did.

"That must be the start of the trail."

"Wait." Maggie followed his finger with her eyes. "It . . . goes straight uphill."

"The initial climb is supposed to be the worst part, at least if it's not muddy. And according to Phil, it shouldn't be muddy."

She was still gawking. "Shouldn't there be steps? Or a ladder? A funicular, maybe?"

"It's not that much of an incline." It wasn't flat, either, though. Maybe this wasn't really a novice hike.

Maggie still wasn't moving. After a second, she said, "How am I going to do that?"

From a woman who'd remade her life after getting sucked into a bad publicity tornado, it was a puzzling attitude. "One foot in front of the other. You go first."

With a humph, Maggie started up the trail. For all that she was skeptical, she set a punishing pace. He almost warned her to slow down, conserve some energy, but he was so glad she hadn't turned back that he let her go.

When they reached the end of the first stretch of climbing, Maggie stopped and set her hands on her knees, breathing hard. "I'd like to file a—a complaint with . . . the hiking board."

"There's no such thing." Cole swung the pack around under his arm and began digging inside. He located two bottles of water, and he offered one to her.

She took it from him and tipped her head back, drinking deeply. He tried, and failed, not to notice some water that escaped her mouth and trickled down the length of her neck.

"There isn't, like, the North Face Council?" she asked when she came up for air. "A Patagonia Principate? A Columbia Congress?"

"No, no, and no."

"Then who the hell gets to decide if something is a hill or a mountain? Because, my dude, this"—she gestured with her hands at the geologic feature they were climbing—"is definitely a mountain."

"It's a hill. You saw the map."

"It lied to us!"

He had to laugh.

"Don't mock me, I'm perfectly serious. My complaint, where should it go?"

"I'll pass it along. And I'll buy you dinner to make it up to you." He wasn't sure why he offered—but that was a bigger lie than the hill-mountain distinction. The truth was that Cole wanted to eat with Maggie. He wanted to tug on the end of her braid while she yelled at him about the hiking board. He wanted to cover her smart mouth with his.

Luckily, she saved them both when she said "Dinner is not enough, James." She shook a finger at him. "Not nearly enough."

"Do me a favor and turn around."

"Why would I—oh my God."

The slope fell away from their feet, all green fields and scrubby heather, before the city materialized. From this distance, Edinburgh was a neat patchwork of gray city blocks and red brick. And beyond that was the blue smear where the river poured into the sea.

The climb had been killer, sure. But that was some view.

"That's the Firth of Forth, right?" she whispered.

"Sure."

"Odd name, but it's really pretty."

"It is."

But he wasn't looking at the scenery. He was watching Maggie, the hanks of her hair that had escaped from her braid whipping around her face in the wind, her cheeks flushed pink, and her eyes bright green.

She'd been legitimately annoyed with him, or with the situation, a minute ago, but now, that had blown away, like a sprig of heather in the window. All that was left on her face was awe—she was actually awestruck.

With a cackle, she spread her hands wide. "Okay. Okay. That's really . . . wow. This has almost been worth it."

"It has been."

Maggie caught his attention on her. Suddenly it wasn't too cold. The wind wasn't too hard. His thighs weren't burning too badly.

Cole turned squarely toward her, took a step forward.

But she wasn't feeling the same tug, clearly, because Maggie only shoved her water bottle at him before taking off again up the trail.

He stowed their stuff, gave himself a brief lecture about not getting swept away because of some pretty vista, and followed her.

"I withdraw my complaint," she said when he'd caught up. "I mean, I still think this is a mountain and I was misled, but the view is nice even if no one told me the trail would be vertical."

"Maggie, there are sheep hanging out all around us. Sheep don't do vertical."

"Sheep are very nimble. They're basically puffy goats."

"I bet there wouldn't have been sheep at the castle."

"Probably not. But even still, this is no Glasgow Botanic Gardens."

"Are they supposed to be amazing?" For all that he'd filmed around the world, he hadn't seen much outside his trailer. The odd hike here and there was all the sightseeing he managed.

"I didn't make it to Kew Gardens when we were in London. I was too busy. But these are that same Victorian glasshouse style, and I'm obsessed."

When they passed the remains of an old fort, they snapped a few pictures. Then they were into another climbing section, and they were both too breathless to talk. Cole and Maggie stopped for water a second time when they reached a big pile of stones and a historical interpretive plaque.

"This is on the map," Cole said, checking his phone. "We've done almost all of the climbing now." Which was good because they'd been walking for an hour and a half. It was good that he'd told Phil they were going to be four hours.

Maggie pointed to the hilltop at the end of the ridge. "Um, that looks higher."

"It's only about twenty meters higher than we are now, and it's all downhill after that."

"Meters? I'm an American," she whined.

"Trust me, it sounds better in metric." He didn't have the heart to do the conversion for her.

"In that village, at the end, you are buying me beer and french fries."

He would've rather stuck with his original offer of dinner, but as long as she was letting him feed her, he'd take it. "Deal."

The next bit of the walk wasn't as hard, but the wind whipping over the crest of the ridge was wicked, and several times he had to grab Maggie's jacket to steady her. They encountered more and more sheep, who watched them placidly, until at last they arrived at the summit. They were greeted by a small column made of stacked stones, topped by another plaque.

The Scottish people clearly liked their plaques.

"How is it possible we're only 1,617 feet above sea level?" Maggie almost shouted into the wind.

"Wait, first you insist this is a mountain, then you're pissed it's *not* taller?"

"I'm tired, James. I'm allowed to contradict myself." She fished her phone out of her pocket. "Take my damn picture."

He did. Then, "Let's get one together. We can send it to Tasha."

"Sure."

Trying not to think too much about it, trying not to sense the curves under her jacket and sweater, Cole pulled Maggie into the crook of his body. She came up to his shoulder, which made him feel bulky and awkward. But when he cinched an arm around her waist, when the warmth of her pressed against his chest, when he saw them on her phone screen, looking for all purposes so *together*, Cole melted.

Right there, on the top of that frigid Scottish hill, he went to goo.

Cole let his chin rest against Maggie's temple. He could smell her hair, the clean soap of her shampoo mixed with the fresh air, and it was—peace. They might only be 1,617 feet higher than when they'd started. They might only be friends. Their hearts might be racing for very different reasons. But for a moment, Cole felt at peace.

He snapped a picture. Then another. Then a third, not because their eyes were closed, but because when this was done, she was going to step out of his arms.

"That's good," she said.

He let go of her and handed Maggie her phone. Then he turned and wiped his eyes, feeling just so silly. It was ridiculous for him to go soft over anyone right now. He needed to stay focused. And besides, Maggie was doing her job—a job she cared about as much as he did his.

"Be sure to send that to me." Goddamn, but his voice sounded scratchy.

"Will do. It's all downhill from here?"

"Yup. It should be a piece of cake."

That was usually a lead-in to disaster, but compared to the first half of the hike, they practically galloped into Swanston. Their quick pace kept them from talking too much—and Cole from stumbling into some other kind of mess. Clearly he couldn't be trusted where this woman was concerned.

"Jeez, this is cute." Maggie waved her hand at the whitewashed cottages and thatched roofs.

"I'm surprised we're not filming here." Cole was pretty sure pictures of this exact village had been in the packet Zoya had sent him when he'd signed the contract. Or maybe all adorable Scottish villages that seemed untouched by time looked the same.

"I can't tell if it's more Walter Scott or *Brigadoon*."

"I'm just glad there aren't bagpipes." Brett, his publicist, had forbidden Cole from ever admitting it in public, but he couldn't stand the things.

They found Phil waiting for them in the car, playing a game on his phone.

"We were a little slower than I'd expected," Cole said. "Sorry about that. Is there someplace to get a drink around here?"

"There's no pub in Swanston," Phil explained. "But I know something nearby."

Ten minutes later, Maggie was cooing her way through a plate of french fries. The noises she was making were next door to obscene.

"Don't even think about rushing me," she told Cole and Phil, gesturing with one of her fries. "I may get two more orders of these."

"Was it that bad?" Phil asked.

Maggie shot her eyes at Cole. Back in civilization and with an audience, she'd reassembled her self-control. There was no more undisguised awe—and there was definitely no excuse for Cole to hold her.

Civilization kind of sucked.

"No," she admitted. "And the view from the top was pretty special. But I might not be in scaling-a-mountain shape."

"Whether it was a hill or not is a matter of debate." That was the only controversy he could see. Maggie's shape was perfect.

"I'm going to write REI and ask them to weigh in. I may include a small bribe to make sure they rule the right way."

Phil's quizzical expression had Cole and Maggie dissolving into laughter.

But even after they'd tried explaining the story and Maggie had polished off her fries with what seemed like an entire bottle of ketchup, the warmth of the shared joke had Cole breathless the entire drive back to the hotel.

Chapter 12

INT. REHEARSAL SPACE

"So when do you think Geordie started having sex?"

Cole, perched on the edge of a mound of vinyl tumbling blocks, sputtered in response to Maggie's question. "I . . . have no idea."

She hadn't seen him since their hike. She'd texted the picture he'd taken of them to him, and he'd replied, Thank you for coming. I had a good time.

In between the prep work she'd done for this blocking rehearsal, she'd given too much thought to every single one of those words. Was the euphemism intentional? Was *good* too muted? If he'd really meant it, would he have said it had been a wonderful time? An extraordinary time? In the picture, he looked elated, but he posed for pictures for a living. Projecting emotions was what he did.

Even so, it was possible Maggie had made the pic her lock screen and then had switched it back to one of Savannah and several of their fellow teachers at a boozy book club.

And then had gone back to Cole.

Then back to Savannah and the book club.

Making the safe choice didn't help when she was still imagining the moment when every cell in her brain had been shouting that he was going to kiss her. Absurd. Totally absurd. But they'd been on the top of a mountain, for crying out loud, and the view had been breathtaking, and the wind had been pushing them together, and—

Maggie had to delete that memory somehow. To get in there with a Brillo pad and brain bleach and scrub those moments away. Because this icy-winter-molten-lava shimmer Cole set off in her gut was unprofessional and pointless and . . . confusing.

She was going to get it together. Starting now.

Tasha cleared her throat. As per usual, she was not amused, but now, her ire was directed at Cole, not Maggie. That was new.

"But don't you think that matters?" the actress snapped. "Take Effie. She's definitely a virgin. I think she's kissed other men. Maybe fooled around. She's never had an orgasm with a partner before, though. This is all new to her. This scene has to feel like a fucking revelation. I mean that literally: fucking is a revelation for her." None of those ideas were in the script; that was entirely Tasha's backstory for her character. Since Tasha had decided to get on board with the intimacy coordination, she was all the way on board.

"Okay, okay. Sorry for laughing." Cole considered this. "Geordie's definitely not a virgin. He has some sexual history, and not just with Madge. Sleeping with a woman like that—someone who isn't in his social class, someone he doesn't really care about, and also not taking any precautions for birth control—that's careless. It's selfish. I think he's done it before. Right?" He looked up, wanting confirmation.

For several months now, Maggie had watched him hedge and downplay his insights into the character. He had an obvious inferiority complex. His youthful missteps had scarred him, and he dealt with it by not always taking himself seriously. It was defensive, and it hurt her to see him do it.

Cole was intuitive about his work, collaborative, and always, always kind. Those were rare qualities. She wished he could believe in himself as much as she'd come to.

"Yeah, I can definitely see that," she said. "So what's different with Effie? Why does he approach this affair differently?"

It helped the work when the actors could empathize with their characters and be vulnerable with each other. This was much easier with Cole and Tasha since they were already so close.

"She's his match in every way," Cole said. "He's going to be a lot more careful with her, and more open with her, than with the other women he's been with."

He was watching Maggie closely, so closely that she almost wasn't certain what they were talking about.

An invitation to be reckless, that look.

Oblivious to Maggie's racing heart, Tasha said, "Which brings us back to Maggie's question. What's his number?"

That broke the spell, and Cole snorted. "A dozen, give or take. Before he left home, when he was still the young rich guy on the prowl, I'd guess he hit a brothel. Maybe had a mistress. Then he rejects that world to become a smuggler, and it's different women. He's still not, like, emotionally available with them. Sex has been just a release for him for a long time."

"But that changes with Effie?"

"Yeah."

"But *why?*" Maggie asked. "And don't say it's because she's not like other girls."

"Yeah," Cole agreed. "That's a good point. She could've been another Madge to him, if they'd met earlier. Why is he ready now?"

A few seconds ticked by while they all considered this.

"I wonder if the failure of the Jacobite rebellion matters," Maggie asked. "Like, things aren't going well resisting the British. The writing's on the wall, even if the Battle of Culloden hasn't happened yet. So Geordie's thinking about what he wants from his life. Is he going to stay with the common people, or is he going to return to his estate? And that's when he meets Effie."

"Yeah, so he's *prepped.*" Cole picked up Maggie's thread. "He's grown up a little, but he's also had something not work out. This has worn down his pride, made him emotionally vulnerable in a way he wasn't before. But then Effie blows his heart up, and he wasn't prepared for that."

Maggie's pulse was up, and she felt fizzy all over. This collaboration—it was everything she loved about theatre. "Exactly. So when they end up in this hayloft together, do you think they both arrive here planning to consummate this relationship?"

"For him, yes," Cole said. "But I don't think he realizes how intense it's going to be, or how the sex will crack his heart open."

Tasha nodded. "Yeah, I know we've talked about her, how this is her first time and how into him she is, but I think we have to get the mirror of that for him. He likes this woman, he wants to sleep with her, but then it's more. That has to stun him."

"I love that," Maggie said. "How do we communicate it?" Because at the end of the day, that was the goal: How could they use this love scene to do the character work?

The script simply read, GEORDIE AND EFFIE MAKE PASSIONATE, EMOTIONAL LOVE IN THE HAY LOFT.

Um, thanks, writers!

"Well, they both have to be naked," Cole said. "It needs to be very different than with Madge. A lot more foreplay, a lot of eye contact, a lot of checking in. And I think he needs to perform oral sex on her, the opposite of with Madge."

Zoya had mentioned that, edited, she wanted this scene to clock in at least two minutes. Since the show's previous love scenes had averaged about twenty seconds of thrusting postpenetration—Maggie had checked; she'd made a spreadsheet and everything, an actual fucking spreadsheet—unless they were going to play strip poker, simulated oral would definitely be involved, along with a lot more foreplay than was normal for the show.

This was like the Mount Everest of on-screen sex scenes.

"Yeah, the consent piece is really important," Tasha agreed. "We don't have to add lines"—that would mean calling in one of the show's writers—"but we need all of those little beats of waiting for a reaction.

You know when you're with someone for the first time, and you aren't sure what they like. You don't know what they want and don't want."

"Um, yeah. Totally."

When Maggie had been fired and the mess of the last year had begun, the man she'd been dating—a real estate agent—had broken up with her. He hadn't wanted to deal with the bad press, meaning that he was afraid he'd lose business if he was involved with the most notorious woman in town. Those hadn't been his precise words, but the implication had been clear. He'd enjoyed dating Maggie, sleeping with her, but he hadn't really cared about her. He certainly didn't want to risk anything for their relationship.

After the jolt of disbelief had passed (*"I got fired at eight a.m., and you're dumping me at five p.m.?"*), Maggie understood. She enjoyed having dinner with him a few times a week. It had been a relief to have an assumed date for events and holidays. The sex had been fine, but she hadn't thought they were in it together for the long haul either.

Hell, he'd probably done them a favor. If she hadn't been fired, they might have gotten married out of inertia, which would've been tragic. She could barely remember what his laugh sounded like or how he'd made her feel, other than vaguely content. You shouldn't marry someone whose best quality was having a pulse.

Since the breakup, she hadn't had the time to date. What did you put on your Bumble profile—*My interests include fighting theatre censorship in high-profile lawsuits*? No, her drought was pretty much exactly what vibrators were for.

Suddenly, Maggie wanted a first time with someone. The intensity of someone else's hands being where only yours had been for so long. The smell of someone's skin, the press of their weight, amplifying every emotion. The sheer intimacy of letting someone else see you come. The nakedness beyond nakedness when you took off your clothing with someone for the first time.

She missed sex.

Well, she missed *good* sex.

Maggie shook the thought off. She was working. "Totally," she repeated. "We have to get all of that into the choreography, especially his tenderness with her and then the way this is going to just explode both of their expectations. Let's walk through what we have."

Cole rolled his shoulders and got to his feet. He'd changed into another one of those flowing linen shirts, but he'd also put on a pair of breeches this time. It made him look more than a little bit like a pirate.

Tasha was wearing her full costume: gown, corset, petticoats, and stockings. Since removing her clothing was such a big part of this scene, the actors needed it for the blocking.

Maggie attached her phone to a tripod and pulled up an app that let her approximate the camera's viewfinder. After David, the DP, had explained that he found the shorthand version of her choreography incomprehensible, he'd shown her how the app could create a more formal, but stick figure–free, version of the storyboards.

"After the dialogue," Maggie said, checking her notes, "we start with Effie in Geordie's lap, and they're kissing. He unbuttons her gown; then we have the sequence with his mouth on her cleavage. He strips her gown off; then he hikes up her petticoats, and he brings her to orgasm with his hand."

"That's the place where I have to show unbridled joy?" Tasha deadpanned.

"Yup, as if it's the first orgasm in the world."

"Lucky me."

"I'm assured the light will be dewy and prelapsarian, which should help." Maggie checked her list. "Then I'd guess he strips her totally and performs oral sex on her. Kneeling or with them both on the hay?"

"Kneeling." Cole was firm about that. "It's not submission, but it's something like that. He's worshipping this woman."

"I like that. Is there anything else we can do to show it?"

"Well," Cole said, "when we get to the penetration, he needs to take care of her. Like . . . use his hand on her clit to make sure she comes."

"Yes!" Maggie exclaimed. "That's so rare in a sex scene." She was already adding it to her notes. "I love it."

The show was clear that the characters' sex was orgasmic, but other than lovingly filming everyone's bodies and showing some oral sex, there'd been shockingly little clitoral stimulation in *Waverley*'s sex scenes—until now. Apparently Cole James was even better at making sure the love scenes were going to be awesome than Maggie was.

She was absolutely not going to think about what that suggested about what kind of lover he would be in real life.

At least she wasn't going to think about that right now.

"But can you even find the clit?" Tasha asked Cole.

"Hey," Cole protested. Then he looked directly at Maggie as he said "I have *never* had a problem locating—"

"Tasha," Maggie interrupted, in part because she didn't want to ponder Cole's ability to locate the pleasure center. "What are you actually saying?"

Tasha sucked on her teeth. "How would that . . . work? He wouldn't actually touch me there, right?"

Aha. Tasha might have gotten on board, but she still had a few hang-ups. "No, definitely not. We can use forced perspective so that if his hand is just above the merkin"—the pubic wig the makeup people would paste over Tasha's mons—"it'll look like he's stimulating your clit."

Tasha absorbed this. "Sorry, I know it'll be fine. You wouldn't ever cross the line—"

"I would *never*," he said.

"But it's still pretty intimate."

Maggie didn't know if Tasha had talked to Cole yet about what had happened to her on the *Cosa Nostra* set, so she was running them through the blocking as if he were in the dark. It wasn't her place to force a confidence Tasha didn't want to share.

"I get that," Maggie said. "I know it's in my title, so I'm supposed to be the expert, but I keep thinking about the word *intimacy*. I thought I knew what it meant—something like closeness and connection—but if it's a thing we feel inside, how do we show that on screen? How do we make the audience believe in something they can't, by definition, see?"

"And the answer is some clit rubbing?" Tasha asked skeptically.

Cole huffed out a laugh, and Tasha, followed by Maggie, dissolved into giggles. There were some moments of this work that were, frankly, absurd.

"It's that he cares about her pleasure," Maggie said, once she'd regained some composure. "And that she—not you, *Effie*—would welcome that kind of touch from him on a part of her body she's never shared with anyone, in a way that's going to make her feel out of control. And there's risk here for her. She could get pregnant, she could *die*, because they have sex. But how she feels makes that risk worth it."

Tasha considered this.

Maggie pushed on. "If we don't put the sex on screen, if we don't take her pleasure seriously, I wonder if Effie's actions even make sense. It would be a hole in her characterization."

"We're compelled to show the banging?" Tasha was only half joking now.

"I don't know about that, but I don't think it's merely titillating. I can see how the choice is justified for the writing *and* the art." And Maggie could also see how the crafting of the scene, the very stuff they were doing in the rehearsal room, was important too. "There's also a level beyond the characters. For you two, and I guess the crew, too, to film this scene right, we need to have a level of comfort with each other. The audience might not see or know about everything that's going on behind the scenes, but we have to be intimate. If you sell them on Effie and Geordie's love, and I know you will, it'll be because of you and Cole's intimacy. Not in a sexual way, but in an emotional one. That's why you were well cast."

"I don't think anyone else sees it that way." Cole gave Maggie a wry smile.

"But they will when they watch the show." Maggie turned back to Tasha. "Look, I don't mean to put pressure on you. I like Cole's suggestion, but if you aren't comfortable with that blocking, we don't have to do it."

Tasha shook her head. "No, I trust that we can do it in a way I'm cool with, and I get your point that seeing Geordie as an attentive lover adds to *why* Effie would take the risks she does."

"I'll keep checking in with you about it when we rehearse. Also, I chatted with her this morning, and Zoya would like to film the thrusting portion in one long shot—no cuts. It makes the blocking a little trickier, but she thinks it'll feel more real if it's not a montage."

"Yup, I can see that," Tasha agreed.

When Maggie had started to break down the show's love scenes, it had amazed her how short most of them were and how many different cuts were involved. They were marvels of editing as much as anything else. But this particular scene was the emotional core of the season. If the audience didn't believe that these characters were soulmates, the rest of it wouldn't work.

"And Cole, Zoya feels pretty strongly about seeing your butt in this one." Geordie had kept his pants on for the scene with Madge, so this was different. "She'd like to see you naked from the back, both for this scene, and for the, um—"

"Sex fest?" he asked.

"Yup." After this scene, the characters' first time, there would be a montage of subsequent encounters. Geordie and Effie were clearly not holding back.

"I've been doing lots of lunges and squats," Cole said confidently. "My gluteus maximus is pleased to be of service."

Given how easily Cole had scaled the mountain, Maggie wasn't surprised. He was certainly in shape. Lana Larkin would be ecstatic.

Maggie wanted to press her water bottle to her burning cheeks, but she refrained. She could only hope they'd blame her flushed face on the stuffiness of the room and not her ridiculous crush on Cole. "Excellent.

The real question before we start blocking is for you, Tasha." She held up a strapless thong. "Are you cool with this?"

"Yup."

"They'll paste the merkin over it on the day of filming. And Zoya's fine with side boob and side butt only for you, but how do you feel about frontal nudity above the waist?"

Tasha gave a long sigh. "Let's try the blocking and see if we can make it work without."

"Absolutely."

They walked through the blocking for the kissing, then moved on to the portion where Geordie was fingering Effie.

Maggie was watching through her camera, trying to see it like the DP would. "The key is timing his forearm thrusts with your gasps, Tasha. It's really acting with your cleavage as much as anything else."

"I don't have enough bust for this."

"Your bust looks great," Maggie assured her.

When they'd perfected the choreography so that it looked real, they decided Effie should keep her corset on for the oral sex for modesty—"Not that there's much that's modest about this!"—and then would lose the rest of her costume only for the penetration-and-thrusting portion of the scene. Cole and Tasha didn't strip all the way for the rehearsal, but at least they'd planned every beat, just like you would with dance choreography. Really, really sexy dance choreography.

Then they ran it several times.

Cole and Tasha had a rapport—frankly, a *chemistry*—that made it mesmerizing. If some part of Maggie's heart throbbed, dull and jealous, watching it, then that was exactly why it was a bad idea to get a crush on a coworker.

Silly heart.

After another run-through, Maggie said, "That's not enough practice for you to memorize the blocking, obviously, but we'll schedule a few more rehearsals before filming. The only real decision left to make is stockings on or off."

"One on and one off?" Tasha mused. "Maybe we need to see cute options for the ribbon garters."

"I like the idea that she knows he's going to see them. It shows her planning this encounter, wanting it."

"Yes! They should be different garters than what she wears earlier in the flashbacks."

"I'm making a note to email Alexa."

"Thanks, Maggie." There was a long pause, and then, more heavily, Tasha said, "Thank you." It was clear she was trying to communicate several things with that, and Maggie appreciated every one.

"You're welcome" was all she said. Tasha obviously didn't want to have an in-depth conversation about each and every one of her feelings. At the end of the day, Maggie could only be pleased that they'd finally gotten to a productive place.

When Tasha left to change and return her costume to the assistant waiting outside the rehearsal room, Cole shrugged back into his regular shirt—which was a bit of a shame. Those were a lot of lovely muscles.

Maggie felt a little guilty about even noticing that. When this was over, it would be nice to go back to ogling him without feeling an uncomfortable twinge.

"That was great," he said enthusiastically. "This is going to be awesome."

"Yup, it'll be instantly iconic. It's going to launch a zillion GIFs."

At minimum, Maggie was certain that she'd be watching it on repeat.

"Your notes today," she told him, "they were really good. You get this guy, and you have great instincts."

He scratched his cheek. "I don't always feel great about weighing in."

"You're doing amazing work on *Waverley*, Cole. I get the sense you don't always feel confident about it, but you should. I'm here anytime you need to be reminded of that."

"Anytime?"

For a second, the question hung between them, crimson and glowing as a brand fresh from the fire.

I wish I could be. That was how she wanted to answer.

But as always, Cole saved her. He let the heat drop from his eyes; then he kicked his feet into his shoes and scooped up his bag before leaving Maggie alone.

Which was exactly how she didn't want to be. Not anymore.

Chapter 13

INT. COLE'S TRAILER

There was an ancient Hollywood joke about how you did the acting for free; the paycheck was for the waiting around. As Rhiannon would probably say, *Where's the lie?* Two hours into twiddling his thumbs in his trailer, Cole was grateful for the distraction when his phone rang.

"Drew, you're up early." As far as Cole could tell, his agent never slept. He seemed to rise with the sun, spend the entire day in the office, and make appearances at parties late into the wee small hours—every night.

The man might actually be a vampire.

"Gotta hustle for my favorite client."

The next time he was at a Hollywood party, Cole was going to ask around and figure out by what order of magnitude that was a lie. Cole knew it wasn't true, and Drew knew Cole knew. The compliment was that Cole was important enough to be on the receiving end of the ass-kissing.

"What's up?"

"I strong-armed Brett into letting me make this call. But honestly, this is thanks to me."

Parsing these things was impossible. Drew could be telling the truth, or he could be taking credit from Cole's PR guy. Drew did that sometimes. But then again, he was the person Cole was supposed to be able to trust the most. It wasn't that big a deal if Drew assumed the wins and the losses for the entire team.

"Look, right after you finish *Waverley*, you're going to shoot"— Drew paused for dramatic effect—"the cover spread for *GQ*."

"No way." That was legitimately a big deal. Cole had done *Men's Health* several times, but there seemed to be some barrier keeping him from the higher-profile stuff. A *GQ* cover was several rungs up the ladder.

"Yup. It's happening because Videon is thrilled—I mean *thrilled*—with the footage. They're talking a big Emmy campaign, For Your Consideration ads everywhere, the works. This cover would just be the spear tip of what they want to do. And here's the best part: Jake Cloobeck can do it, but it has to be two days after the wrap party."

Damn it. Cloobeck was one of Cole's favorite photographers, but they'd never been able to work together. Cole tended to get stuck with folks who were a little less established and who had less of a vision. That was the reality of life on the almost-B-list.

"What if the shoot runs over?" Zoya was keeping things on track, but Scottish weather was unpredictable.

Frankly, prior to this conversation, Cole had been rooting for rain. He was having such a good time working with Tasha and Maggie and Ryan that he didn't want it to end. Besides, they were only halfway through *Waverley*'s shoot, and already the commitments for afterward were starting to pile up. There was something appealing about staying in this moment for as long as possible.

He didn't want to think about how much of that had to do with a certain intimacy coordinator.

"If we can't schedule it then, you'll get stuck with some Terry Richardson knockoff who'll go for fake wood paneling and washed-out polyester or who'll want you to jump in a pool in a suit."

That was annoyingly true. The two main looks for guy-fashion editorials were low-budget '70s porn and wet dress clothes. He'd much rather have Cloobeck.

"Why aren't you happy?" Drew asked. "I thought you'd be psyched."

What Drew was really saying was *Why aren't you fawning all over me to thank me for all my effort?* Cole usually never missed a chance to fluff Drew's ego.

In all the years they'd worked together, Cole and Drew had argued a few times. Drew thought Cole was sometimes too nice, which he'd blamed on overcompensating for when Cole had messed up as a kid. He also thought Cole sometimes went for the lower-profile project for the wrong reasons—such as liking a director. *Whatever your instinct is, run in the other direction,* he'd teased Cole.

Except it hadn't felt like teasing.

For so long, Cole had needed Drew, and he hadn't wanted to risk losing him. If this worked, if *Waverley* hit, the gravity might shift.

Maybe it already was.

Not wanting to be ungrateful, Cole told him, "I know you've worked hard to get this for me. The *GQ* cover? That's huge. It's what we've wanted for so long."

"But?" Drew was no dummy. He'd picked up on Cole's mood.

"I feel . . . I feel more myself than I have in forever." Because this wasn't actually about Drew or whether Cole was appreciative enough for him. It was about Cole.

It was odd to find yourself while pretending to be someone else, but that was the job. In this part, on this shoot, Cole felt like he was becoming the person he wanted to be. It was the way Zoya and Maggie were treating him. The way the younger actors on set looked to him for guidance and advice. Everything about *Waverley* had combined to make him feel like a grown-up, not like a frat boy.

"That's probably why the work is good," Drew said pragmatically. "But I still need you back here right after you wrap."

Cole felt an argument rising in him, but he smothered it. They were way too far into this thing for Cole to start having second thoughts.

Acting demanded everything from you. You didn't get to have days off. You didn't get to linger in Scotland, hiking after the TV show was done. You were into the next project, into the promo, into whatever it took to get the next job. If you were lucky, it was an endless treadmill. The only other option was irrelevance.

He had to keep toeing Drew's line. He owed him this.

Which was why Cole didn't even sigh when he said "Will do."

"Also, Vincent Minna's little protégé, Malik Dennis, is doing a space movie next year, and Vincent got you a reading."

Hmm, that was odd. Tasha had always been far more Vincent's pet than Cole had been, for all that Cole had appeared in several Silverlight projects. Oh well, it was a good opportunity.

"I'll get that on the books for the day after the cover shoot," Drew said. "They're moving on this, but they're eager to meet you."

Everyone wanted an IP movie franchise. Cole had auditioned for a hundred of them, but no one had considered him seriously for one before. His part in *Waverley* was going to change everything.

Cole and Drew had already agreed that his next project should be a movie—he didn't want to get stuck on television—and it needed to be either awards bait or something very splashy and big budget.

Or Drew had made the case for that, loudly and repeatedly, until Cole had finally relented.

"Send me the sides as soon as you get them."

"Will do."

"And look, I didn't mean to sound ungrateful. I'll be back in California as soon as we're done. I know how hard you've worked."

"How hard we've *both* worked."

And that was the truth. If Cole wasn't changing people's perception of him, then Drew's efforts would go nowhere. They'd both made a bet when they'd gone into business together. It was time for it to pay off.

"The world's your oyster, Cole. If you don't want the space flick"—he hadn't even been offered it yet—"there's also a boxing one, *Palooka*. It's more training, but you're in shape already. I trust you've been keeping up with the regimen we agreed to, eating well and all?"

About that, there could be no negotiation. "I am."

"Good. *Palooka* is more serious. More awards-y."

Cole didn't want to take projects just because he might get nominated for something. He wanted to keep growing in the ways that this project and the team behind it, specifically Zoya and Maggie, were helping him to. "Is there anything literary on the horizon?"

"Ha, let's not get ahead of ourselves. It's not like *Waverley* is Shakespeare."

Because he didn't think Cole could do Shakespeare.

Cole tried not to take it personally as he said "I'll take a look at the boxing one too. Gotta run."

The only thing he had to do was wait some more. But at least that didn't come with the smack of low expectations. Drew meant well, but sometimes their conversations made Cole feel as if he were still a twenty-four-year-old dudebro instead of a forty-year-old not-quite dudebro who had learned at least a few things from his mistakes.

Partially to figure out what was causing the delay and partially because he knew it would annoy Drew, Cole went in search of the craft-services table. It wasn't petulant snacking if it was potato chips. But at the food table, Cole found something better than carbs to calm him down.

Maggie was perched on a stool, stirring a bowl of oatmeal and chatting with one of the catering assistants, a guy in his twenties with a sleeve of colorful tattoos down both arms.

"Cole!" Maggie said excitedly, and his heart skipped a beat. "Come, settle a bet."

Oh. That was disappointing. He wanted to be exciting all by himself.

"Are corn dogs and beef Wellington in the same food group?" She tossed this off lightly, without any indication of how she wanted him to rule. While she put the proposition to him, she added a generous pat of butter, a handful of Craisins, and a squeeze of honey to her oatmeal.

Cole gestured to her bowl. "Aren't you just making deconstructed granola there?"

"Perhaps. Oatmeal is mostly a blank canvas for what you add to it anyhow. But don't get distracted, James. Lives are at stake."

Feeling far, far less antsy than when he'd left his trailer, Cole reached for a handful of baby carrots. "Lives, huh? Well, corn dogs and beef Wellington are both protein wrapped in carbs, but corn dogs don't have the mushroom layer."

"Ha!" Maggie raised a fist in triumph. "That's what I said."

Cole was irrationally happy that, by sheer luck, he'd picked Maggie's side.

"Okay, but what about this?" The caterer leaned a hand on the table, which conveniently brought him into Maggie's personal space. He was watching her with what might be called erotic interest, but thankfully, Maggie seemed immune. "Have you ever had Korean corn dogs? Some have dog, a layer of cheese, and then the rice-flour coating." He ticked these attributions off on the fingers of his free hand. "What about those?"

Maggie took a big bite of her "oatmeal" and chewed thoughtfully. "I think we'll have to allow it." She shot Cole a look as if she knew that they agreed on this exception to the rule. "But only multilayer Korean corn dogs are related to beef Wellington. Not the regular kind of dog you find at American state fairs."

"You are as wise as you are beautiful, Maggie, my love." Then the caterer tweaked the end of her ponytail before winking at Cole. "I better go get that case of water bottles."

As the guy left, Cole chewed his carrots a bit louder than was necessary, just to prove some kind of idiotic point.

"How are you?" Maggie asked when they were alone. "I heard that the new bulbs arrived and they're hoping we'll be underway soon."

"Oh, good." Cole had been worried about that before Maggie had distracted him with her important food questions and the less important matter of the crew flirting with her.

He searched his gut. He wasn't feeling impatient anymore, that was for sure.

"How are *you*?" he asked.

"Fine. No, better than fine." Her smile felt more real for the fact that it was soft, quiet. "I didn't expect the crew to be so . . . varied. They all have such great stories. I don't know who I thought ended up on movie sets, but it feels like a pirate ship's crew."

It was such a perfect description, it took a second for him to know how to respond. "That's my favorite part," he said finally. "A lot of people end up making movies because they couldn't do anything else. Everything else just feels . . . boring. Colorless."

"That true for you?" She was staring into her oatmeal, but Cole had the sense that she was deeply interested in his answer.

"I'd like to think I could find something else that would make me happy, but obviously I'm working pretty hard to stay in the industry."

"Maybe because it's your calling."

Certainly Drew wouldn't say that. Drew would say . . . well, Cole honestly didn't know. For all that he treated Drew's advice like gospel, Cole didn't necessarily understand how or why his agent did what he did. The man's image was so finely polished, Cole had no idea what was underneath it.

Maggie hopped off the stool. "I'm going to check with Kevin, see what the estimated filming time is. But"—she set a hand lightly on his forearm—"are you sure you're okay? You seem a little quiet."

Just that tiny bit of warmth from Maggie's hand soaking through his linen shirt helped melt the last bit of chill that his conversation with Drew had left behind.

Cole wrapped his fingers around her wrist. Her skin was smooth and alive, and her pulse under his fingertips was racing—like his own. "I was getting in my head a bit. But this—this shook me out of my funk. Thank you."

"My pleasure."

Cole didn't want to contemplate how much he wanted that to be true.

Chapter 14

INT. BARN HAYLOFT

"I'd like to do this in a bed at some point," Cole deadpanned to Zoya.

They were standing in the actual hayloft of an actual ancient barn somewhere in the Scottish Highlands about to film the first Geordie-Effie love scene. Outside the weather was gray and misty, but thanks to the magic of Hollywood, it was a lovely spring afternoon inside. The crew had arranged for diffused light to pour in, making everything golden and romantic.

The crew had been small the night they'd filmed the Geordie-Madge love scene, but today, it was even more sparse. Maggie had ensured that.

"I mean, I've heard about the birds and the bees," Cole was saying, "but I don't want to see them while getting it on."

Maggie had to bite the inside of her cheek to keep from laughing.

Zoya was clearly having the same reaction. After the director had smothered her grin, she gestured to the romantic spread Geordie was supposed to have arranged for the seduction. "It's going to be iconic." The quilt over the straw, the flowers, and the basket with food. Alas, someone had had to convince the set decorator that lanterns were a bad idea, what with all the straw.

Cole wasn't convinced. "It's giving me nineties-country-music-video vibes."

"Cottagecore is why the show is a hit. You're going to get tagged in a million barn-inspired-boudoir photo shoots on Instagram."

"I'm certain my assistant will thank you."

Cole caught Maggie's gaze and rolled his eyes, and she knew he was thinking the same thing she was: *That Geordie, what a charmer.*

Knowing she was blushing, Maggie made herself check her clipboard.

"Now pout." A tech was doing a final touch of Tasha's makeup, which was pointless because Cole was about to kiss all that lipstick off.

"Do you have any last-minute questions?" Maggie asked Tasha quietly. "Any concerns?"

"Nope."

Tasha didn't seem nervous. With the crew around, the actress went quiet, deadly focused. Maggie had had trouble imagining how she'd filmed all those action movies, because with Cole, she was chatty, profane, and even silly. But Maggie could see it now. Honestly, she'd believe Tasha was an actual CIA assassin and that acting was her cover.

The tech stepped back from Tasha with a firm nod. "You're all set."

Tasha fluffed the skirt of her soon-to-be-cosplayed-to-death blue gown. Despite the careful details that were meant to make it looked lived in—the faux mended hem and mismatched buttons on the bodice—it was too nice a dress for a Scottish farm girl in the early eighteenth century. The sprigged-muslin petticoat and the full draped skirt over false hips would *not* be practical while milking goats or mucking the barn.

But that wasn't the point. The show was a fantasy, and everything about the scene they were about to film was drool worthy: from the beautiful actors in it to the rich colors of their costumes to the shine on the heirloom apples and the crust on the artisanal sourdough in the basket.

And especially the multiorgasmic sex they were about to fake.

"How do I look?" Tasha asked Maggie.

There was no response but to say "Perfect."

Maggie crossed over to Cole. "Everything good?"

For a second, his eyes were on her, and Maggie felt an urge to fiddle with her hair, to straighten her top. She had no idea what he wanted from her, but it felt—ridiculously—as if he were looking for something.

But then the moment was over.

"Yeah, I'm ready," he said.

"I'll be here the whole time."

"Yeah."

It felt as if he was mad at her, but she couldn't have guessed why, and anyhow, that was asinine. He wasn't mad; he was focused.

Which he ought to be.

"Let's get started!" Zoya called.

They shot several takes of the first bit: Geordie and Effie climbing the ladder; the characters stumbling into the hay, kissing; Geordie fumbling with the buttons on Effie's dress. But when they reached the portion of the sequence when things got more intense, filming imploded.

"It's looking good, Zoya." The voice came from the ladder up to the hayloft. Vincent Minna emerged from the aperture, followed immediately by an apologetic-looking Esme.

Vincent Minna. Here. On set.

For an instant, it was hard to believe that this was happening. That it wasn't the wax figure of him from Madame Tussauds, sentient and walking.

But when the shock had made a circuit around her body, Maggie realized this was real. Real and terrible.

Zoya was obviously processing the same shock. She left David, the camera, and the monitor and stumbled toward him. "Vincent, what the hell are you doing here?"

"It's my money, isn't it?" He looked around as if he expected to get a rousing laugh or cheer of approval.

The crew only gawked at him. Even they appeared to be starstruck—star-paralyzed, more like—and they didn't even know what Maggie knew. This man was a monster.

"It's Silverlight's money," Zoya said.

Maggie had recovered her ability to move, and she turned toward the actors. Cole appeared to be bored, even slightly annoyed, by the interruption. But Tasha resembled a corpse. Her skin was ashen. Her eyes dull.

A grenade might as well have detonated in Maggie's chest.

No. This couldn't happen. It was actually, literally her job to prevent this from happening.

"This is a closed set." Maggie positioned her body between Vincent and Tasha, and she began marching toward him.

"Excuse me?" Vincent shot a glance at Zoya.

"She's right," the director said, though her tone was soft, accommodating. "And—"

"You need to leave," Maggie said. "Immediately."

"Who's this?" Vincent still wasn't talking to Maggie at all.

He probably had a list of who it was worth interacting with, and Maggie was certain that she wasn't on it. But that couldn't have mattered less.

"I'm Maggie Niven. I'm the intimacy coordinator."

"Oh, of *course*." It was obvious he thought that was a ridiculous notion.

The disgusting condescension of this man. Tasha was right: it was incredible that no one had knocked out his teeth. But they'd have to debate *that* ridiculous situation later. For now, Maggie had to get him out of here. She'd promised Tasha that she would keep her safe, and she was going to keep that promise.

Maggie put her hands in front of her; they were hovering a few inches from Vincent's chest. "You should leave now."

For a bare second, Vincent's gaze flicked to Maggie. His predator eyes made her want to crawl out of her skin. In a second, he'd sized Maggie up and decided she wasn't even worth contradicting. She was worthless.

Talking, quite literally, over her head, he said, "I have every right to be here, Zoya. It's in the contract. Someone from Silverlight can supervise—"

"You cannot supervise this." Maggie had absolutely no idea if, legally speaking, her words were true. But she also knew that she was not going to allow filming to happen if this man was in the room.

"Zoya." Vincent clearly assumed he'd get his way. He was one of those people who quite simply could not imagine a world in which they didn't get their way. And what evidence would Vincent, with his money and his Oscars and his power, have to suggest that was a bad assumption? When he'd hurt Tasha, and countless other people, he'd likely done it because he could. Because who on earth was going to stop him?

So the effect when someone did was almost palpable.

"Maggie's right," Zoya said, and it was like a shock wave.

Vincent Minna's brows shot up. He blinked. He licked his lips. He crossed his arms over his chest, and it was a relief he didn't throttle whoever was nearest to him, given that that was Maggie.

At last, with something approaching cool composure, he managed to say "I can call my lawyers, and—"

"Call them." Maggie answered for Zoya, because she was done, absolutely done, with this. "But you will not do it here." She began walking forward, willing, if necessary, to shove him.

But he . . . fell back a step. And then another one.

That was when Maggie knew she'd won.

She had no illusions. At the height of his power, one insignificant person saying no to Vincent Minna would've had no effect. But today, with him being older, with Zoya's evident discomfort with his presence, it had been enough. Just enough.

Vincent's glare was lethal as he and Maggie did the two-step all the way back to the ladder. But she stood there, arms folded, until he'd descended.

When he disappeared, Maggie pointed to one of the sparks. "You. Can you stand at the bottom of this ladder and yell if that man tries to come back?" She was fairly confident that no filming was going to occur for a while. This guy could leave the light he was supervising for a few minutes.

"I'm getting security," Zoya called out. Even now, Esme was muttering into her phone. It didn't sound as if she was using nearly enough profanity for Maggie's taste.

"Get them faster." Maggie began marching back to the actors.

"Maggie Niven, bouncer extraordinaire," Cole was saying, but when he turned to Tasha to presumably share a laugh, he caught his best friend's expression.

He was there before Maggie could be, wrapping Tasha in his arms.

Maggie was certain everyone in the room was shocked when Tasha pitched forward against Cole's chest and began sobbing. Not crying. Not something quiet and demure. But absolute-bottom-of-the-pit, great racking sobs.

Goddamn, it hurt seeing Tasha's pain. Hearing it.

Cole twisted, putting the bulk of his back and shoulders between her and the rest of the room. And in that moment, in that elegant gesture of protectiveness and empathy, Maggie fell a little bit in love with him.

The knowledge dropped through her like a hot knife through butter. She loved Cole. But like so many other things, that was a problem she'd have to solve later.

Maggie whirled on her heel and signaled to everyone else. The crew retreated as far across the barn as they could in order to give Tasha privacy.

"What was that about?" David muttered.

Maggie gave him a look that she hoped would mute if not maim.

"Sorry!" he said, putting his hands up in a mea culpa. "Obviously there's some story there, and that—is absolutely none of our business."

"No, it's not," Maggie gritted out.

Zoya and Esme joined the circle. "Security's here. Vincent ran them off earlier."

Maggie didn't have any problem imagining how it had gone, but she was also sure that Tasha wasn't going to feel safe on set anymore. How could she, when the security people quailed at the first sign of a dude in an expensive suit?

"And they won't do that again?" Maggie asked.

"I'll put the fear of God in them."

"What did they fear before? Waffles?"

Zoya glared at her.

"Should we save the lights?" David asked. "Are we going to film?"

"Yeah, kill the lights. We're going to take a break and then reevaluate." Zoya sounded confident about that, and Maggie would guess that making immediate, firm decisions was a life skill for her.

"Maggie," Cole called. "We're going to Tasha's trailer. She wants you."

"Of course."

When Tasha emerged from Cole's chest, her eyes were red and puffy, but she still had more self-possession than most queens Maggie had seen. She led the way, with Cole and Maggie behind.

A security guard joined their procession at the bottom of the ladder, and when they arrived at the trailer, he stayed outside. Inside, Tasha took a seat on the daybed. With her dress, she didn't fit anywhere else. She took a tissue from the box on the counter and dabbed at her eyes.

Cole leaned up against the kitchenette. Maggie stayed by the door.

"It's okay if you want to postpone filming," Maggie said when no one else spoke. "Zoya will understand." The set's safety had been breached. Maggie wouldn't blame Tasha if she wanted to leave the show altogether.

The contract—that might be another matter. But Tasha's agent could get into all that.

"No. I just need ten minutes," Tasha said. "Well, and a cold pack for my eyes."

"I'll bet the hair and makeup team has some." Maggie leaned outside and relayed the message to the security guy.

When she came back, Cole looked at Maggie and raised his brows, as if he expected her to provide an explanation.

Maggie shook her head. Whatever was going to be said here, Tasha was going to say it.

Tasha rolled her shoulders back and cracked her neck. Then she faced Cole. "So you know how I told you Vincent was a shit?"

"Yes."

"That might not have been . . . the whole story."

"Clearly."

"You're not going to like it."

"I'm sure I'm not."

And then, Tasha told him.

Cole didn't interrupt her. He didn't hurry her or ask questions. But by the end of Tasha's narrative, he was basically a towering inferno. The rage was leaking out of him, poisoning the atmosphere in the trailer, like radiation after a nuclear meltdown.

"He. Did. What?" Cole finally ground out.

"I'm not repeating it. It was bad enough to get through once. Twice, I guess. I told Maggie the other day."

"And one of the only things Tasha requested was for Vincent Minna not to be on the set," Maggie explained. "I am just so sorry that he showed up."

"God, Maggie, this isn't your fault. I didn't even realize he'd try it when I said it. I was making a joke."

"Sick joke."

Tasha managed a harsh laugh.

But in between them, Cole was still seething. "We do not have to film this scene. And we sure as hell don't have to do it today."

"Yes, we do." Tasha stood and adjusted her skirts. "It's done. I have given that ghoul in man's skin too many years. I cannot fucking believe I cried. I fucking cried!" Tasha set her hand on Cole's arm. "You cannot kill him."

"Like hell I can't—"

"No. You—or Geordie, I guess—have to make love to me. That's what matters. The past, it's done. Let's go earn some Emmys."

There was a pause, and Maggie wasn't certain if Cole was going to accept this or if he was going to find Vincent and pound him into powder.

Cole still looked so, so angry, which made sense. Maggie had had several weeks to adjust to the story, and she still wanted to introduce the producer to Sweeney Todd and his meat grinder. But this was Tasha's story, Tasha's pain, and right now, Cole and Maggie needed to take their cues from her.

After a few seconds, Cole scrubbed his hands over his face. The deep outraged breaths that had had his rib cage working like a bellows slowed. When he dropped his hands, his eyes were no longer brutal, and his cheeks weren't so red. He threw an arm around Tasha, pulled his friend close, and kissed her temple. "Jeez, no pressure."

And with that joke, everything was better. Things weren't okay—there was no way for things to be okay—but it was like the wind on the top of that mountain he'd made Maggie climb: the foul stench that Vincent had brought whipped away, leaving only sweet potential behind.

Shooting this scene was what Tasha wanted, so they were going to do it.

Back in the hayloft, Cole changed into a clean shirt, and a H/MU tech held an ice pack to Tasha's face until the swelling went down. When they'd touched up her makeup, no one could've guessed she'd been crying.

Movies, they were magic.

"You ready?" Zoya asked them.

"Yes."

Cole and Tasha settled on the hay, her in his lap. Zoya yelled, "Camera set," and the scene started again.

Maggie wanted to stay outside of it. To see it as a performance. To know it was choreography. They'd planned every touch, every kiss, every gasp together, but her insides didn't seem to comprehend that . . . probably because Tasha was faking one impressive orgasm. Startled and luminous and worth wrecking your life for, just like they'd practiced.

"Cut! That was great," Zoya said. "Let's get one more just for fun."

"Sure thing," Cole said. "You okay?"

He pitched that question to Tasha, who nodded.

The actors didn't take their eyes off each other during the break. Not when the makeup techs swooped in to fix them up. Not when a spark had to climb up on a ladder to replace a bulb.

And they didn't once look up at Maggie.

Which was fine. They didn't have to. It was a sign that they'd all done the right amount of prep, so even when Vincent exploded the plan, they were still able to move on.

This was good. It was good.

Their insularity continued when Zoya declared the second take to be perfect and said the camera should move for the next sequence.

Cole and Tasha stayed wrapped up in each other while shooting the bit where Geordie knelt and "worshipped" Effie. It went on once they'd moved onto the straw for the long, intense frontal sequence. For all that Maggie was there handing them props, neither made eye contact with her.

"You both doing okay?" she asked quietly while she placed the exercise ball that helped the actors simulate thrusting.

"Yup." But Tasha's nod was for Cole, not Maggie.

That was *fine*—Cole was her scene partner. Their palpable intimacy felt like an iron curtain, keeping out anything that might detract from the performance. Maggie's slapped-face feeling only came from the fact that she'd thought she got to be inside the process with them but realized now she wasn't.

When she dropped back behind the camera, the script supervisor sidled up to her. "They're really focused today."

"Yeah." They had to be, she reminded herself.

When at last every shot was done and Zoya said "That's a lid. Great work, everyone," Maggie knew that the compliment included her.

What they'd filmed would later be described as the hottest scene of the year, and sometimes one of the hottest in television history. In giving this performance, Tasha was saying Vincent didn't matter—that she wouldn't let him matter—and Cole was saying that he would be there for his friend, no matter what.

It was the bravest thing Maggie had ever seen anyone do . . . even if watching it had also made her feel like the help.

Chapter 15

INT. CROWDED PUB

The pub in the hotel was overpriced, but it was convenient, and so the crew had started assembling there nightly. After his teeth-gritting performance following Vincent freaking Minna's appearance, Cole most definitely needed a beer.

No alcohol during filming: that was what Drew would've told him. But that's why Cole didn't ask for permission.

Besides, dehydration made for better muscle definition.

In the back corner, with an order of french fries and a cider, was Maggie Niven. Around her were half the crew, all trying to ask without asking why Tasha had lost it.

"I'm merely saying, she's usually an awful-*ly*"—David put the emphasis on the second syllable—"cool customer."

"Hmm." Maggie dragged a fry through a puddle of ketchup.

That seemed to be her main source of vegetables. Someone ought to take better care of that woman. Too bad it wasn't going to be Cole.

David wasn't going to let it go. "It's hard not to read something into it."

"Hmm."

The only free seat in the cluster was next to Maggie, so Cole wove through the chairs, fist-bumping this key grip and high-fiving that spark. He slipped onto the bench, then he draped his arm along the back, wanting Maggie to know he was here to help.

She was small under his forearm but fierce.

"Hey, guys," he said.

And . . . crickets.

It made Cole feel like a TV dad catching his children planning a rager. What a one-eighty from *Central Square*, when he'd been the one organizing the party.

"Fry?" Maggie pushed her plate toward him.

"Thanks." He took a pass on the ketchup, though. He usually went for barbeque sauce, but he'd discovered the British didn't really know what that was supposed to taste like.

"How are you all doing?" Cole asked when the silence in the group got to be too much.

"Good," David said in a way that meant *curious*.

Cole should've had the beer in his room.

"Shooting went well," Maggie said, faux chipper and trying to change the subject. "I mean, we made our day, right?" Meaning they'd gotten all the shots on the schedule.

"Barely." Of everyone on set, David was most on top of things, the most likely to remind them that a mandated break was coming up or that they had moved into those sweet, sweet overtime hours.

Television could be brutal. Cole had endured his share of eighteen-hour days. Today, it was Vincent's fault they'd gone ten hours.

"Some things take time." Maggie turned toward Cole. "You . . . doing okay?"

Cole had the sense she wanted to ask about Tasha.

He'd checked in with her before coming down. Tasha was in for the night, with room service. Merrit—who'd been running her errands and had missed all the drama—and two hefty security guys were standing guard outside her room. Tasha kept insisting she was fine, but he suspected that was code for *Fucked up IN the Extreme.*

If everyone else would give Cole and Maggie some privacy, he'd share that. Maggie had earned it. The rest of these folks? Not so much.

The production was lucky nothing about Vincent's visit and Tasha's meltdown had leaked to the press—so far. In a few days, they were going to relocate to Inverness for more location shooting, and two journalists would be arriving to spend a week on set. Holy jeez, it would've been disastrous if they'd witnessed today's events.

But Maggie would never allow strangers to be on set during a love scene. That he was certain of.

"I'm . . . good," he said in answer to Maggie's question.

Cole was normally a fairly even-keeled person. He'd created a routine for himself of work, exercise, and mindfulness. For years, it had kept the messiness of his youth away. Contained it. He'd needed the rules and the certainty.

Now those same things made him feel like the Tin Man, hollow and unable to help the people in his life who needed it. He'd thought Tasha was his best friend in the world. But when she'd fallen onto his chest today, he'd realized how little he truly knew about her.

And here he'd thought he was growing into a better person.

During *Central Square*, he'd been too clueless to perceive the toxicity around him. But later on, he'd seen Vincent and other big shots be jerks. Cole had seen them yell at assistants, get handsy with servers, and be crass and mean in a hundred small ways. *Don't rock the boat,* Drew had said—and all too often, Cole hadn't.

What he'd learned today was maybe he still sucked.

Maggie gave Cole a smile that covered a more complex mix of emotions. "Long or not, the scene was terrific. You both really nailed it."

Just as with the Madge-Geordie scene, Cole knew Maggie hadn't been watching the monitor. She was there for the actors, personally and emotionally. She wasn't a judge or critic, which made her one of the only people he trusted on the production.

"Is Tasha well?" David's question was on everyone's minds, Cole was certain, but the DP was the only one bold enough to put it to Cole.

"She's a pro." As far as Cole was concerned, she deserved a medal for what she'd put on film—okay, on digital—today. And that was all he was going to say to anyone about it.

"Glad to hear it." David's eyes shot back and forth between Cole and Maggie, as if he were watching a particularly heated match at Wimbledon. "So . . . mob scenes are coming up. Lots of night filming."

"Yup."

"It's going to be killer."

Night shoots were the bane of Cole's existence. He probably wouldn't feel well rested for the rest of filming, but they had to get the footage.

"No kissing in those scenes," Maggie said, "so I have a bit of a break."

Days off—jeez, he wasn't going to have any of those for months.

He was going to miss working with Maggie for the rest of the time they were in Edinburgh. When they got to Inverness, though, the schedule was pretty much wall-to-wall banging.

But as long as Maggie had downtime: "You going hiking again? Because West Cairn is higher than Allermuir, and the view must be—"

"Nope, nope, nope. That was a mistake." But her expression said it hadn't been.

Cole's attention went to a freckle above Maggie's lip and then back to those bright-green eyes of hers. He could feel her smile square in the base of his spine.

Damn. He liked her.

"We better turn in early, then."

Cole and Maggie both startled like cats when you flicked on the light—which in this case was the blinking eyes of all their coworkers.

David gave an amused cough before draining his glass. "See you both tomorrow."

With a chorus of *yeah*s and *good night*s, the rest of the crew followed. And that finally, finally left Cole and Maggie alone.

Cole could've moved. He had his choice of chairs now, plenty of other places to sit that weren't hip to hip with Maggie.

He stayed where he was.

"How are you really?" Maggie carefully selected another french fry before drowning it in ketchup.

"I've had better days." It was the simplest and most truthful thing he could think to say. "I wanted to thank you, for taking care of Tasha."

When Vincent had materialized, Cole had mostly been confused, but maybe that was good. He would've definitely taken a swing at the asshole if he'd known the full story. For her part, Maggie had almost mauled him. If Vincent hadn't run, tail between his Armani'd legs, Cole had no doubt she would've laid hands on him.

As if unaware of her own intensity, she shrugged. "Of course. That's my job."

He was pretty sure *physically protecting the talent from predators* wasn't in her contract.

"I didn't know. About Vincent and Tasha, I didn't know." It was important to Cole that Maggie understand he'd been in the dark.

Maggie's eyes were soft. "I know. I'm sorry. When she told me, she asked me not to tell anyone else."

Cole had no idea why Maggie was apologizing. The only person who had done anything wrong here was Vincent—and fuck that guy forever.

"Yeah, I can imagine. She's not very open." He was only now realizing how much Tasha had kept under wraps. It made Cole feel like the worst kind of ass that she hadn't trusted him enough to reveal it. "I'm just glad she shared it with someone. I wish . . . I wish I'd seemed safe enough for it to be me."

"I don't think you should torture yourself about that. It wasn't anything about you, but more about Hollywood. I mean, what would you have done?"

"Not worked with him."

"It's not that simple. Here's Tasha, technically working with him."

"That's my fault too." When he said it, he had one of those oh-shit moments. He hadn't even known he felt guilty about Tasha taking this job until the words had popped out, and then there it was, visible from space.

Tasha was lowering herself, working with someone who had hurt her, because of Cole. No one should have to pay for Cole's past mistakes aside from him. But that was only one face of his guilt. He was basically a d20 of bad feelings at the moment.

"And I should've known about Vincent. About . . . probably so many guys I've worked with. I should've stopped it, somehow."

Cole knew he had privilege as a man and a white person in Hollywood. Even on the B-list, people made assumptions about his marketability and potential. He had no doubt that most people wouldn't have gotten the second chances he had.

When he'd taken those chances, though, when he'd been paying his dues, had he looked the other way? Had he heard that someone was difficult to work with and thought *jerk* and not *criminal*?

"Wait, let me get this straight," Maggie said. "You think you single-handedly should've ended sexism in Hollywood?"

"No." Not when she put it like that. "But maybe I should have been more . . . aware."

"Cole, we all could have been more aware. At the end of the day, though, the only person who's responsible for Vincent's shittiness is Vincent."

Sadly, Cole knew Hollywood too well to buy what Maggie was selling. Sure, ultimately, Vincent had planted himself on set to leer at a teenage girl, had tried to manipulate her into his bed, and had tried to make everyone on earth think she'd slept with him. But Tasha's mother, her costars, her director, the people in the crew, her agent, the other folks at Silverlight: they'd seen it all, and they hadn't stepped in. The distinction between the monster and its keepers was swiss cheese. Why make it? There was plenty of blame to go around.

"There's an entire network of people around him, and Maggie, they all knew."

She sat with that for a moment. "Fair enough. But you weren't one of them."

"It doesn't matter. It's still my fault she had to face him again."

"I'd guess that's math she's had to do every day of her career." Maggie pressed her palms into the table for emphasis. "Do you trust Tasha?"

"Yes."

"Then trust she made the right decision. Look, my heart broke for that woman today. I was about as mad as I've ever been when he appeared. But Tasha knew it was possible she might see Vincent while filming or promoting the show. She weighed that against liking the part, liking the team. *That's* why she's playing Effie. Sure, she enjoys working with you, and yes, maybe she did want to support you, too, but Tasha doesn't strike me as a person who would make a four-month commitment—more, really, once you factor in promo—just to be nice."

Cole tried to imagine putting the question to Tasha. She'd probably slug him, and she wouldn't be gentle about it either.

He took a sip of his beer. What Maggie had said hadn't made the queasiness in his gut go away, but it wasn't about to consume him anymore. He bumped Maggie's knee with his. "You're not going to let me feel guilty, are you?"

"Nope. I'm going to try to talk you out of it."

"You're not going to let me wallow in self-pity, and—"

"It's probably bad for your skin, and then Zoya would be mad at me."

The mention of Zoya took the flirtation right out of the conversation. He and Maggie both had a lot riding on this job. Too much for him to be counting the freckles along her collarbone.

Six . . . that he could see.

Maggie ate another fry. "This is not my business at all, but if you have a chance to encourage Tasha to seek therapy, it might be a good idea. I mentioned it to her, but she could probably use some more prodding."

"I'll try."

Tasha would say *fuck* a lot in response to that suggestion. A dozen, heck, two dozen times—he ought to offer Maggie the over/under on it.

Maggie picked up her glass and watched Cole over the rim. Closely. With the kind of deep scrutiny that made him want to sit up straighter and maybe flex his biceps.

"I have no idea how you got through that scene today," she finally said.

When Tasha had said she wanted to do it, he hadn't known if they'd be able to get through it either. He'd had to block everything out that wasn't Tasha. Just let the muscle memory they'd built up over the rehearsals take over and put his body on autopilot.

"This isn't very healthy, but it honestly might have been the best thing we could've done. Acting can be like . . . obliterating yourself. For a few hours, I didn't have to be me. Tasha didn't have to be her." They'd put up a wall between themselves and everyone else. Honestly, when the day had ended and he'd realized how much time had passed, he'd been shocked. But it had been the only way to get through it.

Something flashed over Maggie's features. Pain, maybe.

But . . . why?

"Are you okay?" he asked. "I—"

She wasn't listening to him, though. Maggie was wiping her hands on a napkin and getting to her feet. "Well, you were amazing. You did great work, and I'm so glad you were there for Tasha. I'm going to head up to my room."

It was like running into a sliding glass door he hadn't known was there. A force field. One of those electric fences you use to keep dogs in your backyard.

He suddenly felt very much like a dog.

"You okay?" he repeated, feeling foolish.

"Of course. It was just a long day. I ought to get some sleep." Maggie didn't make eye contact with him, and her voice was higher than normal. Strained.

Cole knew he wouldn't be able to sleep until he figured out what he'd done to piss off Maggie—because it wasn't nothing. He drained his beer. "I'll walk out with you."

She hadn't waited for him, and it was good that his legs were longer than hers because he caught up with her in the breezeway between the pub's interior and exterior doors. When the interior door closed behind Cole, muffling the din from inside, they were left in the dark.

Maggie had stopped walking—maybe she'd decided there was no way to avoid this conversation—and he almost ran into her.

His hands hovered over her shoulders for a second. In comfort? A plea? He didn't even know. "Maggie, it feels like you're mad at me. Just tell me what I did so I can say sorry and fix it."

"You don't have anything to apologize for." She spoke over her shoulder, her voice wry. "If I'm mad at anyone, it's myself."

"Why would you be mad at yourself?" *You're perfect.* He couldn't say that. It wasn't professional. It wasn't his place. But knowing those things didn't stop him from thinking it.

You're perfect. You're perfect.

"You ever have a feeling crop up out of nowhere and catch you in the teeth? Like a—a rock getting kicked up by a truck on the highway that cracks your windshield?"

"Yeah." But those feelings? He tended to have earned them. "What was the feeling, Maggie?" They were on the cusp of something here, something massive and important. He could sense the edges of it in the dark.

"It doesn't matter."

"I want to know."

She sighed.

His eyes had adjusted to the dark, and he watched those small shoulders of hers rise and fall, settling lower than before.

Very softly, she said, "Directing feels like a thing I'm doing *with* actors. Rehearsal and blocking are, can be, collaborative. But when it comes time to do the performance, they're on their own. Mostly, that feels good. We've done the work, and then it flowers. Today . . ."

She didn't have to say the rest.

"We got through today because of you. And I know that Tasha is really grateful, too, and when she's—"

"No, I don't want *gratitude*." Maggie whirled to face him. Only a few tablespoons of light were making it around the door, and all of it seemed to have pooled in her eyes. "I felt jealous, and that's ridiculous. I'm being ridiculous."

"You're . . . jealous?" Cole's heart was doing a burpee in his chest—a throbbing, bounding, squeezing exercise against his ribs—but his palms were dry, and his mind calm. Because something had fallen into place.

Maggie was speaking quickly. "Not jealous, exactly. That isn't the right word. But today, you didn't need me, and that's . . . good. It's good that you didn't need me. It means we rehearsed well, and I got you ready for that scene. So ready that even when it all went pear shaped, you were still able to execute it. And that's exactly my job, right? What happened today means I can do this job. I'm just having some weird emotional glitch. I don't know, I can't explain it. Maybe it's not even about this job. Maybe it's the stress of the last year and a half, but . . . I'm babbling. I'm sorry. Don't worry about me. It doesn't make any sense."

No, it made perfect sense.

Less than a foot stood between Cole's hands and Maggie's waist. In a second, he could have his hands on her. His mouth on her.

It was suddenly extremely important for him to get his mouth on her.

Only his rules kept him from doing it.

He wasn't Maggie's boss. He had no control over her or over the production. But he was famous. Sort of. And he had power. Kinda.

Maggie was new to this job, new to this industry. Kissing her—at least kissing her *now*—wouldn't be fair.

Kissing her later? That was something else entirely.

"Anyhow, you're fine. I'm sorry I'm being weird. But I was thinking about what you said earlier."

"About?" His voice was even, without a hint of what he'd just decided.

"What's it like when your self rushes back in after you're done filming?"

The question was soft, barely above a whisper, but between that and the dark, he had trouble remembering what they'd been talking about. He had trouble remembering anything except why he shouldn't tug Maggie into him.

"Um, it depends on the part I'm playing. It can be confusing, a relief, a—a disappointment." Cole didn't have a problem being himself most of the time. But when you got to pretend to be a superhero, to be perfect, to be larger than life, it was a rude awakening to return to reality where you were firmly middle aged, not exactly famous, and still trudging up the road to career redemption.

It might be easier some days to just go on being a character. At least then his lines were written for him.

Maggie squeezed his forearm, and even through his sleeve, he could feel the warm support there.

Could feel the wanting there.

She might not be willing to admit it to herself, but it was real, as surely as it was in his own chest.

"Real you is pretty darn cool," she said. "If you needed validation about that. I . . . I like real you."

But real him couldn't do what he wanted in response to that, at least not tonight. Which was a crying shame.

Chapter 16

INT. MAGGIE'S HOTEL ROOM

"Videon is apparently thrilled with the footage they've seen."

Maggie didn't know how Bernard had heard that. But even after only working together for a few months, it was clear very little went down in Hollywood that Bernard didn't get wind of. Heck, he might have been hiding in the back of the screening room when Videon execs had watched the *Waverley* footage from Scotland.

It made her want to ask if he'd known about Vincent Minna, but Bernard was still technically her mentor, and implying that he'd known—and hadn't done anything—about a predator who was antithetical to every value Bernard held wasn't going to go over very well.

Instead, Maggie went with a milder response: "I honestly haven't paid much attention to the footage." She'd been so focused on the actors themselves, on how they felt about the choreography and the filming, on all the technical bits of costuming and lighting, the results had begun to feel almost theoretical. It wasn't that she didn't care if the scenes themselves were hot and realistic, but so much was in her head about filming them in a consensual and healthy way, she hadn't been able to see the end result.

Missing the forest for the trees? Please, she was missing the forest for the leaves.

After the first Effie-and-Geordie love scene, when Maggie had had that flash of not-jealousy, everything had gone great. She'd kept a firm handle on her emotions and had shoved everything that wasn't purely professional under the bed where it belonged.

In the Zoom window on Maggie's laptop, Bernard nodded in agreement. "That's normal for your first job. Wait until the tenth one."

Maggie could only hope she'd make it that far.

When Zoya had introduced them and Bernard had agreed to take Maggie on as an apprentice, he'd been clear that not every production needed or used an intimacy coordinator. That while the profile of the field had increased in recent years, there were limitations on how much work was available. "It's not like getting in to some explosive field on the ground floor," he'd said.

But as good reports had begun to come in from filming, his tone had grown warmer, more long term.

It felt good—and scary.

Maggie needed this, she *wanted* it, so badly. Starting over in a brand-new career in her late thirties was worse than climbing that mountain with Cole. One foot in front of the other was well and good, but she had a lot of miles to go before she could feel secure. If she even could still feel secure after the last year and a half.

She was supposed to be over this stage. She was supposed to own a house, be married, and have a firm professional reputation. *Nein, nyet, nee*: she was striking out where those goals were concerned.

Nailing this wasn't optional.

"I gotta get through *Waverley* before projects two through ten."

"You really should sign with my agent or, if not her, with someone else. You'll get lots of offers if you send out feelers."

The idea that Maggie might need an agent—it still seemed absurd. "I'll think about it."

"Don't put it off too long. Season four of *Waverley* will be a big job."

She'd heard some whispers about the season after this one, and it had made her head spin. True, they were halfway done with principal photography for season three, but after filming, there was still so much else to do with editing and music. A PA had spent half an hour explaining the translation and dubbing to Maggie one afternoon, and she'd wanted to cry, it sounded so complicated.

How could they be thinking about the next one? But also . . . how could they not?

"For whoever signs up for it, sure."

"So you wouldn't be interested?"

Maggie watched herself blink rapidly on Zoom. "Wait, I thought you were being hypothetical."

"They're already breaking the next season, scouting locations and the like. As I said, they're happy with our—or really, *your*—work. I was nervous when I broke my leg that you wouldn't be okay on your own, but you've handled it like a pro. You don't need me at all at this point."

Waverley was big business. Big, big business. Given what a hit the show was, it had already been renewed for the season after this one. But because each season was based on a different book, there were different characters and conflicts each time. In the next one, there'd be no Tasha or Rhiannon or Leanne or Owen.

No Cole.

Maggie wasn't going to pretend the highlight of her day hadn't become the late nights in the pub with the crew, the jokes and the camaraderie, the stories about this set and that starlet. One of her favorite parts of teaching drama had been watching those ties grow between her students. The way that kids who never would've hung out in any other context became friends and changed their self-perception in the process. Doing a show together lit relationships and crushes and the entire other rainbow of human connections on fire. When the ingredients were right, a production could forge bonds that would last forever.

Theatre held human nature up to the audience, sure. But in practice, making theatre embodied human nature.

She could feel that happening with and around her as *Waverley* filmed, and the key connection that was building was between her and

Cole. Somehow, wherever they both started, they'd end up side by side. More nights than not, they left the pub at the same time, often long after everyone else had gone to bed. She wanted to hear about his day. She wanted him to laugh at her jokes. She kept falling more and more in love with him.

It was just a production crush, she knew. It was mostly in her head, she was certain. But if she came back for the next season, he wouldn't be there.

She couldn't even evaluate how she felt about *Waverley* outside Cole. He colored everything, like a red sock that accidentally ended up in the wash with your towels. And there wasn't bleach she could use to reverse it.

"I'm really flattered," Maggie made herself say to Bernard. "I'm definitely interested in helping out with season four, but . . . it's a big commitment." Doing another season of the show would be another massive chunk of her life. Yes, it would be a substantial accomplishment, but it would be more time away from the States. More time away from anything that felt real.

But this job was *important*. Maggie knew that she was making a difference here. If Bernard had been on set instead of her, would Tasha have confided in him? Would he have been forceful enough with Vincent?

She didn't know.

Maggie wanted to pay her bills, sure, but she also wanted to get her reputation back and to do work that mattered. This job was giving her all those things, and Bernard's referral—that wasn't something to turn her nose up at, not at all. If she wanted this career, she had to work to have it. That was for sure. "I'll email your agent."

"Good," Bernard said. "You could do this full time. I absolutely believe that."

At least one of them did.

"I do have one quick question." Maggie intertwined her fingers in her lap, trying to stop herself from fidgeting. "Socializing with the crew and some of the cast—it's something I've been doing, and I'm realizing it's become a habit. Is that . . . okay? Or is it unprofessional?"

She wasn't going to get into that moment in the doorway of the pub when she'd foolishly—so foolishly—confessed her moment of almost-jealousy to Cole. She'd covered it up, or at least she thought she had, and he'd never mentioned it again. But the memory of it was there like a bruise on her skin.

"Oh, that's fine—it can even be an asset. You need people to trust you to do your job, and those friendships help. Plus you want to have a reputation for being part of the team and easy to work with, and you're earning that."

"Good. Great. I just don't want to be too . . . familiar."

"I get it. Especially because there can be confusion about what we do—"

Do intimacy coordinators act the scenes out with the actors? That was what Bernard meant. Maggie's brother had asked her that, and the answer was no, of course not.

"So it's good to have professional boundaries. But as long as you're not getting drunk with your coworkers every night—"

"Nope, definitely not."

"Then I don't see it as being a problem. But it's a solid question to ask. Obviously, given the 'drama' in your recent employment history, it's good to be especially sensitive to those boundary questions."

Bernard used sarcastic air quotes around *drama*. He'd always been clear that he thought Maggie's firing had been beyond ridiculous, but there had been an obvious subtext for that support: *Don't step in it again.* One scandal, if it was the kind Maggie had been hit with, was understandable. It made her more sympathetic. But a second scandal? Worse yet, one in which she was at fault?

That would be beyond the pale.

Bernard was saying exactly what Maggie already knew. Hanging out with Cole and the rest of her colleagues at *Waverley* was fine. But that had to be as far as it went.

Whatever she felt sometimes when Cole was leaning close, talking into her ear over the roar in the pub. When his fingers brushed hers when they reached for the same french fry. When his gaze caught hers and held until everything that wasn't him went fuzzy. That had to stop.

"Absolutely. I'd never cross a line."

She couldn't afford to.

Chapter 17

INT. BACKSTAGE ON THE *WAVERLEY* SET

Cole shifted in his seat. "I can see what you're getting at, but I'd never thought about whether Geordie is a . . . what did you call him?"

"A manifestation of male privilege and entitlement." Libby Hansen, the journalist sitting across from Cole, delivered that in a rush, without so much as a pause between the words. She probably used a cute hashtag version in her reviews. #MOMPAE, or maybe just #HeSucks.

Cole knew what she was suggesting about Geordie, though. "Right. Yeah. I mean, maybe."

Libby jotted that onto her pad. She wrote the dot over the *i* as a heart.

Cole had expected this interview to be fluffier. When they'd told him Libby was a freelance critic who had a million followers on TikTok, he'd expected her questions to be of the boxers-or-briefs variety. But this kid hadn't been alive when the boxers-or-briefs moment had happened.

Dressed in pink head to toe, Libby clearly had a fluffy side. But she was also whip smart and shrewd, and it was quite possible she was seeing through Cole right down to his skeleton.

Her brown eyes flicked up to him. "What drew you to Geordie?"

"Not his privilege or entitlement, that's for sure."

Libby snorted.

At least Cole had managed to make the kid laugh. "No, it was his growth. I guess I need to feel like that's possible, that someone could be immature or selfish, and then learn to be . . . better." Cole's voice went scratchy at the end of his answer, and he fumbled for a bottle of water.

When he had taken a long sip, Libby asked, "Is that kind of redemption personal for you?"

One of Drew's rules was Cole shouldn't get into his private life in interviews. He could talk about his workout routine or his diet, but the Cole James brand itself didn't need shadows or cracks. Any reality. Answering her question—at least directly—would be getting into his own feelings and motivations way, way too much for Drew's taste.

Brett took a more balanced approach to these things, saying that Cole could do what was comfortable for him but shouldn't be afraid to draw boundaries. Drew thought that was too complicated for Cole and an absolute ban was easier to maintain.

But look, everyone with a functioning brain cell knew Cole was trying to get back to where he would've been if he hadn't acted like a punk kid twenty years earlier. While that might have been clear as day, if you declared that you were making a comeback, it didn't actually look like you were coming back. It looked pathetic.

It's a universal message, really. That's what Drew would want him to say. Cole understood the logic of Drew's argument. But he wanted to be more than Cole James the brand. He could let people see him sweat.

"Yeah. When I got started, I was young—younger than you are— and I made decisions that were not for the best. I hurt coworkers and friends, and I hurt myself. I'd like to think I've grown. But when I look at Geordie, his mistakes aren't the same as mine."

"No tabloids back then, for starters," Libby said.

"Yeah, he's extremely lucky he didn't have to deal with *Us Weekly*." Cole couldn't express how much he'd hated going to the grocery stores in those days, seeing his worst behavior splashed all over those covers. It was unfortunate *Cole* and *chaos* both started with *c*. So much alliteration in those headlines. "To answer your question, I hope Geordie and I can make amends and end up in better places than we deserve."

Libby wasn't satisfied, though. "Look, I read the book on the plane over here, and earlier, I chatted with Zoya about her changes to the material. This isn't a spoiler to say Geordie eventually drops his disguise, marries Effie, and they're reunited with their baby. He takes up his father's title and moves into the big manor house. It's kind of the ultimate happy-ending fantasy. I mean, he gets *everything*. So first, has he earned that? And second, if you identify with him, is that what you want?"

Wowzer, Drew was going to be pissed.

Around Cole and Libby, the crew were getting prepped for the next shot. Grips were moving lights, David was fussing with the camera, and Maggie was laughing with Tasha about something.

For a long moment, Cole couldn't tear his eyes away from Maggie. She was half a head shorter than Tash. Her hair was tied back into a practical low ponytail, but the ends were slightly curled and bouncy. She was pointing to something on her clipboard, probably a checklist she'd be ruthlessly marking off as they went.

What did Cole want?

That. He wanted *her*.

Here he was, talking to a reporter about how he'd changed, but had he truly grown up if he admitted he'd fallen for someone on set? The lead actor getting involved with the intimacy coordinator sounded like a joke, like something that would've happened to Cody Rhodes on *Central Square*.

Cole yanked his attention back to Libby. *Don't get personal. Stay light. Be charming.* Drew's words cut through the haze, like headlights in dense fog. "Sure." Cole amped the California dudebro in his voice up. "Who doesn't?"

Libby raised her brows. She knew he wasn't being authentic. She would've called him on it, too, except Maggie was weaving across the set, through the crew, toward them.

"We're almost ready." Her smile was droll. She was trying to help him out.

Cole had been half complaining about this interview earlier, and she'd promised to save him if possible. And here she was, doing precisely that. He could've kissed her.

Oops, bad impulse.

"I'm sorry, Libby." Cole offered a dazzling smile. "Duty calls."

"Oh, you have a few minutes. I just want to give you a heads-up."

No, no heads-up. He wanted to get out of this now.

But Libby wasn't paying attention to him anymore. "You're Maggie Niven, right? I'm Libby Hansen. We're scheduled to chat during lunch, and I can't wait. But I have to tell you, I'm going to have a million questions about *Covering the Spread*."

"My old job?" Maggie was puzzled.

"And the musical itself. It's one of my favorites. I played Hailey in high school." She fluffed her hair.

A beat passed, and then Maggie burst into her high, melodic laugh. It was instantly identifiable, and Cole frequently found himself listening for it on set. "Of course you did. You definitely have Hailey energy." That must be a character from the play that had gotten Maggie fired.

"Actually, if you have a second, I want to put the same question to you that I asked Cole."

"Oh?" Maggie looked at him, as if she wanted him to give her some hint of how to answer.

He shrugged in apology. She was on her own for this one.

"We're talking about Geordie's redemption and whether he deserves his happy ending," Libby explained. "What do you think?"

Maggie looked up at the ceiling, which she often did when she was considering how to respond. Cole had gotten used to looking at the soft skin under her chin while she thought. It looked soft, anyhow.

"I've always thought the beautiful thing about happy endings is no one could ever deserve them," she said after a pause. "But sometimes we get them anyway. They're . . . grace. I guess I'm kind of a heathen. I've never been big into the idea you earn love or happiness. That feels so transactional. I'm not saying Geordie doesn't have to do work to try to make right the things he botched, and it's painful he can't really make it up to Madge, right? But in the end, love is a practice. An ethos. Not a product or something you can buy."

Libby liked that answer, clearly. "What would that happy ending look like for you?"

Cole found himself leaning closer, wanting to hear Maggie's answer.

"Ha, well, a life of purpose. I don't really want to talk about my . . . scandal. It feels boring to say anything more about it. But when I realized I couldn't go back to teaching, I lost something I thought I'd do for the rest of my life. My job was so small. More people will see *Waverley* than all the plays I might've directed in forty years teaching high school drama. But that work, it felt vital. When Zoya offered me this job, I wasn't certain I'd be good at it or that it could be a replacement for what I'd lost. The jury is still out on those things, but I can say that I've had moments when I've been certain I'm in the right place." She locked eyes with Cole.

A feeling of satisfaction came over Cole sometimes after a particularly long but good day of shooting or an exhilarating hike. It was a tingling in his muscles, a kind of fulfilled alertness, that only happened when he'd worked hard, pursued the correct thing. He hadn't known it at all until he'd been twenty-five or so. Even now, when he was certain he was on the right path, it was rare. A double rainbow of sensation.

But there it was, spearing through his chest, while he held Maggie's gaze.

She gave a soft smile. "It has felt *purposeful*, this job. And I guess I want to keep feeling that."

He did too. And he was beginning to suspect it wasn't only about purpose or the job, but about them. About him and Maggie.

Oblivious across from them, Libby asked, "And the big house and the husband and the baby?"

Maggie looked down, laughing. "That's a little personal, don't you think?"

"Maybe." Then Libby raised her brows, as if to say *But I'm still asking*.

"Yeah, I mean, everyone wants that stuff." Maggie's voice was quiet. Embarrassed. Heartbreakingly vulnerable.

"That's what Cole said." Libby sounded a bit smug about it.

But before Cole had a chance to defend her or think too much about how he and Maggie had the same recipe for a happy ending, Zoya called him to set.

◆ ◆ ◆

INT. PUB CORRIDOR

"What do you think?" Cole asked.

Cole and Maggie were huddled in the hallway leading to the bathrooms. He'd caught her before she went back to the table they were sharing with Tasha and Ryan. For a reckless half second, she'd hoped it had been for a furtive kiss. But no, the man had a plan to save the day. Of course.

"I don't know," Maggie said carefully.

"I mean, you heard her: Tasha said she'd do anything to even the score with Vincent. *Anything*."

Maggie hadn't realized that anyone knew about Vincent besides Cole and herself, but it was clear that Tasha had shared it with Ryan, too . . . and then had likely had to hold him back from committing what would have been a meticulously planned and technically flawless murder.

The last few days in Inverness, it had become utterly clear to Maggie that Ryan worshipped the ground Tasha walked on. One of these days, when Cole wasn't hell bent on saving the world and fixing Hollywood, she would have to ask him if he'd noticed it too—

Nope, it wasn't any of her business.

These were her work friends. It wouldn't be right to pry into their private lives. As it was, she was pushing up against those barriers that Bernard had warned her about. She'd taken this as far as she could without getting into any trouble.

Starry eyed, Cole was still going on. "I realized it when I was talking to Libby and the other one—"

"Jack," Maggie supplied. Compared to bubbly Libby, the other entertainment reporter was older—and much more old school.

"Yeah, him too. This is what reporters do, isn't it? Libby might've heard whispers about Vincent's behavior before now. Heck, can she really hang around the *Waverley* set for a week and not hear about Tasha's meltdown? Wouldn't it be better if Tasha could share that story?"

"Maybe," Maggie said, trying to look Cole in the eyes instead of staring at the divot at the bottom of his neck.

It was a compelling neck notch, if a bit lawyerly. It'd probably get a deal for its own Videon series soon: Cole James's Neck Notch as *Ernest Osting, Esq.* Maggie would watch it.

But Cole, unaware of his sexy-as-fuck neck notch, wasn't hearing the warning in Maggie's voice. "It's perfect."

"I can see the logic of what you're saying, but—"

"No *but.*" He edged closer. "It *is* a good idea."

Unlike, say, the way Maggie knew she was looking at Cole. That was fruitless and pointless and unprofessional. And if it felt sometimes as if Maggie might perish from the wanting, then it was a good thing she was an adult, a both-feet-on-the-ground, head-firmly-on-her-shoulders adult, who knew you couldn't die from feelings.

Maggie suddenly had more sympathy for all the students who, over the years, had sobbed at her desk about their breakups and crushes.

Right on, kids. Unrequited love is the worst.

"You can suggest it to her, but you have to let her take the lead. If she thinks it's a terrible idea, you have to be willing to let it go."

"Oh, I can be Elsa if necessary."

But Maggie wasn't so sure he could. Cole was not good at being icy or running away. Between him and Tasha, he was far more Anna than the Snow Queen.

When Cole and Maggie started to weave through the thicket of chairs, he moved an empty one out of the way and gestured for Maggie to go first. And there went her heart again, building the bonfire and getting out the fixings for s'mores, perfectly willing to liquefy for him right there.

Maggie knew Cole meant the gesture in the kindest, most chivalrous, most friendly manner possible, and *that was all*. Sure, it could be taken in another way—a hotter, more intimate way—but Maggie had to accept that it was mere politeness, even if his carefulness with her, his awareness of her, made compartmentalizing her feelings for him almost impossible.

"Have you chatted with that journalist yet?" Cole took his seat next to Maggie and across from Tasha. "The one doing the set visit?"

"The woman or the man?" Tasha picked at something on her cuticle.

"Either."

"Nope, but I think it's on my schedule tomorrow. It's fucking exhausting, if you ask me. This thing isn't going to drop for a year, eighteen months—whenever they decide to release it. Why do we have to start promoting the show now? Don't we have enough to deal with?"

Maggie had no idea how actors handled it—the hours the leads worked, the amount of promo and press that was in their contracts, the day-to-day crappiness of fame. She'd decided in her late teens that while she loved theatre, she had no interest in pursuing it professionally. She'd had no idea how wise that decision was until she'd seen the machine up close. It was hard to cry too hard for people in gilded cages, but Maggie could see the cage part more than the gilt these days.

"Well, doing some promo now saves us from having to do more later," Cole said.

"Except it's really both, isn't it?" Then Tasha pulled the rug out from under her best friend. "But you know, as long as they're here, I was thinking . . . What if I told one of them—probably her—about a certain asshole we all know?"

Cole's expression of surprise would've been funny if the subject hadn't been so serious. Tasha Russell was, as ever, smarter than anyone around her gave her credit for being.

"I don't know," Cole managed to get out.

"You think it's a bad idea?" Tasha asked.

"No, it's worth considering." Maggie certainly understood where Cole was going with this plan. Ever since Tasha had shared what had happened during *Cosa Nostra*, Maggie had wondered about who else Vincent might have done that to. Who else might have experienced other shitty behavior from him. And what could be done about it.

A public accounting of Vincent's grossness wasn't much. But it wasn't nothing.

At least if it was what Tasha wanted.

"Agreed," Cole said. "I'm not saying you have to tell Libby, but she might hear about Vincent's visit."

Zoya hadn't made any kind of announcement about it. She hadn't said *Hey, don't talk to the press about that breakdown that we never explained or acknowledged in any way.* They were essentially relying on the discretion of the key crew members who'd been present, which was a lot to ask.

About that point, at least, Cole was right.

"So I might as well try to get ahead of the gossip?" Tasha's gaze swept over Ryan, Cole, and Maggie.

"I don't know how to answer that without sounding like I'm influencing you," Maggie offered so cautiously that she might as well have been edging onto a frozen pond a few weeks into the thaw. "Instead, I'll just say . . . the press helped me a lot in the last year. If my case hadn't blown up, if public opinion hadn't coalesced on my side, I never would've gotten my settlement." *I never would've gotten this job.* "I hated pretty much every minute of it, but it did help."

Tasha drained her mineral water. "Oh, thank you for that incredible insight. I've only been dealing with the press my entire fucking life, and I never realized that they might help you. How astonishing. How novel." She made a sour face and sighed deeply. When she spoke again, her tone had shifted. "I'm sorry. I know you were just answering my own damn question."

By this point, Maggie was so used to Tasha, she only laughed. "No, I totally deserved that. I'm zero percent surprised you thought of it before we could."

"Strategizing about the press is, like, what I do to decompress."

"You shouldn't talk to them unless you want to," Ryan gritted out, his first verbal contribution to this conversation.

"No one is saying she has to. We're just pointing out the obvious," Cole said.

A minute ticked by. The good part about a pub was that lulls in the conversation never truly felt like lulls because there was always the sweep of other people's conversations and laughter. The tink of glasses at the bar. The music on the televisions.

Finally, Tasha asked Cole, "Did she seem reasonable?"

She meaning Libby Hansen.

"She saw through my attempts at bullshit," Cole said. "She didn't ask ridiculous questions. She got personal a few times, but it was about the work. Not just, like, who I'm dating."

He's dating someone?!

"Not that I am," he added quickly, catching Maggie's eye while he said it, and she realized that her panic must have shown on her face.

Maggie wanted to crawl under the table. She'd thought she was keeping her feelings to herself, but apparently, that was just another piece of self-delusion. Awesome.

Luckily, Tasha was weighing this, and Ryan was entirely focused on the woman next to him, so they both missed Maggie apparently dropping her emotional cards on the table for everyone's inspection.

God, what must Cole *think* of Maggie? Other than her foolish outburst about jealousy, she'd been under the impression that she'd kept the rest of her crush to herself. It was mortifying to know she hadn't.

"Hmm," Tasha said. "I'm not going to pretend I haven't considered taking out every billboard in LA to scream the truth about him. But I'm famous, I'm a millionaire. Would anyone care if my life hasn't been all sunshine and roses?"

"Fuck yes," Ryan answered. "Because it's not just about you. This shit happens all the time. I worked on a show once where a PA told me the showrunner threw a binder at her. It cut her cheek open." His eyes suggested that, in his head, Ryan was reviewing a catalog of violent possibilities for holding Vincent accountable. "She was too scared to say anything about it."

"What did you do?" Cole asked.

"Quit." Ryan was absolutely matter of fact about it. "And I told the producer why. The guy's still working, so it didn't do any good." He looked at Tasha and shrugged. "I'm not trying to influence you. I dunno if that's a story about why to talk or why to shut your trap, but it's what I did."

That sat between them for a minute.

"After *Central Square* went off the air," Cole said, "there was one of those oral history articles, and I found out that the showrunner had been a major-league douche to all the women in the writer's room. I was young and stupid and had my head up my ass, so I hadn't known. But I should've, and I should've said something."

Maggie had never heard Cole talk about that before, but based on the man she knew now, she was certain that it haunted him.

"So I talk because I *can*?" Tasha asked in clarification. "Because I'm protected, relatively speaking, versus some peon?"

"Maybe."

Tasha toasted them with her cup. "Well, I'll think about it."

That put a damper on the night, though, and within ten minutes, Tasha left to go to bed.

When she was gone, Ryan got to his feet. "You two don't want me here."

Maggie didn't know if that was true. It helped having other people around, sometimes. Then she couldn't get confused, pretending that this had a date-like vibe when it clearly didn't. She needed the buffer to keep herself in the land of emotional rationality.

Ryan punched Cole on the shoulder and raised his brows. Cole shrugged back. It was some kind of secret language Maggie wasn't fluent in.

"Night, Ryan," she said as he offered a half wave. "What was that about?"

"Eh, he was paying me back for something I said a few months ago. Just an observation."

"About how he loves Tasha?" Maggie would've shoved the words back into her mouth if she could, but she was curious.

"Yup. Which everyone knows . . . except for Tasha."

"She knows too," Maggie said.

"You think?"

"Believe me when I say Tasha Russell of all people is aware when a man is in love with her."

"Then why is she jerking him around?"

"I don't think she is." If anything, Maggie suspected Tasha was mostly in love with Ryan too. She was different with him than she was with Cole. Tasha rarely met Ryan's eyes, but she looked for him in every room. Whatever the conversation, she was more invested in his attitude toward her than she was with anyone else. "But she's your friend. I wouldn't want to speculate. It isn't any of my business, anyhow." Maggie needed to change the subject. This was feeling more than a little like a confession. "We're more than halfway done with the filming. How are you feeling about it?"

"You never really know until you see it."

"Do you watch your own stuff?"

"Sometimes. Drew puts together highlight reels."

Oh right, his agent. Cole mentioned him often. "Well, I heard Zoya tell Libby you're doing the best work of your career. That people are going to feel as if they're seeing you for the first time."

"What do you expect her to say? She's not going to be like, 'Oh, Cole sucks. This season will be totally mediocre compared to season two.'"

"Oh my God, wasn't Callie White great as Lucy last season? That wedding banquet scene in the last episode—I was convinced she was going to kill everyone."

"Tasha told me that's what happens in the book."

"I'm sure that's how Tasha would've liked to play it. But I was glad Lucy got her happy ending." Zoya had been very clear that she saw the series as being romantic before it was anything else and that the main couples would always be happy.

Softly, Cole said, "Me too."

And there he was, watching her again like he had been when he'd been talking to Libby.

Earlier, she'd wanted to ask *What's your dream?* Now was the moment—but boundaries.

She'd kept it together this far, and there were only six weeks left to go on this shoot. So all she said was "Well, I should get to bed too."

Too bad she'd be alone.

Chapter 18

INT. COLE'S TRAILER

One Month Later

Do you need anything else from me?

Cole stared at the last text he'd sent Libby in the encrypted app she liked to use. After Tasha had decided to share everything with her, Libby had been working nonstop on her story about Vincent Minna as filming for season three of *Waverley* neared its end.

Cole and Libby had done several interviews by phone, but he'd also reached out to PAs he knew who'd worked for Vincent and had shared Libby's contact information with them. When he'd asked Tasha about her own conversations with Libby, she had given him vague updates like "The snake is in the henhouse" and "The sparrow flies at dawn." He had no idea if that meant they were about to nail the guy, if it was some kind of spy code, or if Tasha was messing with him.

Probably the last one.

But he hadn't been able to shake the sense that what he'd said to Maggie was true—he ought to have known about Vincent, and he should've done more to protect the people around him. The guilt was sharp enough, heavy enough, that it had obliterated the other issue. The Drew-wouldn't-like-it issue.

Cole was supposed to keep his hands clean and his public face cheerful and inoffensive. This wasn't a story in which Cole was directly involved. He hadn't witnessed the bad behavior, it hadn't been directed at him, and so it wasn't any of his business. He didn't even have to ask; he knew that was what Drew would say.

So . . . he hadn't asked.

When you messed up, and Cole *knew* he had messed up, it wasn't enough to say *Oops*. And the only way Cole knew to make this better was to get the facts out there, all the facts. The public could hold Vincent accountable, at the very least, and everyone would finally know what a monster he was.

So Cole had gone on the record with Libby, and he'd tried to alert other people Vincent might have hurt, who deserved to have their stories told as much as Tasha did. There simply wasn't another choice, even if this conflicted with Drew's code. When Libby's story broke, Cole hoped it would be clear to Drew why Cole had inserted himself into this mess. But, well, he knew he was right, so he couldn't worry about anything else.

Cole's phone chirped with a message from Libby: Nope! You gave me everything I needed. She included a heart eyes smiley face.

He didn't feel very smiley.

Are you sure? Because I'm still willing to cover a PI.

He'd made this offer earlier, and Libby had patiently explained this was not a divorce case in an old Hollywood movie, and journalists had ethical limitations that PIs didn't have. She needed to do the reporting herself, her way. That was the only way she could write about it.

These things came as news to him, but he'd also felt strangely deflated that he couldn't solve this problem with money. What was the point of having dough if he couldn't buy justice with it?

I am absolutely certain.

Part of the appeal of Drew's code, Cole was realizing, was that it had given him action items. *Career in the toilet? Just follow these five rules to turn things around!* Those rules had given him a sense of being able to *do* something at a time when he'd felt as if he had no capacity to move forward. But maybe they had just been a sugar pill for a hypochondriac. He had plenty to do on set, sure, but it felt a little silly when he set it against what Libby was doing right now. The situation made him feel so foolish.

That sinking fog of dread hadn't gone away when a knock sounded on his trailer door.

He opened it to find Maggie and an anxious-looking assistant from the art department.

"Hey, so I'm glad you're around," Maggie said in a singsong voice. "Do you happen to have any athletic tape? Especially of the peach or beige persuasion?"

He quickly scanned Maggie head to toe, but she seemed fine. "Did someone sprain an ankle? Isn't there a medic around?"

"No injury, no, but the medic only has black therapeutic tape, and, well, the baby's head fell off."

"I sincerely hope you mean the plastic baby doll"—which they were using for shots where the kid was in the background—"and not the real baby," who appeared in the close-ups. Trevor—he was a *very* cute kid.

"Yes, Cole, I'm hoping to tape a real baby's head back on," Maggie deadpanned.

The assistant held up the two pieces of the doll, and Cole had to bite his lip to stop from laughing. With its eyes rolling to the side like that and its limbs at unnatural angles, it was like something from a horror movie set.

"Oh no, Humpty Dumpty had a great fall," Cole said.

"I was thinking more guillotine."

"For Chucky here? Wait, you're getting me off topic. You thought I'd be able to fix this . . . why?"

"Because you know *everything*."

Even though Cole realized Maggie was saying it to sweet-talk him, damn if he didn't want to believe it.

In his defense, she had really pretty eyes.

"I saw you had your shoulder taped the other day," she explained more seriously. "And you and the baby have similar skin tones."

Maggie was right. Cole had overdone it during one of the sword-fighting scenes, and an old rotator cuff injury of his had flared up. It was yet another reminder that, well, he wasn't a kid anymore.

"Let me look around." He returned a minute later with the tape. "Here you go."

"Thank you," the prop guy gushed. "It was this or duct tape."

Hopefully once the doll was swaddled up, it wouldn't be too obvious. Cole wanted this show to be good—not campy.

Maggie watched the assistant, his murder baby doll, and Cole's tape leave. "I dunno, they could've stuck with the duct tape. It would've been very metal. Very teenage goth."

"How did you get on the case anyhow?" It wasn't as if props were her problem.

"Eh, he looked really panicked, so I asked what was up and suggested he could ask the medic. When that failed, I remembered your shoulder."

Cole had seen her do that several times now, check in with the cast and crew and troubleshoot problems. She was getting comfortable with her job, more confident about the flow and patter of the set.

It was a good look on her.

"There's probably a chain of command, and it doesn't involve the intimacy coordinator."

"I could help, so I did." She pointed to Cole's shoulder. "How are you feeling?"

Cole rolled his arm. "A little stiff," he admitted. "But I'll make it through."

"Just a couple weeks to go, and we'll be done."

They were in that mad dash to the end, full of small, jumbled scenes and bits. At this point, he had his nose pressed so far up against the glass, he'd entirely lost sight of the bigger picture.

But not of Maggie.

"Yup. Now that we've fixed the nightmare doll, I'm glad you stopped by. We're supposed to make our day at about five p.m."

"What a relief. These late nights are killing me."

"The last couple of weeks always feel like that. Do you have anything planned tonight?" This was probably the last night they'd have off until they wrapped, and at that point, he had to get back to Los Angeles. Back to his real life.

The thought was strangely unsatisfying.

She shrugged. "I'd like to say a long soak in the tub, a massive meal from room service, and a book, but honestly, I'll probably pass out at eight."

That pretty much described every night of his now. "What about a short detour first? Pick you up at seven thirty–ish?"

"Where are we going?"

"It's a surprise."

"If it's hiking, I'm going to be so pissed."

But he suspected she wouldn't be.

EXT. STREET IN FRONT OF THE HOTEL—NIGHT

"Where are we going?" Maggie asked as Cole led her to the waiting car.

"Telling you would ruin the surprise."

Phil opened the door of Cole's town car with a smile. "Ms. Niven."

"It's good to see you, Phil." Maggie slid across the back seat. "Are you going to make me wear a blindfold?"

"Would you?" Cole asked, with the kind of smile she could feel in her inner thighs.

Maggie shivered. "Maybe."

What a rank lie. What absolute evasive bullshit. If Cole asked, she'd do it in a heartbeat.

From the gleam in his eye, he knew it. "No, no blindfold. It's not as if we know where anything is in Glasgow, anyhow."

That was conveniently true. All she'd managed to see of the city was the path from the hotel to the studio. It was really a shame that she'd spent nearly four months in the UK and had experienced so little of it.

When Phil pulled away from the curb, with forced casualness Cole said, "So we're almost done."

"We're almost done," she echoed.

"Have you thought about next steps?"

It felt like that was all she did lately.

Maggie played with one of the buttons on her coat. "Another one of Bernard's protégés had to drop out of a project, a little indie coming-of-age story about a group of college students falling in and out of love with each other, called *The Mid List*. I think I'm going to take that. Filming starts in a month, so I have time to find a short-term apartment. It's a very different kind of production than this. It's shooting in LA, and it would make sense to spend some time there, to meet some people—oh God, I sound like such an industry cliché, don't I?"

"The next thing you know, you'll be complaining about temperatures below seventy degrees and traffic on the 405 and getting juice at Earthbar every day." Cole grinned, and then he turned his attention out the window. "But yeah, that sounds like a good move for you. I think you'd like LA."

He didn't look at her when he said that last part, for which she was grateful. This conversation was, like, 80 percent subtext, and she didn't think she understood everything that was happening under the surface here.

"After that . . . well, they offered me season four of *Waverley*." She still hadn't accepted, but it felt odd that she hadn't told Cole.

The truth was, she saw him almost every day. She'd catch him at the craft-services table in the morning, and he'd tease her about how much brown sugar she put in her oatmeal. They'd talk about the shoot or whatever she was reading. They'd compare Wordle solutions or what they'd watched on TV the night before. Sometimes, he'd chide her into going to H/MU with him, because those folks had the best music and the smartest jokes. Those hours with him were the best part of her day. The best part of . . . everything.

But they'd never talked about the future at all. It had been an endless stretch of present.

"They're already in preproduction?" Cole asked.

"Yup. It's such a big commitment, they want to nail people down."

He considered this. Then very, very carefully, he asked, "What did you say?"

"When I took this job, I was . . . desperate is a strong word, but let's say desperate. And running away from home for four months seemed awesome. I would've taken a mission to Mars if it had been on offer. But Bernard doesn't think I'm going to have trouble getting work after this, and there isn't much attention on me anymore. I mean, I've enjoyed Scotland, but I don't know if I want to be here for such a long time again."

In the front seat, Phil cleared his throat.

"Sorry, Phil!" she called out, her cheeks flaming because she'd forgotten that she and Cole had an audience for this conversation. A discreet audience, but even still. "Your country is gorgeous, but it's not *my* country. Being here doesn't feel like real life."

"That," Cole said, "is kind of the problem with making movies. Nothing ever feels real."

"Nothing?"

But before Cole could answer that, Phil parked. Where the heck were they?

Across a large dark lawn stood one of those Victorian greenhouses, all lacy white lead and shimmering glass, looking more like a Jell-O mold than a place where they kept plants.

"Wait, it's the botanical gardens," she said.

"Yup. Technically, it's closed tonight, but I may have pulled a few strings. It turns out the director is a big *Waverley* fan, and a signed poster is a sufficient bribe. Merrit arranged it for me."

Maggie was fairly certain Merrit could have successfully negotiated peace on the Korean peninsula.

"*GlasGLOW*," she read off the sign.

"It's all lit up. The exhibit's opening tomorrow, but we have some long days coming up. I wanted to make sure you didn't miss it."

Because Cole had remembered some offhand remark she'd made months ago—literally months ago—about how she wanted to come here.

Feeling as if she couldn't quite catch her breath, Maggie followed him out of the car. "This is . . . thank you."

"It's no big deal. Let's go see some plants."

Whatever Cole might say, it felt like a deal. It felt like a very big deal. It felt like an enormous, glowing deal that the astronauts were probably observing on the ISS.

A woman met them at the door, taking the signed poster gratefully from Cole. "You can go anywhere you'd like."

"Thanks. We'll try to be out in an hour."

"Take all the time you need." And then she winked.

Maggie wanted to say *Hey, nothing is happening here*, but it was very clear that something was happening. Something beautiful and life changing and a little scary.

Just inside the door of the plant palace rose a glass dome. Beneath it stood a palm tree at the center of a fishpond. The fronds of the palm were lit a minty green color, and the rest of the dome was awash in pink lights. It was very *Miami Heat* fabulous.

"Wow." Maggie craned over the white metal railing to peer into the pond. The scales of the koi flitting around the water caught the light, making them look like something out of a fairy tale.

"Why plants?" Cole asked.

"You mean why was a Victorian glasshouse at the top of my sight-seeing list? Well, during the pandemic I got really into houseplants."

Cole snickered.

"Yeah, I know. I'd always thought you had to be born with a green thumb, but with nothing else to do and all that stress, that was what I turned to. I've amassed quite a collection. My best friend back in Eugene is watching them for me while I'm here."

"LA's a good place for gardening. You know, if you move there."

With that, Cole dragged the future back in front of them, exactly like it had been there in the car. It was like a neon elephant in the room.

One with the word *if* flashing on its forehead.

And the problem was that Maggie's thoughts were happy to slip down the slide Cole was pointing to: If she took the job on the indie. If she moved to LA. If she told Cole how she'd come to feel about him. If . . . then . . .

Because when the production ended, there wouldn't be a reason not to. No reason not to kiss. No reason not to touch. No reason not to be together.

Except for how they had met.

For some things, the statute of limitations never ran out. This was one of them.

Her breath uneven and her palms clammy, Maggie pointed into the water and changed the subject. "Did you ever keep a goldfish?" There, that helped. Nothing was as boring as goldfish. There was noth-ing tempting about goldfish.

After a beat, Cole went along with it. "Nope, never. My mom's always loved cats, and so that seemed like a recipe for disaster."

"I just realized I don't know much about your childhood." Maggie felt as if they knew each other very well—she'd spent hours with the man while he was practically naked—but they'd been so focused on the job in front of them. They talked all the time, but maybe those conversations had just been small talk. Verbal rice cakes that didn't convey much information or have many calories.

"Eh, there's not much to know," he said as they left the pond and walked through a curtain of vertical twinkle lights, all purple and white and starry. "I grew up in SoCal, and I had a pretty typical nineties childhood."

"I'm picturing surfing, skateboarding, burritos, and famous people."

"That's not far off—except for the famous people."

"Your parents aren't actors?" While she'd read a lot about how Tasha was a nepo baby, she hadn't seen the same coverage of Cole. Maybe she'd missed something.

"Dad manages a hardware store, and Mom's a nurse. I sort of accidentally started doing commercials. My parents weren't pushy about it at all. The truth is I wasn't a good enough athlete to try for a scholarship, and college wasn't that interesting to me. But in high school, I got bitten by the acting bug, and the next thing I knew, I was on *Central Square*."

"And the rest was history."

Cole grimaced. "Yeah, well, you know how *that* worked out."

They stopped in front of a statue of a woman, probably some mythological goddess. She was kneeling on a pedestal, looking a bit distressed about the tropical foliage surrounding her. The lights in this room were various shades of blue. Like if Picasso had temporarily detoured into garden design.

"You played an iconic role and started a career you're still rocking?" Maggie asked.

"That is the absolutely nicest possible way to sum up the last two decades of my life."

"I'm an extremely nice person."

"That you are. No, the thing is . . . I messed up in so many ways, and I feel like I'm still trying to make up for it. People on the set of *Central Square* got hurt because I was too busy being the life of the party to notice." Cole walked away from her as he said it, which should've given his words some lightness, but months of knowing the man had her familiar with this play.

"What does that look like to you?" Maggie asked, following him down the path. "When are you done atoning for some childish mistakes?"

Cole gave her a sideways look. "Are any of us?"

"Isn't that existential?"

She'd been half joking, but he was entirely in earnest. "Humans—we hurt each other in lots of ways. Maybe we *all* need to atone more."

Maggie shouldn't push this. Her interest wasn't about doing her job, and it wasn't about being his friend. She cared because she was in love with him—and trawling these waters with him, it announced it. But he was in such obvious pain, she couldn't let it be. And if they were going to have this conversation, she wanted to see Cole's face.

She stopped and leaned her hip against one of the benches ringing the greenhouse. Because he was polite, he froze and turned toward her. In the indigo light, she couldn't make out his exact expression, but his posture was tight.

"If you're always feeling like you have to make amends for what you did in the past, I wonder where you have the space to just . . . be. I care about living a life that makes a difference, Cole. I care about how my choices affect other people, so I'm not saying that you're wrong. I just wonder how you find the balance. When you stop beating yourself up."

He worked his jaw for a second. "Are you saying I'm too hard on myself?"

"Yes. Maybe."

Cole scrubbed his hands over his face. When he dropped them and spoke, real passion spiked through his words. "I could tell you the same. You go through this intense thing, losing your job for the dumbest possible reason, and then you turn around and remake yourself into this. And you're incredible at it. It's the job you were meant to do. But you still worry if you're making enough of a difference in the world. What is *that*?"

When she said "Well, you got me there," she expected him to laugh. She expected that it would right this conversation, get them back into the light, slightly flirty space that she and Cole generally occupied.

But whether it was because he was tired or if it was the relative darkness, Cole wouldn't budge. "I'm serious: What is that, Maggie? Where does that come from?"

Maggie tipped her chin back and watched the lights playing over the glass dome for a minute before she responded. "My parents . . . my mom ran a food bank," she explained. "And then she ran a statewide network of food banks, and now she works at the UNFAO. She's literally feeding the fucking world. Meanwhile, my dad's a doctor who's spent most of his life in field hospitals, real Doctors Without Borders stuff. Whatever you think about me, believe me, they make me look like a corporate raider. Like one of those guys from *The Wolf of Wall Street* or something. Don't get me wrong, they supported my interest in theatre. They never missed a dance recital or a play, or—okay, my mom didn't. Dad did, but . . . I know I'm lucky. It's just I also know they find me a little disappointing." She looked Cole right in the eye, as if to say *Happy?*

Obviously he wasn't. "Nothing about you is—I can't even say it. You are a miracle, Maggie Niven."

She wasn't feeling like a miracle. She was feeling vaguely pissed. She'd wanted to have a night off. She'd wanted to hang out with her friend. She had no idea why he was pushing her like this. "The lawsuit is about the only time they've ever been proud of me, and it was also the worst thing I've ever been through."

Cole took a step toward her. Then another. Much more softly, he said, "That sounds terrible."

"It was. It is. They are not psyched about this job. If I'd moved into, I dunno, some kind of nonprofit, bringing theatre to underserved urban or rural communities, that would've been cool. Hollywood intimacy coordinator? Not so much."

"You realize that everyone else on earth thinks the opposite."

"But I'm not the child of anyone else on earth. Look, you asked where that comes from, and that's where it comes from. And the worst part is *they're right*. Like, what kind of an ass would I be if I were like, 'No, I don't want to make a difference. I don't want to improve the world'? Of course I should want those things! Of course I should do those things!" She hadn't realized she'd been shouting until she'd stopped and her petulant words were still bouncing around the space.

Oops.

Cole didn't seem taken aback, though. He simply mirrored her posture, leaning his hip against the bench across from her. "I'm just an actor, and my work improves no one's life, so take this with a grain of salt. But maybe it doesn't have to be one or the other."

"Huh, I'd find that a little more convincing if you seemed to believe it."

"I will if you will."

"You really mean that, don't you?"

"I wouldn't say it if I didn't."

He was *such* a good guy.

She closed her eyes and took and released a long breath. "I'll consider it," she said primly.

Two of Cole's fingers settled lightly onto the back of Maggie's hand. It was the most impersonal of touches, not even a caress. It was simply two tiny points of heat and pressure. A handshake was more intimate. But those fingerprints on her skin were a rabbit hole, pulling Maggie down into the earth. Into some alien world where all the things she'd ever imagined about him were possible. Where she wasn't the only one who'd imagined them.

Maggie didn't trust herself to open her eyes. She didn't want to see him touching her.

That was a lie. She absolutely did.

"Maggie." Cole's voice was so soft, he might as well have thought her name.

"Cole." Her answering whisper made her lips tingle.

Slowly, very slowly, he dragged his fingers down the back of her hand. "I think about you, about this—"

Whatever he was about to say, his voice cracked. And it was a good thing, too, because Maggie needed to catch her breath.

He'd done *what*? The surprise was so acute, she almost doubled over.

Her eyes did spring open, and the way he was watching her—the undisguised longing, the hunger—it had her snatching her hand to her chest and stumbling back.

She wanted those things so badly, but she couldn't have them. "I can't. Cole, I *can't*."

She couldn't . . . what? She wanted to go back and figure out what precisely he meant, to hear the full description and all the various options. But she couldn't risk it. She couldn't stand alone with this man in the semidarkness. That was impossible.

"This job—it's the only chance I'm ever going to get."

"Yeah, I understand that." He said it patiently because he was fucking perfect. "But we're almost done, and—"

"Almost." She brandished the word like someone might a weapon. It was unspeakably important that she be seen as having standards. As being a professional. And nothing that could possibly come after *"I think about you, about this"* was professional.

"Okay. But when *Waverley* is done, we're having this conversation. I promise you that."

Sparks—much brighter, much more twinkly than the lights ringing the greenhouse—went off inside her. So Maggie did the only thing she could: she dumped a bucket of water on them. "I can't have a relationship with someone I've worked with."

"I'm not going to argue with you."

It shouldn't have stung so badly, since it was what she wanted. Her position, while necessary and professional and a dozen other good things, was akin to licking the bottom of one's shoe in many other ways.

Maggie turned from Cole then, needing the break from his eyes, which saw too much. "Do you like Venus flytraps?" she asked, pointing to the sign that indicated the carnivorous plants were in the next room.

"Do you think they bring in flies for them?"

"Probably."

As they went to see the insect-eating plants and then the desert plants, they tried to make small talk, actual small talk. It was nice, because being with Cole was always nice, but it was also as frustrating as heck.

Everything Maggie had come to want was there, and she couldn't take it.

An hour later, when they'd seen the entire garden and said goodbye to the staffer, they walked out into the shadowy night. Against the darkness, the glasshouse glowed pink, like some wild, magical castle in a five-year-old's drawing.

"I love it so much," Maggie said. "It's so over the top."

"Why don't they build them like that anymore?"

"It's such a crime, right? Listen . . ." Maggie wanted to touch him. To set her hand on his forearm, hug him, or even press her mouth to his cheek. But she couldn't. It wouldn't send the right signal, and if nothing else, it would confuse her own heart, which was still mighty disappointed she'd said no. "This was a lot to arrange, for you and for Merrit, and I'm just so . . . flattered and overwhelmed that you remembered I wanted to do this."

"I remember everything you say to me."

"Thank you for going to all this trouble, Cole."

"You're welcome, Maggie."

And as they met Phil and drove back to the hotel, Maggie tried to convince herself that the glow of this evening was enough for her.

Chapter 19

INT. HOTEL BALLROOM—NIGHT

Two Weeks Later

Zoya stood just inside the entrance to the party in a black column dress, chugging from a full bottle of champagne.

"I see you all got started without me," Cole said as he walked in.

"Cole!" She flung her empty arm around his waist and pressed her cheek to his shoulder. "Glad you could make it! Congratulations!"

He could hear the exclamation points in her voice. She was already hammered—which, fair. She'd worked harder than anyone else over the last four months, and her drudgery was only beginning. Cole hoped she had one heck of a breather planned before postproduction.

The last couple of weeks of principal photography for *Waverley* had been about what Cole imagined mud wrestling in August would be like, with the mud getting thick and stodgy and the grapplers more and more exhausted. They weren't at the mercy of the weather in the studio, so there hadn't been any interruptions. It had seemed like Zoya found entirely new pockets of time—early midmorning before your second coffee, and after the dinner break but not quite night—and they filmed around the clock. Shot by shot, they'd gotten what she needed, and they'd finished just after lunch this afternoon.

"Thanks." He rubbed her back. "You too."

She released him and took another swig from her bottle. "It's the best work of your career, you know."

He really wanted to believe that, but he didn't. He couldn't. It felt almost too scary to think his *attempt* at getting his career off the ground again was over, and he wouldn't know if it had worked until the show debuted.

He shrugged and tried to play it off. "You have to say that."

"I do not. Take Dale. This was *not* the best work of his career. He was kind of crap, actually. We'll cut as much of him out in editing as possible and blame the studio."

"Champagne is like truth serum for you. Good to know."

"Oops." But Zoya didn't seem particularly regretful.

"Your secret—well, *secrets*—are safe with me."

"Yeah, don't tell Dale. It's true, but it's kind of bitchy. From you, though"—she kissed her fingertips—"amazing. Everyone's going to have so much fun watching you fall."

This felt like tempting fate, and he'd always been a little superstitious.

"Well, I couldn't have done it without you." That was vague enough to say safely . . . he hoped. "Thank you for believing in me. For giving me this chance." Cole signaled to Esme, who was leaning against the wall, casually keeping one eye on her boss. "She's going to need a minder. And maybe don't let her near Dale."

Zoya said, "Pfft," and took another swig of champagne.

"On it," Esme assured him.

"Have you seen Maggie?"

The assistant tipped her head knowingly. "Not yet."

Now that filming was over, in the tiny window before he had to get back to LA, Cole had only one thought: Maggie.

She hadn't been on set today, as there had been no intimacy in the final day's sides, but she'd promised him she would be at the wrap party. His entire plan for the evening involved finding her and getting out the words that he'd tried to say at the botanical gardens: he was wild about her.

The timing was crap. Cole didn't need to be jumping into a relationship right as his career comeback finally hit—assuming that it hit. But this had gone from something he'd thought *Huh, maybe* about to being the only thing in his life he knew with 100 percent certainty.

He was in love with Maggie Niven.

There wasn't any way he couldn't not tell her. And since she'd almost moaned when he'd grazed the back of her hand at the greenhouse, he was pretty sure she felt the same way.

So despite the bad timing, he had to come clean. Falling this hard, this completely, for someone this perfect didn't happen every day. In Cole's life, it had *never* happened. It was unique. She was unique. That surely outweighed something as trivial as how and when they'd met.

Cole made the rounds: shaking hands, distributing good words, and taking selfies. And when he'd begun to worry Maggie was going to stand him up, he finally spied her, chatting with Ryan by the snack table. The tension in his shoulders eased, and he knew he was smiling like a loon as he wove across the room.

Not trusting himself to touch Maggie, he greeted the stunt coordinator first, bumping Ryan's fist with his. "Hey, man. You don't usually hit these things."

Ryan was all about the job and tended not to mix with the talent and crew much, unless—

"I see you're here too." Tasha's expression was pure boredom, as if she wasn't glad to be done and didn't care about any of this. She held a glass of white wine loosely in one hand. If she'd paired it with a cigarette in the other, she would've been ready to play a jaded socialite.

"Gotta celebrate." *He*, at least, was feeling festive, now that he'd found Maggie.

"Do we, though?"

Cole didn't answer that. He just locked eyes with Maggie. He'd gotten used to her typical outfit: jeans and a clingy sweater with practical shoes. Very little jewelry or makeup, and with her hair held out of her eyes with a few bobby pins. He was a *huge* fan of her typical outfit.

But tonight's black cocktail dress, with its deep V neckline? The high-heeled shoes? The smear of pink lipstick? The sparkle around the base of her throat? Yeah, he liked those too. Liked them a hell of a lot.

Maggie met his gaze and gave a little shrug, as if she was embarrassed by her effort and embarrassed by his staring. He couldn't help it. She was the prettiest woman in the room.

"Maggie." His voice was full of grit, like shoes after walking on the beach.

"Cole." She took an awkward step toward him, her hand extended as if she wanted to shake.

But that felt *wrong*. Too formal.

Instead, he set his hand on her waist, so lightly he couldn't feel her body under her dress. That was too intimate. Too far. But the fabric was warm and made him dizzy, and that was enough.

Maggie tipped her chin back to meet his eyes. The fear, the hope, the anxiety, the longing that were shining there: beat for beat, the same emotions were pinging around his chest.

You're not alone in this, sweetheart.

Holding himself in check, Cole brushed his lips over her temple, and she sighed. If they weren't at this party, if they didn't have an audience—but they did. So after one more second, Cole released her and stepped back.

She looked as dazed as he felt. "How was the, um, last day?" she managed to ask.

"Fine. Kind of anticlimactic, if I'm being honest. I can't believe it's over."

"You did such good work." Maggie gave herself a shake and forced herself to face Ryan and Tasha. "*All* of you did. I'm in awe."

"My contributions made the show," Ryan deadpanned.

"Hey, Tasha did some wonderful riding"—the woman in question choked on her wine at Maggie's unintentional double entendre—"and

Cole told me the sword fighting was awesome. And you didn't kill Dale during the execution scene, so you pretty much did."

"And *you*," Ryan said, "slayed your first solo job as an IC."

"The junior IC," Maggie corrected.

Ryan wasn't convinced by this at all. "The senior one was where, exactly? You did all the work."

"Hey, he was recovering from a broken leg, and he did help."

Cole knew that she had emailed, texted, and talked to Bernard almost every day.

"Uh-huh. Welcome to life as a Hollywood assistant." Ryan took another pull from his beer. "Take the compliment, and when the reviews come out, remember it's your work they like."

Maggie, ever humble, waved this off. "We'll see what the critics say."

"Oh, no, fuck the critics," Tasha scoffed.

"Take the compliment, Niven. You were awesome," Cole agreed.

And that was when all hell broke loose in the form of Beth Russell and Vincent Minna, strolling arm and arm into the ballroom.

Rage flamed in Cole's gut, faster and hotter than when you dumped an entire container of charcoal starter on the barbeque. But as he tried to shield Tasha from those assholes and to catch Ryan's eyes so they could go do something about this situation, she pushed him aside.

The first time Vincent had appeared somewhere he shouldn't have been, Tasha had shattered like an egg dropped from a second-story window onto a concrete patio. But now, she drew herself up and shot through the air, elegant and deadly as a thrown dagger.

It was much better to see her in weapon mode than cowering.

With his soldier's reflexes, Ryan was on Tasha's heels, with Cole and Maggie right behind.

"What the fuck, Mom," Tasha said. "What are you doing here?"

Cole shouldered Ryan to the side so they could form a wall of backup together. He wanted Vincent to understand that whatever he might try to do to Tasha, he was going to have to do it to Cole and Ryan too.

Over Tasha, he could see her mother. The resemblance between mother and daughter—both blonde; both blue eyed; both with lithe, sporty figures—was powerful. So much so, it almost stung.

Despite having several decades on her kid, Beth Russell was still beautiful. Tonight, with her hair piled up on her head in her signature America's-sex kitten style and a white sequin-spangled dress, she was the embodiment of a MILF. But Cole knew her, and that shattered the illusion. The woman was poison.

"We're here to celebrate your accomplishment," Beth said, her voice smooth and innocuous, as if Tasha's question didn't make sense. "Yours and Vincent's."

Next to Beth, Vincent was smiling as if the crowd were happy to see him. The guy was a decent actor, given that Ryan looked feral and everyone else was stony faced.

"Vincent didn't do shit," Tasha said. "Actually—he did *lots* of shit. But it isn't worth celebrating. You need to go."

"Yes." Zoya had handed her bottle of champagne off to someone, and she was in full showrunner mode. "This is a closed party."

"Paid for by the production, and I am the production," Vincent said.

"Let's talk about it out in the hall—"

But Tasha interrupted Zoya's attempt to end this quietly. Looking Vincent directly in the eye, she spit out, "Don't you realize you're the shit in the punch bowl? You're so used to being the most powerful man in the room, you can't see how things have changed. You don't have the same kind of clout you once did. You're not on top anymore. Without the constant string of hits and new Oscars every year, you're just a creepy, decaying producer, like dozens of others in Holmby Hills. You can't smother all the whispers, not with social media. It isn't like in the old days, when the magazines and the papers didn't want to risk pissing you off. Those whispers are a gathering storm, and you know it.

That's why you're scared under that suit. So get out—and while you're running, know I'm done being quiet."

Vincent *did* look scared, and while Tasha talked, his complexion got greener. Everything Tasha was saying? He knew it was true.

But Beth Russell didn't seem to understand, or she was better at bluffing. When Tasha finished, she scoffed. "Can you believe I raised such an ungrateful child?"

Tasha shot her mother a lethal glare. "I can't even look at you. Him? Him I get. I mean, he's evil, but I understand. He thought he could get away with it. The way you served me up on a platter for him, though? That's unforgivable."

"And we're done." Zoya stepped in between Tasha and her mother and signaled to security. "Vincent, Beth, please leave."

The security guys began to approach, but Vincent clearly understood that he'd lost this battle, if not the war, and he tugged Beth along with him toward the door. As he went, he made a hand motion of curt dismissal to Tasha, to Zoya, to the room. But the gesture only seemed pathetic, because he was the one leaving. He was the pimply kid at the door of the club, screaming that he hadn't wanted to go anyhow when they wouldn't let him in.

When the door closed behind the monsters, Zoya melted away, conferring with Esme, probably to figure out the security situation and to get herself another big bottle of champagne. This left the little knot of Cole, Maggie, Tasha, and Ryan alone again.

"Do you want me to take care of that?" Cole gestured toward the door. "Or I could back Ryan up while he takes care of it?"

Actually, letting him take the lead seemed like a better idea. Ryan looked as if he was about to explode.

Tasha set a hand on Ryan's arm. The message was clear: *You are not, under any circumstances, allowed to follow the predator.*

"No, it's okay," she said to both of them. "You'd just get sent to jail."

"It'd be worth it." Besides, Cole had an excellent lawyer on speed dial, a relic from his younger and more irresponsible days. The guy could earn his retainer.

"Trust me, he's definitely not worth it."

As hard as it was, Cole needed to respect her wishes. Being the bigger person sucked sometimes.

He knew Tasha would want him to keep things light, so Cole said, "You were really impressive. This chapter in your memoir is going to be amazing."

Ryan, though, wasn't able to make a joke. His voice was gruff when he asked, "You okay?"

Tasha looked between them. She took a deep breath, released it, and then drained her glass of wine. "I'm actually fine. Good, even. Now it's a party."

At this declaration, Cole had to laugh. "That's all it takes? A solid-to-excellent brush-off?"

"Not all." She set her glass on one of the tiny tables ringing the room. Then she flung her arms around Ryan's neck and planted her mouth on his.

The stuntman rocked back on his heels, but then he got with the program and set about kissing Tasha back. Really, really kissing Tasha back.

Cole locked eyes with Maggie. Her smile was wry . . . and maybe a little bit jealous.

If that's what she wanted, he'd be more than happy to oblige.

But before he could raise his brows in a question, Tasha broke from the kiss and asked Ryan, "Do you want to get out of here?"

"Hell yes."

Taking Ryan's hand, Tasha gave Cole a brief glance. "Make my apologies to Zoya."

"Will do."

For Cole's ears only, Ryan said, "I'll take care of her."

"I know you will."

After tonight, Cole hoped that the job would belong permanently to Ryan. Cole would always be there for Tasha, but he'd happily take the demotion if it meant she finally had a partner who was worthy of her.

They left, and Maggie turned to take in the rest of the party. Conversations were getting started again, but everyone was still agog, staring at the space where Tasha, Vincent, and Beth had been a few minutes before. It was going to be *extremely* hard to keep a lid on this. Libby was going to have to get her story finished soon if she wanted to break the news about Vincent.

And the cat had not just escaped the bag on the Tasha-and-Ryan stuff—it had vaporized the bag for good measure. Everyone on earth was going to know they were together by tomorrow. But he suspected Tasha had been aware of that when she'd kissed Ryan. No one was more aware of being watched at all times than Tasha.

"I honestly can't believe that happened," Maggie said. "I can't believe Vincent had the nerve to show up here. And with her own mother? Horrific."

Since Cole had previously met both Vincent Minna and Beth Russell, he was less surprised. "Beth Russell is one of the most selfish human beings on earth. And Vincent Minna? He might not even be human." But Cole didn't want to talk about them, not right now. "I'm going to check with Zoya, make sure she has everything under control, and then I'm going to head out."

He probably ought to chat with some more folks and distribute more thanks, but after that scene, any possibility of having a normal night had vanished. All anyone was going to want to talk about was Tasha, and Cole had no intention of gossiping about his best friend.

The only conversation he wanted to have was with Maggie.

She looked wistful. "Sure. Of course. It's been a long four months."

"Ride back with me."

Okay, so he hadn't been as direct as Tasha with Ryan. He hadn't kissed Maggie, but that was mostly because when he finally got his hands and his mouth on her, he wasn't going to take them off for a long,

long time. And while Tasha might be ready to take things with Ryan public, he doubted Maggie was.

Maggie watched him, weighing what he was offering. They both knew it wouldn't be just a car ride if she said yes.

After what felt like an eternity, she whispered, "Sure."

At that, Cole could breathe again. "Give me two minutes."

Cole touched base with Zoya and Esme, and once he was certain they were good, he headed to a side door. He locked eyes with Maggie and tipped his head. Maggie had said she couldn't get involved with someone she was working with. He didn't want to cross that boundary by leading her out of the party by the hand. Not until she was ready for that.

Maggie met him in the dark, quiet hallway a minute later.

"I texted Phil. He'll meet us out back."

They didn't talk while they waited in the alley. What kind of small talk could they have made? The words they needed to say to each other, they weren't light.

When the town car arrived, Cole opened the door for Maggie, and inside, he pushed the button to put up the divider between Phil and them. With the tinting on the windows, it felt as if they were in their own private bubble.

Maggie looked at him quizzically. "Another secret?"

"Kinda. I wanted to ask you a question."

"Shoot."

If she'd said "Action," it would have been better because he would have had a script for this. Would have known the ending. He was all alone here, hopeful but not certain.

"In the last few months, we've gotten to know each other pretty well. And there have been times when I . . . that is, we're friends?"

"Yes?" She seemed confused, probably because he'd made it into a question.

"You're amazing. You're smart and hardworking, and you make everyone around you better. The entire production is better because of you. But it's not just about the work. It's really not about the work at all. Because I like hiking with you, and relaxing after a long day with you, and taping props back together *with you*. These last few months, you've been . . . everything to me. And sometimes I look at you, and it's like there isn't enough air. And I—I think we might not only be friends."

"We're coworkers?"

Maybe she didn't understand what he was saying—which would be fair; his words were pretty incoherent—or maybe she was deliberately pretending she didn't understand because she didn't feel the same way.

But he was in this now. He had to finish it. "Were. We *were* coworkers."

"Because my contract expired at five p.m."

"Yeah."

Maggie licked her lips. Most of her lipstick was gone, but they were still stained berry. It took every bit of restraint he had not to lunge for them.

"Some days," he finally managed to get out, "kissing you is the only thing I want to do. Filming, eating, getting in my reps—none of those things matter. I just want to kiss you."

A pause. An endless, endless pause. Then, "*Cole.*"

He could've slurped the relief down like ice water after a marathon. "Tell me I'm not imagining this." Because as inevitable, as obvious, as *right* as this felt to him, he didn't know what Maggie wanted.

He knew that at the end of a long day, she wanted french fries and thought it was a tragedy that you couldn't find proper seasoned fries in the UK. He knew her Wordle starting word (*READY*), and her favorite indie band of the aughts (Stars). He knew she was smart and strong and sarcastic but that it hid her soft heart. He knew her in every way you came to know someone when you worked hard, stressful hours making television together.

But despite all those details, he didn't know if she wanted him enough to overcome her doubts—her reasonable doubts—about how they'd met.

She was playing with the hem of her skirt and not giving him her eyes. "You aren't. But . . ."

"Let's go back to 'You aren't.' I liked that better."

Her gaze shot up to his, amusement lighting her expression. "You couldn't have thought it was all in your head."

"I did. So tell me." He didn't normally feel this needy. But because it was Maggie, because he was in so deep, he wanted the words. The assurance that her heart got as tripped up as his did when they were together.

"When we met, I thought you were sweet. Impossibly sweet, especially because you're so hot. I couldn't figure out how you could exist in this industry. But now I know, it isn't an accident. You made yourself this way because it was the best and most honest way to be. Because of whatever mistakes you think you made when you were young, you made yourself better. And I think that's why I find you so hard to resist. Your goodness is intentional. It comes from discipline and values. When I see you working so hard to make sure Rhiannon keeps herself safe and Tasha is protected, you make me want to be better at my job. To be more . . . fierce."

Thank God it was dark, because he was smiling like a loon. "You can't resist me?"

"I *should*. Because this won't be easy, Cole. I see the way you're looking at me—"

"Like I adore you?"

"Yes. Like if I were to crawl into your lap right now, it would all work out."

"It will." He simply couldn't believe that something that felt this good with someone who was this good could be wrong.

For years, after the mess that was his days on *Central Square*, Cole had distrusted his feelings. When you were selfish and good at rationalizing, you could do some dumb and destructive stuff, thinking it was okay. But he'd thought this one through, from front to back, and he couldn't see how it hurt anyone. The production was over, and he and Maggie weren't going to work together again. This wasn't anyone's business but theirs. The only risk was to their hearts, and he was going to treat hers like gold.

So Cole let the strength of his feelings leak into his voice. "Let's make it simple. This is about us, Maggie, you and me. You either want that, or you don't."

"And if I do?"

"Then come kiss me."

Her hands were shaking when she unbuckled her seat belt, but that tiny act of assent was all he could take. Cole pulled her across the back seat and into his lap.

The lights of the city streaked passed the window, painting white and yellow light over her face. Over her cheekbones and the slope of her nose. Over the accent marks of her eyebrows and the line of her chin.

Carefully, she rested one hand across his nape, her fingertips shifting into his hair. He pushed into the contact. She was touching him, intimately, on purpose. Finally, finally touching him.

The car went around a corner, and her nose grazed his. A streetlight lit every ridge of her irises, every curl of her lashes—and he wanted to drink them all in.

At least after he got to taste her.

"Sometimes," he whispered, "I think you're the only one who sees the real me. Not whoever I'm playing. Not whatever mistakes I made in the past. But me, the way I am now."

"You hide in plain sight, wearing a Cody Rhodes costume," she agreed.

"And you strip it off." Hopefully literally.

"All I can see is you. Even on set, it got to where I couldn't see your performance. Only you."

"You see me, and you still want me?" It was scary, being seen for himself without any buffer. But he would learn to live with it, if he got Maggie in the bargain.

"Of course I do." She resettled, bringing her mouth closer, but she still hadn't crossed those final millimeters.

Patience. He needed patience here. Cole ran his hands over her thighs, the curve of her hip, the dip of her waist. All PG-13 touches, but because it was with her, nothing had ever been hotter.

"Can we really make this work?" she asked.

"Yes."

"No doubt about it?"

"None. It's us." If he wasn't breathless and aroused and anticipating, he'd say it better. Say that he knew it wouldn't be easy, but it would be worth it. But he'd already come damn close to begging here, and ultimately, the end point would be the same.

When he kissed Maggie, he wouldn't be hoping that maybe she'd be the one. He'd *know* she was. And that made whatever speed bumps lay ahead worth it.

A beat passed. Another.

Then very softly, she said, "Okay."

The first touch of her lips to his was like falling asleep in the sun. Every cell of his body went heavy and warm.

She moved her mouth over his slowly, like a surveyor wanting to understand every inch of the topography. Her kiss was careful, so gentle his eyes watered behind his lids.

Being known was . . . intense.

Maggie parted her lips and clung to the corner of his mouth, breathing hard. But now that the starting bell had sounded, he was in this.

He threaded his hands into her hair—so soft—and kissed her. His efforts were clumsy in comparison to hers. Plodding and clumsy and . . . wet. The next time they did this, he'd be better. More restrained.

Except Maggie didn't seem to mind. She matched him stroke for stroke. Moan for moan.

Cole got bolder then, exploring the curve of her ass, the swell of her breast. She pressed herself into his lap—because the same hunger that

Emma Barry

was gnawing in him was in her. His body was hard, straining. Revved up by this, but not satisfied by it. Not by a long shot.

A sharp corner had Maggie shifting on his lap, but he hadn't taken off his seat belt, so he stayed in his seat. He sunk his fingers on her to keep her anchored.

Maggie tipped her chin back with a gasp, and he set about kissing her neck, her collarbone. All the parts of her that he'd watched so many times and wanted to kiss. Now he had, and it was better than he'd dreamed.

"Should I, um, go back to my seat?"

"Nope." He ran his hand down her stomach and over the juncture of her thighs.

She twisted against him like a live wire. *"Cole."* It was a plea, it was a warning, and it was almost desperate.

But they weren't alone.

Cole lifted his hand from her body and his mouth from her shoulder. "Will you spend the night with me?" He was asking a lot more than that, a hell of a lot more. And Cole knew that Maggie understood.

Silence.

Then, unsteadily, she answered, "Y-yes."

Chapter 20

INT. COLE'S HOTEL ROOM—NIGHT

Cole hadn't even asked "My room or yours." He simply led Maggie to his suite.

When he opened the door, it was all Maggie could do not to gasp. Her own hotel room was nice, but it could've fit inside his suite's living room twice. In the next room, the streetlight coming in through the windows outlined the bed. It looked massive. Monumental. As if it should have been a stop on the hop-on, hop-off bus for tourists.

It was a bed that carried *expectations*.

Now that they'd made out like teenagers in his town car, Cole's movements were confident. Feline. The way he moved, the roll of his shoulders, the cock of his hips: it was the most goddamned erotic thing she'd ever seen.

He unfurled himself on the couch. Just poured his body over it, draping one arm along the back of it. "I want to make love to you."

"I, um, suspected as much." Honestly, if she hadn't been acutely aware of Phil in the front seat of the town car, Maggie would've ravished Cole already. She'd known they'd had chemistry, but that kiss had been—wow. She'd had entire sexual relationships lasting months or years that had left her less hot and bothered than that single car ride.

"Good. So what gets you off?" The way Cole was watching her was probably illegal in several countries. It was definitely a fire hazard.

Maggie couldn't make herself sit down. First, there was the problem of where. On the couch next to him? There was no way. She was still recovering from the kiss. Honestly, she wasn't certain her knees could bend any more. Every cell in her body was still squealing as if she were a personified exclamation point.

She squeezed her thighs together. Nope, that wasn't enough. Not enough pressure, not enough contact, and not where she needed it.

"You're blocking this scene in your head?" she joked.

"I've been doing that for the last few months."

Smoke should be pouring from her ears like in an old cartoon. What was she going to say to that? That she hadn't been doing the same thing? She didn't want to lie to him. She wasn't sure she could.

"So you want my sexual history? To know about my fantasies?"

"The second one, yeah."

Maggie fought an impulse to look away. "I haven't . . . done this in a while. Like a year and a half." She omitted the vibrator that was in her suitcase. Nothing helped insomnia like a good orgasm or two. "But since I got to the UK, my fantasy has been . . . you."

Cole's eyes blazed. Realistically, Maggie knew that was ridiculous. That a bonfire had *not*, in fact, flared in his eyes. But in that moment, she would have sworn that it had.

Yeah, whoa, he liked that.

"I understand. Like, exactly. So in the bedroom, what gets you there?"

"It isn't always penetration," Maggie admitted, her voice feeling gawky.

It was hard to believe that she'd spent the last seven months learning to be an intimacy coordinator and having no-holds-barred conversations about sexual positions and pleasure and freaking pubic beards with strangers while choreographing and helping to film some pretty steamy on-screen sex. But this felt utterly different. It wasn't for a scene.

It wasn't for work. It wasn't about characters. It was real. And she was going to do it.

She was going to do it *with Cole*.

Maggie had always been better at directing than she had been at acting because she was extremely self-conscious. Was it possible to get stage fright before sex? Because that seemed like the only explanation for her nerves.

Right, she had to keep talking. "I mean, so unless there's been *a lot* of foreplay, mostly, I come from . . . rubbing."

"Like oral sex?" He licked his lips.

It took a second for Maggie to be able to answer. The thought of Cole's face between her legs had her feeling messy, breathless. "Sometimes. But, um, nipple play and dry humping. That usually gets the job done." At this point, it wasn't going to take much at all.

Cole half sat up. "Do you not like penetration?"

For maybe the first time in her life, Maggie knew that if she said no, this partner would respect that absolutely. "No, I do. At least—I enjoy it, and I want my partner to get off." *I want you to get off.* "But thrusting alone doesn't usually do it for me." It was very hard not to pull the curtain of her hair in front of her face, but Cole clearly wanted to watch her, wanted her blushes, and cared very much about what she wanted. And that was going to be enough to carry her past the worries and the bashfulness. "What about you?"

"Maggie, when I touch you"—Cole relaxed against the couch, fully confident once more—"it's going to be hard not to go off like a rocket."

"Right. But after the first time . . ."

"There will be a second time, and a third time, and a bazillion other times." That was as fast and firm as the fuck he was offering her—and it was a glitter cannon inside her gut. "There will be many, many nights and mornings. Lots of days. Bunches of afternoons."

"I, that, yeah. I'm on board with that. So what's your ideal?"

He raised his hand to his mouth and bit his fingertip, and she wanted to offer him hers instead. But the second they touched, things were going to get intense. They needed to finish this conversation first.

"No bondage or *Fifty Shades* stuff. No anal, no groups. Toys can be fun, maybe, and yeah, I can see that you like that idea. But what's going to make me come is getting you off. I want to bury my face in your hair. I want to kiss the underside of your chin. I want to feel you laughing against my chest. I want to learn how you taste."

Which wasn't exactly a road map to sex. It was more like the recipe for a happy relationship. Though that sounded good too.

Needing more specifics, she asked, "Do you like blow jobs? Hand stuff?"

"Yes and yes. The last few years, I haven't had time for this. For dating. For . . . getting to know someone. With you, I'm in deep. And I can't say I've felt like this—ever, really. But when the connection is this deep, the rest tends to be mind blowing. We're going to be mind blowing."

"How can you be sure?"

"I just am."

His certainty was intoxicating. How could she keep clinging to her worries in the face of his belief in them?

"And penetration?"

He blew out a long breath. "The thought of your pussy makes my dick throb." He ran a hand down the front of his pants, and it was . . . holy shit, she could make out his length and girth. "I mean, that's normally what makes me come, but I don't need that if you don't want it."

Maggie had to close her eyes then. There were too many sensations, too many emotions. The body stuff, yes. The hammering of her pulse in her clit. The way her pussy was swollen and wet. The hardness of her nipples against the lace of her bra. But it was also her heart, squeezing at his concern for her. His respect for her.

"I want you to be inside me," she whispered. "I don't know if I'll orgasm that way, but I'm . . . aching for you." She'd never been as hungry for food as she was for *him*. Every way she could have him, she wanted him.

It was almost scary, feeling that. Admitting it. If they'd known each other any less well, she would be standing here, trying to play it cool. To pretend that she wasn't a pile of Jell-O where he was concerned. That emotionally, sexually, physically, she was desperate for him.

But his grin—cocky, hot—let her know it wasn't embarrassing to feel like that.

Like he was equally worked up about her.

Like she'd made his life by letting him turn her into a puddle of want.

"Just tell me what you want, what you like, and what you don't, and we'll be fine." He said it as if it were that easy.

But maybe with him, it would be.

"I will."

"Then I think we've about covered things."

"I think we have."

"Unzip your dress and come 'ere."

With shaking hands, Maggie did. She'd only been standing five or six steps away from him, but it felt like an epic journey.

Cole folded into her, pushing his face into her stomach and biting her through the fabric of her dress. One of his hands stole up under the hem. "So soft," he said of her thighs.

And even though she knew her skin was . . . regular, she suddenly felt soft. Desirable.

She parted her legs for him, and he cupped her mons.

"I'm pretty wet." That was a massive understatement. She might not have ever been so ready before.

But rather than diving in like she'd expected him to, Cole pulled her up onto the couch until she was straddling him, and then he peeled her dress open, revealing her cleavage. Maggie had debated between this bra, which got scratchy after a few hours, and a more practical cotton one, and she was glad she'd gone for the lace. His approving smile let her know she'd made the right choice, and then he licked her cleavage. Actually licked her. And then his mouth was on her bra over her nipple.

He used his lips and his tongue and his teeth—exactly the right amount of teeth. Rough in a way that had her bucking against his hand, digging her nails into the back of his neck, whimpering in her own mouth, struggling to keep the inarticulate babble inside. The *Oh my God, yes, just like that* and *Don't stop, don't ever stop* and *I love you*. Mostly that last one, because it was just too soon for that last one.

Entirely too soon.

Cole didn't let up. Not consuming her breast, not working his fingers over her panties, and definitely not with the heel of his palm, blunt and firm and punishing against her clit. Exactly what she needed.

She came quickly, loudly. Like a malfunctioning firework that detonates the entire box all at once.

"How was that?" he said, lifting his head from her.

"Oh, you know, pretty good." Maggie sprawled on her back across the couch, feeling boneless and embarrassed and desperate to come again.

"We'll have to do better than that, then." Cole started to strip off her dress, then stopped. "Can I take this off?"

"Yes, please."

Once he'd dropped her dress to the floor, her bra followed. The way he looked at her, the way he stopped and kissed the lower part of her stomach, the stretch marks on her hips, it made her feel precious, perfect.

He left on her panties, which were soaked and messy, but he stood and stripped himself down to his boxers. "All night," he vowed, settling between her legs. "I want to do that to you all night."

Cole kissed her as if they were going to be tested on it later. Hungry, ravenous, consuming kisses. One of his hands was on her breast, and the other was on her ass. His hold was controlling. Acquisitive.

Which . . . of course. She wanted him to touch her like that, to be his and to trust it would be forever. She felt like clay in the hands of a master.

He dragged himself over her, blunt and slow. "This good?"

"Y-yes."

He made another pass and another and another. Each time it was harder and faster, and Maggie's restraint disappeared.

She was rocking into him, her calf pulling him into her, until he ground against the spot that had her head rolling back. "There, there. Right . . . oh God, please, harder, please."

They, this, were probably hurting his erection, and she was probably being too loud, but Cole was kissing her neck and telling her that she was beautiful and that he wanted to see her fly again. She couldn't help it, she couldn't stop. She could only take and take and take.

Her orgasm, when it came, went on for forever. Her eyes were watering, and every cell in her body was vibrating. The things she said then, she couldn't help them, but she'd never felt so good, and all control fell away. She was begging, begging him not to stop, and he was saying he wouldn't ever stop, and she believed him.

She believed him.

When she was done, she would've rolled over, hid her face, but Cole pinned her hands to the couch. "That was . . . you're beautiful."

He kissed her, sunny and assured, and then he scooped her up and carried her to the bedroom.

After depositing her on the colossal bed, he flipped on the light on the nightstand and then dug around in his suitcase for a box of condoms. He held them up. "Yes?"

"Yes."

His boxers came off—and that was a *lot* of Cole. *A lot* a lot. Maggie swallowed, and then he was putting the condom on. "I know I said all night, but I have to—that is, I want to, and—"

"No, please, I'm ready. I don't think I can wait any longer."

He slid her panties off, taking a moment to inhale them. "Damn, you smell good."

She wouldn't have trusted those words from anyone else, but all the most private and needy parts of sex—the things she'd tried to hide from her other partners—he seemed to revel in them.

He climbed onto the bed. "This is okay? It's what you want?"

She knew he cared about the answer, which made it so easy to say yes and mean it.

For the first time all night, he parted the lips of her pussy. His finger worked into her flesh, and she whimpered.

"Good? Bad?"

"Good." She was panting, lifting her hips, pleading for him with her body.

Then his cock was there, pushing into her, and in the best way, it was hard to catch her breath.

"Goddamn, you're wet." The way he said it, it was the highest compliment.

"That's what you do to me."

"That's good."

"*So* good."

He didn't release her gaze while he slid all the way home and ground himself against her. While he began to move, fast and certain. While his eyes went glassy and unfocused. While he stroked her clit—because of course he was determined to take care of her too. Again.

Then his thrusts went wild, and his hands on her were hard, like he wanted to make sure she was real.

The orgasm hit him like lightning. His groans filled her ears and his chest filled her vision, and Cole filled her. Every nook and cranny of her.

Afterward, he cradled her against his chest. "That was . . . that was something else."

No, it was everything.

Chapter 21

EXT. AIRPORT CURBSIDE PICKUP/DROP-OFF ZONE

Two Weeks Later

Cole leaned up against his car outside the arrivals terminal at LAX, trying not to fidget. The heather-blue T-shirt had been the right choice. Much better than the black Henley and not as obvious as the red.

He tugged on the hem. Damn it, maybe he should have gone with the white.

No, it was fine. Well, it had to be fine. He hadn't brought a backup choice with him. At least he'd gotten flowers.

He hadn't seen Maggie since waking up after the greatest night of his life, when he'd unwrapped himself from her soft body and gotten on a plane back to the States for the *GQ* cover shoot. It had been far too many days of emails (so impersonal) and texts (basically shorter emails) and a few hurried phone conversations (which were hardly better).

They'd seen each other on set virtually every day for four months. While Cole thought he'd made a good case for them being together the night of the wrap party, he did worry that the distance might have allowed her doubts to creep in, like ants at a picnic.

For him, the distance had proved that he had absolutely no self-control when it came to Maggie. He'd had to stop himself from texting her about every meal he'd eaten and everything he'd seen and laughed about. He could only hope it had been the same for her.

He exhaled for the first time in two weeks when Maggie emerged from the terminal, dragging a suitcase behind her, struggling with a bulging canvas bag under one arm and a bulky backpack on her back. She scanned the crowd, her mouth breaking into a wide grin when she saw him. If he hadn't been in love with her before, that response would have sent him over the edge.

Maggie wove through the crowd, narrowly avoiding clipping a metal bollard, before stopping in front of him. "Hey." She was trying not to look ecstatic. She was failing.

"Hey yourself." He shoved his hands into his pockets so he didn't reach for her. He'd explained how paparazzi tended to stalk LAX, but it felt wrong not to pounce on her immediately.

Play things safe. Follow the rules. He'd done it for so long, he could keep doing it now. He'd keep doing it until she was ready to be public.

"How was your flight?" he asked.

"Fine."

If she kept biting her lip like that, he was going to snap. That was just . . . physics. That Isaac Newton dude probably had a law about it.

"And Savannah is going to keep watching your houseplants?"

"Yup, until I figure things out."

Until Maggie decided whether to stay past the job she was starting tomorrow—and until he could convince her to move in with him. But he was waiting to spring that part on her until he'd plied her with more orgasms, a few fantastic meals, and several weeks of perfect weather.

She was going to be putty in his hand. LA had him on the assist.

"Let's get your stuff in the car."

They left the airport a minute later, but once they were in Inglewood, Cole pulled over into a neighborhood and killed the engine.

"Here so fast? I assumed stars weren't fans of jet noise."

"Nope, I want to greet you properly." He hopped out of the car and strolled around to Maggie's side.

She watched, amused, as he opened the passenger door and offered her a hand. "You don't have to seduce me," she said. "I think we've pretty much cleared that hurdle."

No, they'd incinerated it.

"But I want to."

She stepped out and into his arms, and he finally, finally got to kiss her. It was familiar and jolting at once. His body immediately went into overdrive because, yeah, they hadn't done this enough. That night in Glasgow, he'd be dreaming about it for the rest of his life. But that had been *one* night. Okay, so they'd tallied more than half a dozen orgasms together, but that wasn't enough.

Not nearly enough.

So not enough that he couldn't resist deepening the kiss and tipping her backward over his arm, like something out of an old movie poster. At last, he lifted his head. "How am I doing?"

She reached up and traced his lips. "Tell me we're close to your place?"

"Ha, no. You'll have to wait about another hour, give or take the traffic." He straightened them both up and retrieved the bouquet he'd gotten for her from the back seat. He'd kept it, quite literally, under wraps. "These are for you."

Maggie pulled the white paper back with a gasp. "Wow."

"The florist told me flowers have a language."

"I've heard that, though honestly, ferns and houseplants are more my style."

"Well, these are red tulips, daisies, and apple blossoms."

"Which mean?"

Cole couldn't quite make himself say *I love you, I love you truly,* and *I prefer you before all others.* But as certain as he'd been that night in Glasgow, some doubt had crept in. Could she possibly want this life forever?

She'd taken the job on *Waverley* to run away, and she'd been great at it. But was working in Hollywood really what she wanted forever? He wouldn't blame her if it wasn't. As much as this was his world and he couldn't imagine leaving it, she still had a chance here. The bug hadn't bitten her yet.

So "You'll have to look it up" was all he said.

Her expression was intrigued and a little frustrated, and it revved him up like an engine.

They chatted as they drove, the kind of meaningless banter that was easy with her, about his photo shoot and the scripts he'd been looking at, about the weather in Oregon and the conversations she'd had with the director of the movie she was going to start working on tomorrow.

When they turned into the Beverly Hills Flats, Maggie plastered herself to the window to gawk at the palm tree–lined streets. "I feel like Eddie Murphy in *Beverly Hills Cop*."

"I can't believe you'd admit having seen *Beverly Hills Cop*."

She flipped him off, and he captured her hand and kissed her knuckles.

"I'm glad you're here." That seemed safe enough to admit. Besides, it was written all over him. There was no way he could hide it from her.

"Me too."

Cole pulled into his driveway. A few years ago, when his career had started showing signs of life, he'd bought a bungalow that might have started out humble. But someone had added an enormous back wing and tricked the thing out like a home-improvement catalog on steroids.

Inside, Maggie took in the undercabinet lighting and ultra-high-end appliances and closet engineering and state-of-the-art security system without emotion. "Over the phone, you emphasized that your house has three different burrito shops in walking distance. I wasn't expecting, well, this." She gestured at the glass-bubble chandelier over the dining room table.

"I bought it primarily for the access to high-quality burritos. I've been meaning to change that out for something less gaudy."

She snorted. "And I thought the real draw would've been that it's close to Hollywood."

"Well, I do work there sometimes. And you do too." He'd been showing her the house as if he were a real estate agent trying to sell it to her, as if she might decide to stay based on the house and not because of him.

"For the moment."

"Let me show you the bedrooms." He hoisted her suitcase and shuffled down the hall. "This is the guest room. I asked my housekeeper to make up the bed and stock the bathroom, because I didn't want to presume. But . . ."

"You can presume."

Thank God. "Noted." And with that, he led her back to the master suite.

He heaved her bag up onto a luggage rack while she sat in a huge leather armchair and slipped her shoes off. "You're certain I'm not putting you out?"

"Not at all. I would've been hurt if you'd gone to a hotel." Or if she'd gotten an Airbnb, which she'd discussed. "And you gotta take one of my cars."

"You have two?"

He felt his cheeks darken. "Yes."

"More than two?" she pressed.

"Cars might be my weakness." He'd bought a cheaper house than he could afford, painfully aware that his current level of success wasn't guaranteed. But he hadn't been able to resist the lure of several very sharp sets of wheels.

Maggie laughed. "And there it is, he owns an unspecified number of vehicles. I knew you couldn't be perfect."

He could've told her that. Presumably everyone on earth knew he wasn't perfect. "I plead the fifth. But we could also get you a car service if you don't want to drive."

"No, if I'm going to move here, I have to learn to deal with it eventually."

Oh, he liked the sound of that. Trying to keep things light, he said, "What do you want to order for dinner?"

"Burritos."

"The sky's the limit, Maggie. We could get something fancy, something with Michelin stars and courses and stuff—"

"I don't need fancy, Cole James. I've already got you."

He really, *really* liked the sound of that.

INT. COLE'S HOUSE

Maggie almost didn't let herself into Cole's house after her first day of work. It felt so *intimate* to use his security code and key. Then again, if she hadn't used them, that would have felt like a rebuff. She didn't want to insult him, so as much as it pained her, like literally pained her, she let herself in the back door.

"Cole?" she called, her voice sounding small in the marble-floored sunroom.

It, like the rest of his house, was beautiful, but also . . . sterile. There were no plants, no piles of magazines or books on the side tables, no rumpled throw blankets on the couch or shoes in the mudroom. He'd just been on set for four months, true, but was it always like this? And if so, could it honestly feel like home?

"In the kitchen," he called back.

The smile in his voice was unmistakable, enough to melt her worries.

She found him setting the table—that gleaming Scandi edifice under the most beautiful chandelier she'd seen outside a theatre—with stark-white plates and minimalist silverware. He had really good taste, or he'd hired an amazing decorator. Probably both.

And it still felt unreal when he took her face in his hands and kissed her until she was breathless.

He had good taste, and he'd chosen *her*.

Coming up for air, he asked, "How was the first day?"

"Good."

"Let me get the food."

He brought in massive bowls of chickpea pasta with roasted veggies and salad while she told him about the director and the production. Compared to *Waverley*, this was low to the ground, though no less professional.

"Honestly," Maggie said, sipping her ice water, "I wish I could've started with something like this. I don't feel out of my depth at all. I feel like . . . I know what I'm doing."

"Of course you know what you're doing." Cole seemed so offended on her behalf—offended at her own low opinion of herself. "You were amazing on *Waverley* from day one."

"Oh yes, day one of rehearsal, when I pushed Tasha away?"

"That was not your fault, and you got her back. Got her back *and* supported her in going public with her story."

"Which may blow back on her and on you and everyone else who's helping her."

"It won't. And even if it does, I'd still talk to Libby again," he insisted.

"I know you would, that's why I"—she stopped herself from blurting out *love you*—"think you're the best." She smiled like a doofus, hoping that he'd bought her misdirection.

It wasn't that she doubted loving him. And it wasn't as if it were too soon in an absolute sense. She'd known the man almost five months. But she'd only kissed him for the first time sixteen days ago. You had to give these things at least the same amount of time it took for a bag of carrots to go soft in the fridge.

"Anyhow, that's enough about me. Tell me about your day."

He'd started training for a boxing movie, so his day had been stuffed with working out, meeting his trainer, and carbo-loading. Maggie wanted a nap by the time he'd reached the end of it.

When he'd finished explaining everything she'd never wanted to know about punching bags, she leaned forward. "Can I ask you something?"

"Anything."

"Why do you want to revive your career? That sounds like a skeptical question, but I'm honestly curious. You don't seem to love being famous. And it's a *hard* job, one without the promise of success even if you work your butt off and are good at it—and you do both. So why?"

He wiped some condensation off his glass with his thumb. "I'm usually too focused on the plan, on putting one foot in front of the other, to think about that. Sometimes I make the mistake and look down, and it's like when you're rock climbing. It makes me dizzy. I think . . ." He eyed her. "You're not going to yell at me about how I shouldn't feel guilty again, are you?"

"I didn't yell. I cajoled with feeling."

"Right, of course. Important distinction. But there were things I got that I didn't earn. Good things, like jobs and publicity, but maybe also bad things, like tabloid headlines and broken self-esteem."

She raised her eyebrows at him, and he laughed.

But his expression fell serious again. "Restarting my career would be a chance to balance the scales. I want to get back to the top by being a good person. Doing things the right way. I want to be a good coworker and a good friend. For me, but also for the industry. I mean, I'm selfish, don't get me wrong. I want to pay this house off and save for retirement, and I like getting to write my own ticket. But when I'm in something like *Waverley*, it's hard to believe that *Central Square*—with all its mess—existed, you know?"

"I can imagine," Maggie said. "But if it's about the system, like movies and television itself, do you ever wonder if there's another way?"

"Buying a movie theater?" he asked, confused.

"Producing. Directing. Something like that."

"Oh, the dark side."

"Hey." She flicked his forearm with her finger. "I live on the dark side. I just wonder if the problem is people like Vincent Minna. Could you make more of a difference if you became the anti–Vincent Minna?"

"Drew is always telling me that I'm an 'entrepreneur.'" Cole put the word in sarcastic air quotes, as if nothing could be more ridiculous. "And look, acting is only part of my income. Endorsements, side hustles, those are part of the gig. But I became an actor because I didn't want a real job with memos and, like, TPS reports."

"Sadly, I can confirm that real jobs do in fact suck. I just . . . wondered if there's another way. Or maybe an *additional* way."

"What, you're saying my performance as mega-hottie and mega-asshole Geordie Robertson can't change Hollywood?"

"Alas, no. But in fairness, your ass is totally revolutionary."

"That's probably why Zoya cast me." Cole set his hand over Maggie's. "You know, Drew has never asked me why I want this. He just took it for granted that I did, and . . . I did. For nearly two decades, it was always about what we were going to get, how we were going to get it. That was what I needed, so I didn't mind. But I'm glad you're here now to ask me those hard questions. Because I don't think I've ever answered them out loud. Maybe I was afraid to."

She flipped her hand around under his, linking their fingers together. "You say that like it's good *now*, but give it a few months . . ."

"No, I'll always appreciate it." His words were firmer and more serious than the Pledge of Allegiance.

Maggie knew she should treat his vow lightly, act as if it were pillow talk because it was just too soon, but it was all too easy to see how they could sit and talk like this every night. How he could tease her out of her tendency to take things too seriously and pick them apart until they were threadbare. And how she could take him seriously, asking questions and validating him in the ways clearly no one else in his life did.

If only it weren't for how they'd met, because *Waverley* was always going to be there. It would always be the first line on her résumé, and it would always be the vehicle for his renaissance. That was never going to change. Cole and Maggie meeting on that set, even if they hadn't touched until filming was over, was always going to be a little bit sketchy.

Maybe more than a little bit.

But despite her fears about how they'd gotten started, all Maggie could do was squeeze his hand and ask, "So what do movie stars do on weeknights?"

◆ ◆ ◆

INT. COLE'S BEDROOM

Maggie hadn't ever seen a K-drama. Like . . . ever. So after dinner, Cole introduced her to the glory that was Hyun Bin and Son Ye-jin—"No, seriously, no one on *Waverley* has ever had this kind of chemistry"—and then they headed to bed.

The night before, Maggie had gone on and on about his shower—"Seven jets? Like, as many as Snow White's dwarf friends?"—and it looked like they were in for a second round of her oohing and ahhing orgasmically while he lay in bed and tried to think calm, nonerotic thoughts.

"I could move in with you just for that," she called to him in the bedroom when she'd turned the water off.

His heart tripped in his chest. *Be cool, be cool, be cool.* "Then my evil plan is working," he shouted back.

"Your plan to ply me with luxury?"

"That's how I get you."

"And how do you keep me?"

He probably didn't. Compared to Maggie, Cole felt hopelessly flat. For decades, he'd been so focused on saving his own butt and career, while at dinner that night, Maggie had proposed fixing the entire industry.

God, but he loved her. Now that she was here, with him, in his own house, it was so hard to keep that inside. His plan, because he honestly did have one, was to make her giddy with happiness. To feed her every night. To hold her every night.

And to give her as many orgasms as she could handle.

Last night, she'd passed out on his chest as soon as they'd gotten in bed. Which meant he needed to work overtime now. He marched into the bathroom.

She was at the vanity, brushing her wet hair. She locked eyes with him in the mirror and raised her brows as if to ask what he was doing there.

He strolled over and set one hand on her waist. The fingers of his other hand trailed down the white towel she had wrapped around herself. It was thick, plush, and soft—but also just scratchy enough to catch on his fingertips.

A riot of sensation, really.

"The way I keep you is by doing this." He pressed the heel of his hand against the V at the top of her thighs, and Maggie's eyes went wide with understanding and heat.

Her palms smacked onto the marble vanity, the brush clattering to the floor. Cole nudged her feet wider apart with his toe. He squeezed the towel into the space she'd made for him. The space where he hoped she was aching for him.

"*Cole.*"

"That a yes or a no?"

"Yes."

"I thought so." In the mirror, he watched his forefinger rub over the towel, feeling for her cleft. He traced it, pressing the fabric, soft and scratchy at once, into her flesh.

Maggie was breathing hard now, and her green eyes were huge. He bit her shoulder. Sucked her flesh until it pinkened. He wanted to leave a mark right there. Something permanent and bright red that everyone could see.

This woman is mine.

But she hadn't said that, not yet.

So he set about kissing her neck, her ear, her temple, all while he watched himself rub her into oblivion. Working her into a frenzy of feelings, until she was buckling between his hand and his crotch. Until she was crooning. Until she was begging him to fuck her.

Maggie kept her eyes open, holding his gaze. Then she was nodding frantically when her release started. Her lids slammed shut, and her face became a mask of pure ecstasy.

He'd done that, he was doing that, to her. Maggie was so contained, so poised, that the way she absolutely lost control when she came, it made him feel ten feet tall. Like a real-life hero, not the ones he played in Tinseltown.

"Don't stop, don't stop, God, yes."

The sweetest melody on earth, right there.

When she collapsed forward onto the counter, he gently pried the towel open, revealing the column of her spine, the flare of her waist. Her body was a miracle. An absolute miracle. He dropped the towel to the floor.

Against the counter, she mumbled, "That was . . . holy cow."

He turned her around before boosting her into his arms and setting her, naked, on the counter.

She looped her arms around his neck with a smile that was a little drunk. "What are you doing now?"

He set about kissing her until they were both breathless. The kind of kissing where nothing is held back, more like fucking than kissing. A grappling, sweaty thing that you did with your whole body. And it would've been embarrassing, how desperate he was for her, how needy she made him, if Maggie hadn't been clinging to Cole just as hard as he was to her.

His lips skidded down her neck. "I'm going to die if I don't get your sweet tits in my mouth."

"No one has ever died from that. And Cole, I—" Whatever else Maggie was going to say turned into a moan, because the woman really, really liked that.

Sadly, with his face buried in her skin, he couldn't see her expression anymore. But he still had her noises. Her legs wrapping around him, trying to pull him closer. Her fingers in his hair, holding him in place.

When he couldn't take it any longer, he released her nipple with a pop, and he began digging in a drawer for the condoms he'd stashed there. He didn't normally make good choices, but when he did, they involved Maggie.

He stripped off his boxers and sheathed himself. "This okay?"

"God, yes, please."

Cole scooped Maggie up again, turning her toward the vanity. He plunked her feet onto the tile and bent her over the counter. "Watch me fuck you."

There was that blaze in her eyes again. She liked it when he talked like that to her. She liked it when he gripped her hips and pushed into her, firmly, a little roughly. When he set a pace that was a bit too fast, a bit too hard. Because he could see the pleasure in her hands gripping the vanity, the hunger in how she met every thrust.

"Touch yourself," he instructed.

She nodded, choppy. Then her fingers were there, on her most sensitive flesh and the place where he entered her, stretched her. Her eyes closed, and now he was the only one watching. The only one who saw his expression: snared and desperate and down for the count.

Which was probably why he buried himself in her and said against her neck "I love you." One last thrust; then he choked out "I am totally in love with you." Because he was, and there was nowhere he could hide. He didn't even want to. He adored this woman.

When the last shiver had racked through both of them, he disposed of the condom and pulled Maggie back into the shower. He held her under the jets until his legs were strong again, until the emotions that had been churning him like a storm were back in place.

"Sorry, that was too much. Sex with you—it's intense." Every time he touched her, it was going to be like this, of that he was certain. He just had to get used to it.

"Did you mean it?" She tipped her chin back, watching him steadily.

"Yes." He shouldn't have said it, but it wasn't because he didn't mean it.

"Then don't you dare take it back." Maggie popped onto her toes and kissed him. A kiss so sweet, he almost felt guilty for fucking her over his bathroom counter. Or at least he almost felt guilty until she broke from his mouth and said, "Because I love you too."

Her words were a day at the beach and runner's high and Christmas morning, all hitting him at the same time.

"Thank God." He kissed her back hard, slamming his hand on the wall to keep them both upright. "Thank God."

Sometimes, you got everything you ever wanted—and wasn't that a kick in the pants?

Chapter 22

EXT. PARKING LOT

Cole was leaving the gym when his phone rang. It was Drew.

For once, his agent couldn't have any complaints. The early buzz about Cole's work on *Waverley* was terrific, Brett had been scheduling all kinds of interviews and photo shoots Cole wouldn't have been offered two years ago, and Cole had taken the job Drew had wanted him to take—he had the sore muscles and the Boston-accent coach to prove it.

Applause had to be coming, right?

"Hey," Cole answered, trying not to sound smug. "Long time, no—"

"You knew about this Vincent Minna hack job, and you didn't tell me?"

In all fairness, Cole hadn't talked to Libby recently, and in his last conversation with Tasha—who'd spent the two weeks since filming had ended hiding out in the Azores with Ryan—she'd said it would probably drop before the end of the month.

Which was, like, next week.

Damn it.

Cole glanced around. No one was near him on the street, and since the story was apparently close to dropping, there wasn't much risk if he had this conversation here and now. The avalanche might not be coming down the mountain yet, but the snow was shifting under the hardpack. Destruction was inevitable. Cole had helped make it so.

"I get that you're pissed, but . . . I thought you'd try to talk me out of it." Cole was important to Drew, but he would never be as important to his agent as one of Hollywood's top producers. It was a simple question of math.

Cole got *why* Drew opposed drama, but not all drama was equal. This wasn't getting into some dumb feud with an ex or starting a fight at an Oscars party. It was supporting his best friend as she came forward about one of the industry's biggest villains. Helping Libby tell Tasha's story was the right thing to do. Period.

"Of course I would've said not to do it!" Drew shouted.

So Cole had been right.

They'd fought a few times in the years they'd worked together. Or more precisely, Drew had been snide to Cole about what he'd wanted and why until Cole had given in and gone Drew's way. But this was an entirely different level of venom.

"I did talk to Quinn and Brett." His lawyer and his publicist. "But bringing you in? I don't really see the career angle here."

"You don't see the career angle?" Drew didn't bother to hide how angry he was. "Vincent Minna is one of the most powerful men in Hollywood. Don't you get what you're doing?"

"Was. He *was* one of the most powerful men in Hollywood." At least if Cole had anything to do with it.

"Don't be stupid. There may be time to kill your quotes. I've heard they're still a few days away from publishing. Let me call this Libby Hansen person, and—"

"I don't want to kill my quotes." Drew's reaction was just so beyond the pale. While Drew certainly did have a stake in Cole's career, it was still exactly that—*Cole's* career. "I stand by everything I said."

Drew inhaled, and then didn't say a thing. Maybe he had finally realized that this particular time, Cole had found his backbone, and Drew wasn't going to be able to sway him.

"But do you have to talk?" Drew finally asked.

So much about life was confusing. Was happiness real, or just a chemical reaction? Where were people before they were born? What the hell did the phrase *act naturally* mean?

Look, Cole didn't know if he'd ever have all the answers. But this—it had been so easy.

"Yes. I know that you're trying to take care of me." At least that was what Cole was hoping this was about. "But this conversation, it isn't your job. Let Brett and me worry about the publicity angle." Even if the publicity angle was awful, Cole didn't care. There were situations that demanded you act in a certain way, even if you had to pay a high price. Standing by Tasha: it wasn't something he could choose not to do.

Maggie had asked why he wanted this, and as he stood next to his car, he knew for sure why he didn't want it. Cole might not be an A-lister—maybe he wouldn't ever be one—but success was absolutely freaking meaningless if it stopped him from speaking up.

After a few more seconds, during which Cole was certain Drew was searching for another line of attack, Drew finally said, "Okay."

But Cole suspected they weren't done with the discussion.

For the better part of two decades, Drew had said jump, and Cole had jumped and then asked if that had been high enough. He'd taken Drew's advice like a habit, one that might not be so good for him anymore.

Well, okay, that wasn't fair. Drew had picked up Cole when there had been very little benefit in doing so. Cole was certain he'd been a drag on Drew's books for a long time. And if it hadn't been for Drew and his advice, Cole wouldn't have booked *Waverley*, and he wouldn't have met Maggie.

Drew had been caught off guard, that was all. And even though Cole knew he'd done the right thing, it was a *big* thing. Vincent Minna had been the most important producer in Hollywood for a long time, and opposing him had been unthinkable for years and years. That was exactly why he'd been able to be a monstrous asshole for so long. But once Drew got used to the fact that Cole had gone public, he'd come around.

Cole was almost certain of it.

◆ ◆ ◆

EXT. THE HOLLYWOOD HILLS

On Saturday morning, Maggie contemplated the trail she had, quite ridiculously, agreed to tackle with Cole. "You're *really* confused about the whole 'What is a mountain?' thing."

"Aren't you from Oregon?"

"Yes, but I didn't go hiking there. I'm a drama nerd."

"So am I. Besides"—he gestured at the vista—"we're still in the city."

"That doesn't preclude this from being a mountain."

"'Preclude'? Maggie Niven, how dare you talk dirty to me when I can't do anything about it?" From the twinkle in his eye, it was clear he was only half joking.

Cole had explained that Runyon Canyon was a popular trail, and so if they didn't want to start any rumors, he'd need to keep his hands to himself. It was the same reason they'd eaten at his house every night. The same reason she'd told the director of *The Mid List*, her current project, that she was "staying with a friend" and had omitted who it was and, oh, that he was making her come every night. It would've made her feel like a dirty little secret, but she was the one who didn't want to go public.

She needed to talk to Bernard, and one of these days, when her mentor was praising her in glowing terms, saying how she really didn't need him anymore, she was going to do exactly that. *Oh, and by the way, I'm dating Cole James.* Cue the explosions.

But she wasn't at that point, and she might not be for months. Once this news was out, there wasn't going to be any stopping it. So she had to be absolutely sure, and absolutely secure, before they let that cat out of the bag.

"Are you properly sunscreened?" Cole was absolutely fanatical about SPF and fancy chemical sunscreens. Maggie hadn't even realized there were different types.

"Yup."

"You have your hat and sunglasses?"

"Check and check."

"And we have plenty of water." Cole's backpack was sloshing. He'd filled it with canteens, more water than Maggie drank in a weekend, saying something about how he needed to get in some strength training.

Better him than her. As Maggie's strength was more of the inner variety, it needed no training.

"After you." Cole waved his arm gallantly to usher Maggie forward.

What she hadn't realized about the mountain they'd climbed in Scotland was that they'd done it in the spring. *Early* spring, and Scotland wasn't that far from the Arctic Circle.

Now it was September, which was still basically summer thanks to global warming, and LA was suspiciously close to the equator—not to mention located in a desert. Maggie was sweating before they'd made it ten steps. By the half-mile mark, she might as well have been melting.

"I feel like the Wicked Witch after Dorothy gets her with the bucket," Maggie groused as they started up the trail again.

"Except you're just beautiful without any wickedness."

Maggie didn't even have the energy to roll her eyes. As she stumbled up an incline, she stuttered out, "I've always, always appreciated that even as she's, you know, wasting away, the witch has healthy self-esteem." She stopped, breathing hard.

Cole ran his fingers up her spine, which was a definite violation of the no-touching rule, before he set about digging in his backpack. "You'd expect that from a supervillain."

Maggie held one of her hands out, and he placed a canteen of water in it. She suddenly appreciated that he'd frozen these last night. He really was perfect.

She chugged, grateful. When she felt vaguely human, and not like a desiccated mushroom, she said, "And see, I would think—"

"Oh my gosh, you're Cole James!" a woman with a long blonde ponytail squealed.

Cole rearranged his features into what Maggie recognized as his Cody Rhodes face. "That's me."

"Team Cody forever!"

"Yeah." He reached out a fist, and the fan bumped it.

"And you and Tasha Russell are back together—wait, is she here?"

"No, no, I'm with a friend."

Maggie gave a little wave, but the woman didn't even see her. She only had eyes for Cole. Maggie tried to remind herself that was a good thing. That the last thing she and Cole needed was for news of their relationship to leak out before she was ready for that. So what if her heart protested at the word *friend*? This was the way she wanted it to be.

"Well, I can't wait for *Waverley*! I have no idea why people were saying you were miscast."

Cole winced. "Thanks."

But so starstruck was the fan that she didn't notice. She, like so many others, saw the brand, not the actual man. "This is so cool. God, I love LA."

"Yeah." Cole was still smiling, but it was hollow. "We should, probably, um—" He gestured to the trail.

"Oh, of course. See you!" She waved and kept hiking.

Maggie was annoyed. But wanting the fan to be out of listening distance before she spoke, Maggie turned her attention out across the view. The trail was sandy, bordered by scrubby green brush. Where the mountain tumbled down into the valley, the city grew up, all red roofs and a wash of gray and white and blue buildings in a neat grid. The towers downtown might as well have been a play set; they didn't look real. Like so many things about Maggie's life in the last year and a half, for all that this seemed to be an illusion, it wasn't. It was every bit as real as the man next to her.

When the fan had made it far enough away, Maggie gestured at her retreating back. "How often does that happen?"

"Sometimes. More now than a few years ago."

"And you *want* it to happen more?" she asked, because that hadn't exactly seemed like a pleasant exchange for Cole.

"Not for its own sake. I promise, getting clocked in public is not my favorite. But I want . . . what it represents."

So they were back to *why* he was invested in his career comeback again. Maggie had been grateful the other day that he hadn't turned her question back on her. It had kept her up at night, actually, pondering what motivated her.

She'd never been an ambitious person, at least not as far as her parents were concerned. Ambition had always seemed like a dirty word to her. The reward of high school theatre was in the doing. Fame and riches weren't in the cards, and most of her students would never do another play in their lives. Maybe they were building some self-confidence and public speaking skills, but mostly, she'd wanted them to understand the arts better. To understand *themselves* better.

When that had been taken away from her, she'd been focused on basic questions: affording her mortgage, her health insurance. But those were no longer immediate concerns, at least not this morning. So what the heck did she want, and why did she want it?

She shot a look at Cole's profile, so handsome against the blue sky. Maggie wanted *him* because she loved him. But as delightful as their relationship was, it didn't pay her bills. It was the best thing in her life, but for so many reasons, it couldn't be the only thing in her life.

When Zoya had first offered Maggie a job, it had solved the champagne problem of how she was going to feed herself. But now, it was more. Maggie wasn't going to get rich or famous as an intimacy coordinator, but she had made a difference to Tasha, to Cole, to Rhiannon.

To the actors in her current project, and perhaps to the ones in her future projects.

The meaning of art was in making it. The meaning of life was in living it.

Maggie wanted Cole, and she wanted to do work that mattered.

Okay, she was ready for the damn test.

Maggie started back up the trail. The faster she got to the peak, the faster they would get to the coming-down part—and hopefully a big plate of french fries. "If you don't like getting recognized, why are we on what's clearly a super-popular trail?"

"Well, I normally arrive at dawn and jog, so I get stopped less."

"Hey, it's not my fault that you wanted to—"

"Yeah, I know." He gave Maggie's own, much shorter, ponytail a tug.

"You're not very good at the whole keeping-your-hands-to-yourself thing."

"I'm complete crap at it."

And she didn't want him to get better at it. She wanted to be confident enough that them being together wasn't a problem.

"Let's finish this damn thing so you can take me home and be crap at it some more."

Chapter 23

EXT. TASHA'S HOUSE—EVENING

With its crisp-white stucco, red tile roof, and wrought iron Juliet balconies, Tasha's house appeared to be a sophisticated Mediterranean palace built for a silent-movie star. But when she opened the front door for Maggie and Cole, it was Tasha's outfit that was the real shock. She was wearing an apron and holding a chef's knife, like an assassin who'd gone undercover as June Cleaver.

"Nice apron." Cole gave his best friend a hug. "It took you long enough to get back to the States."

"Would you have voluntarily left paradise?" she demanded.

"Probably not. So why did you?"

"Libby's story drops in a few hours."

Cole looked at Maggie grimly. They'd known this day was coming. A sick feeling roiled Maggie's stomach. She'd been on board with Tasha talking to the reporter, and she'd supported Cole in doing the same thing. God, but she hoped that would prove to be good advice.

"In that case," Cole said, "I'd think you'd want to stay inaccessible."

"Eh, they would've found me. At least I have more control this way."

Cole and Maggie followed Tasha through her house. While Cole's bungalow was extremely nice and located in a seriously chic neighborhood, it still felt normal, like the regular-people houses on HGTV.

But this was a flat-out rich-person house. Every room was gigantic, and every piece of furniture was clearly luxe. Huge bouquets of fresh flowers graced the rooms, spilling out of gorgeous chinoiserie. The house was even sprinkled with actual marble columns and carved mantelpieces.

In the last six months, Maggie had gotten used to some stuff that would've had past-Maggie gasping, but this was almost too much. At some point, she was going to have to ask if Norma Desmond used to live here.

Tasha led them out the back door. On the covered veranda by the pool house—because Tasha's house needed a second, smaller house, presumably for company—surrounded by the most perfect landscaping Maggie had ever seen, Ryan was grilling. When Tasha handed him the knife, he set his hand on her nape and stooped to kiss her cheek in thanks. It was utterly chaste, and yet so possessive and intimate Maggie looked away.

Those two were a matched set, as beautiful and deadly as throwing knives. But Maggie suspected that with each other, and probably only with each other, they could be soft.

Tasha poured a glass of iced tea and handed it to Cole. "I think we have to talk strategy."

"For what? The story will break, and he'll respond. And then we'll figure it out." Libby had insisted it would be better if Cole didn't see the story ahead of time. It would add to the credibility if the sources hadn't vetted it.

"Do you think I'm going to need a war room?" Tasha asked.

"Why? It's Vincent who's in trouble."

"He's going to try to torch us. You know he will."

Secretly, Maggie hoped Cole and Tasha would only be a small part of whatever Libby had found. Vincent might be on the way out, but from the little Maggie had seen of him, she knew he could still do a lot of damage.

Had Libby sent her story to him for comment by now? Probably, if it was dropping soon. Maggie scanned the sky, as if she were expecting to see a funnel cloud forming above Vincent's head, wherever he was.

Nope, no spontaneous tornadoes in sight.

"I know you want to prepare, but you gotta wait for him to make the first move," Cole was saying. "Maybe he won't get personal."

Tasha poured another glass of tea for Maggie. "The fuck he won't. The whispers are already starting."

Well, that was hard to deny.

"Drew found out somehow," Cole admitted. "Maybe from the fact-checking? I dunno, but he wasn't happy."

Maggie had been livid when Cole had explained how his agent had reacted to the news. She hadn't met Drew yet, but she already hated him.

From the look on Tasha's face, it was clear the other woman felt the same way. "He never did like risk."

"Me talking to Libby wasn't about taking a risk," Cole said dismissively. "It was about doing the right thing."

Maggie loved that Cole saw the world in the same approximate way as a Boy Scout did. To him, things were right or they were wrong, and there was no excuse for not intervening on the side of right. That was lovely. It was admirable. But she worried the complexities of life might catch Cole in the teeth if he wasn't careful.

"I'm so anxious that this is going to go badly," Maggie said.

"And you missed your chance to stop us?" Tasha rolled her eyes. "Maggie, I haven't done a goddamned thing I didn't want to do since I went to the Oscars with Vincent Minna. Every step after that one, it's been one hundred percent me."

It didn't make Maggie feel *better*, but it did help. A little.

"This is a game Cole and I have been playing for a long time. So whatever happens, it's on us. If we nuke the bastard, that's ours. And if we whiff, that's ours too. Come on." Tasha gestured to the platter at the center of the table. "This cheese plate won't eat itself."

One of the things that was definitely true about California was that the produce was out of this world. This spread could easily have been on a food blog. There were three kinds of cheese, plus artisan meats, multiple types of crackers, a dip, and several kinds of fruit and veg. It was all perfect and unblemished and intensely colored; it was basically model food.

Because Tasha was Tasha, she launched into a lengthy explanation about where everything had been grown and how long the cheeses she'd picked had been aged. As she monologued on, Cole went to dive in, only to pull himself back. At some point, Maggie became convinced that Tasha kept making it longer to torture him.

"And then, because Stiltons are back," she was saying, "I got—"

"I didn't realize Stiltons had left," Cole stage-whispered to Maggie.

Tasha pelted him with a grape, which he caught and ate with a smug smile.

"You are a peasant," Tasha told Cole, falling into her chair.

"So am I," Ryan put in.

"But *you* have so many other qualities," she replied.

That had Maggie blushing into her iced tea again. Were she and Cole that obvious?

Cole caught her eyes, and from how her body immediately reacted—every bit of her perking up simply because he was watching her in that bedroom way—she knew the answer was yes.

"Arg, you're all hopeless," Tasha said. "Eat. It's cheese, and figs, and grapes, and moutabbal—"

"Which we will never confuse with baba ghanoush again."

"Thank fucking God." Cole dragged a slice of pita through the roasted-eggplant dip and ate it with a satisfied moan.

With the aquamarine water lapping next to them—seriously, was it dyed? Maggie had never seen a pool that color outside of a movie—and the pink-and-gold sky and the actual movie stars, it was hard to believe that Maggie belonged in this scene. But when Cole squeezed her fingertips, just to check in, it was harder to believe she didn't.

Somehow, she'd fallen into this life. And she loved it here.

When she gave Cole a warm shake of her head to say that she was fine, he turned back to Tasha. "Have you talked to Libby? How is she feeling?"

"Tired." Tasha gave a shrug, as if to say *What would you expect?* "That girl has worked her tail off. She has Jack doing all her follow-up calls now."

Cole cocked his brows. "What's the story there?"

"Well—" Tasha matched his salacious tone.

"You gossips." Ryan snapped a tea towel at Cole and caught him on the arm. From the tang, it sounded like it had landed with some force.

"And proud of it." Cole rubbed the back of his arm, laughing. "I like Libby and Jack, but they trade in gossip about us. It seems only fair that we get to do the same thing. And speaking of romances, I don't think I've gotten enough credit for this." He wiggled his finger between Tasha and Ryan.

Tasha was aghast. "You deserve no credit."

"Hey, I chased off other guys for years before you were ready to admit how you felt about Ryan, and I talked him into—"

"Arg." Ryan fell back in his chair, covering his face with the tea towel.

"Well, the rest of us helped *that*"—it was Tasha's turn to wiggle her fingers now, in Maggie and Cole's direction—"by not teasing you about how you and Maggie were salivating over each other."

"That was very helpful, actually," Cole said.

Tasha shot Maggie a look. "Is that what real people do when they're not making movies—sit around and give each other the business?"

"Pretty much."

And if Maggie set aside the mansion looming against the sunset and the high-level discussion about publicity and famous predatory producers, she could almost imagine spending a lot of evenings like this.

◆ ◆ ◆

"You as nervous as Maggie about Libby's story?" Tasha asked Cole as they carried the dinner dishes into her kitchen.

"No." Cole wasn't. "Vincent will try to snap back at us, I'm sure. But he's going to find out that a lot has changed and he's got less sway than he used to."

Tasha made a face. She wasn't convinced by Cole's prediction, even though he was just echoing her own words from the *Waverley* wrap party. "He still might be dangerous enough to cause trouble."

But here was where Cole thought they were all getting it wrong. Why worry about something that hadn't happened yet? It wasn't as if there weren't real, actual things—inflation, wars, whether Hollywood was finally going to stop making superhero movies—to concern them.

"I've learned you don't have to go looking for trouble. It either finds you or it doesn't. So I'll wait to see how this turns out, thank you very much."

Tasha bumped his hip with hers. "When did you get to be so wise?"

Cole didn't think he was being especially insightful, but he'd spent a lot of time at the bottom of the heap, trying to understand how he'd gotten there. It was enough to make someone philosophical. "Probably around the same time that Cody Rhodes was training to be an MMA fighter." As far as mantras went, *What wouldn't Cody do* wasn't a bad place to start.

"That was your worst storyline on *Central Square*. Hands down."

"In fairness, there are a lot to choose from." But they ought to be talking about something that mattered, and Cody Rhodes definitely didn't.

Cole nodded to the window. Outside, Ryan and Maggie were dousing the firepit. Maggie was laughing at something Ryan had said, her nose wrinkled up and her head thrown back, and Cole's chest squeezed, vise tight. She was so pretty.

Next to Cole, Tasha regarded the same scene, but she clearly only had eyes for Ryan.

"How are things with him?" Cole asked.

Tasha blushed. Like, she actually blushed. The sex must be radical. "Good. Except . . . he tried to convince me to detour through Vegas on the way home."

"To visit the Liberace Museum or the twenty-four-hour drive-through chapel?"

"The second one. Ryan has a thing against rhinestones."

Cole whistled, but he wasn't surprised. Ryan didn't seem like the type to do anything casually, and it was clear that Tasha was it for him. "And you said?"

"That marriage is a broken institution."

"So you're thinking about it?"

She snorted and played with the ties on her apron. With infinite carefulness, she said, "The thing is . . . I love him." The line *I totaled my car* was usually delivered more cheerfully than Tasha voiced her feelings. But since Cole knew Tasha's mother and the example she'd set for her daughter, he knew that Tasha must be terrified by the depth of her love for Ryan.

She, of course, wouldn't want him to reveal that he knew that.

"My condolences," Cole deadpanned instead.

"Shut the fuck up."

"My advice? Spring for the Elvis impersonator. Do it *real* classy."

"That's the secret to long-lasting marital bliss?"

"Of course." Cole suspected the real secret was to marry the right person, and though he would never, ever say it to Tasha when she was in this mood, Ryan was the right person for her. Bar none.

Tasha raised her brows and did her own head-nod out the window. "And things with Maggie?"

"I'm done for." Cole at least didn't have trouble admitting *his* feelings.

"She know?"

"Yeah, I have absolutely no chill where she's concerned." He hadn't meant to blurt out *"I love you"* while taking her over his bathroom counter, but it had popped out all the same. And besides, he did love her, so it had been bound to happen one of these days.

He'd had three massive bouquets of roses delivered the day after his surprise confession to balance the scales. Maybe he'd have to get a guy in a white jumpsuit to croon "Love Me Tender" to her in case he was on to something here.

"Hey," Tasha said, jumping in to defend his honor. "You managed not to get together until filming was done. Well done."

"I could star in an anti-sexual-harassment video series."

"Oh no, my friend, that portion of your career is over."

He snorted. Things had never been quite that bad. "Seriously, Maggie and I, we're great. We just need to keep things quiet for a little bit longer." As long as she was sleeping next to him, Cole—like a chalk-painted sign from a craft store—was all about gratitude.

Tasha gave Cole a consoling pat on the arm. "Good luck with that."

His luck had been scary good of late. This had been the kind of night that Cole wanted to repeat every week from here on out, into eternity.

Except Tasha wasn't wrong. Movie stars didn't exactly have stellar track records when it came to saying *I do*. For all that he wanted to believe Tasha and Ryan and Maggie and he were different, that Cole had turned a corner and grown the fuck up, it was hard to trust in it.

"Can we do this?" he asked his best friend. "Be us, and be . . . happy?"

"Goddamn, I hope so."

Cole did too.

◆ ◆ ◆

INT. COLE'S BEDROOM

A few hours later, Maggie was snuggled on Cole's chest, and he was stroking her hair when his phone buzzed for the fifth time in a row.

Tasha had sent the link to Libby's story, followed by a series of flame emoji. I'm going to keep doing this until you write back.

Got it, great work, he replied.

"The story broke." Cole dropped his phone onto his nightstand and went back to playing with Maggie's hair. He managed to sound bored, but his body instantly revved awake. The adrenaline was bitter on his tongue, and his arms and legs were restless.

Under his hands, Maggie stiffened. "You've crossed the Rubicon."

"Is that near Redondo Beach?"

Cole didn't need to read the final version of the story—he'd had enough details about the bastard that was Vincent Minna to cover several lifetimes—but it was wild to know that it was out in the world. That everyone else was learning the truth.

Would it make a damn bit of difference?

Cole had talked to Libby both because it was the right thing to do and also because he wanted things to change. He wanted this industry to be better, and so the absolute least he could do was to speak up when things weren't okay.

Now, making them okay was everybody's problem.

So would they?

Chapter 24

INT. COLE'S KITCHEN

The next morning, Maggie was working from home. They were sipping coffee while watching the cast of *Hear Her* roast Vincent Minna. The women were all insisting that they had *never* heard so much as a whisper about his bad behavior.

"I just don't buy that." Cole gestured with his mug and narrowly avoided sloshing coffee all over the couch. "I mean, I'm not saying it's their fault, but everyone knew he was a dog."

"Should we assume all the men we've heard are dogs are actually criminals?"

"I mean, if the orange jumpsuit fits."

Maggie took another sip of her coffee. "Do you think he'll go to prison?"

"No." No matter what Vincent had done, it was hard to imagine someone like him—rich, lawyered up beyond belief—actually facing consequences for his bad behavior.

And wasn't that the problem? Even once the truth, or parts of it, came out, there never seemed to be any real consequences.

"You still feel good about it?" Maggie asked. *It* being participating in the story, going public, standing by Tasha. The whole shebang.

Whatever came or didn't, Cole's answer would always be the same. "Yup."

But under Maggie's words, he could sense the worry. Despite his and Tasha's best efforts the night before, Maggie was still anxious.

She shouldn't be. He and Tasha could handle themselves.

And besides, Cole might not want to read the story, but as he listened to the hosts on *Hear Her* gush about how brave they'd all been in coming forward, he began to get a bit of a contact high. It hadn't taken bravery, but yeah, he had been right. This had been the right thing to do.

But Cole's rush—was this how Superman felt all the time?—disappeared like the last doughnut at the craft-services table when Brett phoned just before lunch.

"Hey, something's incoming." From Brett's tone, it was clear whatever it was was bad.

"From Vincent? This fast?"

"I can't tell who's responsible, but it's going to require a response. Read the link I'm sending now, and I'm going to set up a call with you, me, Drew, and Quinn ASAP."

"Okay."

Cole had received an embarrassing number of these calls. Not lately, but in the past. And normally, he'd known exactly what had hit the fan. Here, he'd been so good. Had worked so hard. Hadn't fucked up at all.

"Hey, do you want the guacamole?" Maggie was placing their lunch order, and—

Maggie.

This was going to be about Maggie.

Cole dropped onto the couch with a thud. "No," he said, and she took that as an answer.

"You're no fun."

"No, I didn't mean—yes to guac. But my PR guy just called, and—"

Cole's phone dinged. Brett had sent a link to a story on *Boulevard Babble*, the sleazy-blog twin to more serious publications like *Variety*.

Everyone in Hollywood knew that, slimy or not, *Boulevard Babble* had good sources. If you wanted your PR person to start a rumor or drop a blind item, they were your go-to.

Love Triangle on the Waverley Set! the headline screamed, and Cole could've puked. He read quickly.

In the first paragraph, he learned that rumors of "Chaos Cole making a comeback" were "overstated" because "romantic drama" had "sunk" his performance. And there it was: his "close and unprofessional relationship with Maggie Niven," who'd been hired as a "stunt" and "red meat for the woke set," had left Tasha Russell "brokenhearted." Oh yes, the middle part of the article went for the jugular. It was all about how the "ice queen" herself had spent the last two weeks "hiding out" in the Azores, "nursing a broken heart," while Maggie and Cole had whored it up in LA—the same way they'd done all during filming.

What. The. Ever. Loving. Fuck.

Cole was sick to his stomach, and he was pissed—so pissed—and he was confused, and he was sad. He'd worked for years, and this, this absurd "story," might get in the way?

No part of this was true. It stank like three-day-old gym socks. It was comically over the top. But all that made this crap even *stranger*.

Whoever had given these lily-livered anonymous quotes hadn't been content with smacking Cole. They'd gone after Maggie too.

Just why?

And *who*?

Unaware that she'd been shanked, Maggie was setting the table and making bubbly water in the SodaStream and cutting up a mango, all while teasing him about guacamole. Because she didn't know. All the things she'd worked for, they were on the chopping block too.

"Babe." Somehow, Cole packed all the pain and anger he was feeling into that one syllable. Maybe Maggie was right, and he was a better actor than he gave himself credit for being.

She stopped. Her back was to him, and every muscle of her body stilled. Quietly she asked, "Is it bad?"

"Yup."

"How bad?"

"Brett's putting together a call. I'll know more in a little bit. Maybe they'll be able to clean it up fast, or maybe . . ." Maybe it would grow legs and multiply.

He'd seen the stupidest stories act like freaking zombies and refuse to die, infecting everything around them and destroying the media landscape. Cole didn't want to promise Maggie that he'd be able to make this one go away, because he didn't know if he could.

All Cole's choices since *Central Square* had been about trying to put himself back into the driver's seat. To wash off the labels that he'd earned and to show people he was more than they thought he was. If this took hold, he'd be right back at square one. As if the last two decades hadn't happened at all.

"Is it about Tasha, or you?" Maggie asked.

"It's about me—and it's about you."

Maggie whirled around, pure confusion on her face. "Me? Why the hell did Vincent come after me?"

"You better read it." He passed her his phone.

After a minute, Maggie's skin went to ash, and she sank down onto the floor of the kitchen. As if taking the two steps into the living room was entirely too much.

Which was fair.

"What is this?" Her voice was shaky. Every bit of her seemed shaky. Cole dropped to his knees and crawled over to her.

Before he could pull her into his lap, Maggie held up a hand.

She didn't want him to touch her.

These last few weeks, he'd made up for the months of wanting to hold her. Cole had assumed if he filled their days with casual hugs and nudges and caresses and their nights with orgasms, he could get Maggie as addicted to him as he was to her.

Apparently not.

The sting of it left him cold.

"What is this?" she repeated.

"I have no idea." Because he didn't. "It could be Vincent, or maybe someone from the production was . . . jealous? Mad?" He couldn't even comprehend that. Everyone on set had seemed to like both of them. As far as he knew, neither he nor Maggie had caused any bad blood during filming.

Cole had wanted not just for people to *think* he was better but to *be* better. Maggie was one of the only people he knew who cared as much about that as he did.

Unless that change was the problem.

"Maybe it's just my past."

Maggie shot him a knife-sharp look. "Meaning?"

"Bashing me used to be . . . kinda fun for the press. I was a punching bag for a long time. Maybe they wanted to go back to that. I have no idea. I'm sorry."

If that was it, if this was *his* fault, Cole would . . . he didn't even know.

He wrapped his arms around his middle rather than reach for Maggie again. He was chilled, though. Straight through to the bone.

"What can we do?" Maggie had scrolled back up to the beginning and was reading the story again. "Does *Boulevard Babble* print retractions?"

"Probably not." They'd have to have standards first.

"This is so bad. It's *so* bad. I don't even—"

Maggie's phone rang from the kitchen counter.

She handed Cole his phone and, with a wince, answered hers. "Hey, Linda." It was the producer for *The Mid List*. Maggie pressed her eyelids closed. A tear squeezed out and ran down her cheek and splashed onto her shirt.

Cole ought to get her a tissue, ought to apologize again, and ought to fix this. If he could just fix it, she'd let him do the rest, he knew.

He hoped.

"Yeah, I've seen it." Maggie's tears weren't discernible in her voice. She was so strong. All the crap she'd been through had made her so strong. "None of it is true. You've talked to Zoya, and she's so pleased with my work. I mean . . ."

Whatever Linda said then made her body have an earthquake.

Cole set his hand near her foot on the floor. Not on her foot—she'd made it clear that she didn't want that—but near it. He had to offer her comfort. Had to.

When she spoke again, Maggie's voice was strained. Pained. "Yes, in fairness, I am romantically involved with Cole James, but—no, nothing happened on set. Linda, I swear, absolutely nothing happened until after the wrap party."

That was, technically, true. The wrap party had still been going on, probably, but—

That wasn't the point.

Maggie had said she couldn't get involved with someone she'd worked with, and he'd just barreled right over that, assuming that he'd done enough to make up for his past. Assuming that because they loved each other, they should be together.

That "When you assume, it makes an ass out of you and me" thing had never been truer.

Maggie straightened her spine, but another tear ran down her face. "My work has been impeccable. On *Waverley* and on *The Mid List*, I have followed every ethical standard. I have talked to Bernard about all my concerns and limitations and worries. Whoever gave these quotes, this venom, it's just not . . . yes. Yes, I get that. I know, it's such a delicate role, there's no room for drama. Yes, yes, I understand. Bye."

Maggie hung up and scooted back across the floor, farther away from Cole.

So much was wrong right now, but the fact that Maggie wouldn't look at him, that hurt most of all. If she wouldn't let him touch her, she could at least let him see her eyes.

"What did she say?" Cole finally asked after the seconds of silence became too heavy.

"Well, I'm out of a job. Again." Maggie snapped to her feet. It was so instant and so unexpected, Cole almost got whiplash.

"They *fired* you?" Cole couldn't wrap his head around it.

"Yup. As Linda just helpfully explained, with a job like this one, there's no room for error. None at all. I'd guess that when I check my email, Bernard will have dropped me as a mentee, too, and he won't vouch for me moving forward. So that's done."

Her voice was so flat, Cole couldn't tell how she felt. It was probably the same mess of feelings he was having, but she would probably organize them into a spreadsheet later.

She pressed the heel of her hand to her forehead. "I—I messed up. I knew it, I knew I shouldn't get involved with someone I'd worked with, and I did it anyway."

"You did it because—" *We're in love.*

Suddenly, Cole realized that this—they—had been worth it. Even if his career and reputation were spoiled, being with Maggie would have been worth it.

But to her, maybe it didn't feel like that.

"Because I messed up," she finished for him.

Maggie turned and started down the hallway toward the bedrooms. Away from him.

Cole rolled up and followed her. He knew she was . . . mad? Crushed? Sad? Fucking up again made him want to change out of his skin. But somehow, he had to get her to see that there were things they could at least try to do.

"Please, join this call with my team. Brett will be able to do . . . something." It might not make it go away, but he would be able to issue a comment at the very least. "You need to hear what he has to say. I'm certain Tasha will want to make a statement, and then you have to tell me how you want me, us, to weigh in." Cole understood why they'd tried to keep things under wraps, but the horses were so far out of the barn, there was no use talking about how they should've locked the door.

Maggie pulled open the guest room door—the freaking guest room door, not the door to *their* bedroom—and marched inside. "Not right now. I need to be alone." She shut the door in his face.

Cole wanted to fall against it. He wanted to wrench it open. He wanted to pull her into his arms and kiss her until they remembered what mattered—but the truth was, *this* mattered. Her reputation mattered. His career mattered. No amount of kisses, not even his and Maggie's kisses, could make that go away.

But a kick-ass PR team could make a difference.

Cole texted Brett. Read it. What's the plan?

Five minutes later, he was on a Zoom call with Brett, Drew, and Quinn.

"I take it that we're all having an exciting day," Brett said. "Tell me what we're dealing with here, Cole. Is any of this at all true?"

Cole ran his hands through his hair. "The only part that's even close to real is that I am involved with Maggie Niven, but nothing happened until after principal photography wrapped. Not a damn thing. And I have *never* been involved with Tasha, who, by the way, was in the Azores with someone else." And not brokenhearted at all. "The optics aren't great, I know, but this isn't an abuse of power, not from me and definitely not from Maggie. I don't know if this is Vincent, trying to hit back at—"

"Don't get ahead of yourself, Cole," Drew said. "We don't know where the story came from."

"I just—I mean, I don't get it. The buzz about *Waverley* has been so good. If I was such an ass on set, how do you square that? And everyone's been saying that they felt so comfortable filming the love scenes. If Maggie was so unprofessional, how could that be? None of it makes any sense."

"The most important thing is to stay calm." This had always been one of Drew's key rules. *Mismanaged response causes more than half of all PR problems.*

Cole had always wondered how he had figured that out. Like, how did you crunch those numbers?

But since Cole had signed with Drew, he had always followed that advice to the letter. He let Brett do most of his talking to the press for him. They hashed out the language for releases, and they weren't in a rush to talk until they knew what they wanted to say.

For years, that had served Cole. He had to believe it would work this time too. "I know. And I really appreciate having you all on my team."

He'd been annoyed with Drew when he'd tried to kill Cole's quotes in Libby's story, but now that they were facing a potential nightmare that could derail everything, there was nothing but upside to having Drew in his corner. The guy was a machine.

"We know you are. I have a call in to the reporter," Brett said. "In fact, I have four calls in. I'm going to figure out where this bullshit came from, and—"

"I'm less worried about the source than countering it," Drew said, a bit sharply. "We need to get Zoya on record. Tasha might not want to give quotes to the press because she's at the center of Libby Hansen's story about Vincent, but maybe the rest of the cast could speak up."

"And we gotta address Maggie too," Cole said. "We have to clear her name."

"That's not a priority for me," Drew said.

"Well, it is for me. There's no rehabbing my reputation without addressing hers. We're a package deal."

They better still be a package deal.

But honestly, even if she was going to dump his ass, Cole would still make sure that his team erased these false rumors. It would be absolutely wrong to let that stuff stand, and it was his fault that anyone had smeared her in the first place.

"And we need to put that gossip about me and Tasha to bed." Maybe it'd served him at one point, but that was over. For Tasha and

Ryan's sake, and for Maggie and Cole's, that part of the story needed to die.

"I get it, Cole," Brett said. "And I'm working on it, I promise. Right now, you've got to lay low."

"I know, and we have been. I have no idea how this got out." And why it was so *wrong*. It would be one thing for news of his and Maggie's relationship to get leaked. They had been together in public a few times. But where did all the poison come from?

Something about this just didn't add up.

"Quinn, do you think there's a slander angle?" he asked.

"I doubt it. Whoever gave the quotes would have to know they were false. More than likely, it's just someone shooting their mouth off. You know how much people like showing off for reporters, trying to make themselves sound cooler than they are."

Many of the worst stories that had leaked about Cole's past bad behavior had been exactly that. No one had been trying to hurt him, but they had wanted to brag about knowing him, unaware of how proving that they did might spray mud all over him.

"Understood. There's just something so . . . cruel about this, I guess. It feels meaner than regular bragging or gossip."

"Let's see what Brett finds out," Drew said. "And while he's working on that, he can draft a statement."

"I've already started," Brett said. "It'll be ready within the hour."

Cole released a windy sigh. "Okay, okay, fair enough. Thanks for helping me out with this."

"Of course."

After the call, he almost knocked on the guest room door, but wanting to respect the line Maggie had drawn, he opted for a micro training session instead, where he pummeled the bag three times harder than he had yesterday.

Chapter 25

INT. A GUEST ROOM IN COLE'S HOUSE

Maggie hadn't cried when she was fired from her teaching job. That was confusing and humiliating and enraging, but it happened so fast and had been so shocking, she didn't have time to sob about it. She'd had to act.

But somewhere along the way, she'd processed the pain of losing her teaching career. Add in the emotions Cole had grown in her and the fact that she'd started to enjoy working in Hollywood and feeling competent again, and it all mixed together, overwhelming her tear ducts.

Today, Maggie cried like she hadn't cried in years.

She cried because the situation was embarrassing. She didn't like thinking of herself as being proud, but it turned out being fired twice in two years was mortifying. *You suck in* all *industries*: that was the message. And she was going to have to tell her parents—her *parents*—about it. Yet again, she'd let them down, and now she could add Zoya and Bernard to the list of people she'd disappointed.

She cried because she didn't know what she was going to do now. To stave off financial ruin, yes, but also just . . . generally. What else did she like? What else was she good at?

Nothing. The universe was strongly suggesting she was good at nothing.

She cried because she'd messed up and couldn't blame anyone but herself. Falling for someone she'd directed was a bad, bad idea. She hadn't been confused about that. She hadn't even thought she was going to get away with it, not really. Maybe this blowing up in her face wasn't that surprising. The world had sucked so much the last few years. Of course this had gone wrong too.

But mostly, she cried because she loved Cole. She loved him so damn much.

This situation would've been easier, maybe, if their relationship had simply been lust. But it wasn't. They had been good together. *Were* good together.

Stupid as it was, this story was going to hurt him, and it was going to drag down the show. Maggie believed so much in the work they'd done on *Waverley*. And Zoya . . . she must be livid at them for endangering all that. As well she should be.

When at last Maggie's tear ducts had run out of cry juice and she felt as dried out as beef jerky, she stumbled into the shower. The guest bathroom was less impressive than Cole's. It only had one showerhead, which honestly seemed kind of unfair now that she'd gotten used to luxury.

After her shower, Maggie had to face another problem: all her clean clothes were in Cole's room. The room she'd begun to think might be *her* room too. Because if she'd been able to keep the intimacy-coordinator job, it would've made sense to sell her condo in Eugene and move to LA. And if she was going to be with Cole most of the time anyhow, it would make sense to move in with him.

The funny part—funny in a way that made Maggie sick—was that she didn't doubt that Cole loved her. She didn't doubt that she loved him. She didn't doubt that they could've made it work.

Maybe still could?

She was in the barrel roll, and until the world stopped whipping madly around, she couldn't get the context she needed to know what the future might look like.

But it required clean underwear.

Wrapped in a towel, she tiptoed down the hallway to his room. After she was dressed, she headed to the kitchen for food. Cole was wearing sweaty workout clothes, pacing and talking quietly into his phone, when she came into the living room.

"I'll call you back," he told whoever it was.

"I see the burritos arrived." Maggie's sobbing and shower break had been more than an hour. Way more than enough time for their food to be delivered.

Honestly, they were truly amazing burritos. She understood why he'd bought the house.

Cole watched her tear into one. Sobbing your guts out was hungry work.

Maggie wanted so badly to know what he was thinking, but she was also so tired, and this conversation—it wasn't going to be easy or good. The future was a muddle, and Cole was going to demand certainty from her. A certainty that she didn't have. At least she had rice and beans and really good guacamole.

When she'd finished and drained not one but two glasses of water, he said, "Your phone has been blowing up."

She'd forgotten to take it with her into the guest room, which had probably been a blessing. She didn't want to see what people were saying about her. "I'm sorry I couldn't talk to you right then. I was . . . overwhelmed, and I needed a minute to process it."

"And you've done that?" He seemed darkly amused by the possibility.

From her previous experience having her life wrecked, she knew that it would be months before she'd understand all the things she was feeling right now. "Nope. I'm so . . . mad. At myself. At whoever gave those quotes. But there's so much more. It's like an ocean of feelings inside me, and I'm not ready to talk to you about them. I need some time, Cole."

The moment stretched and stretched between them. He wanted to press, she could tell. But he was trying to give her space. Maybe he was afraid if he pushed, he wouldn't like the answer.

She knew if he pressed, neither of them would like the answer.

"Okay." He wasn't happy about it, but he accepted it. That had to be enough. "Let me tell you what Brett said."

As Maggie had assumed, there wasn't much news. His team was looking into the story and writing up a response, which would go out very soon. Cole had texted with Tasha and Ryan, who were figuring out how to comment, and he'd talked to Zoya. The showrunner was furious. She'd gotten her own people on the case, along with the production company's team.

Because everyone Maggie knew now had "people."

But everyone's main focus was rehabilitating Cole, as it should be. He was the face of the upcoming season of *Waverley*, and they didn't want him to be damaged goods.

Maggie didn't rate. She didn't have people—not that kind of people.

"The story isn't getting much traction outside of town, not yet," Cole was saying. "So far, people on social media seem skeptical about it. We might be able to contain it."

Contain it? The damage had already been done, at least as far as Maggie was concerned. She'd been fired. Her reputation had taken a crushing blow, and she wasn't going to be able to recover.

Still, she said, "I'm glad." And she was. For him. "I'm going to call Savannah." Cole might have a lawyer and a publicist and an agent, but the only person Maggie wanted to talk to was her best friend. "I was going to see if she could catch a flight down. Is that okay?" *Is it okay if I invite someone to crash at your house?* That was what she was really asking.

"Of course." Cole didn't hesitate, didn't waver. If anything, he looked more hopeful. More happy.

Maggie wished—she wished so many things. That the story hadn't broken. That she hadn't been fired. That she could be as certain as Cole that this relationship had a future.

She knew she loved him, and right now, that was about it. The river of tears had swept through her and ripped everything loose. The life she'd put back together was a pile of junk sitting in the gutter. She was going to have to sort through it all and see if something, anything, could be salvaged.

"Thanks."

And with that, she offered him a sad smile before retreating back to the guest room to dig through the flotsam of her life all over again.

◆ ◆ ◆

EXT. COLE'S HOUSE

Cole had arranged for a driver to pick up Savannah at LAX the next morning and bring her to his house. But Maggie was surprised when she climbed out of the car with one of Maggie's pothos in hand.

"You brought my plants?"

"I smuggled this one in. I thought you might need a friend." Savannah flung her free arm around Maggie.

Maggie sank into the hug. She'd never needed one more. She hadn't been comfortable touching Cole, not when touching Cole had been the thing that had set all this in motion in the first place.

"I can't believe you came. Thank you."

Savannah pulled back, her expression incredulous. "Of course I did. You think I was going to pass up a chance to sleep"—she dropped her voice to a whisper—"in Cole James's house?"

"I hope it will be exciting enough to justify the trip. Come on in."

Maggie took the plant, which honestly did make her feel better, and Savannah collected her luggage.

Ten minutes later, they were sitting in Cole's backyard, drinking lime water. Even with the short notice, Savannah had somehow managed to wrangle together the perfect SoCal outfit: a drapey minidress in a bohemian fabric and cola-tinted sunglasses. With a scarf tied around her ash-blonde hair and a tangle of necklaces around her neck, she could've doubled for a young Stevie Nicks.

For the moment, at least, they were alone. Cole had left to train with Ryan just before Savannah had arrived, so they had some time to process things before he showed up and was . . . perfect.

Because Maggie had no doubt that with Savannah, he would be, as ever, perfect.

"Do you want some sunscreen?" Cole had a basket by the back door with enough of it for a small army.

"I already have some on, *Mom*."

"Cancer protection is one of Co—it's important to take care of yourself."

Savannah regarded Maggie over the top of her sunglasses. "Oh, is that one of Cole's bugaboos?"

Maggie knew Savannah would never give quotes to the press, but she also reveled in juicy details about the life that Maggie had—at least until yesterday—fallen into. Who wouldn't?

Besides, Maggie had walked right into this one. "Yeah, he's really on top of UV blockers. He might be rubbing off on me."

"A professional thing, I'm sure. But is he rubbing anything else?" Savannah asked that with the same casual tone she might use to ask if Maggie had eaten a peach or changed brands of facial scrub.

"From time to time," Maggie said, equally casually.

"From time to time?" Savannah was almost offended. "It'd be a shame to be fired if you aren't hitting that on the regular. Please tell me that you have stroked those glorious abs."

Maggie chuckled for the first time in twenty-four hours. It was good to know that her sense of humor wasn't broken. "I have."

"And?"

"They're amazing." Everything about Cole was amazing. His amazingness was *so* not the problem.

"Also, tell me Tasha Russell is single and you're going to introduce me."

"This has to stay under the cone of silence because it isn't public yet, but I regret to inform you that Tasha is not single."

"Boo."

"I take it that Emily is not back?"

"Sadly, I think this breakup is going to take." Savannah seemed to be over it, though Maggie was going to have to push later to figure out if that was real or a front.

"That sucks."

"It does." Savannah rearranged to get more sun on her face. "So are we going to talk about it?" *It* being Maggie's abrupt lack of a job.

"Can we stick with Cole's abs?"

"Firing first, abs later."

"Fine. I can't believe this happened to me again. I used to be so *good*. How have I stumbled into multiple work scandals? Like, I have now been fired by two different industries. That's impressive for someone who likes to follow all the rules." Her sense of self had been broken by the second firing, but despite what everyone thought of her, at heart, she liked to color inside the lines.

"You're right, most people settle for one. What did your parents say?"

"I'm ignoring their texts and calls." They would be outwardly sympathetic, but their horror would be palpable under the surface. Maggie couldn't face it, not until she wasn't feeling so shattered.

"I bet the podcasts and the morning shows are hollering at you again."

Oh yes. "*Hear Her* called."

"Oh my God."

"They wanted Cole and me to come on together." She hadn't told him because he would be all for it. He was desperate to fight someone on her behalf, but she had to take care of him, to make sure that he got what he wanted, even if she couldn't.

"You should do it," Savannah said.

"You have to understand, I worked with Cole. It's a major violation for us to be involved even if nothing happened on set. This position is so new, and there are still people in the industry who doubt that intimacy coordinators are necessary. We have to walk on eggshells and be total professionals to legitimize the field. What happened isn't just about me but also about the value of what I do. Or did, anyway. Being an IC hangs on . . . vibes and your reputation, and I seriously damaged mine."

Linda on the phone and Bernard in her email had made it sound as if Maggie's relationship with Cole was the worst thing anyone in Hollywood had ever done or could ever do. That was exactly why she'd resisted getting involved with Cole in the first place.

"I love you, Maggie, but you didn't cross any lines," Savannah said. "You weren't his boss, you didn't have any power over him. And vice versa. You're two adults who met at work, and then, when that job was over, started dating."

"But this job means holding yourself to a higher standard. How could someone else trust me again?"

"I'd think they'd have *more* reason to trust you because you and Cole specifically chose not to start a relationship until after *Waverley* was done filming. You treated yourselves, your coworkers, and your workplace with respect. That shows judgment."

Was that good sense, or was it rationalization? Maggie was so mixed up, she didn't know. "I want to believe you, but that's also the way of seeing it that lets me off the hook. I mean, I blew up my life for a second time in as many years because I couldn't resist a *man*. Granted, Cole is a very kind, very funny, very hot man, but I literally threw it all away for love. I'm a pop song! A *clichéd* pop song! I just . . . Does that sound like something a serious person does?"

"It sounds like something a happy person does."

Happy. Now there was a concept Maggie tended not to honor.

The old version of her life, the one where she worked twelve-hour days for ten months a year—had it made her happy? Maybe.

Sometimes. But a lot of teaching had been a grueling routine, with fleeting moments of sheer joy mixed in.

The life she'd been trying to build in Hollywood, had it been better? Yes, but there was no way to go back to that. The news of Maggie and Cole's relationship had broken something that couldn't be mended.

"Is it enough, to be happy?" Because being with Cole, it probably meant rebuilding her life all over again another time in some other industry. Maggie could have him, but she couldn't have him and have that job.

"Yes." Savannah at least had no doubts.

That made one of them.

So what then? Oh God, she was really contemplating this? Even with none of the practical questions answered? "What about my 401(k)?"

"You work at Starbucks, and you love that man, and you thrive. Seriously, Mags, I thought you were smarter than this."

That didn't sound all bad. Except: "But I want my life to matter."

"Stop this. It's like your mom's voice is coming out of your mouth, and it's freaking me out. Your life does matter! It clearly matters to you and to him. What are you, greedy?"

"No. But I might be a little bit . . . proud." A lot bit proud.

"Ah, well, if Mr. Darcy can get over that, you can do it too."

"There you go, making sense."

Savannah smiled smugly and tipped her face back into the sun. "So tell me more about this man you can't resist. How jealous am I going to be when I meet him? Because even if you're denying me Tasha Russell, I am meeting him, right? I'm only here until tomorrow night."

"Cole should be home in the next few hours. And you're going to be . . . incredibly jealous."

The thing was, Maggie didn't doubt Cole's worth for an instant, just as she didn't doubt her feelings for him.

So what exactly was the problem?

Chapter 26

INT. GYM LOCKER ROOM

Ryan sparred better with his fists than with a sword, that was for sure. After an hour in the ring with him, Cole was exhausted, which had been the point. He didn't need to train that badly. But he did need to make his mind stop its constant whirring.

He dropped to a bench in the locker room, breathing hard. "You fight well, man."

"That's my job." Ryan, as ever, couldn't take a compliment. "How you holding up?"

"I'm climbing the walls."

In between wondering if Maggie would ever forgive him, Cole had taken a few swings at himself. His blunder had put everything he'd worked toward for almost twenty years in jeopardy. He still didn't know exactly how he'd misstepped, but he knew he had.

Brett had sent him a roundup of the responses that morning, and it boiled down to this: If Cole had seduced the intimacy coordinator for *Waverley*, well, wasn't that exactly what Cody Rhodes would do?

It made him want to break cinder blocks apart with his bare hands.

All he'd wanted to do was shed his irresponsible reputation, and instead, he'd confirmed it in a way that had wrecked Maggie's career.

"How's Maggie? Tasha wants a full report. She's worried."

Tasha didn't bring a lot of people into her circle, but those who made it, she would fight for, tooth and nail, hammer and claw. Cole suspected Maggie was, or might soon be, in Tasha's flock. And heaven help whoever was responsible for this story then. They'd have to deal with both Cole *and* Tasha.

That would make a good subject for their next movie together—if they got to make another movie together.

"She's not great," Cole admitted. "After she got fired, she cried for a long time. Her best friend is flying down from Oregon this morning."

"Good. She didn't want to come hit things with you?"

"That's not her style." Cole kept to himself that she'd slept in the guest room last night, and that their conversation over coffee this morning had felt more like they were roommates. That he hadn't kissed or touched her since the story had dropped. He was trying to be patient, but frankly, he was down to his final drops of the stuff.

"She ought to try it. It might help."

In Cole's bag, his phone sounded. It was Brett. "I gotta get this," he said to Ryan before answering. "Hey, do you have any news?"

"I do." His publicist said it extremely carefully, and Cole's gut dropped into his shoes.

"Was it Vincent Minna?" Cole demanded. "Because I will go on every talk show on the planet and burn his world down if he hurt Maggie." He'd restrained himself in the UK at Tasha's command, but he would not do it again if the guy was responsible for this.

"It wasn't Vincent."

That brought Cole up short. "Someone from the production?"

"It was Drew."

Like in an old screwball comedy, Cole almost checked his ears for wax. Because he was certain he hadn't heard that right. "It was . . . Drew?" he repeated back to Brett. "Drew *Bowen*? My agent?"

That simply couldn't be right. It had to be another Drew. Or maybe Brett was misinformed.

"I didn't believe it either. But he pitched the story to someone else, too, a reporter named Hope Acosta, and she forwarded me the email."

"Wait. You're telling me he didn't just give some quotes but that he planted the story? He sent someone a fucking *email* about it?" Cole yelled that bit, and Ryan's brows shot up into his hairline. "He meant for this to happen? It wasn't like—like, a mistake?" For a second, Cole tried to imagine what kind of mistake could've resulted in the *Boulevard Babble* story, but not even the wildest screwball comedy had plot twists that unexpected.

No, it had to have been pure malice.

"I wish it was," Brett said. "Look, I can't believe it either. But it's real."

Cole had assumed that finding out the source of the quotes would make all the rest of it clear, but this—this made no sense. "Do you understand this?" he finally asked after what felt like an eternity. His mind felt like a computer that wouldn't boot up. He couldn't put the pieces together. Not at all.

"No," Brett said. "I've been doing this for a decade, and I've never seen an agent plant a story to discredit their own client. Not ever."

"He didn't like that I talked to Libby Hansen," Cole said slowly. And there had been other disagreements, too, smaller ones. About potential parts, publicity. For so long, Cole had obeyed every one of Drew's instructions. And this time, he hadn't. "Maybe he didn't like my independence." It sounded almost funny, but it also sounded a lot true.

"Frankly, he would've made a lot of money off of your success—and I still think the career renaissance is going to happen. Now that I know what I'm dealing with, I can probably smooth this over. But look, we gotta bring Quinn in, and you—you have to fire Drew. It's going to be an ugly fight, but you have to shut him up, and fast. Then we can start the damage control. I know you've worked together for a long time, but—"

"I have zero problem firing his ass." It was going to take a hell of a lot of self-control not to pound him too. "I'm leaving the gym now. I need to get cleaned up, but I'll call Quinn on my way home. Can you send him the evidence?"

"Yup. I'm on it."

"Thanks, Brett. I'm sure we'll talk again in a few hours."

Cole got to his feet. He was beyond pissed, but for the first time since yesterday, he knew what he needed to do. As terrible as he felt, at least there was that.

This betrayal was—God, Tasha would understand what he was feeling. This was why she hated her mom more than Vincent. When someone who was supposed to be on your side turned out to be operating only for themselves, it was like setting a cup on the counter and watching it float to the ceiling.

What could you trust, if not that?

Maggie. He could trust Maggie.

And if he could fix this, maybe she could trust him again.

"Did I hear that right?" Ryan asked. "It was your agent?"

"Yup. That son of a bitch. At least Brett thinks he can clean it up. I'll give you and Tash a call when I know more."

Cole broke into a jog on the way to his car. Now that he could see the path in front of him, he didn't have a minute to lose.

INT. BRETT'S OFFICE—EVENING

Brett brought Drew into a conference room at his PR firm where Quinn and Cole were waiting . . . along with some hidden recording equipment.

Drew beamed behind the aviators he hadn't bothered to take off when he'd come inside. "How's my favorite client holding up?"

"Favorite?" Cole couldn't keep the sarcasm out of his voice. But because that wasn't part of the plan, he quickly added, "I'm fine."

Compared to that morning, he was. And they had a script here. He couldn't just tear into Drew, as much as he wanted to.

"That statement from Zoya was fantastic." Drew took a seat and pushed his sunglasses to the top of his head. "It sounds like the smoke is already starting to clear. Now you've got to get out there—on your own, not with Maggie. You really ought to break up with her if you haven't already. She'll just remind everyone of these rumors, even if they are false."

There was the patented Drew Bowen advice. He'd dropped so many little nuggets over the years, all of which Cole had taken. Cole could only hope Drew hadn't been playing him like a guitar the entire time.

Cole assumed that Drew had done this because he wanted to get Cole back in line. Maggie had just been collateral damage, and Drew had probably assumed he'd never be caught.

What an asshole.

"They *are* false, and I'm not going to discuss Maggie with you." Cole wasn't going to put up with that, script or no script.

Brett signaled to him: *Simmer down.* But Cole's simmer was as down as it was going to get.

"If you don't break up with her, you're making a big mistake." Drew had said that mistake line to Cole a time or ten. In Drew's estimation, Cole had messed up by taking certain projects and turning other projects down. Mostly by *not* kissing this ass or keeping his head down.

Cole was going to spend the rest of his life second-guessing all those decisions. He'd caught Drew this time. How much other stuff had he gotten away with?

"The other thing is," Drew said, as if he were about to impart some crucial secret, "you have to be careful."

If anyone needed to be careful here, it wasn't Cole. "Why?"

"The Vincent Minna thing." Drew said this as if it were the beginning, middle, and end of an argument, all packed into one tight phrase.

Which, well, Cole knew that for him, it was.

Drew, clearly realizing that Cole didn't get it, looked to Brett and Quinn for support. When neither said anything, he went on. "I know that it wasn't your fault, but your fingerprints are on it."

"By *Vincent Minna thing*, do you mean supporting Tasha while she revealed a predator to the world?"

"There's no need to accept that framing. That's what those feminists on social media would say. The ones who talk so much about 'accountability.'"

Cole almost laughed because Drew was about to get a first-class lesson in accountability. But the implication underneath Drew's words was gross. "The industry could use a lot more accountability. Vincent Minna hurt my friend and a lot of other people." Cole said it as evenly as he could, given that he wanted to scream it at the top of his lungs. "I watched him bully half of Hollywood, and I feel like an utter ass that I never called him on it. Of course my fingerprints are on it. I had to make things right. I'll frame it however I want to." Cole didn't like feeling anger, the pulsing in his gut, the bitterness in his mouth. But he liked even less how Drew saw Cole and his career.

The worst part was that this conversation was goddamn familiar because they'd played some version of it a dozen times. As they'd gotten ready for this meeting, it had been all too easy for Cole to remember the times Drew had steamrolled him. The conversations in Drew's office, on a film set, once in the hallway at a crowded party. The details had changed, and the stakes had never been this high, but the flow was the same. Cole was naive. Cole was messing up. Drew was going to steer him right.

Every other time, Cole had gone Drew's way. But today—today was different.

Across the conference table, Drew's expression was one of pure pity, and it made Cole want to charge over there and knock that smirk off his face. "Well, a lot of people are pissed."

"Worried. You mean that a lot of people are *worried*."

"Your problem is that you've always had the soul of an elementary school crossing guard. You gotta grow up about this business."

"You think I'm too nice?"

"Yup."

Cole shot a look at Brett. It was time. "You're wrong, and I'll prove it."

"How?" Drew asked, his skepticism thick as the icing on a birthday cake and every bit as sickly sweet.

Drew was going to relive this moment a hundred times in the next few months, wondering how he'd missed what was about to happen. At least Cole would have this as consolation. He was going to live rent-free in Drew's head for forever.

"I know about Hope Acosta."

"The entertainment reporter? What about her?" Drew didn't so much as blink. He had no idea the trap was closing around him.

"The jig is up. We have your email," Brett said.

Drew, who'd been smiling slickly at Cole, whipped his head toward the PR guy. "Excuse me?"

Brett pushed a piece of paper across the table. "She reached out to ask for comment on a story about Cole, a story similar to the one *Boulevard Babble* ran. But unlike those turds, she didn't think it was worth running. She was mostly trying to give me a heads-up."

A sheen of sweat had appeared on Drew's upper lip. "I didn't email Hope. I haven't talked to her in months, and—"

"You've emailed me from that address before," Brett interrupted. "When you were on vacation. It's not your official one, sure, but I know it's you."

"You're speculating because you want to give Cole an answer, and this is—it's dangerous."

Quinn spoke up for the first time. "You're in breach of your agency agreement with Cole." He opened the manila folder he had with him— and honestly, nothing good ever came out of a manila folder.

Drew ought to make a rule about that.

"I am not. You can't even prove that I emailed Hope, and—"

"I'm going to step out now and let Quinn handle the legal details. But Drew? I'm firing you. I don't want you on my team."

For an instant, Drew's poise crumbled. A wave of surprise and anger washed over his face. For the first time in their almost-twenty-year relationship, he was shocked.

The man recovered quickly, though. His smug, impervious mask slipped back into place in an instant. "You can't do that."

"Quinn thinks I can, and he's better at his job than you are."

Cole stood up, shook hands with Brett and Quinn, and headed for the door. They'd agreed that Cole shouldn't be around for all the sordid details. And besides, he had to get home and tell Maggie that it was handled. That even if this was his fault in the first place, he'd handled it.

As he was leaving the room, Drew shouted after him, "You'll regret this."

But Cole was absolutely certain he wouldn't.

Chapter 27

INT. COLE'S HOUSE

Cole's voice froze Maggie in the hallway leading to the open-concept kitchen / living room.

"I haven't normally discussed my personal life with reporters," he was saying. "But given the *Boulevard Babble* story, I know I have to."

"Zoya Delgado, Tasha Russell, Rhiannon Simmons, Owen Roy, and Leanne Archer have all released statements disputing the story and standing behind you and Maggie." Jack Davis's voice sounded weird.

Maggie peeked around the corner. Cole was sitting on the couch with his laptop open on the coffee table. He was giving Jack an interview—an open-book, all-subjects-included interview, by the sounds of it—over Zoom.

He was doing it for her, even though he hated that stuff.

She folded back against the wall, smiling. She'd just taken one of his cars to drop Savannah at the airport, and the whole time she'd been driving back, she'd been impatient—more impatient than normal—with the traffic. She needed to see Cole.

It wasn't that she had all the answers. But she had one of them.

"I appreciate the support of the cast of *Waverley* so much," Cole said.

Their statements had been gushing and genuine, even Tasha's, and she despised the press even more than Cole. When she'd read them, Maggie had almost cried again. Late yesterday, *Boulevard Babble* had deleted the story and published a terse retraction.

Cole's lawyer must be very scary, and it turned out that was valuable in this business.

"The original story didn't match with what I saw during the week I spent on set either," Jack said. "I don't think anyone could take it seriously. But now there are reports that you split with Drew Bowen because he gave those quotes to *Babble* in the first place."

Maggie smacked her hand over her mouth to smother her gasp.

"For legal reasons, I can't comment on who was responsible for the leak. But it's important to me to clear things up, not only for my sake but also for Maggie's."

Last night, Cole had come back from his meeting with his team, and all he'd told her was that he'd found the culprit and that things were going to work out. Since they'd been having the conversation under their breaths in this exact spot while Savannah chilled in the kitchen, it had been a brief discussion, but that had been the gist. Then he'd been charming, if a bit distant, with Savannah, melting away after dinner so that they could have girl time.

And here he was, trying to save Maggie. Not knowing if she wanted to be with him or if she blamed him for all of it, but trying to save her anyhow. Because he loved her.

On Zoom, Jack asked, "And you and Maggie are . . . ?"

Cole wouldn't confirm their relationship without Maggie telling him that it was okay to do so. Maggie knew that as surely as she knew the sun would rise in the east and set in the west. He thought this was his fault, and so he had to fix it.

Two careers had blown up in Maggie's face. One had been absolutely not her fault. And the other . . . had been a little her fault. But ultimately, she couldn't change who she'd fallen for. And she couldn't change the bad timing. She could decide if she wanted to rebuild her life with or without the man she loved. And having done it once without him, she knew that it would be better with him.

Infinitely better.

In the living room, Cole said, "I care about Maggie deeply. And I—"

When Maggie breezed in, he stopped talking and went statue still. Jack probably thought the internet had hiccuped.

Maggie sat next to Cole on the couch and waved at the camera. "Hey, Jack. It's good to see you. I'm sorry to be late. I was taking a friend to the airport. I didn't know Cole had scheduled this for now." She linked her fingers with Cole's and squeezed his hand.

It wasn't that some magical rightness stole over her when she touched him again. But as he returned the gesture, she knew that whatever came next, she wouldn't have to face it alone.

That was the thing about being in love: you had a person who was ready to slay dragons—or reveal his personal life to the press and unleash his scary lawyer on jerks—to take care of you.

She turned her attention toward the computer. It seemed right—perfect, actually—that Cole had put her pothos on the console table behind the couch. It was the only thing of Maggie's in the house, and displaying it there was his way of saying *I want you to put down roots here. No matter what else comes, I want you to stay.*

"Cole and I are together," she told Jack, and Cole's fingers contracted, hard, around hers. "I know that people are curious about the timing, and I do want everyone to know it happened *after* filming. We both take our professional responsibilities very seriously. But that detail is all that I think we owe anyone."

Jack bit his lip to keep from smiling. "Fair enough. And Tasha?"

"Tasha is one of my closest friends in the world, but we've never been romantically involved," Cole said.

"Yeah, her email to me reads 'If anyone watches *Waverley* and thinks Cole and I have chemistry, that's because (1) we're actors and (2) Maggie Niven is an incredible IC. Kissing Cole is about as exciting as folding my laundry.' I skipped several words in there I won't be able to put in my story about this conversation. It ends, 'And FYI, the only man who could ever break my heart is my partner, Ryan Baris.'"

"Which Ryan would never do," Maggie said. Wanting to change the subject, because honestly, they'd all given the press more than enough today, she asked, "So how's Libby?"

Cole had been right the other day: if the press was going to gossip about actors' love lives, turnabout was fair play. Besides, the thought of bubbly, Gen Z Libby with stodgy elder-millennial Jack was delightful.

That broke Jack's control, and his grin popped out. "Making trouble. I've lost track of how many interviews she's done the last few days."

Because while Cole and Maggie had been wrapped up in this drama, Libby's story about Vincent had been out there, steamrolling the entertainment media. Part of why they needed to get this wrapped up was to get the focus back where it belonged: on taking down that predator.

"She's amazing," Maggie said.

"Yeah," Cole echoed, "she's definitely worth holding on to."

Maggie had a feeling that he wasn't only talking to Jack and that he wasn't only talking about Libby.

"I intend to," Jack said. "Thanks for talking to me, you two."

"Our pleasure."

Maggie pushed Cole's laptop closed and twisted to face Cole.

He was staring at her with a rapturous expression. "*Our* pleasure?" he echoed.

"Yup." Then she kissed him. Softly, then . . . less softly. When his arms came around her and he half hauled her into his lap so that he could really, really kiss her, that was when the magical rightness stole in.

It made sense that Effie Deans had wrecked her life for the love of a roguish man. Maggie couldn't blame her in the least.

"I'm sorry," she whispered against his mouth between kisses. "Getting fired again, it was triggering for me, and I—"

He pulled back. "No, it's okay. I understand. And *I'm* sorry. It was my freaking agent who caused the entire mess."

"I can't imagine how much that must have hurt." What little she'd known about Drew, she hadn't liked. But the guy being a little suspicious wasn't the same as him actively hurting Cole.

"It did," Cole admitted. "And even if he was trying to get me back in line, I cannot believe he included you in the mess. I'll never forgive myself for what he did to you."

There Cole went again, diving on any and all grenades that happened to bounce past him.

"*I* forgive you. Actually I don't think I even need to. It wasn't your fault."

"I'm just getting started. I'm going to have my lawyer reach out to the director of *The Mid List*. There must be something we can do, and—"

"No, I don't want you to do that. The more I thought about it, the more I could see their position." Maggie hadn't messed up in the way that, say, Vincent Minna had. But given how delicate on-screen intimacy was, her conduct had to be above reproach. And some reproach wasn't misplaced here. "I think it would be better for me to find something else to do." The words made her stomach queasy, but Cole's hold on her—firm and certain—meant she could face it. Maggie believed in herself and in her relationship with Cole strongly enough to know she could handle it.

But he was still fighting for her. "You know Zoya will still want you for season four of *Waverley*."

"Except I don't want to spend four months in Scotland next year." Four months without Cole.

He watched her steadily, let what she wasn't saying out loud soak in. "Is that why you told Jack we were together?"

"I told Jack we're together because we *are*. And being with you—it means more to me than that career. I can start over. I've done it before, and if I need to, I'll do it again after this. Reinvention doesn't scare me. But a life without you, that does."

Cole pressed his mouth to hers. It wasn't a sweaty, grappling kiss but one of firm sweetness. The kind of kiss that sealed a vow. The kind that was a down payment on something.

Like maybe a life together.

He leaned his forehead against hers. "I was pretty freaked out the other day when you pulled away from me."

"I'll try not to do that again." Hopefully they weren't going to go through many more disasters like the one they'd just lived through. But if they did, she would try to handle it differently. "You deserve to have me reach for you, not to . . . isolate." Even if for a few hours there, moving into a blanket fort in the woods had seemed like the only option.

"If I had to choose between you hiding out in the guest room for a few days and you leaving me, I'll take the isolating."

"I wasn't going to leave you. I honestly never even considered it." She slid down until her head was resting on his shoulder. "I was feeling just so, so alone, and it took me a moment to realize that I have people."

He began playing with a section of her hair that had escaped the bobby pins she'd fastened it back with. "And you're gathering more all the time. Tasha is ready to hunt Drew down."

Maggie scoffed. "Yeah, he's toast." She tipped her chin back so that she could look up at Cole. "But that's enough about me. What about you? How are *you* doing?"

"I'm . . . okay. Brett thinks we've reversed the damage, but I realized I may never get away from the himbo label. Falling for the intimacy coordinator, being betrayed by my agent—those sound like plotlines on *Central Square*."

"In the last few days, I've seen you stand by your best friend against abuse in your industry. I've seen you deal with someone on your team who was lying to you and lashing out at you. I've seen you defend your girlfriend, giving up pieces of yourself to do it. If those are the actions of a himbo, then himbos seem pretty awesome to me."

"I just want to feel . . . grown up. And I thought I'd finally gotten there."

"You *are* there. You've dealt with all of these messes calmly and maturely and beautifully—while I was breaking down, by the way. That's pretty damn grown up. Time and again, I've seen you do the right thing, even when it was hard. Even when it wasn't what you wanted to do. You are a good man, Cole James. The *best* man. Loving you is an honor."

Cole's smile then was boyish. It wasn't Cody's smile or Geordie's smile. It wasn't the mask he used for fans or for the press. It was real, and it was hers.

Theirs.

"You'd never settle, Maggie. Not ever. And so, you loving me, you wanting to be with me above, like, your job—a job you were so great at—makes me feel worthwhile. Even if no one else can see it, winning you makes me feel like I've redeemed myself. Washed the past off. You asked me once when I could stop atoning, and it's now."

"And now for my next trick, I'm going to help you see that you don't need me to feel that way about yourself."

"But I get you as a bonus, right?"

"You bet."

Epilogue

EXT. THE EMMY AWARDS RED CARPET

Almost Two Years Later

Cole was tired of red carpets. He was tired of the banks of photographers and the coordinated pocket squares and the fake conversations. So many fake conversations. He was tired of all the travel and of sleeping in a different hotel room every night. Why did *Waverley* have to hold premiere events in New York, London, Edinburgh, Paris, Rome, Tokyo, Mexico City, *and* LA? And why did he need to wear a different suit to each event? They were tuxes, for crying out loud. They all looked the same.

But he wasn't tired of people saying nice things about *Waverley*, which had dropped its third season six months earlier. He wasn't tired of the fact that it had received the best reviews in the show's history, and apparently the best ratings, too—though Videon never gave anyone, you know, the numbers to prove that. He definitely wasn't tired of getting nominated for things for the first time in his career. Like, say, an Emmy, which was what they were here for. And he extra-specially wasn't tired of the outfits Maggie had worn to all those fancy events. Tonight's slinky electric-blue column dress—high-necked in the front but swooping so low on her back that he'd wanted to know how it stayed up—was a particular favorite.

"Did you visit the set during filming for the fourth season?" Maggie was asking Libby.

At least for this conversation, Cole liked the reporter involved.

"I did," Libby said. "It looks very sexy, even if you turned them down when they asked you to come back."

Thanks to Drew's leak, Maggie had become something of a minor celebrity. She was the most famous intimacy coordinator in the business, even if she'd only worked on a handful of projects. The Guinness World Records people ought to certify that.

"Well, I had other things to do." Maggie gave Cole a knowing smile.

It took Cole a second to realize that she meant something appropriate for public consumption and not just what they got up to every night.

"As the VP at Instep Pictures?" Libby asked. "Remind us what your mission statement is."

"Well, Cole and I started Instep to build on what we'd learned making *Waverley*. We believe that great art grows out of great environments. Rather than a top-down model, where you have a genius who's so devoted to their vision that they treat everyone around them badly to achieve it, we wanted to support creators in building diverse, nurturing sets. Making movies doesn't have to wreck everyone involved. Creativity thrives when you're good to each other. That's really the core of it for us."

She was saying *we*, but Instep had been all Maggie. Cole had helped her get meetings with financiers, and he'd lent her his name, but the production company was entirely her vision.

Maggie had kept insisting that she hadn't learned enough on set to do this, but he'd convinced her that she didn't have to make the movies herself. That producing was really about assembling a team of cool, smart, creative people, and then figuring out what they needed to do their best work. And honestly, Maggie had spent her entire life doing that in different ways. Once she started to believe in herself, he hadn't been at all surprised when Instep had taken off.

"And your first projects drop soon?" Libby asked.

"At the Snowshoe Basin film festival in Montana at the end of the month. We're really excited."

For all that she'd told him what really mattered was that the two of them were together, he knew she wouldn't have been happy if she didn't also have a career that made a difference. Cole was confident that now, in her third job, she'd found a way to do it that was as big as she was. More than as a high school drama teacher and more than as an intimacy coordinator, Maggie was changing the world as a producer.

He was so damn proud of her.

Tasha Russell bumped Cole's shoulder with hers. "Are you wrapping up here, or is Maggie still in the middle of her Darryl Zanuck routine?"

"She's almost done."

Or not. Maggie was in the middle of describing every project Instep had in the pipeline to a rapt Libby. They might be here awhile.

"Ryan has a flask if you need it," Tasha muttered.

Ryan held open the lapel of his own tux, revealing it tucked into an interior pocket. "Gotta be prepared."

"And if you're nervous—"

"I'm not," Cole told his friends.

"Sure." Tasha didn't, for a second, believe him.

But as always, he was telling the truth. Being nominated was actually an honor. It wasn't something he would've been able to imagine just a few years ago. And at some point in the future, after he did some more serious roles, well, who could say? But for the moment: "I'm not going to win."

"Everyone loves a comeback kid," Tasha said.

Which had turned out to be true. People had loved Cody Rhodes, and they had loved watching Cole playing a grown-up role. Even if they still sometimes treated him like a frat boy, even if no one believed him when he told them that he'd finally managed to read all of *The Heart of Midlothian*, even if sometimes the way they loved him was limited, the outpouring of support meant a lot.

"The ceremony will be boring, and when it's done, I get to just be me." Cole James, fully grown up, no longer a reckless kid.

"Until you have to promote the next one."

Tasha did have a point.

Heck, Oscar buzz was already starting to build around *Palooka*. And the parts Cole was getting offered these days, they were meatier. If he hadn't managed to entirely reinvent himself, he'd gotten most of what he wanted.

"Isn't that right?" Maggie turned around, giving him the "Help, I need you" look.

He was only too happy to oblige, especially because joining her meant he got to slide his hand up the bare skin of her back, exposed by that most excellent dress. "Isn't what right . . . pumpkin?"

He and Maggie didn't really do terms of endearment—and from the expression on her face, he had a feeling that she was going to remind him of that later on.

"That you're going to produce a documentary about the tabloids of the early 2000s and how they affected the celebrities from that period?"

"Oh, yeah." He wasn't planning to go on camera, but it had been all too easy to find people who'd been coming up at the same time he had been to go on the record about how toxic that environment had been and how the stench of it had lingered. It felt like the last thing he needed to do to truly make things up to the cast and crew of *Central Square*.

Maggie was beaming at him as if he'd just invented the moon and gifted it to her, and that—that made it all worthwhile. So Cole kissed her temple, which resulted in a blinding smattering of flashbulbs, but you had to give the people what they wanted in this job sometimes. And what they wanted was Cole James, deep in love.

Emma Barry

It was what he wanted, too, so it wasn't a hardship or anything.

"That sounds amazing. I can't wait," Libby said. "Tasha, do you have any comment on the latest news coming out about Vincent's trial?"

Once Libby's story had broken, more and more of Vincent's victims had come out of the woodwork. It turned out that some of them had cases that the district attorney thought were actionable. Cole hadn't been following the story too closely, but it sounded as if Vincent might actually face some real consequences.

Cole had never been so happy to be wrong.

"Yeah, they take the trash out on Mondays," Tasha said. "And I wish all his victims the best."

"Succinct," Libby said. "I love it. Before I let you all go, I do have to ask about that." She gestured at Maggie's left hand and the sparkly ring that Cole had planted there at a vineyard in France, while Ryan and Tasha had watched and clapped, a few months ago. The show's absolutely grueling promo schedule had had at least one upside.

"I figured it was time to put a ring on it," Cole told Libby, before dropping another kiss on Maggie's temple, this one far longer and much less chaste.

Tasha leaned past them to say "Cole refused to follow Ryan's and my lead and get married by an Elvis impersonator in Vegas. I had a half-off coupon for them to use and everything."

Ryan had managed to get his way and lead Tasha down the aisle more than a year before. He was a persistent mofo.

"So those rumors are true?" Libby asked.

"Abso-fucking-lutely." Tasha was a marvel: confirming a story that had been rumored for more than a year in the most profane manner possible.

Cole had to get things back on track. "Yeah, well, Ryan had to lock you down, and I had to do the same before Maggie realized she can do better than me."

Maggie gaped at him. "There's absolutely no one who is better than you, Cole James."

296

"It's handy that I feel the same, Maggie Niven."

When he looked back at Libby, she was rolling her eyes. But when she said "Congratulations, you two," it was sincere.

"Thanks, Libby."

As they turned to walk away, someone in the crowd shouted, "Cody! Cody!"

Cole leaned into the crowd and fist-bumped the fan.

"You don't have to answer to that name, you know," Maggie muttered when he returned to her side.

"I spent a long time running away from that guy, but Cody will always be a part of me."

Cole had realized that his fans didn't just like cheering on their favorite actor from the early aughts; they were also nostalgic for younger versions of themselves. They liked remembering who they'd been when *Central Square* was still airing new episodes and life had seemed . . . simpler. If Cole didn't share his fans' impulse to live in the past, that was okay too. They were on their own journeys.

"I don't resent Cody anymore. And besides, if I hadn't played him, I never would've ended up on the path that led me to you."

Maggie's smile turned melting. "Have I mentioned that I love you?"

"Not often enough."

And with that, he led his wife up the red carpet.

AFTERWORD

To write *Bad Reputation*, and specifically to write about the challenges of filming love scenes, I had to develop an in-depth understanding of the structure, plot, and characters of the fake show that Cole, Maggie, Tasha, and the rest of the cast and crew were making. Like way, super in depth.

Thousands of words in depth.

While I hope the book stands alone without these notes, I thought readers might enjoy getting a sneak peek into the world of *Waverley*. Here's a snippet, prepared for you by one of my favorite minor characters: Zoya's assistant, Esme.

MEMO

To: The Cast and Crew of *Waverley*, Season 3
From: Esme McCullough
Subject: Season and Series Overview

Since we have so many new folks joining the production this season (including the entire cast!), our illustrious showrunner, Zoya Delgado, asked me to write an intro to the production binder with summaries of all nine season 3 episodes and an overview of how they fit into her five-season plan.

In case you've been living under a rock, Sir Walter Scott wrote the Waverley novels in the early 1800s. The first season was based on *Rob Roy*. In it, Francis is sent to live with family in Scotland after getting in some trouble in England. He falls in love with a woman named Diana, who's facing an unhappy arranged marriage, and they both get tangled up in the Jacobite Rising of 1715. When her fiancé is killed, Diana is free to marry Francis. Convenient for him!

After the overwhelming success of season 1, Videon green-lit us for seasons 2, 3, and 4. It was an unprecedented deal for them, and it demonstrates how Zoya Delgado is as skilled at negotiation as she is beautiful, talented, and committed to equity on set. (Hi, Zoya, is it a good time to talk about that raise?)

Anyhow, Zoya based season 2 on *The Bride of Lammermoor*. She shifted the setting to make it about a noble family who lost everything for supporting the 1715 rising. The daughter, Lucy, is in love with Edgar, a revolutionary, but her mom wants to break up the engagement and force her into a political marriage with someone else. This one originally had a tragic ending, but I'm sure you all agree with me that the changes Zoya made that gave Lucy and Edgar an HEA were improvements.

For season 3, we've moved forward in time two decades with *The Heart of Midlothian*. We start with Effie in prison for the murder of the out-of-wedlock baby she had with the smuggler/disguised nobleman Geordie. In reality, the baby was stolen by his ex-mistress. Their story plays out against the Jacobites losing hope and a sweet secondary love story. Zoya has again fixed this book because Walter Scott liked his tragedies, the sad, sad man.

Next season, we'll arrive at *Waverley* itself. This one focuses on Edward, an English soldier, who's torn between two women: the aristocratic Rose and the Jacobite Flora. When their plot fails and the rebels lose at Culloden, Flora dumps Edward for accepting an English pardon, and he marries Rose. The production values and battle scenes are going to be WILD. I know you can't wait.

Should we get reupped for a fifth season (fingers crossed!), Zoya wants to close things out with an adaptation of *The Antiquary*. William has two problems: he's illegitimate and he's in love with a woman who won't have him. He assumes a new identity in order to win her heart, and eventually discovers that he's actually the son of an earl. As you've probably guessed, he gets the girl. And this season would have an around-the-world feel that would take us out of the UK (!!!).

With all of that in mind, here's the episode-by-episode breakdown for season 3:

◆ ◆ ◆

Episode 1

In the opening scene, Andrew Wilson is hanged for smuggling. We cut to Geordie, disguised in the crowd. He feels guilty he escaped from prison while his partner didn't. The English commander overreacts to the crowd's jeering, ordering his soldiers to fire into the crowd and setting off a riot. This part is based on true events. The rest . . . not so much.

Meanwhile, in prison, Effie overhears the riot and reflects on her terrible situation: she's been accused of killing her baby. In a cottage in the countryside, we meet Effie's sister, Jeanie, and her boyfriend, Rueben. They're good and boring and can't afford to get married. They're wondering how they can get Effie out of jail, or if she's going to die there.

At the end of episode 1, Geordie leads a mob into the prison to lynch the English commander for firing on innocent civilians. The rioters force Rueben to come along to hear the commander's confession before they kill him. Geordie breaks into Effie's cell to free her too, but she refuses to leave because it would confirm her guilt. They have hot sex against the wall of her cell—proving that Zoya is willing to give the people what they want because she's an artist.

Episode 2

This one is told through flashbacks. We start with scenes from Jeanie and Effie's childhood. Jeanie is quiet and good, and Effie is loud and rebellious. Then we meet Geordie. He's the bad boy son of a nobleman who likes smuggling and resisting English control of Scotland. This section introduces Madge, Meg, the Jacobites, and Andrew Wilson. We see Geordie and Andrew as swashbuckling smugglers. And at this point, Geordie and Madge are in the full bloom of their destructive love.

But at the conclusion of the episode, Geordie and Effie meet at a local ball and sparks fly. Jeanie realizes this is going to be trouble.

Episode 3

This is also a flashback episode. The Geordie and Effie romance develops. Jeanie disapproves but tries to support her sister. Geordie breaks things off with Madge. Then Geordie and Effie become lovers—and Cole James and Tasha Russell make millions of fans happy.

Meanwhile, Jeanie meets Rueben. While it's clear they're soulmates, they have no future because he's poor. Effie discovers that she's pregnant, and she decides to hide this from Geordie because she believes in his politics. She confides in Jeanie, however.

Episode 4

Back in the present, Effie prepares for her trial. Everyone in Edinburgh is depressed because they realize how deeply entrenched English control of the system is. They're not going to get those wily Brits out easily. Geordie sneaks into prison to see Effie again. He later tries to convince Jeanie to lie in order to save her sister. Ever the saint, Jeanie refuses.

Meanwhile, back with the Jacobite rebels, we find out that Madge kidnapped Effie and Geordie's baby. Cue gasps everywhere.

Episode 5

Effie's trial begins. Geordie is in the courtroom in disguise, listening to his lover testify. He considers exposing himself, but he wouldn't be able to clear her and he'd only be arrested and probably executed.

Jeanie takes the stand. Her testimony is intercut with flashbacks of young Jeanie and Effie. Jeanie refuses to lie. Rueben reacts with relief, and Geordie with horror. This episode ends with Effie's conviction. She's stoic, and Jeanie feels awful.

Feel free to email Rajesh Ram, our music supervisor, with suggestions for the closing montage song. I'm sure he'd love that.

Episode 6

Jeanie vows to save her sister and sets off on foot for London with a letter from Rueben for the Duke of Argyll. Meanwhile, Geordie goes to see the Jacobites to enlist their support, but Madge refuses to help in any way. She throws herself at Geordie, but he rejects her. He doesn't yet realize she has his baby. Poor Geordie: he isn't the sharpest spade in the shed.

At the end of this episode, Jeanie is captured by Madge and the Jacobites. She realizes that Madge has Effie and Geordie's son.

Episode 7

Jeanie tries to negotiate her release, but Madge won't hear of it. This is personal. Meanwhile, back in prison, Effie accepts that she's going to die. Outside, Geordie realizes how many people he's hurt and resolves to be a better man.

Basically, everyone gets an epiphany here.

Using her wits, Jeanie escapes from the Jacobites. Once she crosses the border into England, she faces discrimination from the English (boo). She meets the Duke at an inn and gives him Rueben's letter. The Duke offers to help her.

Episode 8

At the start of this episode, the Duke orchestrates a makeover for Jeanie, and we blow our remaining costume budget for the season. Then he takes her to meet Queen Caroline. Jeanie gives an affecting account of the events to the Queen, who issues a pardon for Effie. The Duke and Jeanie begin the journey back to Edinburgh.

Meanwhile, Rueben gets word from Jeanie, and he tells Geordie about the baby. Geordie goes back to the Highlands to confront Madge and the Jacobites. He recovers his son. Madge is heartbroken and loses her grip on reality, though Geordie apologizes to her. Meanwhile, Effie languishes in prison with her execution date looming nearer and nearer (!!!).

Episode 9

Jeanie and the Duke arrive back in Edinburgh. Rueben is overcome with Jeanie's beauty and kisses her—in public. The Duke offers Rueben a job as the minister on his estate, which will allow him and Jeanie to marry. Effie is freed from prison and reunited with Geordie and their son.

We close with dual weddings and dual wedding nights, and happy endings for both Effie and Geordie and Jeanie and Rueben. The book has a tragic ending for Effie-Geordie, but as Zoya would say, forget the haters. Love always wins.

And in case you missed it, here's the production team. Please give an extra big welcome to Ryan Baris, who's taking over as the stunt coordinator, and to Bernard Caldwell and Maggie Niven, who'll be serving as our intimacy coordinators.

Principal Cast

Tasha Russell as Effie Deans
Cole James as Geordie Robertson
Rhiannon Simmons as Madge Wildfire
Owen Roy as Rueben Butler
Leanne Archer as Jeanie Deans
Dale Bridges as Andrew Wilson

Department Heads and Key Crew

Zoya Delgado: Showrunner/Head Writer/Director for Episodes 1, 4, and 9
Kevin Combs: Director for Episodes 2 and 3
Jamal Garrett: Director for Episodes 5 and 6
Eileen Banks: Director for Episodes 7 and 8
David Keith: Director of Photography
Hugo Burch, Lottie Morrow, and Jorge Ochoa: Second Unit/Assistant Directors
Rajesh Ram: Music Supervisor
Gene Dillon: Head of Editing
Abbas Briggs: Head of Production Design
Rosanna Hensley: Head of Art Decoration
Sachin Fox: Head of Set Decoration

Alexa Pratt: Head of the Costume and Wardrobe Department
Rachel Dotson: Head of Hair and Make-Up
Sebastian Bell: Head of Production Management
Mariya Reeves: Head of Script Supervision and Continuity
Marley Porter: Head of the Camera and Electrical Departments
Lili Best: Supervising Sound Editor
Ryan Baris: Stunt Coordinator
Leonard Pierce and Amin Cordova: Sword Fighting and Combat Experts
Bernard Caldwell and Maggie Niven: Intimacy Coordinators
Shirley Todd: Location Manager
Logan Finch: Head of the Transportation Department
Edna Fitzpatrick: Horse Master
Georgia Pierce: Catering
Esme McCullough: Assistant to Zoya Delgado and Jack of All Trades

Acknowledgments

Bad Reputation rises from the ashes of my 2015 NaNoWriMo book, *Star Struck*: set entirely at a film festival, it was the tale of a sweet actor named Cole attempting to make a career comeback and falling for a hardware store owner / amateur photographer, while several other love stories played out and an abusive producer got his comeuppance.

It never quite worked, but I could never let go of it. Probably because what *Star Struck* needed to be was *Bad Reputation*. I'm grateful to the folks who read and commented on the earlier version, including Deidre Knight, Jenny Holiday, and Erin Satie. You helped me to believe that someday I'd be able to write Cole and Maggie's story properly. I hope that I finally have.

I'm indebted to my long-suffering critique partner, Genevieve Turner, who reads all my drafts and anxious my-book-is-terrible emails and who's always able to talk me back to rationality and gives me helpful notes. Without her, there would be no conflict in this book. None at all.

I wrote much of *Bad Reputation* during FaceTime work dates with Olivia Dade, whose humor, kindness, and goodness inspire me. When I have trouble believing in myself and my stories, Olivia always convinces me to keep going. She is the best writing friend I could imagine, and I adore her.

If I got the Hollywood details in *Bad Reputation* right, the credit goes to Janine Amestra, my subject matter beta reader. Not only did she keep me from making several egregious errors, but her notes were sensitive and thoughtful, and she helped me tie together several of the emotional arcs beautifully.

I am also grateful to the folks whose memoirs, novels, and reporting informed how I think about the entertainment industry and moviemaking, including Maureen Ryan, Tom Hanks, Viola Davis, Alan Sepinwall, Nell Scovell, Sam Heughan, Jenna Fischer, Emma Thompson, Alan Rickman, Danny Trejo, Carrie Fisher, Jennette McCurdy, Cary Elwes, Jodi Kantor, Megan Twohey, and Jen Chaney. Any remaining mistakes rest on my shoulders alone.

In a literal sense, this book would not exist without Sarah Younger. I have already apologized to her for giving Cole a bad agent, but let me say again that I was able to write a terrible, controlling agent because I have been blessed with a protective, brilliant, and fierce one.

Lauren Plude has been my champion and guiding light for three books now. Without her what-if questions, I never would've been able to transform *Star Struck* into this form. Lauren is hilarious, talented, and kind, and I appreciate having her on my team so much.

Over several books, Kristi Yanta has proved herself to be an editor extraordinaire. She always understands what I'm trying to do, and her notes always help me find the way I should've written the darn book in the first place.

I cannot say enough good things about the production and marketing team at Montlake, especially Karah, Jenna, and Elyse. They've helped me fix typos beyond numbering and are unceasingly cheerful and professional. I can't believe I get to make books with you.

Finally, I wouldn't be able to tell stories without the support of my family. You're the best movie-night companions ever, and I appreciate that you're always up for lengthy heated arguments about whether—for example—streaming has yet to produce an A-list star, or what really *is* an A-list star. I love you very much.

About the Author

Emma Barry is a teacher, novelist, former political staffer, and recovering academic. Emma lives with her high school sweetheart and a menagerie of pets and children in Virginia, where she occasionally finds time to read and write. You can visit her on the web at www.authoremmabarry.com.